IN
THE
DEEP

OTHER MONTLAKE TITLES BY LORETH ANNE WHITE

In the Dark
The Dark Bones
A Dark Lure
In the Barren Ground
In the Waning Light
The Slow Burn of Silence

Angie Pallorino Novels

The Drowned Girls
The Lullaby Girl
The Girl in the Moss

PRAISE FOR *IN THE DARK*

"White (*The Dark Bones*) employs kaleidoscopic perspectives in this tense modern adaptation of Agatha Christie's *And Then There Were None*. White's structural sleight of hand as she shifts between narrators and timelines keeps the suspense high . . . Christie fans will find this taut, clever thriller to be a worthy homage to the original."

—*Publishers Weekly*

"White excels at the chilling romantic thriller."

—*The Amazon Book Review*

"*In the Dark* is a brilliantly constructed Swiss watch of a thriller, containing both a chilling locked-room mystery reminiscent of Agatha Christie and *The Girl with the Dragon Tattoo* and a detective story that would make Harry Bosch proud. Do yourself a favor and find some uninterrupted reading time, because you won't want to put this book down."

—Jason Pinter, bestselling author of the Henry Parker series

PRAISE FOR LORETH ANNE WHITE

"A masterfully written, gritty, suspenseful thriller with a tough, resourceful protagonist that hooked me and kept me guessing until the very end. Think CJ Box and Craig Johnson. Loreth Anne White's *The Dark Bones* is that good."

—Robert Dugoni, *New York Times* bestselling author of *The Eighth Sister*

LORETH ANNE
WHITE

IN

THE

DEEP

A NOVEL

 Montlake

Text copyright © 2020 by Cheakamus House Publishing
All rights reserved.

Published by Montlake, Seattle

www.apub.com

Amazon, the Amazon logo, and Montlake are trademarks of Amazon.com, Inc., or its affiliates.

ISBN-13: 9781542019699
ISBN-10: 1542019699

Cover design by Caroline Teagle Johnson

Printed in the United States of America

For Jay and Melanie and their piece of paradise, which inspired this story.

THE MURDER TRIAL

I believe you believe what you saw, but what you saw is not what you think.

—*Harry Houdini*

Now, February. Supreme Court, New South Wales.

I see the crowd as soon as the sedan hired by my legal team turns onto the street. Galvanized by the sight of our black Audi, the mob surges forward. Police struggle to hold the agitators back. I see mouths open wide, yelling. Cameras. Reporters. Microphones. Faces red and hot in the Sydney summer sun. I can't hear them, though. The air-conditioned interior of our car is cool and smooth and silent, but as we near the courthouse, I'm able to discern the text on the placards being waved at us. At me.

KILLER!
JUSTICE FOR MARTIN!
LOCK HER UP

I feel like Alice slipped through the looking glass. *Off with her head then* . . . This cannot be happening. This cannot be real. I press my palms firmly onto my thighs, terrified by the ferocity that my trial has unleashed. I try to keep my face expressionless, as per my legal team's coaching. But a man slams the front page of this morning's *City Herald* against the window near my head. I flinch. My heart beats faster at the sight of the angry black letters that march across the top of the page.

ACCUSED OF KILLING HUSBAND: CRESSWELL-SMITH MURDER TRIAL BEGINS

Below the headline is a photo of me.

Next to my photo is an image of Martin. A graphic artist has created a slash that jags between our faces—like a rip through the page, symbolic of the deadly rift between us. My eyes burn. Inside my belly I begin to shake. He looks so vital in the photo. So alive. I loved him once. I loved him with all my heart.

A female cop in a pale-blue short-sleeve shirt and bulletproof vest, her face ruddy beneath her cap, yanks the man away from the car. I feel the first flicker of real panic.

Our driver slows. Uniformed officers battle to restrain the jostling onlookers as traffic cones are removed so we can park. People line the stairs all the way up to the Supreme Court entrance. At the top of the stairs, more reporters wait with mikes. One of them stands out—a woman in a bloodred jacket. She's tall and her white-blonde hair gleams in the fierce February sun. Melody Watts. I recognize her from the nightly Sydney news. A flock of cockatoos takes flight into the sky behind her, flashes of white and yellow darting up between the buildings into a bright-blue yonder. *A sign,* I think. Because I cannot go to prison. I *will* be free. Like those birds soaring up, up, and away into the sunshine. My lawyers have got this. They'll convince the jury of reasonable doubt. They're the best in the business, and they come with the price tag to prove it. We're going to win this.

I am a victim.

I'm fragile.

I'm not a killer.

This is the persona I must project. I must convince the jury of twelve that this is who I am. I need to put on the performance of my life.

And yes, it will be a show. Because that's what all these people have come for. Theater. Everyone is here for the spectacle that is a salacious Supreme Court murder trial with international implications. And I'm the star. I'm the one who has apparently disrupted the natural order of things, and when natural order is upended, it rattles the human psyche. These folks all want to stare at me now. The car accident. The freak. The evil. They want to see me punished and locked away so they can tuck their children safely into their beds at night and pretend this isn't normal. They want to see for themselves what I look like so that if—in the future—they spy someone just like me coming down the street toward them, they will *know*, and they will cross to the other side of the street to avoid the Monster before it comes too close, where it can brush against them, infect them, beguile and bewitch them.

I glance at Peter Lorrington, my barrister, who sits beside me in his regal black robe and crisp white court bib. His judicial wig rests upon his knee. He has earbuds in his ears. He's watching a live news clip on his phone. I replay in my mind his earlier words.

"Murder consists of two elements—the intention of the accused, and the act. The prosecution must prove both to the jury. Both that you intended to kill Martin, and that you did in fact kill him. The prosecution is missing the key element of that equation. And remember this—anything can happen in a jury trial. Anything. At the end of the day, all we need is to show reasonable doubt. We can do that."

Lorrington's strategy is to both undercut the police investigation and deliver to the court an alternate narrative of events that matches the forensic evidence. A story where I did not murder Martin. A story where the cops screwed up. It will be his story versus the prosecutor's story. That's ultimately what a jury trial is—a battle of two narratives. A fight for the very heart and emotions of the jurors. Lorrington said that, after all, a jury trial hinges on emotion more than logic.

I'm a victim. I was framed. I'm not a killer.

Deep breath. Assume identity . . .

Victim.

I smooth my damp palms over my tan linen skirt. The tan of neutrality. Like my flat, nude-colored shoes. Neutral. My blouse is simple, white. The white of innocence. I adjust my pretty horn-rimmed glasses. They say *hardworking*. My hair has been cut. No polish on my nails. I could be a librarian. I could be your sister, your mother. Your girlfriend. I could be you. Demure. Gentle. Empathetic. Sensitive. Wronged. So very wronged—framed, in fact.

I've played this character well and often throughout my life. I can do it again. I'm adept at masks. An expert, really. I learned from one of the best. My husband. The deceased. Martin Cresswell-Smith.

The car comes to a stop. *Thump, thump, thump* goes my heart.

Lorrington takes out his headphones and turns up the volume on his phone so I can hear. It's the reporter outside, the one at the top of the stairs—Melody Watts. Her Australian accent is blunt.

". . . the accused is arriving now with her barrister and solicitor."

Camera angles change, and suddenly we're looking back down at our car. The effect is surreal. Melody Watts is saying, "Mrs. Cresswell-Smith has been out on bail since her arraignment just over a year ago. Bail was set at one point five million. At the time Magistrate Robert Lindsay found the Crown's case against the accused was 'not weak,' but he ultimately determined its strength was outweighed by a number of factors, including Mrs. Cresswell-Smith's need to prepare for trial with her legal team, plus her lack of criminal history in New South Wales. He said"—Melody Watts consults her notebook for the exact quote— "'While murder is the most serious offense, refusal of bail is not to be deemed as a punishment, as there is still a presumption of innocence in the bail act.'" She looks up at the camera, and the sun catches the whiteness of her teeth. "Mrs. Cresswell-Smith was not deemed to be a danger to the community, and she surrendered her passport."

Lorrington puts on his wig and adjusts his robe. Suddenly my mouth is bone dry.

We exit the car.

Humidity slams me like a wall. Sound is suddenly explosive. The crowd jostles, chatters, jeers, taunts. Mobile phones are held high, recording, snapping photos. Press cameras zoom in with monstrous telephoto lenses. My barrister touches my elbow gently and escorts me up the steps, his robe billowing out behind him. The journalists clamor forward, mikes reaching out. They're after blood. Which will boost ratings in an era of dying media, and their desperation is ugly.

"Mrs. Cresswell-Smith, did you kill your husband?"

"Did you do it? Did you kill Martin?"

A searing flash of memory blinds me and I almost stumble. *Blood. Martin's. The fishing knife . . . the fury in Martin's eyes. The bitter bile of betrayal in my throat.*

"How long had you been planning his murder?"

Anger expands like a hot balloon inside me. My pulse races. My raw hatred for Martin pushes against my carefully constructed emotional walls. I fist my hands tightly at my sides and clench my teeth as I ascend the stairs flanked by my legal team in their flowing black robes.

"Innocent until proven guilty!" yells a large woman.

"Bitch! *Black widow bitch!*"

Rage explodes and shatters my facade into a million shimmering shards and I'm filled with a vileness of fury that makes me want to inflict bodily harm. I swing around, opening my mouth around a ferocious retort.

A camera clicks in my face.

Fuck.

My lawyer grabs my arm. "Do *not* engage," he hisses in my ear. "Do *not* look at the cameras. Do not smile. Do not say *anything*."

But it's done. The cameraman who yelled the disgusting insult has baited me. He captured my tight, twisted face, the ferocity in my eyes.

I'm shaking with adrenaline now. Sweat prickles across my lip. Moisture dampens my armpits.

"Justice for Martin! Justice for the Cresswell-Smith family!"

And suddenly I see them near the doors. Martin's parents. His sister stands on one side of the couple, his brother on the other. Shock stalls me as I meet his brother's gaze. The genetic echo is startling. It's as though Martin is standing right there, looking down at me from the courthouse doors, judging me, admonishing me from beyond the grave. Martin would look exactly like his brother in a few more years if . . . *he were alive.* The idea carves a hollow into my stomach.

How does this even happen to someone?

When did it begin?

Did it start with our move to Jarrawarra Bay, when the spotted gums burst into blossom and the flying foxes came?

No, it started well before that . . .

Watch the shells closely, Ellie, I say in my head, channeling my father's voice, clarifying my focus. *Because life is a shell game, and in a shell game only the tosser wins. Never the mark. You're either the tosser or the loser.*

I plan on being the tosser in this confidence trick. Slowly I glance up at the imposing building that houses the wheels of justice. I imagine the faces of the jury across from me.

You're all going to let me walk out of here. Because I'm going to sell you my story.

Just watch me.

THEN

LOZZA

Over one year ago, November 18. Agnes Basin, New South Wales.

The Jarrawarra Bay police boat carved a smooth *V* into the dark water of the Agnes River. Senior Constable Laurel "Lozza" Bianchi stood on the starboard side of the boat with Constable Gregg Abbott. She watched the deepening shadows among the mangrove trees tangled along the north bank. There were four on board. Constable Mac McGonigle was skippering them under direction from Barney Jackson, the old crabber who'd found the body and made the triple-zero call.

The late afternoon pressed down heavy with humidity. The air tasted fetid on Lozza's lips. Everything lay eerily silent, apart from the growl of their engines and the occasional soft *thuck* against the hull as they hit and sliced through one of the big jellyfish that floated with the tidal currents toward the sea. The jellyfish were the size of volleyballs and trailed frilled tentacles barbed with venomous stingers.

Smaller saltwater channels fed off the tidal river, twisting like a labyrinth into the heart of the mangrove flats. Lozza knew the silty channel bottoms teemed with mud crabs whose shells could grow as broad as a man's head. Both omnivorous and cannibalistic, the muddies were aggressive scavengers with claws powerful enough to crush shells.

And snap fingers. Whatever awaited them deep in the dank shadows of the estuary would not have been left untouched by those muddies.

They passed a listing old jetty. Rotting pilings stuck out of the water. Shags perched atop the pilings, hanging their black wings out to their sides to dry as they watched the police launch pass.

Thunder rumbled in the distance.

Gregg glanced up. "Think the storm will blow in?" he asked.

Lozza followed his gaze. Two fish eagles wheeled high above towering eucalypts, the raptors silhouetted against streaks of clouds turning violent vermillion and orange as the sun slid toward the horizon.

"Hell knows," she said quietly. "But it'll be dark soon. It would help to get a look at that floater while there's still some light."

"Bloody foxes will fly as soon as that sun slides behind those trees," Gregg said. "At least they aren't as bad here as south of Jarra."

As if summoned by her partner's mention, a colony of giant fruit bats exploded out of the eucalypt canopy and swarmed in a shrieking cacophony into the sky. Almost simultaneously, cockatoos and lorikeets began to screech. The earth seemed to exhale and shift, and a slight breeze stirred. The mood on the river changed.

"I hate them," Gregg muttered as he squinted up at the swarming creatures. "They fight the whole night in the spotted gum outside my bedroom window. Like bloody witches bickering in a coven. And they stink."

Everyone was on edge over the giant flying foxes that had mysteriously migrated en masse to the region recently. They'd begun arriving in swarms when one of the gum varieties had suddenly blossomed, and then more and more of the megabats had come flying along the highway like a portent of doom, gradually increasing in numbers until nearly every building, rock, tree, and vehicle in the town just south of Jarrawarra was covered with them.

"Like a Hitchcock movie," she said.

Somewhere, a kookaburra laughed.

The boat rocked as Mac guided their craft into the choppier water of Agnes Basin. The water body was vast—almost forty square kilometers—and full of the giant jellyfish. Like bubble tea.

"You go about another half kilometer up the east side of the basin, over there," Barney said as he pointed the way for their skipper, his voice hoarse and quavery. "And then you turn into a deep, narrow channel. That's where it is." Barney's complexion was bloodless beneath a map of red veins. Sweat sheened the old man's face, and he swiped his sleeve across his brow. Lozza noticed the man's hands trembled. Maybe Barney needed a drink. Or maybe he was rattled. Maybe both.

Barney had gone to check on his "noncompliant" crab traps. Instead, he'd discovered the body of a blond male tangled underwater in one of his lines.

"There—that's the channel entrance." Barney gestured toward a dark gap amid the mangrove trees. "You go in there."

Mac slowed the launch, steering them carefully into the channel. Water slapped and chuckled against the prow. Heat grew wetter. Branches clawed at them from the sides, and twigs scraped softly against the hull. Mac slowed the engine further. It grew darker as they went in deeper. Hotter. Clouds of mosquitoes buzzed over the water, and tiny bugs got trapped in the orange frizz of hair that had sprung out around Lozza's face in spite of her best efforts to marshal it all back into a tidy bun.

Mac switched on the spotlights, and eerie shapes and shadows jumped at them. A sense of a presence oozed out of the swamp, like something hidden, waiting, biding its time to clutch at them. The air smelled foul.

"You think it's him—Cresswell-Smith?" Gregg asked.

"Would be weird," she said.

"Right," he said. "Because if he went overboard ten klicks out to sea, how could he have washed in here? Doesn't make any sense."

Lozza flicked a glance at the newly minted constable fresh off probation. He talked too much. Especially when nervous. Or anytime, really. It annoyed the hell out of Lozza. Her default on the job was to go silent. She also knew her irritation stemmed in part from the fact that Gregg was good-looking and she was secretly attracted to the surfer turned cop. He'd come to policing later than most. He still ran his surf school on the side, and he'd helped teach Lozza's daughter to surf. But good-looking men tended not to notice Lozza in that way. Which tended to make her a little bitter toward them.

Thunder clapped and lightning pulsed, turning their surroundings into a sudden freeze-frame of black and white. A few plops of rain hit the water. Lozza's mind turned to the day she'd first met Martin Cresswell-Smith's wife on the beach. It would be Lozza's task to inform Ellie if this was her husband tangled in Barney's crab-pot lines. Ellie's words from their earlier interview swam into her mind.

"I hope you don't find him. And if you do, I hope he's dead and that he suffered."

"There!" Barney pointed suddenly. "I tied my crab pots to some roots behind that jetty jutting out over there."

Mac cut the engine and they drifted with the current, listening to the small waves chuckle against the hull as they floated toward the jetty. Thunder cracked and silver light flashed. Everything turned darker as the sun slipped below the horizon and storm clouds shouldered across the sky.

Lozza took her flashlight from her duty belt, clicked it on, and panned her beam over the jetty. She saw where Barney had tied some frayed-looking ropes to mangrove roots. The jetty itself was new—constructed as part of the controversial Agnes Marina development, which Martin Cresswell-Smith and his wife, Ellie, were spearheading. Barney had explained to Lozza how he used decayed-looking ropes above the surface of the water to hide the fact that his illegal pots were down beneath. But underwater, the old rope ends had been affixed to bright-orange polypropylene—or polyprop—lines that led to the pots. When Barney had returned to check his pots earlier today, he'd pulled on his lines and one had stuck fast. Rather than cutting the rope and losing a pot potentially full of good muddies, he'd decided to return with a mate's son to untangle the lines. The teen had gone into the water with goggles and fins, pulling himself down to the bottom along the orange polyprop. In the murky water he had come face-to-face with a body tangled in the line.

The kid had flailed wildly to the surface, gasping for air. Barney told him they couldn't leave "it" down there. "It" could be someone they knew. So the poor kid had plucked up the courage to go down once more. He'd cut through the rope with a knife. The body had shot straight up to the surface like a gas-filled balloon, popping out into a small cove behind the jetty, where it had drifted up against the mangrove roots on the far end.

"It got lodged in the roots," Barney had said. "That's when we gapped it back to the open water of the basin, where we could get better mobile reception. And I called you coppers."

Mac allowed the police launch to drift slightly past the jetty, angling his craft so that the spotlights illuminated the shallow inlet. They saw it almost instantly—the gleam of fish-belly-white skin. A khaki shirt. Yellow-blond hair. No pants. The white buttocks cutting like half moons just above the surface as the floater bobbed in the reeds against a tangle of roots, trapped there by the gentle push of the current.

Barney made a rapid sign of the cross over himself.

"Tie up to the jetty," Lozza ordered Mac. "Gregg and I can bushwhack from the end of the jetty to the other side of that cove." Mac fired up the engines, and with a growl of bubbles, the boat surged toward the dock, connecting with a bump. Shadows leaped. The water around the pilings and roots made a slopping sound. Thunder cracked right above them and lightning split the air. Rain started to pummel down steadily, pocking and splashing the dark water, droplets silvery in the glare of the spotlights.

Lozza and Gregg climbed onto the jetty. Both used flashlights to navigate from the end of the jetty into the swamp forest. Lozza expanded her baton and used it to thwack through the tangle of grasses and reeds. Snakes were a concern. She hoped the action would chase them off. Gregg stayed close behind her. He swatted at clouds of mosquitoes, cursing. The bugs seemed to prefer his blood to hers.

It gave Lozz a punch of satisfaction. It wasn't only women who flocked around the Adonis cop.

They reached the floater. Pressure built in Lozza's chest. The body was definitely male. He lay facedown, arms flopping at his sides with the swell. The khaki shirt matched what Martin Cresswell-Smith had been wearing when he'd gone fishing four days ago. The head of thick blond hair was a match. Body was the right size and general shape, too. He'd been a decent-looking bastard—like a rugged and bronzed rugby god, with swagger and charm to match, when he chose to use it. But Lozza had glimpsed something dark and sinister beneath the skin of Martin Cresswell-Smith.

She crouched down at the edge of the bank and studied the scene, taking care not to slip down the slick bank or to touch anything right away. She knew the drill. She'd been with the New South Wales homicide squad for years before she'd relocated to the South Coast and returned to general duties. She still retained her detective status, although she was not referred to as *Detective* because she was not assigned full-time to investigative duties.

Another silvery sheet of lightning pulsed as Lozza tracked the beam of her torch slowly over the body.

Gregg said, "You think it's him?"

Lozza definitely thought it was. But Gregg was right—nothing about that made sense. Martin Cresswell-Smith's boat had been seen leaving the Bonny River boat ramp, which was a half hour's drive down the coast. He'd logged in with marine rescue and told them he was heading out to sea in a southeast direction. If he'd had an accident at sea, there was no way his body could have washed all the way north up the coast and then into the Agnes River mouth and all the way into this channel via Agnes Basin.

"And if this is him," Gregg said, "where's his boat—where's the *Abracadabra*?"

"Gregg, shut up a minute. Please."

He swatted at another mosquito. Flies buzzed over the corpse. Lozza panned her flashlight over to the man's left hand. A wedding band embedded with a red stone encircled the floater's ring finger. She'd seen that ring before. On Martin. But there was no Rolex on the floater's wrist. Martin Cresswell-Smith had gone missing with a very expensive bronze-colored Rolex Daytona.

Gregg clouted another mosquito. His violent movement made the beam of his flashlight dart across the mangroves. A black thing exploded out of the darkness. Gregg sidestepped a terrified shag, his foot going down too close to the edge of the bank. He slipped and fell into the water with a loud splash. Gregg swore and scrambled wildly to get back out, bumping the body. It lolled onto its back.

Gregg froze.

Lozza went dead still.

Empty eye sockets stared up at them. The corpse's lips and nose had been shredded off. The tender areas of the groin were gone. Replaced by a writhing mass of sea lice. But it was something else that snared Lozza's focus.

The hook of a silver hand gaff had been sunk deep into the decedent's chest. On the handle in black letters was the word *Abracadabra*. And what appeared to be stab wounds from a knife punctured the shirt all over the man's torso. He'd been stabbed easily fifteen times. Lozza leaned in, bringing her flashlight beam closer. A dark ligature mark circled the man's swollen neck. There were more ligature marks around the wrists. A rope was still tied around the bare ankles. Lozza's heart beat slow and steady. Her attention shifted down the length of the man's right arm. He was missing three fingers. Cut nice and clean above the joints. Neater than a mud crab's work.

Gregg sloshed and clambered out of the water and up onto the bank. He took two steps into the grass, braced his hands on his knees, and retched.

Lozza returned her attention to the rope around the decedent's ankles. Polyprop. Bright yellow and blue. Not Barney's. If she were a betting woman, Lozza would bet that the rest of this yellow-and-blue line had been used to anchor this victim to something heavy underwater, where crabs and fish and sea lice and other mangrove critters would have picked his bones clean in a few more days. And then the bones would have disarticulated and buried themselves deep in the soft silt. There'd have been nothing left to find of this body. Except Barney and his crab pot had come along and gotten tangled in a killer's lines.

Her mind shot back to Ellie—her apparent memory loss and strange actions. A sick feeling filled Lozza's gut. Had she played them? Was she still playing them all? Every goddamn step of the way?

Because this sure as hell was no deep-sea fishing accident. This was no ordinary husband missing at sea. This was murder.

Lozza reached for her phone to call it in. While she and Gregg were the first responding officers, this would need to be run out of State Crime Command.

And right now Ellie Cresswell-Smith was *the* key person of interest.

THE MURDER TRIAL

Now, February. Supreme Court, New South Wales.

I focus on keeping my hands in my lap as Molly Konikova, the Crown prosecutor, rises. The barrister positions her binder upon a lectern on the prosecuting side of the bar table. She's tiny—birdlike—swallowed by her silk robe, which drapes around her like oversize black wings. Thin lips. Beaked nose. Bony, fluttery hands. Her hair, a dun color, hangs in lackluster strands to her jawline beneath her gray wig. Excitement jabs through me—she's a cartoon, a caricature of ineptitude and weakness. Surely the jury of twelve sensible-looking citizens seated across the room from me in the dock will take my defense barrister far more seriously than this sparrow-creature? My barrister is tall and pale-skinned with a head of thick dark hair, physically toned, his judicial garb more elegant than sinister. A man who radiates a calm and sophisticated intelligence, a man who can read the minds of a jury and spin a con, because he is a magician himself.

Konikova eyes me. Her gaze is cool. Direct. Almost steely. Perhaps I've misread her? No, I don't think so. She waits a beat, then turns her gaze on the jury—seven males, five females. The men average older. My odds lie with the men, I think. Women are the harshest critics of each other. I suspect this is because the flaws we see in other women are flaws we hate to acknowledge in ourselves. Being critical, lashing out at other females, is a way of attacking those traits within ourselves that we detest most.

Silence presses into the courtroom. Tension grows thick. The air is too warm, no natural light. Anxiety blooms in my chest. I flick a glance toward the shut doors. I've never tolerated well the sense of being boxed in. Suddenly the thought of year upon year of incarceration—twenty-five to life—fills me with such a clear and singular dread that I can taste it in the form of bile at the back of my throat. I moisten my lips. I concentrate on keeping my hands motionless. I aim my toes toward the jury bench, as I've been schooled. It keeps me facing in the most advantageous direction, I've been told.

Konikova begins her address to the court, and her voice startles me. It doesn't match her appearance. It's big. Amplified by the microphone. Assured yet friendly. My heart beats faster.

I've been told voice is key for advocacy. A trial advocate with a voice that does not project functions at a constant disadvantage. After all, it's theater. Barristers are performers, consummate story spinners, and not every solicitor has what it takes to become an advocate. My anxiety tightens. Perhaps I really have misjudged the prosecutor. I'm slipping.

". . . and over the course of this trial," she is saying, "what will emerge is a shocking portrait of a woman who grew so embittered, so enraged by jealousy and betrayal, so hateful of her husband, that she cunningly and systematically plotted the ultimate revenge. Murder." Konikova waits a beat. The only sound is the scratching of the court artist's chalk.

"Granted," says Konikova, "the victim, Martin Cresswell-Smith, was no angel himself. By all accounts he was a sociopath who brought out the very worst in his wife, but she also brought out the worst in him. Mr. and Mrs. Cresswell-Smith's relationship devolved into a vicious spiral, a devious battle to the ultimate end. Death." Another pause. The sketch artist glances up, assesses me, and resumes her work. I wonder what—or who—she is seeing.

I am a victim. I am demure. Wronged.

"And this heinous war that was waged between Mr. and Mrs. Cresswell-Smith was not isolated to the couple. They took innocent people down in collateral damage."

There is a stirring in the public gallery. Many of the observers are cops. Newspapers have speculated that one of Lorrington's legal strategies will be to undermine and discredit the key investigators on the case—Detective Senior Constable Laurel "Lozza" Bianchi, Detective Sergeant Corneil Tremayne, and Constable Gregg Abbott. So this is personal for them. The jurors seem to be leaning almost imperceptibly forward. The Crown prosecutor has hooked them. She's begun reeling them in. And they all want to play their part in the resolution. They *want* to see a Villain. They want to see the Villain grovel, go down, and be punished by the might of the law. They *need* to see a Hero triumph. It will make them feel good about the world. Konikova is giving them exactly what they've come for, a chance to do their civic and honorable duty and set right a hideous wrong. I know how this works.

I hate her from this instant and I struggle to refocus on her words, which are suddenly blurring in my head.

". . . and step by logical step, founded on irrefutable forensic evidence, on police statements, on the testimonies of witnesses, and on the expert assessment of a forensic psychologist, the Crown will demonstrate to Your Honor that this defendant"—she swings the back of her hand in my direction, waits for all the members of the jury to look directly at me, to get a good, long look—"is a cunning, cold, calculating mastermind. A chameleon who is able to project a demure countenance. Do not be fooled by her ruse," Konikova says. "Because at the end of the day you will be left with no choice but to find her guilty on all charges."

A rustle of activity passes like an invisible current through the audience. Reporters scribble fervently in their notebooks. I swallow. A drop of sweat slithers between my breasts. I pin my desperate desire for freedom on Peter Lorrington and his legal team.

Konikova tips her wigged head toward Lorrington. "No doubt my esteemed colleague of the bar will attempt to obfuscate matters. Misdirect. He will offer to you alternate versions of events and attempt to match them to the facts. But remember, it's just that. A story—a fiction. Smoke and mirrors. He will likely spin for you a narrative of a victim who fell prey to an abusive and domineering husband who pushed her to the very edge of her sanity." Konikova pauses and nods. "Yes, he thinks you are gullible. Psychologists will tell you that gullibility is deeply engrained in all of us, and when immersed in a story that stirs emotions, it's easy to let your guard down. Your duty is to not succumb, to not let your guard down, to keep your eye on the ball."

Lorrington straightens his gown and glances up at the ceiling, as if bored.

"The defense will attempt to malign the hard work of police officers. The defense will try to serve up surrogate suspects. All just to create the faint possibility of reasonable doubt. To believe the defense will be to allow a woman to get away with the murder of her husband. You cannot do that. You are here to perform a civic role. You are here to correct a wrong. And what has been done here is a serious wrong. Let us set it right."

Konikova takes her seat and reaches for a glass of water.

"Mr. Lorrington?" the judge, Geraldine Parr, says. "Do you have anything to add?"

My barrister rises slowly. His height becomes evident. The atmosphere shifts. His is a commanding presence. Everyone is awaiting his performance, his rebuttal. He smiles. He goddamn smiles. And I almost want to smile, too—from silly relief, from the knowledge that this formidable legal presence has my back—along with a reputation of turning courtrooms and judges and juries into putty in his elegant, pale hands.

"Something amusing, Mr. Lorrington?" Judge Parr peers over the tops of her reading glasses. "Or are we actually going to outline a defense?"

I'm aware that my barrister's opening will be extremely brief and general. It behooves the defense to hear the prosecution's entire argument, and to hear all the prosecution witnesses before committing too rigidly to any specific version of events.

"Your Honor," says Lorrington in his booming baritone as he clasps the sides of his lectern. "It appears that Madame Crown here has taken the liberty of outlining my defense for me."

Laughter erupts from the gallery. I see smirks on a few jurors' faces. The sketch artist hurriedly flips a page, works faster.

"Order," calls the court officer.

"But indeed," says Lorrington, turning to the jury, "Madame Crown is correct in that there is an alternate version of events. One that better fits the evidence. We shall demonstrate to Your Honor that all is not quite what the prosecution might have you believe. Madame Crown is also absolutely correct in something else—keep your eye on that ball. Read between the lines of her argument. And do not for an instant let your guard down, because your civic duty is to not send an innocent person away for a crime she did not do. That is your call to justice. That is the weight that now rests upon your shoulders."

With an elegant flick of his robe, he takes his seat beside his assisting solicitor.

"Your first witness, Madame Crown?" says the judge.

Konikova stands. "Your Honor, we call Detective Senior Constable Laurel Bianchi of the South Coast Police District."

The court door swings open.

A female detective with frizzy orange hair and a freckled, sunburned face enters. Her cheeks are ruddy. She looks overheated in her dress pants, white blouse, and ill-fitting blazer. A tight fist forms in my gut as Lozza makes her way to the witness box. She's stocky and walks with the swagger of confidence, her arms held away from her hips as though allowing for an imaginary gun belt. As she nears I see the scar across her brow.

She takes her place in the witness box near the jury bench. She doesn't look at me.

The court officer calls out loudly to the court, "Silence, please." He turns to Lozza, who has asked to swear by affirmation. "Do you solemnly, sincerely declare and affirm that the evidence you shall give will be the truth, the whole truth, and nothing but the truth? To adopt this affirmation, say, 'I do.'"

"I do."

And you will regret it.

My gaze is fixed on that scar across her temple.

Because your past mistakes, your hot temper, your quickness to violence will help me, Lozza Bianchi. Lorrington is going to cut you down. So I can win.

Too bad your little girl will see what her mother really is. A Monster.

Adrenaline rides hot into my veins. It's game on now. I can taste blood.

Konikova's hands flutter around her folder. "Will you state your full name for the court?"

The cop leans toward the mike. "Detective Senior Constable Laurel Bianchi. Jarrawarra Bay. South Coast Police District."

"Detective Bianchi, can you describe to the court where you were on November eighteen just over a year ago?"

Lozza flicks her gaze to me.

Mistake. I've got you now.

But as the cop's gaze locks on mine, a thin, quiet blade of dread passes through me. Perhaps I've misread Lozza Bianchi, too.

Just like I misjudged how badly things would spiral out of control between me and Martin from that cold January night on the other side of the world over two years ago.

THEN

ELLIE

Just over two years ago, January 9. Vancouver, BC.

It was a blustery day, a sharp wind ticking the bare maple branches against the windowpanes, when I finally folded Chloe's party dress.

I placed it carefully, gently, in a suitcase atop a few of Chloe's other belongings I still could not bear to part with. I stared at the small clothes, listening to the wind, memories welling inside me. The dress had little dancing elephants on it. My daughter, for some reason, had loved elephants.

Chloe had worn that dress on her third birthday. Just thirty-six months old and all of life ahead of her. Her limbs still infant-chubby. Her smile so full. Dewy skin. The sense of promise, of a future, vibrated around her. The memory of her infectious little chuckle when her daddy tickled her tummy filled my soul. In my mind I suddenly saw her fist clutched around wilting wildflowers offered up to me on a lemony-sunshine spring day. I could almost smell my baby girl, feel her body in my arms. A scraped-out sensation gutted my stomach, leaving a hollow of hurt. The sense of loss—it was still physical two years down the road. The accident had happened three months and two days after that birthday celebration. After she wore this dress. Thirty-nine months and two days was her life on this earth.

For what?

What in the hell did it all mean? Why bother to keep going?

For a while I hadn't bothered.

Part of me died—drowned—with my child that day. And in the outfall of the tragedy, my relationship with Doug, our marriage, had withered like grapes never picked on a winter vine.

I'd taken it out on Doug. I'd taken it out on myself. Doug's ultimate betrayal was a punishment I'd brought down on myself, I guess. My therapist had said my lashing out at him was an outward manifestation of my own guilt. She'd said I was hitting at my husband to *make* him hate me as a way of punishing myself, and that I needed to let go of all that guilt because Chloe's death was not my fault.

I wasn't so sure about that.

Perhaps a buried side to me would never be sure.

My therapist had helped me, but not in time to salvage our marriage. Our life together had been built around my falling pregnant, around prenatal yoga classes, celebrating ultrasound images, baby showers, baby shopping, a gender-reveal party, readying Chloe's room, fretting over breastfeeding and introducing solids, reserving a preschool spot . . . just being parents. We were a family of three planning to grow into four, or maybe five. Then suddenly we weren't. The mother, the wife, the *me*, no longer existed. I slowly lost my friends from my mom-and-tot groups. I had no one to read all those beautiful kids' books to. Doug would never get to take the training wheels off Chloe's little bike and teach her to ride like a pro. My job was illustrating children's books, and I was suddenly no longer able to do it, and had to step away.

I closed my eyes and took in a deep breath. It was January. Winter. The hell that was Christmas was over. New year. Soon it would be spring. Fresh start. New me. New Ellie.

Doug had remarried last fall. While it had cut me in two, Doug being with his new woman no longer enraged me. I no longer harbored feverish dreams of doing them both violence. Doug's wedding had shaken something loose. I suddenly abhorred the idea of holding on to this shell of a house and what I'd shared with him and Chloe here while he was busy making a home and babies with someone else on the other end of town. I was suddenly free—desperate, in fact—to let it all go.

I was moving into an apartment downtown next month. It was one of my father's properties, so if it didn't work out, it wasn't as though I'd be committed to a long-term lease or anything. I'd picked up some freelance work to ease back into the illustrating business. I could eventually get more contracts, or I could take off and travel, do anything.

I shut the lid of the suitcase and pulled the zipper closed. The sound was satisfyingly final. As I hefted the case off the bed, I glanced at the pillows on the side where Doug used to sleep, and I was slammed with a need to be held again. For a moment, as sleet pelted the windows and the clouds pressed down low and dark, I tried to recall the last time I'd actually had meaningful contact with another person—a lingering hug, a heartfelt squeeze of my hand. My heart twitched with an ache so basic and raw it made me think of abandoned dogs in cages at a pound, waiting to be adopted, to be touched and loved, and how they paced or pined and withered and died if they were not. A loving touch to an animal, a human, was like sunshine and water to plants.

I shook the feelings and rolled the suitcase toward the door. The movers would be here tomorrow. I was ready for them. At my final therapist appointment she'd said that packing Chloe's last things away was not a move toward forgetting my baby girl, but rather a sign that I was finally finding ways to cohabit with my loss. And I should not expect my loss to be an easy or forgiving roommate. The Grief Monster would still trip me up in unexpected ways, she said. Over and over. Unpredictable. Fickle. Mean. Beguiling. Deceptive. The thing, she'd said, was to try to recognize it for what it was when it struck—the

Monster—and to be kind to myself and not expect others to understand what I was going through because there was no decreed chronology of phases or trials to pass through . . . it truly was different for everyone.

Later, when I left the house to meet my father for a special birthday dinner, just him and me, I was dressed in new knee-high boots with very high heels, a black jersey dress I'd not been able to fit into for ages until now, and dark-red lipstick. My hair was brushed to a shine and fell below my shoulder blades. I felt solid. Bold. Confident.

This time, I promised myself, things would go well between me and my dad.

THEN

ELLIE

The lobby of the Hartley Plaza Hotel at the Vancouver waterfront was busy—mostly people in business attire bearing name tags, apparently all here for the AGORA convention being sponsored by the Hartley Group. AGORA was another of my father's brainchildren. A pitch-fest that sought to match monied venture capitalists with dreamers who needed financial backing for their projects. I made my way through the throngs to the Mallard Lounge.

The lounge was no less busy. Patrons sat deep in leather chairs around low tables with flickering candles. A bar of dark wood and mirrors ran along the far wall. A pianist played muted, jazzy tunes at a baby grand, and a fire flickered in the lodge-style hearth. Floor-to-ceiling windows afforded a view over the floatplane harbor, and outside the sleet was turning into fat flakes of snow.

I waited at the hostess stand, trying to spot my dad among the patrons. I saw him almost immediately. Tall, with a shock of silver hair against a dark tan that screamed of yachts and travel and exotic locales. He was hard to miss, the distinguished Sterling James Hartley.

The hostess took my coat, and I adjusted my sweater dress over my hips. As he saw me he surged to his feet, raising his hand. People turned. Looked. Always. Whenever my father moved, people watched.

His was that kind of energy. He took up that kind of space. I felt a flicker of a thrill.

"Ellie! Over here."

I smiled and wove eagerly through the tables toward him, conscious of his gaze upon me. I'd made an effort and hoped he'd approve, and at the same time I hated myself for even wanting his patriarchal nod. Then I saw the woman seated at his side—the woman who'd until this instant been hidden by the big winged back of her chair. Slender as a rake and maybe just ten years older than I, she had a perfect lob of platinum hair and pouty lips. My mood plunged. Darkness circled.

"Ellie, this is Virginie Valente," my father said. "She's from Milan."

I gave a tight smile as he kissed me on the cheek, and I said softly in his ear, "Happy birthday, Father. I thought it was going to be just me and you."

"Oh, really?" My dad grinned, stepping back. "I thought it would be a great opportunity for you and Virginie to meet."

I sat.

Virginie smiled. "So nice to meet you, Ellie."

"Right. Lovely." I decided then and there not to give my dad the present I had in my purse for him.

"What can I get you to drink, Ellie? Virginie and I are having a whiskey, and—"

"Wine," I said. "The Sloquannish Hills pinot gris. Thanks." I named my choice of poison, suddenly thirsting for it and desperate to put my stamp of control down at this round low table where I was clearly the spare part and resentful for it.

The server brought the bottle and artfully, obsequiously, held the label low for my father to read.

"It's fine," I said to the server. "He's not drinking it. I am."

My father's gaze narrowed and fixed on me. My face went hot. Virginie shifted in her seat and reached for her glass to break the tension.

The server poured a splash into my glass to taste.

"Just leave the bottle. Thanks."

As the server retreated, I reached for the bottle and sloshed wine into my glass. Nice and full. It was beautifully chilled. Little beadlets of moisture formed on the outside of the glass. I took a big gulp. A familiar warmth branched out through my chest. Like an old friend. I felt better already. I took a few more swallows to get the buzz fully going. On some level I knew I'd been triggered. I knew little brain impulses were now flaring down neural channels that had been scored deep by addiction born out of grief over my lost child. Deep down I was already gone, lost to an old coping mechanism. At least for tonight.

My father watched me in silence.

I gave a shrug. And I wondered if he'd bothered to tell Ms. Milan here about his daughter's dangerous descent into booze and prescription medication after the death of his little grandchild.

A depressed drunk just like her mother . . .

Probably not. I took another swig of wine. Dad had probably forgotten he'd ever even had a granddaughter. He'd likely fathered kids and had grandkids all over the world that I didn't know about.

"Shall we take a look at the menu?" Virginie said in her Sophia Loren accent. A Continental femme fatale acting in an old James Bond movie. Made me want to puke. Expensive rings. Expensive French manicure. Perhaps she wasn't even that young. Just well preserved. Cosmetic surgery? I leaned forward for a better look, the booze already making me forthright. Yes, cosmetically enhanced lips, I decided. In fact, I was certain of it. The upper one had been overdone. I hated augmented lips. They made women look like ducks. In fact, I *loathed* filled lips. They made me feel violent, to be honest. A vague image of Doug's new wife shimmered into my mind, and I reached quickly for my glass and took another deep swig.

"I'll have the charcuterie board," said Virginie.

"I'll have the duck," I said, still watching her lips. I knew the menu. Doug and I used to frequent the Mallard with my dad before

Chloe drowned. Doug and Daddy got along because Doug was like him and into real estate, and Daddy had funded some of my ex-husband's big projects, to great mutual benefit.

My father ordered. I made solid inroads into my bottle of pinot gris. The food arrived.

Virginie picked up her fork. "So, Ellie—"

"Excuse me?"

She looked confused.

I circled my finger near my ear. "Sorry, can't hear—you'll need to speak up. Music is loud. People behind me are noisy."

She glanced at the table directly behind me, where a brunette sat in a leather wingback chair silently scrolling through her phone. Across from her another woman silently worked on her iPad as she sipped wine.

Virginie leaned closer to me so her lips got in my face, and she said loudly, "Your father*rr* tells me you'*rrre* moving into one of his apa*rrrtay*ments downtown."

I poured the last drops of wine into my glass. "Did Daddy also tell you he owned the whole building? All the apa*rrrtay*ments in it?"

"Ellie," my father warned.

I ignored him and raised my hand high to summon the server. I pointed to my empty bottle and made a sign for him to bring another.

"Ellie," he said again. "Look at me."

I glanced at him. Flint glinted in my father's keen blue eyes. His white brows drew down. Danger sign.

"Yep?"

"Are you sure you should be drinking so much? After what happened before?"

I glowered at him, my heart suddenly pounding. "You mean, what happened after Chloe died? Is that what you mean, Dad?"

Virginie placed her manicured hand gently on my father's forearm, staying him, and said to me, "I stay at a hotel right downtown when I'm in Vancouver. We should meet for coffee, Ellie, or a spa treat—"

"Right, yep." I reached for the new bottle of wine, poured, and plunked it back down. I picked up my glass and sucked back a mouthful. "Sounds fabulous. I'd love to hang out with you for a while before my father trades you in." I spoke loudly. I felt the people at the surrounding tables listening, but I didn't care if anyone heard the "Unhinged Hartley Heiress"—as one tabloid had referred to me—arguing with Daddy dearest in his namesake hotel. I'd had enough. Of my absentee father. Of his women. Of my old life. I'd had enough of the old Ellie, who just used to suck it all up like a sponge and go home saturated with toxic thoughts and emotions. I'd had enough of Daddy's gold-digger arm candies in their designer outfits jabbering on about luxury cruises or adventure vacations and spa treatments. "He usually lasts about fifteen months per girlfriend, max."

"You should take Virginie up on her offer, Ellie," my father said coldly, firmly. "She's a fabulous weight-loss coach. Could give you some gym tips, too."

Wham. I stared at him, mouth open, glass midair.

"I've lost plenty of weight," I said quietly as I set my glass carefully back onto the table. "I . . . I was hoping you'd notice."

"Ellie." He leaned forward. "You've come far, but—"

"Oh, you two!" Virginie laughed breathlessly and waved her hand as if to brush away the tension. "You remind me of my own father and myself. We'd have the most terrible rows over—"

"Ellie doesn't row," said my dad. "Ellie is passive-aggressive. It's the quiet ones people forget to worry about. Snakes in the grass."

My eyes burned.

Virginie hurriedly tried to change the subject again. "I hear you draw children's book pictures, Ellie?"

"Illustrations," I said, still holding my father's steely-blue gaze. "I have a degree in fine arts and a major in English literature."

"It's so cha*rrr*ming," she said. "Have you ever thought of starting your own publishing business? Publishing children's books?"

I inhaled, broke eye contact, and poured more wine, considering carefully what to say. Because yes, I had thought about it. It had been a dream very near and dear to my heart, something that had been seeded into my soul while I read Chloe bedtime stories. Something that had died when I lost my baby girl.

"Virginie's right." My father dabbed at his mouth with a linen napkin and reached for his Scotch. "It would be a fabulous idea. Kids' books to start with, and then when you find your legs you could branch out into some real books."

"Real books?"

"You know what I mean." He took a sip.

"No. I don't. You mean children's books are like training wheels for some more important work?"

"What I'm saying is, don't let what you are used to doing hold you back from growing into the future, Ellie. Just because something is easy, or comfortable, doesn't mean you have to stay there. Change is hard. Always. But you can be whoever or whatever you want to be." He leaned back into his leather chair, cradling his drink. "What I'm saying is you cannot allow yourself to be shaped by your tragedy. Alter the narrative. Be a chameleon. Adapt." He pointed his glass at me. "It's your choice."

Blood drained from my face. A buzzing began in my ears.

"I'm serious," he added. "We all choose our individual narratives in life, the stories we want to believe about ourselves. And if we believe a new narrative strongly enough, others will believe it, too." He sipped his whiskey. "In fact, that's part of the reason I asked you to join me tonight."

Of course there was a reason. How could I have been *so stupid* as to have believed this was to be just a dad visiting with his daughter on his sixty-fifth birthday? A memory quivered like quicksilver—the joy, the wonder, on Chloe's face as I'd read her favorite bedtime story to her. Yet again. Because she'd requested it, yet again. The sound of her chuckles at the funny parts. Her chubby finger pointing at the illustrations. Emotion welled hot inside me. Those moments I'd shared with

Chloe *were* real. Those books *were* real. Life lessons through fiction. My job helping to create children's books was valuable.

I'd made a colossal error in judgment coming here tonight. I'd thought it would be the two of us, and the "narrative" I'd imagined was my dad saying: *Hey, you look good, Ellie. You've lost weight. You look strong. I'm so proud of how you've managed to pull through after everything . . .* How could I have even let that enter my head? What woman in her midthirties needed her father's approval, his love? What woman needed a husband, a man's touch . . . the smell of her child's hair, the feeling of her toddler's body in her aching arms? Tears coalesced in my eyes.

"I'm serious, Ellie. Bring me an idea—any idea—a publishing venture, art business, a gallery maybe, a retail outlet, and if you put together a half-decent business proposal, I will finance it. You've won the game right there." He waved his drink across the room. "Half the people in this hotel would like to be in your shoes right now and avail themselves of this opportunity." He leaned forward. "You could start your own little bespoke company, selecting only the projects you want to champion . . ." His words dissolved into a drone as the music went louder and the sound of rising voices blurred in my head.

Little.

Bespoke.

Bespoke was right up there with cosmetically enhanced duck lips. I stared at him. He'd never respected what I did. He'd never respected *me.* He'd seen me as a little thorn in his side ever since my mother died when I was nine. I grabbed my glass and sucked back what was left inside. "So that's why I'm here?" I said quietly as I poured more. "You want to throw some money at me—at your little *Ellie problem*—before you and your new lady here embark on some yearlong, age-crisis-fueled adventure?" I'd known he was leaving on a big trip. I hadn't known he was taking a woman. But of course he was. "Like you've always just thrown money at me, or parked me somewhere expensive, ever since Mom died, thinking that covered your paternal obligations."

He blinked.

"Yeah." My voice started to rise, surprising even me. "I should have had the guts to say it to your face long ago. I should have been less . . . what did you call it? 'Passive'? You think if you throw a few millions my way"—my voice turned shrill and I couldn't seem to stop myself—"that if you dangle some venture capital in front of me like I'm one of these speed daters looking for cash—like all the others here for this conference—that you can wash your hands of your little Ellie problem and finally be free now that you've hit some benchmark birthday and want to enjoy your end-of-life decades?"

Virginie shot a terrified look at the people seated at the tables around us. They'd fallen quiet and were actively listening. One or two glanced our way, then quickly averted their eyes.

I could imagine the gossip headlines already. *"Hartley Heiress" has another public breakdown. Sterling James Hartley and his trust-fund daughter row at his famous AGORA convention in his namesake hotel.*

Shaking slightly from the adrenaline building in my system, I said, "You really do think money is everything, don't you? Maybe if you'd just once *tried* to read me a story at night when I was little, or seen how your grandchild—"

"Lower your voice," he growled.

"Oh, not *passive* enough for you?"

"I'm simply making an offer, Ellie. Something to keep you busy, to help keep your mind off . . . things. To get you out and about and meeting people. Freelance work is so solitary. You're all alone in your studio. It's not good."

I glowered at him, heart pumping. I wanted to say that I *liked* being alone. But he was right. I needed company. I needed family. Not financing.

Virginie and my father exchanged a look. My father nodded and raised his hand, calling for the tab. He then leaned close and took my hand in his. Big and warm, and the little nine-year-old inside me ached.

"Virginie and I are going to leave now. We have another engagement tonight."

I nodded, mouth tight.

"I'm going to call you a cab."

I said nothing.

"I just want you to know the offer is on the table. Whatever you want, whatever it takes. Maybe you want to try something in real estate, like you were doing with Doug—"

"That was Doug's thing. Not mine."

His jaw tightened. He nodded again. "Phone me. Virginie and I are leaving on the tour tomorrow and could be out of cell reach a lot of the time, especially in the Sahara and while on the Antarctica leg of the expedition, which will be toward the end of the year. But even if you can't reach me personally, get in touch with Sarah Chappel—she's my new personal assistant at the office. I'm leaving her instructions, and I'll do the same with my legal adviser. He can look through your proposal, get the ball rolling, and set you up."

He got to his feet. Virginie followed suit. Finality. I could feel it. I was thirty-four, supposedly over my grief crisis, and my father was paying me off because he wanted to focus guilt-free on his world trip. His duty was done. The notion echoed through my skull like a resonant steeple bell. Sterling Hartley was signing the final check. His conscience could be clean.

"Don't bother about a cab," I said.

"Ellie—"

"I'm staying, going to have another drink."

He regarded me.

"Hey, you said I should get out more. Well, I'm out now."

He hesitated, then placed a perfunctory kiss on my cheek. I motioned for the server. I ordered a martini while I watched my father going up to the bar. He leaned across the counter and said something to the barman, who had a shaved head and dark stubble, and was built like a wrestler. The Rock glanced my way and nodded. My all-controlling father had likely told the barman to keep an eye on his wayward adult child. For a moment I wanted to believe he cared. But my sociopathic father more likely was worried I'd make a scene that would embarrass him.

I turned my back to them and faced my reflection in the big windows. Long shiny hair so dark it was almost black. Pale skin. My fitted dress. Knee-high boots. I didn't look half-bad. I crossed my legs in an attempt to look more elegant. My martini arrived, and as I took my first sip, my phone rang.

I set my drink down and ferreted in my purse. *Dana.* My heart squeezed. I'd missed Dana hugely. I missed all my old girlfriends—our nights out on the town. It had been far too long. I hurriedly connected the call.

"Ellie," Dana said as soon as I picked up. "What are you up to tonight? I could use a couple of drinks."

"Tom?"

A dark laugh. "How'd you guess? Yeah, we had another dustup. It's his work. Stress."

I smiled, happily drunk now. Delighted at the prospect of seeing Dana. "Meet me in the Mallard Lounge at the Hartley," I said. "I'm already here and warmed up and I sure could blow off some more steam with an old friend."

Dana said she'd be there in a few. She lived nearby. I killed the call, and as I slipped my phone back into my purse, I noticed in the window reflection the brunette still seated behind me. She seemed to be watching me as she spoke quietly into her phone. I glanced to my left. A man sat there. Also watching me. I looked across the room and felt a twinge of unease. How loud had I really been?

THEN

ELLIE

Dana downed another tequila shot and plonked her glass down hard on the bar counter, cheeks flushed, eyes bright. "Screw men!"

I laughed. My boho friend turned men's heads. She was a woman who liked to read tarot cards and meditate and measure her pulse after a "forest bathe," otherwise known to ordinary people as a hike in the woods. Her hair was thick and wavy and chestnut brown, her complexion clear. She wore a long skirt tonight, leather boots, big hoop earrings, and a wide smile. Dana was vital where I'd been so crushed. Her presence tonight awakened a squidge of envy in me and a whole lot of love. I wanted some of her fire. I wanted to stay out of the depression-and-grief abyss that had yawned open in front of me again at the sight of my father's new girlfriend.

"Screw everyone!" I concurred with matching gusto and downed my own shot. I motioned to The Rock for another round. We ordered more food and yet more drinks. And we laughed. Great big belly laughs. Flushed with warmth and friendship. When I checked my watch, I was startled to see the time. The movers were arriving in the morning. I needed to wrap things up here and get myself into bed.

"God knows I needed this, Dana. Thanksh."

She pointed her finger at my nose and snorted. "You're shlurring."

"Did you just snort? You snorted!"

"I did not."

"Yes you did."

We guffawed and leaned our heads in close. The Rock paid keen attention. I whispered into Dana's ear. "How mush do you think Daddy tipped him?"

"Who?"

I gestured with my thumb. "The Roshck."

She giggled, hiccuped, then pulled herself together and sat upright. "We're grown women, Ellie. Adults don't behave like this." She tried to keep a straight face, but her mouth twitched.

We collapsed into giggles again. Then I said, "Does one ever really grow up?"

She reached for her purse on the counter. "Supposedly."

"No, I mean it. Sometimes I still feel like a kid inside. It's like my nine-year-old self is the real me, just living in this older body."

She stilled and her face turned serious. She hesitated. "My gran said something similar right before she died. She said she was always the little girl inside, but people treated her like this stupid old woman who was too slow for their fast, young world."

"And I revert to my inner kid every time I see my father. It's like he pulls a trigger."

"Don't fight it, Ellie. Just do your own thing. Don't worry about him."

I nodded again and scrabbled in my purse for a tissue. I blew my nose. The woman seated on the other side of Dana at the bar caught my eye. She was busy on her phone and sitting a bit too close. She appeared to be eavesdropping on our conversation. There was a vacant stool on her other side—she could have moved over a bit. Something inside me grew quiet. Was she the same woman who'd been seated behind me during dinner? My brain felt thick. I couldn't be certain. Her gaze met mine briefly, and she looked away. Her elegant bob brushed her shoulders. Designer jacket and skirt. Slender in an athletic way. A businesswoman. Probably here for the AGORA con. A soft hunger filled me. To be more. To be like that sophisticated businesswoman, or more like Dana. My father was right. I *could* be that woman. I could be anyone. I just had to choose.

"You know, Ellie, I think you should do it."

I shifted my attention back to Dana. "What?"

"Take his money."

I looked at her.

"No, I'm serious. Like how much cash are we talking here?"

I gave a dry laugh. "You know how much he's worth. *Forbes* magazine listings and all. I could probably have as much as I wanted."

"Like . . . several million?" Dana looked suddenly sober.

I nodded.

"Well, what *do* you want?"

I glanced at myself in the mirror behind the bar. What *did* I want?

I wanted Chloe back. I wanted what I'd had with Doug. To be that little family. I wanted someone to be proud of me. Just human things. I wanted to keep doing my art. My needs were not extravagant. "Hartley Heiress is a title wasted on someone like me," I said softly. "A waste of a lot of money."

"Yeah," she said. "Privilege sucks."

I snorted.

"Seriously, Ellie, think about it." She looked at her watch. "Oh, crap. I need to get home. I've got an early thing tomorrow. You going to get home okay?" she asked me as she slid off her stool.

"Just a cab ride over the bridge away. You?"

"I'll walk. I'm just a block away. I'll be fine. That's the nice thing about living right in the city—close to everything. You'll love it."

I nodded.

She gave me a kiss on the cheek and we hugged.

"Oh . . . oh, wait, wait." She rummaged in her purse, took out her phone. "Gotta commemorate this." She called The Rock over. "Could you?"

He smiled, took Dana's phone.

Arms around each other, we beamed drunkenly for a photo, the lounge behind us.

"Mine, too." I handed the bald barman my own phone.

He shot, zoomed, shot. We grinned like silly Cheshire cats.

Dana paused, looking strangely sober again. "Don't be a stranger, 'kay?"

"I won't. Promise."

And I meant it. Letting loose had been the right thing. We hadn't done this in far too long. I watched Dana weave through the tables toward the lounge exit. The place was getting empty. There was a shift in the tenor of the patrons. I felt another sharp sense of being observed. I glanced at the bar. The Rock's dark eyes were on me as he spoke on a cell phone. Was he talking about me? To whom? I shook the sinister notion and went to retrieve my coat. I carried it as I headed tipsily through the lobby toward the washroom.

As I neared the bathroom, my heel snagged on a raised section in the flagstone tiles and I stumbled forward. A man lunged forward and caught my elbow, steadying me.

My face heated with a rush of embarrassment.

"I . . ." I made a face and gestured to the floor. "Paving is uneven. Caught my heel." His eyes were a startling blue against olive-toned skin. His gaze intense, direct. His hair was thick and Scandinavian blond. "I haven't worn such high heels in a while—guess I need practice." A bubble of laughter burbled up from my chest. I tamped it down, trying to appear serious.

"Why not?"

"What?"

"Why have you not worn heels?"

38

I regarded him and felt a quickening in my heart. There was something about him—an intensity, an aura of warmth and quiet strength.

"Never mind, I'm sorry—I didn't mean to be forward," he said, removing his touch from my elbow. "I just meant . . . they suit you. Heels. I mean." He ran his fingers awkwardly through his hair. He looked embarrassed. His fringe flopped back over his brow. He stood taller than I was in my heels. Well built. Perhaps more girth than he needed, but I've always liked a bit of a bulk in a man. I especially liked thick thighs, and his swelled under his business pants. He wore the kind of clothes Doug might wear—the Doug I'd fallen for. And whatever my feelings were now about Doug, they remained conflicted and horribly confusing, and I found myself attracted to this man.

I hooked my purse strap higher over my shoulder and cleared my throat. "Thank you."

"What?"

"The . . . uh . . . the heels. The compliment."

He laughed. I liked the way his eyes crinkled and dimples appeared in his cheeks. And I laughed nervously in return.

"Look, could I . . . can I buy you a drink?" He gestured to the dark and intimate little pub entrance to his right.

"I was just on my way out."

"Of course. No worries."

"And . . . I've had a couple already."

"Something to eat, then?" His smile deepened. "To help soak it all up."

I realized his accent was Australian. With maybe a hint of British. Underscored by Canadian, or was it American? And there was no judgment in the way he said "soak it all up." The moment—his manner—was curiously intimate, casual, easy. Simple. I hesitated as some vestigial thing reawakened deep inside me. I glanced back in the direction Dana had gone. I thought of my cold North Shore house across the bridge. All packed and boxed up and hollow. Chloe's empty room.

How long had it been since a man had noticed me in this way? I'd put on so much weight after Chloe, and it was not all off yet, but he didn't seem to care. What I saw in his eyes was approval. It felt good.

"I'm in town for this convention," he explained, "and it's been a brutally long day. I need to decompress, and I could do with your company."

I knew they served brandies by the fire in the dark pub, and one wall was lined with bookshelves of first editions behind glass doors. The chairs were deep and comfortable.

"I'm Martin." He held out his hand. "Martin Cresswell-Smith."

"Ellie Tyler." I placed my hand in his.

"So, Ellie Tyler, how about the drink and a bite to eat?"

I hesitated and held his gaze. Had I sent out the wrong signals? Inadvertently invited the wrong kind of attention? He didn't look like a serial killer. And I was safe inside this hotel, right? How wrong could this go?

You can be whoever or whatever you want, Ellie . . .

I smiled. "Sure. Why not?"

THEN

ELLIE

I looked for a ring. There was none. It didn't mean he wasn't married, but I'd decided in the washroom that if he sported a wedding band I was out of here. The server arrived bearing a cheese board with two glasses of port. Martin had selected a low table in front of the fire with two chairs turned partially toward the hearth. It felt private. Intimate.

"I hope you don't mind me taking the liberty," Martin said, gesturing toward the food and drink. "We can change the order if you don't like—"

"It looks wonderful." I reached for a glass, relieved to see he also seemed a little nervous. It suggested to me that picking up women on the way to the bathroom was not something he did routinely. Perhaps he really had seen something special in me.

He raised his glass. "Cheers," he said, clinking his glass to mine. "To chance meetings."

"To chance meetings."

I liked the shape of his hands. And in spite of the hint of nerves, he possessed the air of easy authority that often came with established wealth. Thanks to my father, I'd met many men who carried that aura. And judging by his bronze Rolex and gold cuff links engraved with the initials MCS, combined with the elegant cut of his clothes and the

Bolvaint shoes, Martin Cresswell-Smith was accustomed to financial success. I felt something inside me begin to open up. Hope. A possibility that I could live—really live—again. Laugh. Love, even.

"What are you thinking, Ellie?"

"That you don't look like a serial killer."

He laughed. Loudly. The sound rich and infectious. He leaned forward, a mischievous light twinkling in his eyes. "But I *could* abduct you. I could take you away from here to a dark and remote place."

"Too risky. Too public. CCTV cameras." I wiggled my hand toward the roof.

He glanced up. "Are there?"

I hesitated, not yet ready to share with him how much I did know about this hotel that bore our family name. "Well, I imagine there might be. In the lobby, at least. And you'd have to take me through the lobby, right?"

"Hmm." He swirled the rich burgundy liquid in his glass. It caught the glow of the fire. "Maybe a rear service door?"

"Opening a back door would sound the fire alarm."

He made a wry face. "Okay, you win. Abduction is out."

I chuckled, reached for an artisan cracker, topped it with soft cheese, and popped it into my mouth.

"So where is the accent from?" I said around my mouthful.

"The better question is where isn't it from." He fell silent for a moment and I had a sense he was debating how much to tell me about himself. "I was born in Australia. Melbourne. My mother was originally from Canada. My father is in property development. Shopping malls. International resorts. So we traveled a lot when I was growing up. We spent three years in England, and I went to school there. Some time in the States—Nevada, New York. Then Portugal and France. A year in the Caribbean. Some months on the Red Sea living at a diving resort for a project my dad was working on there. A lot of time in Toronto. I live there now. My business is based in Toronto."

"And you're here as part of the AGORA convention?"

He nodded. "A chance to pitch a development proposal in New South Wales. We had backers, mostly out of China, but red tape between the Australian and Chinese governments recently forced my financiers to pull out." He sipped his drink. "So now I'm looking for some new equity partners and have done a few pitches here."

"What sort of development is it?"

He looked into my eyes, weighing me, and I wondered what he saw—a tipsy and brainless female unworthy of an in-depth explanation, or someone seriously interested.

"It's a resort and residential development along the coast about four hours' drive south of Sydney," he said. "A very high-end marina with a lodge and rental-cottages component on an estuary." He glanced at the fire for a moment, then smiled and said, "It's just north of an area I loved to visit as a kid. We spent several family holidays there. A place called Jarrawarra Bay. We'd go after Christmas each year when I was around nine, ten, eleven, and the last trip was when I was twelve." He paused. "Those years in some ways were the best part—the truest part—of my life."

I chilled inside. I'd had almost those exact same thoughts just moments ago—that the years just before and when I was nine—before my mom died—those had been the truest, most real parts of my life. I'd even mentioned this to a magazine journalist who'd written a feature on the "Grieving Hartley Heiress." It had been a sympathetic piece, for a change. The journalist had lost a child of her own and had understood me. I stared into his baby-blue eyes, memories surging over me.

"What is it?" he said, attentive. "You look like a ghost just walked over your grave."

"It's nothing. I . . . just . . . it's like you read my mind." I smiled, feeling a deepening kinship with this warm, attractive, attentive, charismatic man who shared my sorts of feelings. "I've thought the same thing before. Tell me about those holidays?" I reached for my glass and sipped, absorbing him wholly, the evening of drinking lending a pleasant warmth and evaporating the last of my reserve. "Why were they so happy?"

"Oh, I guess it was because I still got on with my father, before I disappointed him."

My pulse quickened.

"Sounds crazy," he said.

"No, I understand. Really, I do. What about siblings?"

"Older brother and older sister. I'm the baby." He made a rueful face. "And yeah, the family disappointment, as it turned out."

"Why?"

Martin leaned back in his chair and cradled his drink. "My whole family are—or were—über athletic. Glorious human specimens, really. Unlike me, especially as a child. My sister was a minor tennis star before she became a top corporate executive. My brother's sport was rugby. He could have gone far professionally had it not been for a boating accident the family blamed on me."

"What happened?"

"I didn't listen to the 'captain,' which happened to be my father. We were going out from the river mouth, and big waves started to break over the sandbar which had formed at the tidal mouth of the river. When a bar breaks you need to time everything just right—it's when most boating accidents happen—going in or out when the bar is breaking. I didn't listen to an order, got in the way . . . and the end result was the boat hit a wave as it was breaking, and we went nose-up into the air and the boat flipped over backward. My brother was hit, broke his back." Martin's face and voice changed as he spoke about it. Pain showed. Unresolved pain. My heart squeezed.

"Anyway . . . Jeremy—my brother—ended up okay in the long run but unable to play rugby. He went into real estate development with my father, and my dad spent everything on him—time, money, love . . ." His voice faded.

"To make up to him?"

Martin took another sip of his drink. "In part, yes, I think so. And also to shape Jeremy into his own image, equip him to take over the empire, so to speak. I was cut from my father's life. Nothing I did could meet his approval. God knows I tried one crazier scheme after another to get his attention. I just ended up screwing up." He laughed, but there was no mirth this time. "I was the runt, the little black sheep. A tad too tubby, not at all athletic, nor handsomely chiseled, nor quite as tall as the rest of them. Including my mom."

But I liked this runt. I liked the substance of what he'd grown into. I'd never been partial to perfect features or skinny triathlete types anyway.

"End result—I left Aus when I was nineteen and never looked back, really."

"Although you did go into property development like your dad," I said. "And there's the marina project back in Australia."

He laughed again. Warm. Everything Martin did was warm. Engaging. "Touché, yeah," he said in that flat Australian way. "The project of my heart. I should have said that I never looked back until that part of the world started calling a couple of years ago. I realized I still hankered for that coast where we spent such amazing family holidays. Maybe it's the kid in me." He finished his drink. "Or maybe it's because my brother tried to buy that land for development some years back and failed to develop it."

I raised my brows. "So this is payback?"

"Nah. More like, 'I'll show you all that I am not a loser. Jeremy failed but I won't.'"

"Except the China money backed out."

"Yeah. But I'm here. I got some nibbles I hope will pan out."

"Hard to see you as a loser from where I'm sitting, Martin." I reached for my glass.

Something changed in his face. His gaze locked with mine. The air thickened between us, and I felt heat low in my belly.

He broke the gaze, cleared his throat. "Yeah, well, maybe it is just another subterranean way for that kid in me to get Daddy's attention. But it's a damn good project. Enough about me. Tell me about you, Ellie Tyler."

And I did. That I was a children's book illustrator and freelancing. Divorced, because my marriage hadn't worked out. I told him I was moving to an apartment because we'd sold our big, empty North Shore house. I refrained from mentioning Chloe. And I did not mention my father. I needed to protect those parts of myself still. I'd learned the hard way, and I wanted new people to know me—the real me—before they thought of me as a product of the Hartley empire. The most wonderful thing about Martin was the way he listened. He gave his whole attention, as though I was all that mattered to him in the world right at this moment, in this warm cocoon of a cozy bar.

"So you live in Toronto?" I asked.

"It's my base. I travel a *lot*. I'm involved with several developments in Europe at the moment—Spain and Portugal. And in Turks and Caicos. I've got something brewing in the Cook Islands. No wife or kids, so I move around where the work takes me."

Hope burned hotter. And alcohol had loosened me enough to say, "A guy like you, no wife? I'd have pegged you as taken."

"I was in a long-term relationship until very recently. Never married, though. And it's over now."

"I'm sorry."

"Don't be. I . . ." He hesitated, and I caught a flicker of emotion in his eyes. "I wanted a family. Kids—several. I wanted to do the whole white-wedding-vow-traditional thing. She didn't. Simple as that. And when I forced the issue . . ." His voice faded. He adjusted his tie. I felt a twinge of guilt for pressing him. I'd ruined the mood.

"I clearly wasn't her Mr. Right, that's all. I figure down deep somewhere she was reserving options." He changed the subject. "So what brought you to the Hartley Plaza tonight if not the AGORA convention?"

"Oh, just a meetup with a very old and dear friend from art school."

"An event that called for high heels."

"Serious heels." I laughed. "Don't you know that women dress to impress other women?"

"How about your family—you have siblings?"

I shook my head.

He studied me in silence for a few moments, his gaze so direct, so intense, it was like he'd slipped his hand into my shirt and touched bare skin. And I almost wished he would. I felt myself lean in. He lowered his voice to a whisper, and it did things to my insides.

"I've never met a children's book illustrator. I've met a lot of people. But never one who makes children's books come alive."

I took out my phone and showed him some of my work, our heads close. I could smell his aftershave. I could feel his breath against my cheek.

"Whimsical, Ellie. Beautiful." His fingers brushed mine as he returned my phone. He looked at me. Really looked, this man who wanted kids. Who'd dreamed of traditional wedding vows. Who'd loved family holidays by the sea. "Truly wonderful," he whispered. "How did you get into this work?"

I cleared my throat. "I got a degree in fine arts and literature and followed up with art school. I had every intention of being a fine artist— gallery exhibitions, the works. But I found I loved illustration, especially for children, and I . . . I like the freedom that freelancing offers, to travel, move around." My heart beat fast. I felt hot, excited, suddenly. I'd just made a decision—yes, I wanted to travel. I wanted the flexibility. *This* was my new narrative. My choices, my decisions. Adventurous Ellie.

"And no long-term relationship, no kids for you?"

Wham. Just like that he flipped me over.

I tried to smile. My mouth wouldn't cooperate. "I . . . I should go." I reached for my purse at my feet.

He put his hand on mine. "Must you?"

Did he expect sex? Would he be angry if I said no?

"I need to get home. I've got an early appointment tomorrow."

He hesitated, then quickly took a pen from his pocket and scribbled a number on a napkin. "I've really enjoyed talking to you, Ellie Tyler." Not a hint of disappointment in his voice. Which made me like him all the more. Martin Cresswell-Smith was a man who could be my friend. And I realized I would actually like to have sex with him. I wanted it. Very badly.

"But it hasn't been long enough, and I'd really like to see you again." He held the napkin out to me. "My mobile number. Call me. Please."

No threat. It was all up to me. *My* choice to call. Or not. I could just drop this napkin into the trash on my way out. Or I could keep it. I took it from him and our fingers touched. A shiver chased down my spine.

I cleared my throat again. "Are you going to be in town for a while?"

"Four more days at this hotel. I'm checking out on Monday. But seriously, Ellie, call. Anytime. Like I said, I travel a lot." He paused and held my gaze. "But I can make long distance work."

We let those words hang between us—a visceral, ectoplasmic, shimmering sense of promise. I tucked the napkin into my purse.

He called for the check. I saw him sign the tab to his room. I got to my feet and wobbled slightly. He helped me into my coat and placed his hand gently at the small of my back as he escorted me from the bar into the lobby, the pressure of his palm both gentle and firm. Both sexual and benign. Both controlling and charmingly chivalrous.

He accompanied me outside and made sure I got safely into a cab. I nestled into the warm back seat of the taxi, and he waved goodbye from the hotel doors. As the cab pulled away I pressed my palm against the cold window and watched him through the softly falling snowflakes, feeling as though I were in a romantic movie.

"Where to?" asked the cab driver.

Home.

I gave him my address.

Except it doesn't feel like home anymore.

As the taxi started down the snowy street, a traffic light turned red. We stopped, waiting in the softly swirling snow for the light to turn green. I turned to look back into the lighted windows of the hotel. Martin had gone inside and was standing in the lobby, talking to a woman and a man. A memory niggled through me. Martin said something to the couple and they all laughed. The man peeled away and the woman started to walk with Martin toward the bank of elevators. It hit me—the woman who'd been sitting at the Mallard bar counter earlier. Or was she?

A hesitation rippled through my fuzzy memory.

The light turned green and the cab started to move.

"Wait!" I called to my driver. "Stop!"

He hit the brakes. I flung open the door and tumbled myself out into the snowy street. I ran carefully on my heels toward the hotel entrance.

"Hey!" I heard the cabbie yell behind me. I ignored him and pushed through the revolving doors into the hotel, my heart hammering.

THEN

LOZZA

Over one year ago, November 18. Agnes Basin, New South Wales.

Warm rainwater leaked down the back of Lozza's neck as she crouched in the darkness, taking photos, her camera flash throwing the floating body into macabre relief. White skin against black water, the empty eye sockets, the nose-less face, open, lipless mouth. She clicked. Flash. Her brain circled around the words she'd heard shortly before they got this call.

"Ellie is not what meets the eye . . . That kind of woman can be the most dangerous when betrayed or wronged, because you least expect it. They can be deadly. Did you know that she stabbed her ex-husband . . . ?"

The sheer number of puncture wounds in this floater's chest—about fifteen, maybe more—whispered of rage, unhinged violence. Red-hot passion—because you didn't need to stab someone this many times to kill him. But the ropes, the severed fingers—was that planned torture? Sadism? And why no pants? Where was the boat? How'd he get here, into this channel?

Nothing about this made sense.

Lozza came to her feet and waited for Gregg to quit throwing up. Mosquitoes buzzed in clouds about them. Rain beat down steadily, and water dripped off the bill of her police cap.

"You good?" she asked.

He nodded, his face ghostly in the light of her torch.

"Let's get back to the launch."

She'd phoned it in. Reception had been spotty but she'd gotten through. They made their way back to the police launch.

Barney sat beneath the targa cover. Rain pattered and ran off McGonigle's jacket in silver rivulets.

"ETA for forensic services and a homicide squad detective is about two hours," Lozza said as they reached the boat moored to the jetty. "We need to cordon this area off while we wait." She turned to Barney. "There's a path leading off the end of the dock. Where does it go?"

"Abandoned homestead," Barney said. "The Agnes Marina developers erected some scaffolding near the old house. It's for prospective buyers who want to climb up to a platform and survey the view they'll get from the new lodge when it's built."

Lozza turned to Gregg. "Cordon off the immediate area with tape," she said. "We can extend the cordon as we get a better idea of the scope of the scene. I'm going to take a look down that trail. The decedent lost his fingers somewhere. My bet is he didn't drown here, either, but was killed elsewhere, and then someone tried to dispose of him in this channel full of big muddies." Lozza addressed Barney. "Want to show me the way to that old farmhouse?"

"Are you bloody nuts? No bloody way I'm going in there. Not to that place. Not now. In this weather? Hell no." He made another sign of the cross over his body.

Thunder clapped and rain doubled in volume and velocity. Water bounced off the river almost a half meter high, creating a shimmering silvery cauldron as white lightning pulsed through the mangrove swamp.

Lozza left Mac manning the watercraft and radio while Gregg strung out blue-and-white crime scene tape, marking off the immediate area. She picked her way slowly along a narrow and dark path through the tangle of trees. A wet spiderweb caught her across the face, and she started. She wiped the sticky threads off and continued. Reeds snapped back, branches clawed at her jacket.

A lizard as large as a small dog scurried across her path. She stilled and controlled her breathing before continuing again.

Lightning flared simultaneously with a loud crack of thunder, and she saw the house. The thunder grumbled into the distance, the forest went black again, and the rain drummed down even harder, creating little rivers through the swamp. Lozza picked her way carefully along the wet path until she came upon the derelict building.

It was a single story with an old tin roof that clattered under the raindrops. A covered veranda ran around the house. Lightning flashed again and silhouetted the low building against gnarled trees.

She made her way to the front door. The porch floor was rotted, and the door hung on rusted hinges. She creaked it open.

A bat darted out and she ducked. The creature's claws tangled in her cap and hair before it fluttered out into the swamp with a screech and a whopping of wings. Her heart hammered. She entered the building. It was sweltering inside the house. It smelled of urine and excrement and . . . something worse. Like putrid meat. She panned her beam across the room. It lit on a broken table. Two chairs with metal legs. A kitchen area with an old stove. She made her way deeper into the house. The heat and stench grew stronger. Lozza covered her nose and mouth with her arm. Rain clattered on the old corrugated metal roofing and dripped through holes, puddling on the floor.

She entered a room at the end of the passage. Her eyes adjusted as she tried to make sense of what she was seeing.

A chair in the middle of the room. A man's boating shoe lay near the chair. Ropes hung down from an exposed rafter. The rope ends trailed around the chair. New ropes. Yellow and blue—same colors as the polyprop tied around the floater's ankles. The exposed wooden floorboards were stained dark under the chair.

Blood?

Urine?

Lozza looked up and panned her beam along the roof rafter where the ropes had been tied. A sense of horror seeped into her. She entered the room slowly and the air stirred around her, lifting spiderwebs that wafted in the currents her movements created. Heat rose and the stench increased. She aimed her beam into the corner. Her pulse quickened. A pile of excrement.

Human?

She moved closer. Near the pile of feces lay a tangled pair of men's cargo pants and once-white boxers. The pants were blood-soaked. The boxers appeared soiled with human excrement, and the stink was stifling. She moved her light back to the chair and froze as something near the far wall caught her eye.

Lozza inched toward it. Floorboards creaked beneath her boots. A gecko scurried, and something cried outside. She crouched down, her arm still covering her mouth and nose.

The missing fingers from the floater's right hand. Three.

Beside the severed digits lay a pair of secateurs, pruning clippers. On the handle of the clippers was the name of the Cresswell-Smiths' boat. *Abracadabra.*

Lozza came slowly to her feet. She began to back away, not wanting to disturb the scene any further. The heel of her boot kicked something that spun and clattered across the wooden floor. She swung her beam in the direction of the sound. A knife. Fishing knife. Bloodied. And behind the knife, more clothing.

Lozza walked slowly over the creaking floorboards, trepidation filling her throat. She crouched down beside the pile and shone her beam on it. A royal-blue windbreaker and a pale-blue Nike baseball cap. Bloodied. The label inside the jacket was legible.

CANADIAN OUTFITTERS

The jacket came from Canada.

She thought of Ellie and her soft Canadian accent, her big gentle eyes.

"I hope you don't *find him. And if you do, I hope he's dead and that he suffered."*

She thought of all the witnesses who'd seen Martin and Ellie heading out in their boat, Ellie dressed in her royal-blue windbreaker and pale-blue cap, her long dark ponytail blowing in wind that had been too strong to offer a good day of fishing. Ellie returning home.

With a gloved hand Lozza picked up the cap and examined it more closely under the beam of her flashlight. A few long dark hairs—almost black—were caught in the Velcro of the adjustable strap at the back.

Thunder cracked. Lozza stiffened, glanced up. Lightning pulsed outside the broken windows, turning everything inside this room of horrors into a stark image of black against white. She felt sick.

Carefully she replaced the Nike ball cap as she'd found it. Lozza pushed to her feet and backed out of the room along the same path by which she'd entered.

THEN

ELLIE

Just over two years ago, January 9. Vancouver, BC.

I rushed toward the elevators, rounded a corner, and saw Martin step into an elevator. The woman was walking away. Insane relief gushed through me—the idea that he might have been heading off with that attractive businesswoman from the Mallard Lounge had galvanized me. I couldn't wait for life any longer. I needed to grab hold of all the things with both fists and squeeze the glorious juice from them before someone else snatched them away.

The elevator doors started to slide closed.

"Wait!" I rushed forward.

He saw me. Shock registered on his face. He slapped his hand on the elevator door, stopping it from closing. His gaze locked on mine.

"Ellie?"

I breathed fast, both thrilled and terrified. My heart thumped with adrenaline. I saw he was alone in the elevator car.

"What is it, Ellie?"

Out of the corner of my eye I noticed the brunette stop and glance back. A moment of doubt quivered through me. But the woman turned and disappeared around the corner.

I stepped into the elevator and placed my hand against the side of his face. His eyes turned dark. Desire changed the shape of his face.

"Ellie?" he whispered.

I leaned up and brushed my lips against his. The doors slid closed. His breathing quickened. He grabbed the back of my neck, his fingers thrusting into my hair at the nape, and he pulled me close. He pressed his mouth against mine. With his other hand he hit a button for a top floor. I reached for his belt and began unbuckling it.

He ran a hand up the side of my thigh, then up under my sweater dress. The elevator car began to rise, smooth, gliding to the top.

His body was solid, his thighs big. He inserted his knee between my legs. His lips forced open my mouth and his tongue tangled with mine. He tasted of port. He cupped my bottom and yanked my pelvis up against his. I felt his erection against my groin. My vision turned black and scarlet as he moved his hand into my pantyhose and cupped my crotch. I sagged into his touch, melted into it. A small groan rose in his throat as he pushed a finger up inside me. My brain swirled into a dizzying kaleidoscope of pleasure. He thrust up harder, deeper, kissing me more forcibly. I lost myself in the glorious, blinding sensation, feeling like I was going to explode as pressure built inside me.

Frantically, I undid his pants.

He moved fast.

Our sex was animalistic. Primal.

I gasped as he thrust up into me, and I braced a hand against the mirrored elevator walls. I gasped and shattered as he released inside me. I couldn't breathe. I felt blinded. I struggled to focus.

The elevator bell pinged.

I blinked. We'd reached the thirty-second floor. The doors started to open.

He hurriedly extracted himself. As the doors opened wide I pulled down my skirt. My hands shook. He watched my eyes as he did up his pants. Intense. Like a wolf. Sex with Martin was like being eaten by a wolf.

No one waited outside the car. Thank heavens. Martin stepped out and looked down the hallway. The lighting was muted. The hallway was empty.

He turned to me, held out his hand. "Come," he whispered, his eyes still dark pools, the soft blue swallowed by his dilated irises.

"Come to my room, Ellie Tyler," he said.

My lips tingled. My insides felt tender. I felt hot all over again. I felt powerful.

"Be with me for the night, Ellie."

An elderly couple approached down the corridor. They entered the elevator car with me still in it. It struck me—what I'd done. A raw wave of panic, anxiety, rose inside me. What had just happened here? I caught sight of myself in the elevator mirror. A distorted Ellie. Smudged eye makeup. Mussed hair. Kiss-swollen lips. Rumpled dress.

The other Ellie—the new Ellie, the chameleon Ellie, the powerful Ellie Tyler—had been let out, and I wasn't quite ready to deal with the collateral damage she could cause to my old self.

I forced a smile that felt more like a grimace, suddenly both terrified and emboldened by my reckless behavior. I needed to digest what I'd just done. The elderly gentleman pressed the button for the lobby. He glanced at me.

"I . . . I need to get an early start," I said to Martin, who stood waiting outside the elevator, his hand out to me. The doors started to slide closed.

"El—"

The doors closed.

I heard him yell and slap the door. "Call me!"

The elevator car descended. Going down, down, down. I could smell him on me. Smell sex in the elevator. The mirror was still misted from my steamy touch. The couple exchanged a glance and moved farther away from me. The elevator stopped on a lower floor. A man got on. He stared at me. I was filled with a sudden self-revulsion. Shame. He could smell sex on me—I was sure of it. He was giving me a lewd look. Claustrophobia tightened. An old sensation of paranoia resurfaced in me. Like everyone was watching me, knowing things, voices whispering behind my back, susurrations in the wind . . . mocking . . .

Bad mother.

Slut.

Siren.

Passive.

Aggressive.

Mad.

Mentally unstable.

Do you know she stabbed her ex?

Two faces of Ellie. Good Ellie. Bad Ellie. Weak Ellie. Strong Ellie.

The car stopped, and the doors started to open on the ground floor. I squeezed out the crack before they could even open fully. I hurried for the exit.

"Hey!" the man called from behind me.

I turned.

"You dropped something." He came loping toward me holding something out in the palm of his hand. Gold glinted. Martin's cuff link. With the letters MCS.

I snatched it from his hand without a word and rushed toward the hotel doors.

By the time I got home I felt a bit better. I ran a scalding bubble bath and took an Ativan. Just to calm the noises that had started up in my head again. I blamed my dad for that. He'd triggered me. I wouldn't take any more pills after this one.

I sank into the bubbles and let the heat swallow me. I closed my eyes and relived sex with Martin.

I touched myself between my legs. I felt a smile. There was no need to feel ashamed.

Change the narrative, Ellie.

I was no longer Doug's wife. This was not going to be my house. I was not Chloe's mother. I was moving to the city. Single city girl.

"I travel a lot. But I can make long distance work."

I could be Martin's lover. His girlfriend.

But will you actually give me a second thought, Martin Cresswell-Smith, or is this just what you do when you travel, a lot?

I sank down under the hot water and held my breath. As I had done so often after Chloe drowned, just trying to imagine what my poor baby had felt.

Until I came up gasping, flailing for air, my hair streaming down my face.

THEN

ELLIE

Just over two years ago, January 10. Vancouver, BC.

I woke with a sense of something . . . different. My head felt thick, my mouth fuzzy with the taste of stale alcohol. It took a second for the sharp, bright reality to cut in.

I sat upright.

Martin. A stranger. Sex in a hotel elevator.

I got up hurriedly and made coffee with the Nespresso machine I'd left unpacked. I sipped my coffee, watching the garden. The heavy green trees twisting and swaying. The dead heads in the flower beds. The leafless blueberry scrub. The berry bushes made me think of the time the bear had come. Thoughts of sex with Martin folded into a memory of Doug holding Chloe up to the window, him pointing to the bear. Chloe's giggle.

Sucked in deep by the image, I smiled sadly into my reflection on the windowpane. The memory was soft. Like a heavy cashmere coat. Familiar. Comforting. And it struck me—I could handle the memories. I could feel sad but smile at the same time. I didn't *need* the medication. I'd truly, finally, come through the tunnel of grief. I'd even had sex with a new man.

Was this what closure was? Not boxing the loss away but living with it. In a new space. Being able to cherish the memories and still think about tomorrow . . . and hope?

I reached for my purse and found the napkin with Martin's number. I picked up my phone, but nerves bit. I set it down, showered. I picked up the phone again while blow-drying my hair.

I put it down.

As I combed my hair I thought of his words.

"Four more days at this hotel. I'm checking out on Monday. But seriously, Ellie, call. Anytime . . . I can make long distance work."

What if I didn't call? He did not have my number. We'd be ships that had passed in the night.

For a moment I wished I *had* given him my number. So it would be up to him.

But it wasn't. I wandered around my boxed-up house fingering his smooth gold cuff link. It was a sign. I took a deep breath and called him.

The phone rang five times. I heard his voice.

"You've reached Martin Cresswell-Smith. I can't take your call right now. Please leave a message and I'll get back to you as soon as I can."

I hung up, trembling slightly from a punch of nerves that was intoxicating.

The movers arrived and I went out for breakfast while they loaded the truck. I googled Martin from the coffee shop. Of course I did. Who wouldn't? He had a LinkedIn profile that said he owned a private development company—*CW Properties International*. It linked to a company website with his bio. The website looked slick. It listed a portfolio of developments past, pending, and proposed. Images of his various sales teams around the world. A photo of Martin seated behind a massive glass desk in a voluminous Toronto office with a brilliant view of the city skyline. Contact info. He had no social media profiles. I liked that. It showed professionalism to me. Discretion. I broadened my search to the Cresswell-Smith name in Australia. A link to a story came up about Jeremy Cresswell-Smith. The brother Martin had spoken about—ex–rugby player and son of Malcolm Cresswell-Smith. I had his dad's name now.

I searched the name Malcolm Cresswell-Smith and followed the links to a company website and also found news stories about shopping malls and other real estate stuff. Then I discovered a business-magazine feature on Malcolm Cresswell-Smith. From the date on the article, it appeared that Malcolm Cresswell-Smith had retired several years ago. He lived with his wife on a horse farm in the Hunter Valley, not far from Sydney. His son, Jeremy, ran the company—Smith and Cresswell Properties—and his daughter, Pauline Rudd, was involved in marketing. She was also on the company board. No mention of Martin.

I sat back and looked out the window. Pedestrians passed by the coffee shop hunkered into coats, with umbrellas pointing into a brisk winter wind filled with sleet. So Martin really had been cut out. Like he'd said.

I felt a twinge of emotion for him.

I dialed his number again. Got the same message.

I left the coffee shop thinking that at least he had my number now from my missed calls. He could phone me. I was sure he would.

But three days later, on Sunday evening, when Dana came by my new apartment to crack open a housewarming bottle of wine, Martin still had not called.

THEN

ELLIE

Just over two years ago, January 13. Vancouver, BC.

"The *elevator*? You have got to be kidding me."

I shook my head.

"Crap, Ellie."

"I know. Most risqué thing I've ever done in my life."

Dana laughed and raised her glass. "Cheers to that!"

We'd opened a second bottle of wine and were sitting on my new balcony in our down jackets under an outdoor heater, our Ugg-covered feet up on the railing. Beyond the deck cover, rain fell softly in the January darkness. I'd told her about meeting Martin, and that I'd googled him, and he looked legit.

"He sounds too good to be true," she said.

"Yeah. I know."

"Maybe he is—I mean, too good to be true."

I gave a shrug. "Might come to nothing anyway. I hate myself for calling, though. I feel cheap. Stupid for thinking he might have actually wanted to hear from me again." I sipped my wine. "I knew better, it's just . . . hoping, you know? That there was actually some spark, something special."

"Hey, you're doing great. Maybe there's a valid reason he hasn't returned your calls, and even if he doesn't call, just having done this was a big step."

"You think?"

She pulled a weird mouth, as if she wasn't so sure. "Uh . . . yeah. I think so."

We laughed and got happily drunk. We ordered pizza as the night wore on, and just as Dana was about to leave, my phone rang. I froze. My heart hammered. My gaze shot to her.

"Answer it!"

I reached for my phone. Unknown number on caller ID. I cleared my throat. "Hello?"

It went dead.

I stared at the phone. "What the—?"

We waited for a moment, but it didn't ring again.

After Dana left I sat in the dark for a long time, just fingering the engraved letters in the smooth gold of his cuff link.

He'd be checking out of the hotel tomorrow.

This cuff link was expensive. A personalized accessory. One of a pair. Maybe he was upset he'd lost it. How would it look that I'd kept it? I *had* to return it. Surely? A normal person without hang-ups would return an expensive piece of jewelry. I'd drop it off at the hotel tomorrow morning. Early. Before he checked out. If I happened to run into him in the lobby, I could say that was why I'd tried to phone him—to return his cuff link.

I felt better already.

THEN

ELLIE

Just over two years ago, January 14. Vancouver, BC.

"Ms. Tyler, good to see you," said the manager of the Hartley Plaza Hotel as I approached the hotel reception desk in the lobby. I'd taken extra care. Blow-dried my hair. It hung long and shiny down my back, my bangs thick over my eyes. I'd selected a nice cranberry-red wool coat. Boots. Scarf. Black-lace underwear. I told myself the underwear was for me—just to make me feel good. I was not desperate. This was my narrative. I was a woman who wore sexy underwear. I was just returning an item with possible sentimental value to the owner.

"What can we do for you?" He was fawning. I was Sterling Hartley's daughter. This was his hotel. I was used to this behavior.

"I have something that belongs to one of your guests. I'd like to return it before he checks out."

"Leave it with me and we'll see that it gets to—"

"I'd rather hand it to him myself. Can you tell me if he's still here?"

He hesitated. The two employees behind the check-in desk exchanged a glance. It was against protocol. But I was also Sterling Hartley's daughter.

"I'll handle this," the manager said to one of the employees. He took over her computer station and asked, "What is the guest's name, Ms. Tyler?"

"Martin," I said. "Martin Cresswell-Smith."

He tapped at the keyboard. "No one of that name is registered with us."

"He's checked out already?"

He frowned and tapped at the computer keyboard again. "We've had no one of that name in our system."

"Are you *sure*?"

"I'm certain."

"Maybe you spelled it wrong." I scribbled Martin's name down on a hotel notepad using the spelling from the paper napkin, which was the same as the spelling I'd googled. I gave it to the manager.

"That's how I spelled it."

"Could you try again?"

He held my gaze for a moment.

"Please."

He humored me. I scanned the lobby, hoping to catch a glimpse of Martin wheeling his luggage through.

"I'm sorry, Ms. Tyler."

"But I know he was here."

I saw him sign the bar tab to his room. We had sex in the elevator when we went up to his room.

"I really am sorry."

I felt blindsided. I stared at the manager. I had been so certain of how this would work. He'd come down in the elevator. I'd give him the cuff link. He'd say he'd been trying to call me, or that he'd had back-to-back meetings, or . . . something. He'd kiss me. We'd go for lunch before he went to catch his plane.

I rummaged in my purse and took out my phone. I showed the manager the screenshot I'd saved of the photo of Martin sitting at his Toronto office desk.

"This man. Have you seen him? Perhaps he registered under another name?"

The manager regarded me oddly, then glanced at my phone. He shook his head. I showed the photo to the two employees.

One said, "Yeah, I think I saw him the other night. In the Mallard Lounge."

"Who was on bar duty that night—do you remember?"

She frowned, glanced at her manager. He gave a shrug.

"Tony Jarecki," said the employee. "He works the bar most nights."

"Bald guy?"

"Yeah."

I made straight for the Mallard. It was open for breakfast. I found Tony Jarecki sitting behind a desk in a small office off the back of the bar. He looked up from his work, startled to see me.

Without preamble I said, "Did this man come into the bar the other night?" I showed him Martin's photo.

He studied the image, then glanced up and regarded me in silence for a moment. "Yeah."

"Was he a hotel guest, registered here, do you know?"

Tony ran his tongue over his teeth, thinking.

"Don't lie to me," I said. "I can see you're going to lie."

He laughed in an ugly, mirthless way. It made me feel soiled. Mocked. Cheap. I noticed a monitor for a CCTV feed in the corner of the office. A hot, sick feeling suddenly slid through my gut. I wondered if they had CCTV in the elevators. Perhaps Tony and all the other employees had watched me having sex with a stranger. And they were all whispering and laughing behind my back and calling me names.

Fool, fool, fool. Slut, slut, slut.

Stupid, desperate woman opening her legs.

She stabbed her ex, do you know . . .

Hospitalized for a mental breakdown.

I suddenly needed to get out of here.

"For the record," Tony said, his voice low, his words coming slow, "I was not planning to lie, just considering how much a patron might want to protect his, or her, privacy. I'm sure you appreciated that?"

I swallowed, my face going hot.

He angled his head, his black eyes boring into me.

I said, "If it's money you want—"

He surged to his feet. "Please get out, Ms. Tyler. I don't want your money."

"Yet my father can buy you."

His eyes narrowed.

"I saw him talking to you. I'm sure he paid you."

"Your father was looking out for you. He's a good man. He paid me for a service."

I waved my phone at him. "Was this man in this photo here with another woman? Is that why you think he needs privacy?"

"I think you need to leave, Ms. Tyler."

From the look on Tony Jarecki's face I was certain Martin Cresswell-Smith had been in the Mallard with someone else—maybe that woman who'd walked past the elevator. I glanced at the security monitor. I'd bet he was captured on camera with that woman.

"I should get back to my work," he said.

"Yeah. Yeah, you should."

I exited the Mallard Lounge and made my way rapidly through the lobby for the hotel exit. I felt everyone was watching me.

I stepped into the cold air and fingered the cuff link in my coat pocket. *Forget it, Ellie. Move on. You made a mistake and you're embarrassing yourself. Face it, you were just desperate to be wanted, to be needed in that way. It's over.*

I put up my coat collar and leaned into the wind as I stepped off the curb. But even as I headed down the sidewalk with every intention to put it behind me, a deeper, darker, locked-up side of me felt it—something inside had started to go wrong.

THE MURDER TRIAL

Pretrial forensic evaluation session.

"Do you know why you are here, Ellie?"

The psychologist's voice is smooth. Low. He's elegant, almost beautiful in an androgynous way. Sallow skin. Hooded eyes. Long, thin face. Long, tapered fingers. His toes are probably long and tapered, too. Lips not too thin, not too full. Soft-looking. He wears a scarf that probably comes from a market in Nepal. He probably went hiking in the Himalayas, took a side trek to visit some monks in Tibet. He has a corner office with windows that go right down to the floor and lots of natural light. Nevertheless I feel trapped, agitated.

"I'm here because you're a forensic shrink, we're up against a murder trial, and my legal team needs to know whether I can be put on the witness stand. Because that would be a really big gamble, right? To put someone in my position on the stand? They need to know if I might actually help the case or blow it up in their faces, especially on cross."

"And what do you think?" the psychologist asks.

"I'm not the one being paid to think, Doctor."

He regards me. I check my watch. I glance at the door. I'm tightening up with each second that ticks by, afraid he's going to get inside my head, into the deep, dark spaces where my secrets live in shadows. No one is allowed in there. Not even me. I've learned what can happen if I open those doors. But his silence continues. And my chest grows tighter.

So I fill the space, and instantly regret opening my mouth because it's exactly what he's waiting for—this is not my first rodeo. I'm a veteran of therapy.

"I think," I say slowly, "that they would like the jury to see just how much of a victim I am. They want the jury to see what Martin did to *me*, for them to feel sorry for me—to see why he deserved to die."

His brow twitches upward. He moistens his lips as he takes notes. The session is also being recorded. I must be more careful. There are little chocolates in a glass bowl on the table in front of me. Each chocolate is individually wrapped in gold. He sees me looking. He leans forward, pushes the bowl closer.

But I sit back, cross my legs, and wrap my hands around my knee.

"Did he?"

"Did he what?"

"Deserve to die."

I lurch up from the sofa, pace across the room. Stop. Look out the window. We're on the second floor of a brick building. There are people outside on a postage stamp of lawn—mothers or nannies watching kids play on swings. I think of Chloe. I fold my arms tightly over my stomach, and I say softly, "We're all going to die. One way or another. Some people do bad things. I think they deserve to die sooner."

He's silent for a moment. I hear him writing in his notebook, turning a page.

"Did your daughter also deserve to die, Ellie?"

I feel rage building inside my stomach. I'm a hairbreadth from grabbing my purse and walking out. I'm also aware of what is at stake. A guilty verdict or an innocent one. It's not negotiable. I need to do everything I can to help my legal team win this.

"She was too young," I say softly. "Too innocent."

"What about your mother?"

My heartbeat slows, and I say, "My mother died when I was nine, Doctor. Her death has no bearing on this trial."

"It has a bearing on your psyche, Ellie. Nine is a young age to lose a mother. These life events shape what we become. And what you've become is going to matter in court. Whatever can be used against you will be."

Grief can become a Monster that consumes and overtakes you. I know this. I've been told this before.

Outside the window, down below on the patch of grass, a child falls off the swing. Her mother runs over to her, drops to her knees, gathers her child into her arms, and comforts her, stroking the girl's hair.

My thoughts circle back to Chloe. To what we could have had. I think of what I didn't have with my own mother. How my father neglected me before her death and even more so after. The rage swells bigger in my belly, pushing up toward my gullet.

The psychologist moves—I hear the leather of his ergonomically designed chair squeak.

"Do you want to tell me what you remember of your mother's death, Ellie? You were at home with her, right, when she overdosed?"

I swing to face him. "Is this what they're going to do? Find holes in my psyche? Poke at old pain? Trip me up and trick me into saying the wrong things? Just like you're trying to do now?"

"Is that how you see life? People waiting to trick you into revealing yourself?"

But I see in his face that my reaction, my walls, my quickness to anger, have already told him much of what he needs to know.

I'm hiding secrets.

But aren't we all?

THEN

ELLIE

Just over two years ago, January 21. Vancouver, BC.

One week after humiliating myself at the Hartley Plaza, I stopped at a crosswalk in town for a red light, distracted about a meeting I'd just had about a possible job. I carried my large waterproof portfolio case by a strap hooked over my shoulder. It was late afternoon, getting dark already, and the sky was low and full of drizzle. A little girl standing at my side looked up at me. She smiled shyly and angled her head.

Chloe's smile.

My heart stopped, then imploded. My knees almost gave out under me. Her mittened hand held tightly on to her mother's.

She could have been mine. That mother could have been me. Chloe would be five now. If she'd lived. I might still be with Doug. In our old house. Chloe would've just started at the school down the road. I might be standing here right now, holding her hand, waiting to go across the street to meet Doug at his law firm, which was just a block away. We'd be meeting Daddy for his coffee break.

The pedestrian light turned green. The mother tugged the little girl, and they crossed into the street with all the other pedestrians. I couldn't move. Time folded in on itself. It was like I'd glimpsed a parallel universe that would have been my life if I had n0t let go of Chloe's hand in the waves that day.

I managed to step into the road, but the light had already changed. A cyclist almost hit me and veered into traffic. A car swerved for the biker and honked.

"Fucking asshole!" yelled the cyclist over his shoulder. "It's a fucking red light!"

I stumbled backward and up onto the sidewalk, breathing hard. I clenched and unclenched my gloved hands, raw panic circling.

Focus, Ellie. Don't do it—do not become unhinged again. It'll pass. It was just a trigger. A PTSD trigger. Your therapist explained the mechanism of these things.

I turned and began to walk down the sidewalk in the direction from which I'd come. No plan. Just walking. Fast. Focusing on the rhythmic click of my bootheels. Trying to breathe deeply. I kept my head down, averting my eyes from the faces of others. Heat flushed my cheeks. It started to rain more heavily. I decided I'd head for a bookstore near Gastown. Sit there awhile. There was a liquor store one block away from the bookstore. I'd stop in there afterward, buy a bottle of wine or two to take home. I had some pills left. I'd take one. Relax. Sleep it off. I'd be okay by tomorrow.

I rounded a corner. And froze.

On the sidewalk ahead of me a man moved quickly down the hill. It was the blond hair that had snared my attention. Like a beacon. Shiny and thick.

Martin?

He wore a tailored coat and carried a briefcase. People parted around him like he was a shark in a sea of dark tones of gray upon gray upon black. He strode swiftly, heading away from me.

My heart began to hammer. My mouth turned dry.

I jerked into action, pushing and shouldering through a stream of people coming off a bus. Martin turned around a building, disappearing from sight. I began to run, my portfolio bumping against me and flapping out and hitting pedestrians, who cursed at me.

I rounded the corner, panting. Then stopped. Rain drummed down, fine and steady. I glimpsed him again. He was halfway down the block, where the sidewalk was nearly empty. I hurried after him, not even considering properly why I was following him, or what I'd say when I reached him. If it was even him.

He stopped at an intersection ahead of me to wait for cars to pass. He turned and looked directly at me.

I stilled.

It *was* him—it was definitely him. I raised my gloved hand. But he looked straight past me, through me. His face blank.

"Martin?" I called, raising my hand higher, waving. "Martin!"

He looked over his shoulder as if to see whom I was calling to. Then he crossed the street and vanished into the entrance to an underground parking garage.

In shock, I slowly lowered my hand. It was him. I was certain it was him. Or . . . could I be wrong?

I scurried forward and stopped at the entrance to the concrete ramp that led down into the bowels of the garage. He'd gone down there. The garage exhaled a cold, damp smell. I hesitated, then started down the ramp to the first underground level. I rounded a curved concrete wall. From there I could see through a gap down to the next level. *Martin.* He'd stopped beside an orange Subaru Crosstrek. I was about to go farther down the ramp when the driver's door of the Subaru swung open.

A woman got out. I couldn't see her face. She had a woolen hat on against the cold, and a scarf was wound around her neck, hiding her chin. She was bundled into a puffer coat, so I had no clue of her body shape. And the light was dim. She kissed him, and he placed his hand at the small of her back. The memory of Martin touching me in that way slammed through me. I tried to swallow. The woman walked around to the passenger side, got in. The door shut. Martin put his briefcase on the back seat, climbed into the driver's seat, and shut the driver's side door. The engine started.

My brain reeled. He'd said he was leaving Vancouver on Monday last week. The hotel manager said he'd never registered at the Hartley Plaza. But I'd seen him sign that bar tab to his room. Was I going mad?

The car reversed out of the parking space. It came up the ramp, making for the exit into the street. I panicked and glanced around in desperation for a place to hide. A door to my right led to a stairwell. I opened the door and ducked inside. As the door swung slowly shut, the Subaru drove past. Martin looked out the window. I tried to press back against the wall, but he saw me through the open gap. The car continued, and the stairwell door swung shut.

I sucked in a shaky breath. Had I imagined this? No. It had to have been someone else, not Martin. Not the warm Australian developer seeking a backer for his project in New South Wales. Not the man who wanted kids and had been so attentive . . . the man I'd had sex with in an elevator.

I rubbed my face hard.

Mistake—that's all. I'd made an error. He was someone who looked like Martin Cresswell-Smith. A doppelgänger. It was not unheard of. And I'd been sucked into some weird concept of reality after seeing a child that could be Chloe. That was all this was.

Then, as I stood in that cold, concrete, pee-scented stairwell, my phone rang. I fumbled in my purse, checked the caller ID.

Not a familiar number.

I connected the call with a shaky gloved finger and put the phone to my ear.

"Hello?"

There was a moment of staticky noise. "Ellie . . . hello? Hello—can you hear me?"

I blinked. My legs sort of sagged. I glanced through the tiny window that was set into the stairwell door as if the car might still be there. But there was nothing. I felt confused.

"Are you there, Ellie? This is Martin. Have I got the right number?"

"I, uh . . . yeah. Yeah, this is Ellie. Um. Could you hang on a sec? I . . . I'm just . . . in a store, paying for a purchase." I pressed my phone against my coat, muffling the sound. I waited, gathering my wits, trying to organize my thoughts, hoping I could make my voice sound normal. I put the phone back to my ear. "Sorry about that."

"Before you say anything, Ellie, I want to say I am so sorry not to have managed to return your calls until now. I had my phone nicked at Heathrow, somewhere between a fish-and-chips shop, an airport bar, and the plane. It had your contact details. I had to wait until I got home and could get my history and contact information reloaded."

"Where . . ." My voice caught. I pushed open the door and peered down into the lower level of the parking garage again. The spot where the orange Subaru had been parked was still vacant. My mind wheeled. I cleared my throat. "Where are you now?"

"Sea-Tac Airport. About to board a flight up to YVR. It's been a whirlwind of back-to-back meetings since I last saw you. I miss you."

I blinked. "I . . . This is so weird."

"What is?"

"I thought I just saw you."

"Where?"

"Vancouver. Downtown."

He laughed. Warm. Because everything Martin did felt warm. That familiar feeling of attraction, affection, curled through me.

"I must have a double. Look, I'm going to be landing in Vancouver in a few hours. I'll be there for two days. Can I see you tomorrow night, El? Dinner, maybe? I know a special little place in Deep Cove. I'd love to spend longer with you this time."

"I . . . I'd like that."

We made a plan to meet at the restaurant, and the call ended. Dazed, I stood in the stinking, cold stairwell for a moment, trying to regroup. My old therapist's words played through my mind.

"We go through life mishearing and mis-seeing and misunderstanding so that the stories we tell ourselves will add up. We fill in gaps that make no sense because we want to believe something."

That was it. I'd so badly wanted to see Martin that I'd believed I had.

THEN

ELLIE

Just over two years ago, January 22. Vancouver, BC.

"God, you look good, El. More beautiful than I remembered."

"And you—you've been in the sun. Where'd you get the tan?" I'd known the moment I saw him sitting at the table by the window that it was not Martin I'd seen yesterday. The doppelgänger had not had a tan. And the doppelgänger's hair had been longer. Martin was sun-browned and his hair had been trimmed short. He looked good. All my subterranean qualms had evaporated as he stood up and kissed me on the mouth.

"Spain," he said as he poured wine for me. "Five days on a yacht off Marbella." A broad smile cut across his face, his teeth white against his bronzed complexion. "Even in winter the Med weather can be stunning." He set the bottle back into the ice bucket. "I hope you like it. Pinot gris. Sloquannish Hills. It's a small vineyard in—"

"In the Okanagan. I know. Coincidentally, it's one of my favorites." The last time I'd had this wine was at my father's expense at the Mallard Lounge. Two bottles of it.

"Well, then, I approve of your taste." He lifted his glass. "Cheers. To seeing you again. I'm glad you could make it, Ellie. I'm glad you didn't give up on me."

"I'm glad, too." We chinked glasses. "Was the Marbella trip for pleasure or business?" I took a sip and felt the lovely spread of warmth through my chest.

"Business. However, I did manage to conduct it on a friend's yacht. The Spanish financier is backing my marina development in New South Wales. It's all systems go."

"Congratulations."

"I know, right? All the more reason to celebrate."

I opened the menu, but Martin placed his hand on mine. "I've ordered."

"What?"

He smiled. "We can change it if you like, but I've ordered the bouillabaisse. For both of us. It's the specialty here. I want you to try it, Ellie." He paused. "I have a reason."

I felt a vague unease. "What reason?"

He gave a sly grin. "Later," he said. "First we eat. You might not like the dish, then I shall have to restrategize."

I set my glass down. "Actually, I have a reason of my own for wanting to see you again." I took a small box out of my purse. I placed it squarely on the table between us.

A flicker of concern darted through his eyes.

"Open it," I said.

He opened the box. His gold cuff link winked in the candlelight. He glanced up, met my gaze.

"You dropped it in the elevator. It's why I phoned you. I wanted to let you know I'd found it. In case it meant something to you."

He picked the cuff link up out of the box. "Thank you. I was hoping you'd called because you—"

"I went to the hotel to look for you on Monday morning," I said quickly before I chickened out. "To return it."

His gaze locked with mine. I watched his face carefully.

"You weren't there, Martin. You weren't ever registered as a guest at the hotel."

His eyes narrowed ever so slightly. "No? Are you sure?"

"I'm certain."

His mouth flattened at the shift in my tone. "Perhaps Gertrude registered us under the company name."

I felt my cheeks heat. "Gertrude?"

"My personal assistant." He looked at me oddly. "Is everything okay, Ellie?"

I glanced down, fiddled with the stem of my glass. I felt like an idiot. "Was she—does Gertrude travel with you?"

"Sometimes. Depends on the trip. She did accompany me on the Vancouver trip—I needed her to handle a bunch of stuff, and to entertain the wife of an investor from Spain. Turned out well—it was his yacht I was on in Marbella."

"Oh, oh, that's . . . good." I cleared my throat. I didn't dare tell him I'd badgered the barman at the Mallard, too. But it would explain why The Rock might have seen Martin with a woman in the Mallard Lounge. I was spared any further embarrassment by the arrival of the entrées.

The server placed two steaming bowls of bouillabaisse on the table along with small bowls of rouille plus slices of grilled bread. When the server left, Martin took the cuff link box and slipped it into his pocket. "Maybe I dropped it on purpose."

"Excuse me?"

He crooked up a blond brow. "Maybe I dropped the cuff link like a glass slipper at the ball in the hope you'd come and find me."

I laughed, maybe a little too loud, but it was a relief to move on from my embarrassment.

The bouillabaisse was fabulous. We ordered more wine and spoke about art, the galleries he'd visited in Europe, paintings he liked, a work he'd recently acquired for his office in Toronto—he showed me a photo of where it had been hung to the best light advantage, and I recognized the interior of his office from the screenshot still in my phone. I loved that Martin even had a vocabulary around my passion for art. Doug had never expressed interest.

When dessert and coffees arrived, he said, "So, I've told you all about my family and I still know so little about yours, El. When I mentioned that I'd disappointed my dad, you said you understood, and you sounded like you meant it."

I hesitated. Things always shot off on a weird trajectory when people learned I was Sterling Hartley's daughter who stood to inherit billions. I'd perhaps already waited too long to tell Martin, and I feared it was going to look odd. Even so, I hesitated, then started with my mother instead.

"She died when I was nine." I took a sip of espresso. "She was an alcoholic and abusing prescription meds. She killed herself."

His dessert spoon stilled midair. I read something in his eyes . . . unease. I was scaring him off. Perhaps he was wondering if I'd inherited psycho genes. Maybe I had. I sure as hell wasn't going to mention right now that I'd suffered from clinical depression myself and had slipped into a haze of medication and drink for months after Chloe drowned. And then I'd been institutionalized for mental health issues. I also knew the instant I mentioned my father's name that he might actually recall having read some of these things about Sterling Hartley's daughter anyway.

"I'm sorry, El. I'm so sorry."

"It was a long time ago."

"Those things experienced as a kid—they live with you. I know."

I nodded and felt a bond. He covered my hand with his.

"What about your father? Did he remarry?"

"I doubt my dad will ever marry again. He's the eternal Peter Pan—Sterling Hartley."

He stared. Said nothing. Then he cursed softly. "The AGORA convention—you didn't mention it. When I said I was at the Hartley Plaza for the event. Christ, your family namesake hotel and you didn't mention it?" He was angry. There was a rough edginess about him. "Why not?"

"Because, Martin, I'd just met you, and liked you, and I wanted you to get to know me not as my father's daughter. If there was to be any chance of us meeting again, I wanted it to be because you liked *me*. When people find out I'm his daughter . . . it changes things. Like now."

"Christ." He sat back and grabbed his wine. He regarded me like I was some kind of laboratory specimen in a petri dish. I could almost see his brain whirring, slotting pieces together.

"I'm sorry, but . . . please, Martin, don't let this ruin everything, okay?"

His features remained unreadable, then a grin suddenly cut his face and he laughed loud and long. "I had sex with Sterling Hartley's kid in an elevator at his hotel," he said between chuckles. "I don't believe it."

"His *kid*?" I set my napkin on the table. "I really should go."

"No . . . no, El. Stop. Don't go." He wiped his eyes. "C'mon. I love it. Pardon my French but your dad is a first-class a-hole, a business sociopath with narcissism issues. Show me a magazine or news article or Twitter feed that doesn't say all those things about the arrogant billionaire Sterling James Hartley. All those wannabes at the AGORA convention know this about him, yet would never say it to his face, because he's also a rich motherfucker who has the magic and money to make others rich, too."

I pushed back my chair.

"Ellie—"

I came to my feet. "Look, maybe I dislike my own father, Martin. Maybe I also love him, too. Did you think about that? He's all those things, but he's still the only real family I've got, and someone laughing because they think they've screwed him over by screwing me in his elevator—"

"Ellie—" His face sobered, and he caught hold of my wrist. "I'm sorry. Please. Please forgive me. Sit down, please."

I stared at him, a sick feeling dawning. Could this man have already known who I was when he bumped into me?

Slowly, quietly, I said, "Why did you really ask me to dinner, Martin? Is this some game to you?"

He cursed softly under his breath. "No, El. Absolutely not. Please sit. Hear me out."

I seated myself on the edge of my chair.

"Listen, the reason I brought you here tonight—the bouillabaisse—I'm going to be leaving for an eight-week business trip to Europe. One of the stops is Nice, and there's this most gorgeous little restaurant that serves absolutely the best bouillabaisse in the world. I wanted to get you in the mood, get a sample, a taste . . . Would you come?"

"What . . . what do you mean?"

"Come with me, Ellie. To Europe."

"What?"

He leaned forward and took both my hands in his. As he spoke he traced the insides of my wrists gently with his thumbs. "I leave on Friday and I hate that I won't see you for eight weeks. Come with."

"I . . . I can't. I work. I . . . have a new contract."

"Of course." He let go of my hands and sat back.

My brain raced as I hurriedly cataloged all my commitments—freelance projects, deadlines. I replayed in my mind how I'd felt when he'd simply vanished out of my life after the night we'd met, and suddenly I didn't want to let him go.

"How about joining me for just part of the trip, then?" he said. "Maybe a few days in Rome? Venice? Or—" His eyes brightened with an idea. "What about we take a few days in the Cook Islands at the end of the trip?"

"That's on the other end of the world from Europe."

"So? Who cares? Aitutaki—I know a stunning resort on the lagoon there. We can have whole beaches to ourselves, Ellie, a little luxury hut with high-end room service right over the water. Sunshine. Warmth. Who doesn't want some sun at this time of year?"

Thoughts swirled crazily through my brain. Due dates. Line drawings. Concept sketches. Excitement built.

He leaned forward again, a barely restrained energy simmering like electricity around him, and I realized it was utterly contagious. It was crackling over my skin.

"Could you perhaps bring your projects? Maybe you could work on some of your art while I go to my meetings? Then we could meet up for dinners?"

"Martin, I—"

"I know. It's crazy." He raked his hand through his thick hair, and the candlelight glimmered on his exorbitantly priced Rolex Daytona—I'd googled that design. I knew how much it cost. The cuff links, too. I'd searched for the little stamp in the gold on the inside. I wasn't sure why I'd done that. Perhaps it was because I wanted—needed—to know that he had wealth of his own. It made me feel he wasn't after mine.

"The trip would be on me, El. Everything taken care of. Gertrude will make all the reservations and compile our itineraries. Some of the nicest hotels and pensions, because honestly, I like to travel comfortably."

I swallowed. I thought of sunshine and crystal clear lagoons. And being with this man. And sex. Lots of sex.

Your choice. Your story. Pick your narrative.

How wrong could it go?

THE WATCHER

Outside, across the road from the Deep Cove restaurant beneath a leafless tree with gnarled fingers, the Watcher sat in a dark car, watching the lighted windows of the quaint restaurant. The interior of the car was cold, but an engine idling too long in order to keep the car warm would draw too much attention. Martin Cresswell-Smith could be seen inside one of the lighted windows. A candle flickered between him and Ellie Tyler. It was a romantic and golden vignette framed by winter darkness. Martin reached across the table and cupped Ellie Tyler's face. The waiter returned to their table with the check.

The Watcher reached for the camera on the passenger seat, removed gloves, focused the lens, aimed, clicked.

A few moments later a yellow cab drew up outside the restaurant entrance.

The couple exited, bundled in their coats against the cold. Martin placed his hand at Ellie's back and leaned close to whisper something in her ear. Ellie laughed, throwing her head back and exposing a pale column of throat, her long hair shimmering like a dark waterfall under the outside lights. The Watcher clicked the camera. And again.

The couple got into the waiting cab.

The taxi pulled off.

The Watcher started the car and pulled into the street behind the cab, tires crackling on dead leaves and frosted paving. Crystals and ice glistened in the headlights.

The taxi crossed the Lions Gate Bridge, entered the city, and turned into an expensive residential part of town. It stopped outside a new apartment block owned by the Hartley Group.

The Watcher parked in the shadows across the street and watched as the couple exited the taxi, Martin Cresswell-Smith's hand once more at the small of his date's back. Proprietary. The Watcher reached for the camera.

Click, click, click.

The couple entered the apartment complex doors and disappeared from sight.

The Watcher counted up floors. Waited.

Several minutes later lights clicked on in a unit on the twelfth floor. The couple came into view, kissing, shucking coats, pulling at shirts. The watcher zoomed in with the telephoto lens, clicked. And again. *Click.* The couple disappeared from view. Lights dimmed. The Watcher waited. Cold crept into the vehicle.

The apartment lights went out.

Game on.

The Watcher reached forward and started the car.

THEN

ELLIE

Almost two years ago, March. Cook Islands.

The wind blew hot against my face as I gripped my handlebars and sped after Martin's scooter through a plantation in the Cook Islands, clinging to every last drop of our travels before we had to fly back to the cold, wet Pacific Northwest and my old life.

It had been glorious. Skiing in Austria and visits to the spa while Martin met with businesspeople. A side trip to Croatia. A week in a villa in Marbella on Spain's Costa del Sol while Martin took meetings on his friend's yacht and I sketched with windows open to the sea breeze. Two weeks in Nice, where we enjoyed the famous bouillabaisse at the restaurant Martin had told me about over dinner in Deep Cove. There had been shopping and visits to art galleries and museums. And Martin had bought me some exquisitely beautiful Venetian beads. He hadn't allowed me to pay for a thing, and I loved him for it. I was ready to be with a man again, especially one who treated me like a princess. One who was not after my trust fund. I'd paid dearly in losing Chloe. I'd worked hard to pull myself back up. It was time for me to be in a good place. I had a right to be happy, didn't I? Didn't everyone?

We navigated a series of bends on our rented scooters and came upon a lagoon with a sugar-white beach. Not another soul in sight. We parked the bikes and laid out our mats along with the small picnic provided by our resort.

Heat radiated off the sand as we ate and drank wine.

When Martin kissed me, a powerful swell of emotion ballooned up inside my chest and pushed into my throat, shaping words in my mouth.

I love you.

They almost slipped out of my lips, but like secret, pleasureful things, I held them back, cautious. I was generally cautious, and this thought suddenly reminded me of my father.

"Ellie is passive . . . It's the quiet ones people forget to worry about. Snakes in the grass."

Martin moved hair back off my face and looked down into my eyes. I believed I saw in his gaze those same words. *I love you.* My heart squeezed with happiness. On some level I knew it was a drug—endorphins. The neurological chemical cocktail of fresh love. Addictive. I wanted more.

Martin stood and dropped his shorts. "Coming for a swim?"

I hesitated. Suddenly the music in my mind turned discordant, like wrong piano notes. Fear, cold and black, snaked through me.

He saw it in my face. "Ellie?"

"I . . ." I suddenly couldn't talk.

He reseated himself. A look of concern creased his features as he squinted against the bright sunlight. "You know, I don't even know if you like to swim?"

So much you don't truly know about me yet, Martin. And when you do know . . . will you still want to spend time with me?

"Do you?" he said. "Like to swim, I mean?"

I laughed uneasily. But the world had tilted sideways, and my own laugh sounded like an ugly little noise in my brain. A memory reared a demon head. It crashed in a salty wave through my being. I felt Chloe's hand in mine. I felt her slipping. I cleared my throat. "I don't feel like going in. But you go. I'll watch."

"It's cooking hot," he said. "Look at you. You're glowing with sweat. Pink in the face. Tell me you don't need to cool off?"

Conflict tangled with anxiety and a desire to please him. On the back of it rode a desperation to rid myself of these black thoughts that always came when I considered going back into the sea. I *craved* the freedom of swimming in the ocean again, yet I was terrified of the feelings and triggers that came with the notion.

"Come." He reached for my hand and drew me to my feet, this solid, golden, naked man. "No waves. No currents. No sharks or anything. It's a lagoon, El. It's only waist-deep—shoulder deep at max. I'll hold you if you're scared."

No waves. No waves, no waves, no strong currents.

"I . . . I used to swim," I said. "A lot. I was a good swimmer. I was on a team at school . . ." My voice faded as I stared at the expanse of saltwater lagoon. I heard waves booming, but they were in the distance, way out at the reef. They were also in my memory, thundering away. He tried to lead me to the water, but I resisted. Couldn't help it.

He frowned, hesitated, then said, "Okay. Sit. Talk to me, El." He seated himself on the mat and drew me down next to him.

Thighs touching, we sat in silence for a long while. The sun rose higher, into its zenith. I sweated. He was patient. If I wanted to be with him—and I believed I did—I needed to tell him, because he'd find out eventually.

"I know, Ellie," he said gently. "I know about Waimea Bay and what happened there."

I closed my eyes. Emotion burned. Of course he fucking knew. I'd googled *him* after I'd met him. And after I told him I was a Hartley—who wouldn't have pulled up some of the old news stories? He'd probably been waiting for me to tell him myself. On my own terms. Once more, I felt like a total stupid asshole of an idiot.

"There are no waves here," he said again. "But I understand if you don't want to go in." He moved hair behind my ear because I'd allowed it to fall forward to hide my shame. "It's the ocean that brings it back, isn't it?"

I nodded.

"Grief is a funny thing, you know."

"I know. Except some people just seem to get over it and move on."

"Sometimes it just appears that way on the outside."

"Yeah. But . . . I . . . maybe it's because I feel guilt. About not having been a better mother. My old therapist figured unresolved guilt sets us up for poor bereavement prognosis. So maybe that's what happened."

"Do you want to tell me in your words what happened?"

I looked out over the sun-sparkled water. So peaceful. Tranquil. "Her name was Chloe," I said softly. I flicked him a glance. "But you know that, don't you?"

He nodded.

"Then you know she was just three." I paused. It was actually easier saying the words to Martin than I'd thought it would be. He had a way about him that made me want to give, to tell, to be open. He was a good listener and exuded no sense of judgment. "We—Doug, my ex-husband, Chloe's father—went on a holiday to Hawaii. It was supposed to be one of those wonderful family times. My father and his then-new girlfriend were to join us, and Doug's parents were already there. We—Doug and I and his parents—rented cars and drove around to the north side of Oahu, where we stopped at Waimea Bay, which is well known for surfing."

He nodded. But let me work through it, word by word.

"The sea was this incredible indigo, flecked with white foam. Like scallops of lace on water." I stared at the lagoon and listened to the distant boom of surf on the reef. Sweat pooled under my breasts, trickled down my sides. "Utterly cloudless sky. Hot. So hot. We'd bought a pineapple, and stopped at the beach to eat it. There was a fair-sized group on the beach. Lifeguards. People swimming between the flags. Swells big, but rounded and smooth. A small shore break." I paused, gathering myself.

"Doug went in, bodysurfing. But someone needed to watch Chloe, so I stayed on the beach with her. It was nearing noon. Fierce sun. Too hot for Doug's mom, so she and Doug's dad drove on to find a place for lunch. Doug stayed out in the water forever. Chloe was getting irritable and I wanted to swim, too. It was always Doug who . . ." My words faded. I cleared my throat.

"I decided to take her in. There were others with children in the water. There were lifeguards. We stayed in the shallows. It was fun, floating, laughing, bouncing over the small waves. We went in a bit deeper. Then I suddenly lost my footing. There was a dip in the ocean floor, and I found myself treading water, out of my depth. I held Chloe afloat and began to scissor kick back to the beach, but I realized I was in the grip of a current. Powerful. It seemed to come out of nowhere. I kicked my legs harder while holding Chloe up. She was giggling but I'd begun to panic. And suddenly a set of swells barreled in. The first swell was huge. It sucked us up but we sailed smoothly down the back, but it also took us more solidly into the rip. The next wave broke over us, pummeled us right in and down and around and around like a washing machine. I . . ." My hands began to tremble. Memories started blurring, folding, darkening. Hiding. Peeking. Dragging me back into shadows again. I saw Chloe's face in the milky underwater churn. I saw her eyes. Wide. Her mouth open as if calling me. Her hair floating around her face. I felt her hand in mine. Slipping away as the sea tore her from me.

"I tried to hold on to her. Tried so hard. Didn't know which way was up or down and had no breath left. Her little body was slippery from sun lotion. Little slippery fish. She was ripped right out of my hands. And I came up, foam everywhere, salt water and hair in my eyes and I was choking and—" A ball of pain hiccuped through me and strangled my words. I sat silent, breathing hard.

Martin covered my hand and sat silent, too. Giving me time, space. No judgment that I could feel. I sucked in a shaky breath. "I screamed and screamed, and dove down, and searched and I . . . the lifeguards pulled me out. I was hysterical, still screaming for Chloe. Jet Skis and paddleboards went out. Doug came in. He ran up the beach. He . . . he was yelling at me, asking how in the hell I could have done that— gone out so far. Hadn't I seen the signs about rip currents. Why hadn't I stayed in the flag zone. Didn't I realize conditions could change on a dime." I swiped sweat from my brow and heaved out a shuddering breath. "Boats went out looking. A helicopter in the air. Everyone helped. A full-scale search-and-rescue operation was launched. But the surf got really high. You can't believe how big it can get there. From flat to thunderous, murderous, in a heartbeat. They found nothing. That night we waited on the beach while they kept searching with spotlights. And then the next morning, she . . . she . . . my Chloe, my little Chloe, my little three-year-old, my baby, my toddler—her body. All broken and bloodied. On the rocks . . ." Tears slid down my face, turning my sunblock into a horrible soapy chemical taste on my lips. I smeared it away. "It was my fault, Martin. Doug let me know it. He couldn't love me after that. He never touched me after that. He'd adored Chloe. Losing her cost us our marriage. Doug came to hate me and I turned into this awful specter that just *begged* to be hated. I became this ugly, fat shell that housed bitterness and grief, and I got to a point where I just wanted to curl up and die."

He nodded, looking far off into the distance. "Is this what precipitated the . . . pill thing? The self-medication and subsequent psychological spiral?"

"So you read about that—of course you did."

He gave a rueful smile. "After Deep Cove. After you told me that Sterling was your dad. I confess, I looked you up."

"Yes," I said softly. "And I hate that everyone pays sanctimonious lip service to being more open about mental illness in an effort to destigmatize psychological illness, yet a person with mental illness is judged nevertheless. People whisper and gossip behind your back. You become the laughable or embarrassing drunk, or the drug-addled neurotic paranoid with addiction issues who can't keep her looks and who can't hold on to her husband and could you blame him for leaving her anyway. You become this freak who can't move on from a tragedy because all the collateral damage just compounds the thing. You become the salacious tabloid headline. It's so much easier to get pneumonia, or heart disease, or to break a leg. People are comfortable with that sort of brokenness. They understand that." I sucked in a deep breath. "It's like you've got to kill yourself before everyone can say: 'See? We need to talk about mental health.'"

He said nothing.

I watched his profile, waiting for judgment.

"Do you hate me now?" I said quietly.

"Come here, El."

He gathered me into his arms and held. Just held. Our bodies hot and warm and damp and sticky from sweat and sun lotion. But the smell and solidity of him was so comforting. He stroked my hair, kissed my mouth. "I love you, Ellie Tyler," he whispered. "I freaking love you and I am so sorry you had to go through that. You are a good person. A dear and wonderful and kind and sensitive and creative person, and this should never have happened to you and I have no idea how Chloe's father could ever have abandoned you after this, after what you'd both gone through."

I sobbed as he held me—big, jerking, palsied shudders taking hold of my body. I let it come. Like a purge, like a bloodletting, a lancing of some terrible boil trapped inside my soul. Telling Martin, and having him still hold me, still say he loved me—no therapy had come close to achieving this. It was like I was home. Safe with him. He understood, and he accepted me.

When I had finally quieted, he said, "This is why you won't come and swim with me?"

I nodded.

"But it's about surf, really, isn't it? It's about forceful water, moving water, strong currents, big waves that could render you powerless and snatch things away?"

I sniffed, wiped my nose, and nodded.

"So we can deal with that. Look. The lagoon is basically walled off by sand. It's calm as a bath. No currents here. No sharks. It's shallow. Not even a ripple of wind on the surface. Perhaps if we go in together, and you survive, and perhaps if it doesn't feel so bad, it would be a big step. Would you try it? With me?"

I bit my lip and nodded. It was time. Time to step back into the sea. I wanted to conquer this—make it go away. And maybe I could do this as long as there were no waves or strong currents. He was right. As long as he was there with me. And it would be a first step. It would be empowering if I managed it.

With Martin holding my hand, we entered the lagoon. The water was silky and warm. We went knee-deep, then waist-deep. We lolled and rolled about, and floated, him naked, me in my bikini. He kissed me, and I smiled, then laughed. He hugged me tight, undid my bikini top. Slid off my bikini bottom.

We made love in the water. In the shallows. In defiance of my bad memories.

We swam some more, never going out of my depth—I could stand anytime I wanted. My limbs eased. My heart and soul lightened. It was pure bliss.

We exited the water together and ran hand in hand back to our beach mats. We lay on our backs, drying in the sun, fingers laced.

"Thank you," I whispered as I stared up at the impossibly blue and clear sky. "For being you. For hearing me." I rolled onto my side and trailed my finger down his tummy toward his belly button. "I think I really do love you, Martin Cresswell-Smith."

◆　◆　◆

Later that evening, as I was seated in front of a mirror doing my makeup for dinner, Martin brought me a drink. He kissed me on the forehead.

"It must have been so awful when they found her little body all battered along the reef like that. The police questioning you on top of it all, as if they thought you could be guilty. As if you could have let her go on purpose. I am so sorry, El."

I went cold.

I watched him go into the bathroom to have a shower. The palm fronds outside rustled and whispered against the roof of our hut as an evening wind stirred.

Later that evening over dinner, I said, "I didn't tell you about any police questioning me, did I?" I didn't think that part had made the papers. It had been kept pretty quiet, and the cops had dropped it.

"Yes, you did." He looked puzzled.

I held his gaze. Unblinking, he continued to look directly at me.

"What's troubling you, Ellie?"

"I . . . I guess . . . I . . ." My voice faded. "Memory lapse, that's all." I reached for my wineglass.

His expression changed from puzzlement to concern as I sipped. I felt a bolt of panic. Was it a mini blackout? That's how they'd started. Followed by longer, more serious memory lapses. In the depths of my darkness, I had not even remembered stabbing Doug when I'd found him in the restaurant with that woman. I only knew for certain that I'd done it because it had been caught on a security camera and the establishment was full of witnesses, more than one of whom had filmed or snapped bits on a cell phone.

"You okay, El?"

"Yeah. Yeah, it's nothing."

"You sure?"

"Yes. Can you pass the salt?"

That night I lay unable to sleep while a hot wind bent the palms outside and the muslin drapes sucked in and billowed out onto the balcony. Thunder rumbled in the distance. A memory filled my mind. The police station in Hawaii. The detective's voice . . . *"Did you purposefully let her arm go . . . Why did you take her into the water?"*

I sat up sharply, heart thumping. I glanced at Martin. Bluish in the pale moonlight shining through the skylight, he lay sleeping. Big, steady breaths. Peaceful. Worry clamped a cold hand around my throat.

I never would have told Martin about the cops . . . surely?

THEN

ELLIE

Almost two years ago, April. Vancouver, BC.

Dana and I sat on the sofa in my apartment, our socked feet up on the coffee table.

"Like old times," she said as we toasted each other. She'd brought snacks, we'd made popcorn, and I'd provided the wine. We were watching a tacky horror movie at my place because the view was stunning and Dana's place by her own admission was a bit of a dive.

I'd been home over three weeks and had been feeling really out of sorts since our trip—couldn't seem to get over the jet lag, having trouble sleeping and focusing on work, and remembering things. Perhaps I'd picked up a bug. Martin had stayed over a few times but was back in Toronto. He called every night, though—said he was worried about me. I told him I was suffering from Martin withdrawal, missing the adrenaline rush of being with him. Deep down it was more—I had a niggling fear it was over with him, that he'd had his fill, was tired of me, and would move on to a new fling. Like my father always did.

Near the end of our movie, when we were happily tipsy, my phone rang. I glanced at the display.

Martin.

My heart kicked. "I need to take this," I said as I rose from the sofa and padded toward the bedroom.

Dana stopped just short of stuffing a fistful of popcorn into her mouth. "Who is it?"

"Martin."

"Are you *serious*?" She stuffed the popcorn into her mouth, reached for the remote, and hit pause. She stared at me as I connected the call. "Tell him you'll call back, Ellie," she said around her mouthful. "We're just at the good part. We're almost at the end."

I held up my palm as I said into the phone, "Hey, Martin, hi. Dana's here and we're in the middle of a movie—can I call you back later?"

He laughed, but I heard an edge. "You always forget the time difference, don't you, Ellie? It's already past midnight here."

I checked my watch. "Oh, I—tomorrow morning, then?"

"I'll be on a plane. Look, I need to know stat. I'm going to Nevada for a week—Reno, Vegas—got some people I need to see about a development down there. Do you want to come?"

"I . . . When are you going?"

"I just said. Tomorrow."

Dana held up the wine bottle and gestured to my nearly empty glass. I held up two fingers and mouthed, *Wait two minutes*. A dark look entered Dana's features. She turned her back on me and poured the rest of the wine into her own glass. She hit play.

I went into the adjoining room. "Can I think about it? I've got some work that—"

"There's no time, Ellie. And what's to think about? Vegas, you, me. A couple of nights on the town gambling. I need a yea or nay right now, so Gertrude, who's handling the reservations, can ensure us seats together on the plane."

"*Ellie!*" Dana yelled. "Do you want to watch the end of this movie or not?"

Tension tightened. I was not good at decisions on the fly. I preferred to think things through ad nauseam.

"Yes or no?" Martin pressed. "I'd fly into YVR on the red-eye—be there early tomorrow morning. Gertrude is holding us seats together for the Vancouver–Vegas leg. I need to tell her either way stat."

I ran my hand over my hair. "You've booked already? For me?"

"Sort of. Hedging bets. You can always say no and she'd cancel."

My mind spun. I could do my concept sketches while in Vegas. And if I put in a few extra hours when I returned . . . I could pull off my deadlines.

"Yes or no? I've got a call coming in from our Indonesia sales office, and I need to take it. If—"

"Yes."

A beat of silence. "Yes?"

"Yeah. I'm coming." Delight burst through me. He'd expected me to say no—I heard it in his voice. I'd surprised him and I loved that. I'd been in a funk. And I craved seeing him like a drug. I relished this feeling of recklessness. Like when we'd had sex in the elevator.

"Oh, I do love you, girl," he said. "Pack something dressy, sexy. We're going to live it up, babe. Gertie will be in touch about your tickets. Can't wait."

The phone went dead.

I stared at the phone in my hand, a little dazed. I went into the living room. The movie credits were rolling. I plunked myself back down on the sofa beside Dana and reached into the bowl of popcorn.

Dana angled away from me, gulped down the last of her wine, killed the TV, and tossed the remote onto the coffee table. She got up and dusted potato chip and popcorn crumbs off her pants. "I've got work tomorrow. I need to go." She fetched her purse from a barstool at the kitchen counter and padded on her socked feet into the hallway. She reached for her coat hanging near the door.

"Dana—"

"Don't." She punched her arms into her sleeves and grabbed her boots. "Do not *Dana* me—you couldn't call him back?" She sat on the bench and shoved her feet into her boots. "Just once, Ellie? Does this Martin guy have so much pull over you that you can't enjoy a date with your girlfriend—your *oldest* friend? The one who hung around for you when you were at your very lowest?" She came to her feet and reached for her woolen hat.

"Oh, come on, Dana. You can't possibly resent my relationship with him. Do you? After all I went through with Doug and—"

"I resent being treated like a doormat and shunted aside for a rich prick."

"Christ, he's not a prick."

Her gaze locked on to mine. I saw hesitation in her features. Her eyes softened, but just a little. "Ellie, you're vulnerable right now. You're just getting back onto your feet. You shouldn't make any huge commitments."

"It's not a commitment."

She regarded me. "What did he want this time that couldn't wait?"

I felt my cheeks heat. "He wanted to know if I'd join him in Vegas."

"And that couldn't wait like one second?"

"The flight is early tomorrow morning."

She blinked. "He booked you a flight before asking?"

"He's got a high-powered and fast-moving job, Dana. He's just that kind of guy."

"Like your father? Like Doug?"

My face began to burn. Anger rushed softly into my chest.

"You've barely gotten back from Europe and the Cook Islands. What about your new contract?"

"I'll manage."

She buttoned her coat. "Everything is always on his terms, have you noticed that? And he's isolating you from everyone, including me. He's monopolizing all your time. He goes all out, spends every minute with you, then he pulls back and disappears and makes you pine for him. Then just when you're getting really desperate to be with him, he clicks his fingers like this"—she drunkenly snapped her fingers—"and you drop everyone, come running. Like a puppy dog. He forces you to make a snap decision to commit to being exclusively with him in some distant locale, no time to think or even call him back?"

"I'm the one who *chooses* to be with him, Dana. He's not forcing me to do anything."

She stared. "Really? So you *chose* to speak to him during the rest of the movie, during a time *I* had set aside to spend with you? What am I? Some . . . some old toy that you take out of a box for amusement and then drop when something better and shinier comes along?" She reached for the door handle, but then swung back to face me. "I canceled a prior arrangement to hook up with you, you know that? Do you not see . . . Wait—never mind. I'm not looking for sympathy. Just—just don't bother to ask me over again unless you actually want to spend time with me, okay? I've got a life, too, you know. I'm not some piece of shit you can just walk all over." She reached for the door handle.

"Dana, that's bitter."

"Yeah, whatever." She opened the door, stumbling slightly. She'd had more wine than I'd thought. That was all this was—just the booze talking.

"How are you getting home?" I asked.

"Fuck off," she muttered.

"Excuse me?"

She barked a small laugh but had a sad look in her eyes, like she wanted to cry—Dana did that sometimes—got all weepy I-love-you drunk sometimes.

"Stay here tonight, Dana. The sofa is a pullout and—"

"Be careful." She pointed a finger at my face. "Be very careful, Ellie."

A feeling of coolness washed over me at the way she said it, at the sudden change in her face.

"What do you mean?"

"I mean, I . . . I've got a bad feeling about that man. Your aura is weird after you've been with him. Dark. Wrong. Something is badly off with that guy."

"You've had too much to drink."

"Just don't come crying to me when he's screwed you over. Not this time." She swayed slightly. "This time you're *choosing* to be a victim."

"I cannot believe you just said that. After everything I've been through with my marriage, with losing my child—"

"You know what? I'm tired—we all are—of your victimhood. It's always all about you, Ellie. All about *your* losses. When did you last ask me what's really going on in *my* life? Huh? When did you last ask me about Tom?"

I swallowed. Guilt pinged through me.

"Have you ever considered you might be using your mental breakdown, your loss, as a crutch, and that you *like* to milk empathy? Because you've gotten used to playing this role and actually thrive off the attention?"

"What has made you so angry, Dana?"

"Tom was laid off last month. I told you that night at the Mallard."

My mind reeled. I vaguely recalled her mentioning that now, but I must have been too drunk to properly encode that snippet of information. Fear whispered through me. I'd remembered all of Martin's conversation later that night—had I not?

"Yeah. Well. We still don't know where his next paycheck is going to come from. Have fun living it up in Vegas." She stepped out of my apartment into the corridor, spun around, swayed for a moment, reached for the wall to steady herself, and said, "Maybe those Oahu police should have dug a little deeper, huh?" She shut the door.

I began to shake. I stared at the closed door, half expecting her to walk back in and say sorry, but also knowing she wouldn't. I didn't do conflict. I didn't like conflict. My father was right. I'd do anything to avoid it if I could. How could she have dared say that about the police—what in the hell could she mean?

I dimmed the lights and hurried to the window. I waited until I saw her exit onto the sidewalk below. She popped open an umbrella and stepped into the rain. The streetlight glistened on the raindrops. She crossed the road. Anger, hurt, guilt—it all swirled in a toxic cocktail inside my chest. Dana was jealous, I decided as I watched her move into the shadows on the far side of the road. She stopped suddenly beside a parked car with its engine running—exhaust fumes puffing out the rear and crystallizing in a soft cloud in the cold air. I tensed as I watched her bend down near the driver's side window as if to talk to someone inside. Dana then looked directly up to my window. My heart quickened. I stepped back. Was it the same car that had been parked in that same place yesterday? The car that had been there when I'd arrived home—an orange Subaru Crosstrek with misted windows obscuring the occupant? I'd noticed because it was the same model and color Subaru I'd seen in the underground parking garage. It was not a common color. Dana straightened up and continued down the sidewalk under her umbrella. The Subaru pulled out of the parking space, did a U-turn across the lanes, and drove off in the opposite direction.

A chill crawled down my spine, and I felt a sort of *tick tick tick* along the edges of my mind, like dry twigs against glass, trying to get in.

THEN

ELLIE

Almost two years ago, May. Las Vegas, Nevada.

"You put a spell on me . . . I was bewitched by you . . ." A curvaceous lounge singer with a sultry Billie Holiday voice crooned the words into her mike. Martin and I sat listening in a plush booth in a corner farthest from the stage. Alongside the songstress a male magician in a Charlie Chaplin outfit performed pantomime magic tricks aided by a young woman with eerily white skin. She wore a twenties-style bathing suit. A bloodred slash of ribbon around her pale neck and her red Cupid's-bow lips were the only splashes of color on the black-and-white set. It was like watching an old silent movie, only alive and choreographed to the beat and cadence of the song.

This late-night magic-show-cum-cabaret was being performed at the Abracadabra Club downstairs in our Vegas hotel. Martin and I cuddled in a comfortable alcoholic haze, flush with our night's wins and too many complimentary cocktails from the Second Chance Casino.

The song and tempo changed. "Luck be a devil tonight . . ."

I laced my fingers through Martin's and leaned my head back against the padded seating. I felt blissfully buzzy and, yes, beautiful. For almost two weeks I'd spent days by the pool, or at the spa, while

Martin had his meetings, and the nights had been ours. Dressing up. Shows. Fabulous food. Trying our luck. I was tanned and so much thinner now than when I'd met him on that blustery January day. I was relaxed and in love, and it showed in my face and body. I really felt as though I'd turned a corner. I'd gone down into the abyss of loss and grief and managed to crawl out. I had overcome.

The Charlie Chaplin magician waved his wand with jerky movements that replicated the choppy, almost comical action in early silent movies. He reached up to remove his hat, as he'd done several times during the show, and pulled out a live rabbit. I gasped.

Martin laughed at me.

"What's so funny?" I said, punching him playfully. "That was brilliant! There was nothing inside his hat—I saw. He tipped it to the audience several times."

Martin's eyes danced in the light of the little candles in jars on the tables. He cupped my face and looked at me with kindness in his eyes.

"My Ellie. I do love you."

I snuggled against him, and he put his arm around me. But I felt a whisper of unease. He was being patronizing. Or was that just me being sensitive? Like my father always accused me of being. Doug, too, sometimes. A memory washed through me—Doug chiding me for letting Chloe play with a toy that had loose buttons. One of the buttons had come off. She'd put it into her mouth and nearly choked.

"You can be such an idiot sometimes, Ellie . . ."

"Passive-aggressive Ellie."

Martin didn't mean it like that, I decided. He wasn't like that.

"I still didn't see the trick coming," I said, unable to let it go. "He'd been wearing that hat on his head the whole time when he wasn't tipping it to the audience, and when he did, you could see it was empty."

Martin considered me, something strange, foreign, forming in his eyes. "Like Houdini once said, El, you saw something, but it's not what you thought you saw." He reached across the table and plucked an olive from a plate of snacks. He popped it into his mouth and chewed. "That's the best thing—what I love—about magic, about trickery," he said as he swallowed the olive and reached for his glass of Scotch. "The trick is to misdirect, to make us all look and think one way while something is slipped past us another way."

"You're making me out to be a fool."

"On the contrary." He took a sip, set his glass down, and leaned forward. "When we step into a magic show, we arrive actively *wanting* to be fooled. Magic is . . . It's a kind of willing con. You're not being foolish to fall for it. If you *don't* fall for it, the magician is doing something wrong."

I glanced at the stage. I supposed I had been distracted by the assistant's choker—she'd drawn attention to it moments before the rabbit trick. The choker had made me think for a moment her white neck had been slashed and the ribbon was blood.

"We crave the deception," Martin said. "We want to see our world as a tiny bit more fantastical and awesome than it is. That's why we go to the theater, or movies, read books. The magician is much the same as a storyteller—a trickster who uses misdirection, sleight of hand, to manipulate a person's beliefs about the world. And we see storytelling everywhere—marketing, politics, religion, over the garden fence."

I regarded Martin. He had a strange feverish quality in his eyes as he spoke of magic. He'd had too much to drink, I reckoned. The weather had been too hot, the sun too fierce, when he'd sat with me for a while by the pool.

"Another cocktail, ma'am?" I jolted at the sudden intrusion and glanced up to see a server who'd appeared out of nowhere. Just like magic. He bore a tray with a pink champagne fizz and another glass with whiskey and a single block of ice.

"I'll regret it," I said, looking at the champagne fizz.

"Come on, last one," Martin said. "It's our last night."

"Oh, all right."

The server placed the pink fizz on the table in front of me.

"And you, Mr. Tyler?" the server said to Martin. "A refill?"

"It's Cresswell-Smith," Martin said coolly and sat up straight. He reached for his glass, threw back the last of his drink, and plunked the glass down hard on the table, his mood suddenly dark.

The server set the fresh whiskey on the table and silently left with the empties.

"What was that about?" I asked quietly, watching as the server disappeared through a dark door in the black wall.

"He must have assumed we were married when you gave him your name," Martin said.

"I didn't give him my name."

"You must have. When you made the reservation for tonight."

"*You* made the reservation."

"Somewhere else, then—you must have given it to someone somewhere. I don't see why they'd assume I had the same name as you. Why not assume it was the other way around—that you had *my* last name?"

I frowned at him. "Martin, I didn't give my name. I'm certain I didn't. Besides, what's the big—"

"You didn't use a credit card over the past few days? You didn't call down to the front desk using your name? You didn't make any reservations at the spa, the pool?"

"I . . . maybe." My head felt thick, woozy. "I just don't understand what the fuss is about. The server made a simple mistake."

"These people keep tabs on everything, Ellie. The more they know about guests, the easier it is for them to sell you something that you didn't even know you wanted. These small things matter to them."

I hiccuped, pressed my hand to my mouth. Giggled.

"What in the hell is so amusing?"

"You. Being so annoyed by being called *Mr. Tyler.*"

He stared at me with an unnerving intensity that reminded me of a cat stalking a bird. And suddenly I knew what was bugging him. Yes, he'd had too much alcohol, but I figured the reason he'd been knocking drinks back so hard and fast had something to do with the way he'd appeared edgy when he'd returned to the hotel after his business meeting this afternoon. Something had upset him. Things hadn't gone as he'd hoped, but when I'd pressed, he'd said it was nothing. In hindsight his malaise had been hovering just below the surface all night, despite the good time we'd had. And now the alcohol was chipping away his facade.

"Talk to me, Martin," I said gently. "This mood—it's because of bad news you got at your meeting, isn't it? Did something not come together as expected?"

"It's nothing." He looked away as he sipped his fresh drink. His neck muscles were corded, his jaw tight.

I took his hand. "Hey, it is something. If we're going to be a team, you need to know you can off-load on me."

His eyes locked with mine. "A *team*?"

I felt a frisson of unease. When Martin let his filter drop and unleashed his full focus on something, it almost felt too intense. Dangerous. Like the sun when you got too close. But it was also this intensity that attracted me, like a honeybee to a bright, burning flower that promised life-sustaining pollen. I held his gaze, trying not to blink.

He broke eye contact and watched the lounge singer for a while, his profile set in tight lines.

"Martin. Please."

"I don't want that meeting to affect our last night in Vegas," he said in a monotone without looking at me. "I'm trying, Ellie, but you keep poking at it like a goddamn boil. It's not the end of the world, okay? One of my financial backers fell through."

"Which one? Which project?"

His eyes narrowed and he sipped from his glass.

"Martin?" I poked deeper. "Which one?"

He cursed softly and swigged back the remaining contents of his glass. He faced me. His eyes watered. I racked my brain, trying to recall who he'd said would be at the meeting this afternoon. And it struck me.

"The Marbella guy?" I said quietly. "It was him, wasn't it? You were meeting with him to talk more about the financing for the marina proposal in Australia?"

He sat in unmoving silence. The song changed. "You pulled the wool over my eyes . . ."

I touched his arm. He flinched, then heaved in a deep breath and said, "It was all but done. One final signature from one of his board members, but that particular member had veto power. She pulled the plug this morning."

"Why?"

"She felt Australia was risky for them. It wasn't in keeping with their company mandate."

"Are you going to be in trouble?"

"No. Heavens, no. It's . . . It was just, you know, a personal project."

"Because it's where you used to spend family holidays? Because it was the land your brother couldn't develop—a project he couldn't make happen?"

He nodded.

"So this kills it? Like totally?"

He gave an irritated shrug. "It's the second backer to pull out after everything was almost in the bag. Could give others cold feet. Sometimes these things are all about perception and timing."

"Is it a risky proposition, then?"

"Hell no, Ellie. This could be one of the top resorts and residential marina developments south of Sydney. It's an ideal location. It's got everything. It'll cost to get it off the ground, yes, and the global economy plus the current real estate climate in Australia has made investors twitchy. But it could pay off huge." He waved his hand in the air and motioned for another drink. The waiter appeared in seconds and set it down in front of him, ice clinking against glass. Martin sipped again. The rate he was drinking, this was clearly gutting him. I had not seen Martin like this. It set me on edge. I *needed* to make him feel better.

"Hey. It'll be fine," I said. "You'll find another—"

"Oh, Ellie, shut up, will you."

I blinked. Hurt washed through me.

"How much?"

"What?"

"How much were they in for?"

He narrowed his eyes. "Why?"

"Just tell me."

"Twenty-six million to start."

"Describe the project to me."

His brow lowered. A small muscle pulsed along his jaw. I felt anger radiating off him. Caution whispered, but I insisted. "Tell me."

He moistened his lips. "In a nutshell, three phases. One is proposed residential—very high-end marina properties. All the lots would be an acre or more. Waterfront along channels that would be cut into mangrove flats. Access would be via the Agnes River into Agnes Basin. That's where the big expense is—digging the channels into the flats. Another phase would be a luxury eco-lodge on the beach behind the dunes between the ocean and Agnes Basin. The third phase would be rental cottages. Plus a large section of estuary land would be donated for an environmental park. The environment and ecotours would be a big part of it."

I watched his face closely as he spoke. For a moment I saw the glimmer of excitement return to his eyes.

"Do you have environmental approval? Development permits?"

He gave me a slightly condescending look, as if I were asking a child's questions. "The enviro consultants' report is in the works—they've told me it's going to be positive. Obviously with some mitigation measures taken for environmental protection. The local mayor and shire councillors are on board. Apart from one greenie councillor who is objecting very loudly, but he objects to any development. The local trades in the community are hungry for business, and those contractors and their families tend to support new developments like this because it'll bring more rates to the shire, more jobs for the foreseeable future. Those surfies and fishermen who live along that coast in that rural area do so because the wave breaks are spectacular and uncrowded, and the fishing is good. The weather is great. The beaches deserted for the most part. They love the lifestyle, but work is hard to come by. They see the Agnes Marina development as a godsend, to be honest. Apart from a small but loud faction of greenies—you always get someone trying to save the last toad or fish eagle. But this project would bring additional ecotourism to the area, and the greens will still get a chunk of protected parkland from the deal. We were all but ready to start presales."

"Until this afternoon?"

"Yeah." He eyed me. And a feeling began to grow inside me. A desire to share this part of him, this part of the world, his dream project, the memories of his past, the things that made the fires come alive inside this man. The magic show ended. Applause sounded. We finished our drinks and went up to our room. But that night we did not make love. He was too drunk and fell asleep snoring. I lay there listening to him, looking up at the ceiling. Through a small gap in the thick drapes, the never-sleeping coruscating lights of Las Vegas pulsed. And I felt something was slipping quietly from my grasp, and that if I didn't grab on tightly now, or take some firm action, I would lose this new Ellie unfolding like a butterfly inside me.

My father's words echoed through my brain.

"I'm serious, Ellie. Bring me an idea—any idea . . . I will finance it. You've won the game right there. Half the people in this hotel would like to be in your shoes . . ."

I turned my head on my pillow and looked at Martin. He'd woken up. He lay flat on his back, unmoving, eyes staring up at the roof. I rolled onto my side to face him.

"I'm going to help you," I said.

"What?"

"I can help finance the marina."

He propped himself up on his elbow. "No. No way. You can't do that."

"Why not?"

"I don't want you tied into my business ventures."

"Well, then—"

"El, wait, I didn't mean it like that."

"How did you mean it?"

"I'm a gambler. I win some and I lose some. I don't want to tie you to a loss. I can't let you take my risks."

"But you win more than you lose, right? Like my dad. It's the very fact that he's a gambler, and a smart one, that has made him one of the wealthiest men in the country." As I spoke, the urge in me to fix things for Martin—and thus for us—grew fierce. It almost became a panic, an unarticulated, raw fire in me to ensure that Martin did *not* lose this dream, because then we would lose us.

"Yeah, but—"

"I *want* to do this, Martin. I *can* do this. Not just for you, but for me, too. And you're going to accept me as a financier. You're going to help me help you, and you're going to make me a true partner in this marina venture." My father had encouraged me to pick a venture. He'd offered me his real estate lawyers. I trusted that my dad's lawyers could help me set up any partnership to my best advantage. Sure, I knew next to nothing about property development, but Doug had gotten good at it without experience and with my father's help. I had access to those same experts, who could deliver to me what I needed to know in layman's terms. Twenty-six million in equity was a mere drop in the bucket for the Hartley Group. I had my massive trust fund on top of that—I wouldn't even have to touch it.

"Make me an equity partner, Martin."

"No, Ellie."

I stared at him in the dim light, hating the resistance that pulsed around him. He was pushing me away. I got out of bed and pulled on my nightgown. I paced and thought about my idea until dawn was a faint glow on the Nevada horizon. I yanked back the drapes fully, allowing the beautiful desert light to flood into our suite. I made coffee.

"What are you doing?"

"Making you coffee." I brought him a mug and sat on the edge of the bed, sipping my own, watching the sky brighten.

"Tell me what it would entail," I said.

"No."

"Why not? Give me an honest reason why not."

Back and forth we went until he threw back the covers and went into the shower. When he came out, something in his face had changed. There was a glow in his eyes, as if the serum of my idea injected into his veins had spread and was taking hold.

"It would entail living in Aus for a while, El," he said, rubbing his hair with his towel. He was naked and glorious apart from a skimpy towel around his waist. "We'd need to be on-site to see the whole thing through. At least in the early phases."

"I've already thought of that. I want to try it, Martin. At least for a while. My work is portable. I could secure some new contracts before we leave. I could do the work over there."

"But—"

I went up to him and pressed my fingers against his lips. "Shh. No more buts, *Mr. Tyler*."

He didn't smile.

My own smile faded. I regretted trying to make a joke.

"I like the sound of that," he said very quietly, darkly, drawing my body against his. Surprise rippled through me. He felt damp from the hot shower. Warm. I felt his erection against my belly. He smelled of good soap, of shampoo.

"You *like* the sound of *Mr. Tyler*?" My voice caught on a wave of desire as his erection hardened.

"I'd prefer *Mrs. Cresswell-Smith*, though," he whispered over my lips.

"Martin—" I grew wet and hot in my groin. He kissed harder, opening my mouth. The idea sank talons into my heart as he cupped me between the legs, parted my folds, inserted a finger. I could barely breathe—"Let's . . . let's do it."

"What?" he murmured against my mouth.

I pulled away. "Get married. Chapel—I saw it downstairs. The Second Chance Chapel next to the Second Chance Casino."

His jaw dropped. "Wha—"

"Now! Let's do it right now. Mr. and Mrs. Cresswell-Smith!" I was positively busting with the idea bubbling up inside me. Intoxicated with it. "Think about it, Martin—it was a sign last night—*Second Chance* Casino? Where we won big. So why the hell not tie the knot, cement this team thing. Go to Australia as true partners. Why should we not both get a second chance at love? Why *not* take the gamble? I'm divorced. You've just ended a long-term relationship. Why shouldn't we score this time around?"

He forcefully shoved me backward onto the bed. I bounced against the mattress and my nightgown fell open. He dropped his towel and leaned over me, opening my thighs. And he took me in a way that was more ferocious and animal than that first night in the elevator. I matched him thrust for hungry thrust, my fingers and nails digging into his flesh with a surprising force of my own, the aggression just driving me higher until I climaxed with a cry, and he came, and we both fell back on the bed laughing, panting. Spent. Sticky and sweaty and delirious with my idea. The sun burst over the horizon and gold light exploded into the room.

By lunch we'd bought rings—his a platinum band inset with a ruby, mine a simple platinum band. And we'd filled in all the requisite forms. By that evening Martin and I stood in front of a legally ordained wedding officiant, as promised by the Second Chance Chapel website. Our "rush package" included a "fresh floral bouquet," which I clutched in front of me. A photographer snapped photos, which he would give to us in "high-resolution JPEG files with a copyright release" so we could easily print them off to frame later. We opted out of the live online broadcast, preferring to break our news to friends and family in person later.

"Forasmuch as you, Ellie Tyler and Martin Cresswell-Smith, have consented to join in wedlock, and have before witnesses and this company pledged vows of your love and faithfulness to each other, and have declared the same by joining hands, and by the exchange of rings, I now therefore, by the authority vested in me by the State of Nevada, pronounce you wed. Congratulations! You may now kiss the bride!"

We kissed. The camera flash popped. Silver confetti rained down from the ceiling and swirled around us with the aid of a fan. I laughed. I felt deliriously happy.

Just after midnight we boarded a red-eye for Canada as husband and wife, a new marriage certificate in hand and plans for Australia in our hearts. I'd already sent an email asking to meet with my dad's lawyers.

THE WATCHER

A red dot pulsed on the computer monitor. The app installed on the cell phone was broadcasting their GPS location. They'd landed at YVR. The Watcher stared at the dot for a few moments in the dimly lit room, a glass of whiskey in hand, then leaned over and clicked on a desk lamp.

A halo of yellow light fell upon a pile of news articles that had been printed off the net. Amazing what a well-rounded and intimate psychological profile the World Wide Web could yield if the target had not been overly careful, or had lived a relatively public life. In this case—for a period—it had been a very public life.

Hartley Grandchild in Fatal Drowning Accident

Hartley Heiress Suffers Mental Breakdown

Daughter of Sterling Hartley Stabs Husband in Restaurant

Ellie Tyler Arrested

Hartley Heiress Divorces

Some of the raunchier tabloids featured photos of an overweight and disheveled Ellie Tyler covering her head with a jacket as police led her out of a Vancouver restaurant. Blood spattered the jacket. Another showed an unflattering image of a haggard and very overweight Ellie Tyler under a headline that read:

Court-Ordered Addiction Counseling for Hartley Heiress

Trust-Fund Daughter Spirals into Booze, Pills, Depression

One tabloid had captured Sterling Hartley and a Swedish girlfriend rushing through an airport after hearing that his daughter had been hospitalized.

In a kinder *Vogue* magazine feature titled "A Mother's Grief," Ellie Tyler spoke about recovering from the drowning death of her toddler. She was candid about her mental health and the need to destigmatize mental illness and the addictions that arose around it. And yet . . . the stigma dogged her.

Next to the pile of news stories was a file folder titled ELLIE. It had come from a PI who had also quizzed Doug Tyler's new wife. Another file folder was titled MARTIN.

The dot began to move. They were leaving the airport.

THEN

ELLIE

Over one year ago, October 25. Jarrawarra Bay, New South Wales.

The small prop plane dropped as it slammed into another wall of turbulence. I gritted my teeth and clutched the armrests. I was flying on my own to meet Martin, who'd gone ahead of me three months ago, once our financing had come through. I'd been traveling for more than thirty-six hours over several time zones, and I felt sick and dehydrated from too much wine and too many lorazepam pills taken in an effort to quell my anxiety. The air vent above my seat was not working. And now the storm. And the plane was too tiny. My claustrophobia was tilting toward panic.

The plane plummeted again. We were beginning a descent. Something fell with a dull thud at the back of the cabin. The object rolled down the aisle and came into view—a bottle of water. My thirst was suddenly fierce. The bottle was out of my reach. I thought of the Ativan in my purse. Another bump and rattle and the wings rocked. The clouds seemed closer. Denser. Darker. Lightning jagged through the blackness. I lunged for my purse under my seat. Hands shaking, I hurriedly rummaged in a side pocket, found the container, and popped a sublingual pill under my tongue. I closed my eyes and put my head back, waiting for it to dissolve. Sweat pearled on my brow and dribbled down the sides of my face. I struggled to breathe in, counting to four before I exhaled slowly, purposefully. A soft fuzz gradually began to soothe the sharp edges of my panic. I took in a deeper breath, exhaled more slowly. Calm began to wrap around me like the familiar arms of an old friend. I yielded to the drug. My muscles softened. My mind eased, and to help further distract myself I glanced around at the other passengers. They seemed unperturbed.

Most were casually dressed—shorts, flip-flops, T-shirts, summer dresses, jeans. A couple in more businesslike attire. All deeply tanned. Some more weathered, sun-spotted, sun-bleached than others. A range of ages. They fit with Martin's description of Jarrawarra Bay—a rural seaside hub, historically a center for local sawmill operations and wattlebark production, dairy, beef, and oyster farming, as well as "epic" deep-sea fishing. He'd said the locals either worked in one of these industries or fell into a camp of telecommuters, retirees, holidaymakers, and second-home owners. Even Nicole Kidman, he'd claimed, owned an estate just north of Jarrawarra in one of those secluded, scalloped bays where lilly pilly trees grew tall and attracted flocks of lorikeets in startling rainbow colors.

Despite my malaise, or because of my meds, happiness began to bloom softly in my chest at the thought of being with Martin again, at seeing the newly constructed house he'd bought for us on the banks of the Bonny River. He'd sent photos. It looked spectacular. The house was an architecturally designed double story with lots of glass and clean lines, and there was a boathouse with a dock, he'd said, which would be ideal as my studio.

A streak of lightning speared through the clouds, and the plane tilted as we headed into a steep, bumpy descent toward a bay fringed with yellow sand.

The lone flight attendant ordered us to restore seats to the upright position and stash loose belongings beneath them. She'd remained buckled into her fold-down seat next to the door for the duration of the short flight from Sydney's international airport. The pilot announced we were about to land in Moruya. He said it was unseasonably hot and that the storm was moving south of us. Moruya was a short drive from Jarrawarra Bay. Martin would be waiting.

Crosswinds buffeted us, and my stomach surged as a foreign landscape whirled up to greet us—a twisting chocolate-brown river and estuary thick with mangroves. Spindly gums bowing to the wind. Oyster beds in the river with decaying pilings and docks. A crane flew low over the water. As we lowered, I saw kangaroos grazing along the side of the airport fence. We hit the runway with a jolt, bounced, and hit with another hard bang, and then the plane rattled and shuddered all the way to the very end of the runway, right past the tiny airport building. After the pilot finally managed to bring us to a stop, we turned and taxied slowly back to the building. The heat grew stifling inside the cabin. I peered through the tiny window at the squat, tin-roofed structure that passed for the Moruya Airport. A patio in front with tables. A fence. A gate . . . I saw him. My heart kicked.

Martin.

Tall. Deeply bronzed. Wearing shorts. His hair gleaming like gold. He shaded his eyes, scanning the windows of our plane as we came in. I could barely restrain myself from unbuckling and ferreting my stuff out from under my seat. I wanted to see it all. Right now. I wanted a hot shower, a clean bed. I wanted to feel my husband's arms folding me into this new and exotic adventure of a life we'd chosen.

The seat belt sign pinged off.

The flight attendant opened the door. I could smell the sea. She extended the foldout stairs. We all waited, sweating, as the pilot and copilot climbed out first.

I was the first to descend after them.

Hot wind slammed me as I stepped onto the stairs. It carried the scent of eucalyptus trees and a tinge of smoke from distant forest fires.

Martin's hand shot up as he saw me. He waved wildly, and I hurried down the stairs, over the tarmac, and in through the arched gateway. He lifted me off my feet and hugged me as he spun me around in a circle and kissed me. Tears poured down my face—of happiness, relief, pure exhaustion. I was done.

He set me down, moved my bangs back off my brow, studied me a moment, then gripped my face in both his hands. Looking at me, right into me, his blue eyes all the more blue against his deep tan. He said, "Welcome to our new *home*, Ellie Cresswell-Smith. I have missed you *so* much. How was the trip?"

His accent was markedly Australian—much stronger than when I'd seen him last.

"It was . . . okay." The baby who had screamed the entire way from Vancouver, the claustrophobia at being stuffed into a flying tin can, the anxiety bordering on panic, the zero sleep . . . It all fled my mind. "You look so tanned, so . . . Australian."

"And what does that look like? Crocodile Dundee?" He wiggled his eyebrows.

I laughed, thrilled to be back in his aura and feeling the throb of his energy once more. "Thank heavens, no. I'm dying to see our new place. The photos looked *amazing*." I pointed out my bags on the trolley that had been pushed from the plane. Martin dragged my two suitcases off the cart. His flip-flops flapped as we made our way from the airport building to his truck—our truck. All this was mine, too. This life.

Kangaroos watched us from sparse, dry grass near the parking area. Heat pressed down. I heard beetles. Birds screamed—harsh and unfamiliar sounds. Sweat beaded and trickled between my breasts. My hair felt sticky against my scalp and cloying down my back. I could smell the old sweat on myself. I literally ached for a hot shower, a firm bed, fresh sheets.

"Our new ute," Martin said proudly as he drew back a tarp that covered the back. He hefted my bags into the high bed. They landed with a thump. I wanted to tell him to be careful with the suitcase that contained my art supplies, but I held back.

"I cannot wait for a shower," I said, moving toward the passenger door. "And sleep. I don't even know how many days I've been awake now."

"Oh, babe—" He hesitated.

I stopped with my hand on the door. He looked crestfallen.

"What is it?" I asked.

"I brought us a picnic. I thought we'd drive straight on up to Agnes Basin so I could show you the site office and development right away. After all, that's the whole reason we're here, doing this thing, right?"

My heart sank. I wavered, feeling dizzy suddenly. "I . . . I hope we're here for more than just the development."

His gaze locked with mine. His features turned unfriendly. I blinked. I was imagining it. The world—the sunlight—everything was too harsh. Too bright. Too hot. Too discordant. The meds, my hangover, the jet lag suddenly making my ears ring. I dug into my purse, found my big sunglasses, put them on. "It's fine." I cleared my throat and focused on speaking with an easy, breezy tone. "I'm just hella tired, that's all. And maybe a bit hungover." I laughed lightly. "I thought some drinks on the plane would help drown out a screaming baby. But no luck." I forced another light laugh. "Poor mother."

I didn't mention the lorazepam.

Martin didn't need to know about that.

There was something veiled in his eyes as he watched me, which unsettled me further. "So shall we go up to Agnes, or not?"

"Sure we should. It'll be fine—I'm fine. I want to see it now," I lied. I was reluctant to displease him. Not on our first day back together.

THEN

ELLIE

A big grin cut across Martin's face the moment I said I "wanted" to drive up to see the development right away. His eyes and body danced back to life, like those of a child who'd just been handed back a new and prized toy that had been in imminent danger of being confiscated.

"And I've got just the thing for that hangover!" he announced as he drew back the cover on the ute bed again, exposing a cooler box. He popped the blue lid off the cooler and like a magician pulled out two bottles of chilled cider. Beads of moisture slid down the outsides of the glass bottles. My thirst was suddenly ferocious.

"Hair of the dog." He wiggled the bottles, his grin deepening to reveal his dimples, then cracked open a bottle and offered it to me. I took it and immediately glugged down a quarter of the contents as he opened his own.

"Got plenty more of these in the esky," he said as he closed the cooler. "And wine. And roast chicken. Potato salad. French bread." He clinked his bottle against mine. "Cheers and welcome *home*, babe. Here's to our new life."

We took long swallows together, climbed into the ute—me almost getting into the wrong side. We set our ciders in the cup holders, and Martin started the engine.

"We won't be at Agnes long, I promise. We'll be home before dinner." He pulled into the road on the "wrong" side and tossed me another smile. "Besides, if you try to adapt to the new routine right away, it'll help head off the jet lag."

I took another deep swig of my cold cider, feeling the buzz of alcohol spreading fast through my weary lorazepam-addled veins and sleep-deprived brain. But he was right. Hair of the dog. It worked. And who cared about jet lag—this was our new world, a new adventure. And the development was the reason we'd come. I could sleep later.

Just go with the flow. No rules. Shape your own narrative.

But by the time we were on the Princes Highway and driving through a narrow and never-ending tunnel of monotonous gums with dry, drab, sharp-angled leaves, I'd finished my drink and was nodding in and out of a syrupy stupor. Martin put on the radio. Music played softly.

I must have drifted off deeply, because suddenly my head slammed against the window and I jerked awake in shock. My eyes flared open. I struggled to orient myself. We'd swerved to avoid roadkill. I winced and rubbed my face. My chin was sticky with dried drool. My body odor smelled strong. My face was sweaty. Martin cast me a quick glance. Something like distaste flitted through his features; then it was gone. Perhaps I'd imagined it. He returned his attention to the road, but I saw his hands fisting the wheel.

I sat in fuzzy silence for another several kilometers as the forest whizzed by. Occasional kangaroos and wallabies lay dead along the side of the road. A sick feeling filled my stomach. I should have insisted Martin take me home first.

"How far is it?" I asked as we passed yet another massacred roo, or whatever the tawny-colored creature was.

"I told you already. Agnes is about a twenty-five-minute drive north of Jarra." His voice was cool. A sense of doom spread black and oily through my chest. My father used to use that same tone when I was unable to live up to his expectations.

I looked out the window, then jumped as a giant prehistoric thing with dragon wings over three feet in span came flapping down the side of the highway along the fringe of gums. It was followed by another, then a whole swarm. "What in the hell?" I spun around in my seat to watch them, my heart hammering.

"Flying foxes," he said, voice clipped. "They're a species of giant fruit bat. Largest flying mammal there is." His gaze remained fixed on the road ahead, his neck muscles taut. "Bloody things started migrating into the region in swarms when some of the gums started to blossom early due to this weird hot weather. More than one hundred thousand at last count have set up camp in this area—like a fucking megabat epidemic."

I blinked. I'd not heard Martin swear in casual conversation. Once again I noted the thickness of his Aussie accent, the changes in his features. Or was I seeing things crookedly through my haze of malaise? A thread of fear curled through me. Paranoia had been a side effect of my drug and alcohol abuse after I'd let Chloe slip through my hands and drown. I'd fought back from it. Maybe I should not have taken the sedatives on the plane. Maybe I would slip again.

"The shire has set up a task force to figure out how to deal with the buggers because they're a protected species and you can't just kill them. They shit over everything. Foul-smelling orange guano."

I stared in horror as another mass of giant bats flapped along the line of gums where the trees had been cleared to make way for the road.

He slowed and put on the indicator as we approached a sign that pointed to the Agnes Basin. We turned off the highway and onto a smaller road that led toward the ocean. We passed a placard affixed to a post. It was torn and flapped in the wind. Letters big and black.

STOP AGNES MARINA!

"Martin?" I turned in my seat. "Is that aimed at us?"

"It's nothing. It's normal. Every development gets that stuff. Bloody greenies."

I saw another poster, edges torn and snapping in hot wind.

NO! TO AGNES MARINA

A few hundred meters farther, several placards had been hammered into trees.

**MAKE A PARK, NOT A RESORT FOR MILLIONAIRES,
SAVE THE ENVIRONMENT, STOP AGNES!
SAVE THE FISH EAGLE
SAVE OUR FISHING HABITAT**

Martin took the ute onto a smaller side road. As we rounded a curve, we were warned by a forest of red signs planted like election banners into the dry verges.

**STOP, STOP, STOP, STOP.
DEATH TO THE MARINA.
VOTE MAYOR OUT!**

Kangaroos grazed between the signs, looking like giant rats with malformed hands. Wind gusted. Branches and twigs crashed down from the gums, and leaves dry from drought scattered across our path. My head felt thick, as though I weren't really here and I were seeing all this through some viscous filter from far away. Pressure began to build inside my ears. A heavy sensation pressed down into my gut. My own words to my father when I'd told him about our venture filtered up into my memory.

Besides, how wrong can it go?

"Martin," I said softly, trying to pull myself into focus, "this seems—"

"Most people in this shire, Ellie, including the majority of councillors plus the mayor, are *more* than pleased at the prospect of construction jobs," he said crisply. "They're pro the development. And new jobs mean more votes, and the new houses will bring more taxes for the shire coffers, and new houses will mean more residents for the constituency, and that means more state funds."

Another tattered sign flapped on a fence.

SAVE THE FISH EAGLES, KILL THE MARINA

"But the environmental study is—"

"In the bag, dammit, I told you! The consultants were chosen because they're on *my* side. They've promised it will be positive. It'll be good."

"I thought environmental consultants were supposed to be neutral."

He swore under his breath. "You can be so naive. Don't worry about it—I said it's fine, okay? Everything is going to be okay." His voice turned quiet. But his neck was corded and so were his arms. He flicked a glance at me, and he must have seen the extent of the shock in my eyes because his features softened almost instantly. He sighed. "Look, I'm sorry, El." He took in another deep, regulating breath. "I realize this development stuff is all new to you, but every project has to jump through these hoops, and it always comes with bumps. And those bumps can be frustrating. Creating a marina that requires deep channeling into an estuary thick with mangroves where local fishermen hide illegal crab pots and do what in the hell they like—of course you're going to get objections. But the bottom line is, approvals are on track, presales are going gangbusters. I'll show you the numbers when we get home." He forced a smile.

We passed a shed with corrugated metal siding. Painted in bloodred, angry letters were the words:

DEATH TO THE CRESSWELL-SMITHS!

THEN

ELLIE

"This is it! What do you think?"

I stood with Martin in front of a prefabricated building that squatted on a freshly paved parking lot next to a sullen tidal river.

A sign creaked in the hot sea wind: AGNES MARINA SALES OFFICE. Sulphur-crested cockatoos, white and surreal, screeched in the branches that hung over the building. Surf thundered in the distance. A shag—a black bird some might call a cormorant—perched atop a rotted piling, wings spread out to dry like a cape. A flotilla of pelicans bobbed on the surface, eyes like giant marbles watching us.

I shielded my eyes against the glare. The sky had turned hazy but no less harsh, even from behind my shades. I was disoriented, wobbly on my feet, and the world seemed to sway with the ripple and push of the river. Topmost in my mind was that slogan in dripping-blood paint.

DEATH TO THE CRESSWELL-SMITHS!

"They threatened us both personally, Martin," I said quietly.

"Oh, come on—it's just some nutjob. I'm sorry you had to see that."

"Did you tell the police?"

"It's not even worth it."

"Are you sure? And why drag *me* into it? It said, 'Cresswell-Smiths.' That's both of us."

"You're my wife. We're equal partners and some crazy is trying to spook us, that's all."

"Well, it's working."

"Don't be ridiculous, El. Come." He took my arm and opened the door.

The air-conditioned interior was cool and furnished with a gleaming white desk, leather chairs, and a marble-topped counter that hosted an espresso machine and was fronted by barstools. Television monitors screened footage that showed laughing couples on yachts, private marinas, surfers in barreling waves, deep-sea divers, aerial shots of the inlet and estuary, exotic meals, flowers, fancy drinks, swimming pools, tanned girls in bikinis, men with smiles that belonged in toothpaste ads, and children who grinned from ear to ear.

Stacks of brochures covered glass-topped tables, and posters showed sunny images of an idealized lifestyle. I picked up a brochure. It advertised the various ownership models available, from a quarter share to a half share to full ownership, with potential to put properties into a rental pool.

"This is Lennin, my on-site sales ace," Martin said proudly.

I looked up and blinked as Lennin exited an adjacent office. Lennin was female. In her mid- to late twenties. She wore a red T-shirt and white shorts. Really short shorts. Her legs were long and sunbrowned, her arms lean and muscular. She sported a huge white smile and a mane of chestnut-colored hair that bounced softly around her shoulders. I was momentarily stunned by her in-your-face radiance and the fact that Lennin was a young woman. When Martin had told me he'd hired a terrific salesperson named Lennin, I'd just assumed it was a guy. And older. She reminded me of the ubiquitous ever-youthful employees at high-end health clubs where—despite my wealth—I'd never felt I fitted in. Or one of those reality television stars who crewed on exotic boats and looked totally unreal.

"G'day, El," she said in a hearty Australian accent. "Martin's told me *so* much about you." Lennin offered me her hand. "So great to finally meet you."

I shook her hand and was suddenly acutely conscious of my wintery jeans, the damp perspiration marks under my armpits, my unwashed hair. The fact that I could do with a shower. The notion that I'd never in my wildest dreams have a body like hers. Martin watched us as though he was weighing us, one against the other. For some absurd reason I felt he'd done this on purpose—juxtaposed, contrasted me against Lennin—so I could take note of my own shortcomings, my age, against Lennin's youth and vitality. Even while I knew it was an absurd idea, resentment pulsed through me.

"It's Ellie," I corrected. It was fine for Martin to call me El, not her.

Her smile wavered, but just for a nanosecond. "I'm so thrilled to be part of a Hartley Group project, Ellie."

"Excuse me?"

A tiny frown crossed her brow. "The Hartley Group," she repeated.

"The Agnes Marina project has got nothing to do with the Hartley Group."

She glanced at the brochure in my hand. I followed her gaze. The back page was covered with a glossy photograph of my dad, a copy of his signature in bold black underneath.

"Your father's backing is a huge sales point for us," said Lennin. "Sterling Hartley has . . . well, he frankly has a sterling reputation. Our association with him has been a super-hot selling point."

My heart beat faster. I shot a look at Martin. He'd turned away from me and was using a remote to flip through advertising collateral on one of the monitors.

Heat burned into my face. I said to Lennin, "My father isn't a part of—"

"Ellie!" Martin called. "Come over here and see this." He aimed his remote and clicked. Aerial footage filled the screen as a drone moved over long stretches of beach fringing endless mangrove swamps with dark, twisting rivers. "We're going to need more of these drone shots, I think. See there?" He pointed the remote at the screen. "The marina channels will be dug into the mangrove flats at the north end. And over there, that's where the eco-lodge and wildlife viewing platform will be. We've already constructed temporary scaffolding with a platform near an abandoned homestead so prospective buyers can climb up and see the view potential. I'll take you out there now."

"Martin," I said quietly, "my father is not backing or endorsing this project. His company—the Hartley Group—has nothing to do with Agnes Basin. This is my—*our*—financing. It's an Agnes Holdings development, not a Hartley Group project."

He flicked a glance at Lennin. She quickly went into the adjacent office and shut the door. Martin waited for her to disappear, then lowered his voice to a whisper. "Our association with the Hartley family is a fact, Ellie. *You* are a Hartley. Your dad financially backed *you*, knowing what this was all about."

A buzzing grew loud between my ears. "That's not an endorsement. You can't use his name. This is *my* fund. My father basically invested me *out* of his life. He threw this money at me because of some paternal guilt thing. He did *not* invest in Agnes Basin."

"It was his lawyers who helped you set up the financing and the holding company, El." He nodded at the brochure. "It's just semantics. Juxtaposition. We don't actually say in there that he's our backer. It's just the illusion that he is. Nothing is a lie."

"It's misleading at best, fraud at worst."

His eyes narrowed sharply. His jaw tensed. His gaze ticked to the closed office door. Quietly he said, "We'll talk outside. I'll explain how these things work. This is all new to you—a children's artist with a literature background. I appreciate it's a steep learning curve."

Anger sparked through me. "I might not be informed about the real estate business," I replied curtly, "but I'm not an idiot."

He grabbed my upper arm, hard. Shock ripped through me. "Come, now," he growled as he forced me out the door. He slammed the door shut behind us. Hot wind tugged at my hair. Martin ushered me into the parking lot well away from the building. He bent his head close to mine.

"The fact is, you are a Hartley, Ellie. And I—"

"I'm your wife, Martin. I'm *Mrs. Cresswell-Smith*. Before that I was Ellie Tyler, Doug's wife. Using my maiden name in advertising collateral is deception."

"Oh, for Pete's sake, it's not deception—that's who you are. The 'Hartley Heiress.' Anyone who reads more into that, well, that's their fault. They don't have a legal leg to stand on. Think about it like a lawyer."

"I'm not a lawyer. Neither are most of the buyers who'll be misled by this."

"It's goddamn marketing. Buyer beware. It's how the world works, from photoshopped models in everything from soap and toothpaste to car commercials. Do you think the guy on TV in a white lab coat is really a doctor? Do you think the model with nice skin got her complexion that way from using the product she's shoving down your throat? Do you think the shampoo really gave the actress her nice thick hair? Jesus. Grow up, Ellie. The Hartley name is like the lab coat. It inspires subliminal confidence. It's helping kick-start presales. And if we continue with this volume, we *will* make headline numbers, and it'll force the big banks to take notice, and they'll clamor to throw more equity at us for the next phases." He dragged his hand irritably over his hair, making it stand up. Sweat gleamed on his face. "Look, I understand. You don't get it. You've never had to hustle for your next paycheck because you've lived your entire life in an ivory tower. People like you can afford shallow philanthropy—you can afford to sit on a high horse. But this is how you hustle."

"People like *me*?" Sweat trickled down my belly into the waistband of my jeans. Heat pressed down thicker, wetter, stifling. The world around me swayed with the movement of the river alongside us. I felt like I was going to throw up. "What about *you*, Martin? From the postnup figures your lawyer put on the table, you can afford a pretty high horse yourself. Or was that a lie, too? Perhaps my father was right and I was an idiot for not thinking of a prenup before we tied the knot in Vegas."

He blinked. Alarm sparked across his features. His eyes darted toward the sales office. I followed his gaze. Lennin stood in the window watching us. A gust of hot wind creaked the sales office sign, and a memory prompted by Lennin's hair speared through me. In my mind I saw the man I'd mistaken for Martin kissing a woman with chestnut-colored hair before they climbed into an orange car in the underground parking garage. That memory oozed into another of an identical car parked outside my apartment on the rainy night Dana had last visited. I'd never managed to ask Dana who she'd spoken to inside that car. Dana had refused to take any of my calls after that night had ended our friendship. I missed her suddenly. Like a big hole in my heart. The world tilted around me and my knees buckled.

Martin caught me as I sagged.

"Are you okay?" he asked, supporting me by the arm.

"I . . . Just exhausted. Dehydrated. I . . . feel weird. Need to sit down."

"I'm so, so sorry, Ellie. I'm throwing far too much at you at once. Let me take you out on the boat. It'll be cooler on the water." He helped me away from the sales office, away from the watchful eyes of Lennin. "You must be hungry, too."

"Just exhausted and a bit ill."

"We'll take the boat up the inlet, anchor, have a picnic, and then see the viewing platform before we drive back to Jarrawarra Bay."

"Martin, I . . . I'm really not feeling so good. I need to get some rest. I—"

"You can nap on the boat. I'll anchor us somewhere in the shade." He walked me down to a jetty.

"What about my suitcases in the back of the truck?"

"I've got a cover over the box. Lennin will keep an eye on the ute."

I swallowed. My tongue felt thick, foreign in my mouth. I felt like I was slurring my words. "Where did you find Lennin?"

"She's great, isn't she?"

I wanted to say more about my father being used in the collateral, but I couldn't think straight enough to argue more coherently, and my fuzziness was my own fault. I shouldn't have taken the lorazepam and then the cider on top of that. I was suffering now because of it, and craving another hit to make this feeling go away.

He helped me along the dock. I stumbled again. Alarm pinged through me. Something was really wrong. This felt like more than jet lag and sedative withdrawal. He hooked his arm around my waist and led me up to a boat moored against the dock.

"There she is. Beautiful, isn't she?"

The watercraft was white and blue. It nudged against the pilings and tugged gently against the ropes.

"It's a Quintrex cuddy cabin," he said. "Good all-rounder. Very small but usable cabin. Has plenty of room at the rear with a fold-down lounge seat. Windscreen is higher than a runabout. Good for deep-sea fishing as well as spending a night somewhere. Almost seven meters in length. Nice stability with the blade hull, too."

I saw the name emblazoned on the side. *Abracadabra.*

Another memory swam into my fuzzy consciousness—the magic show on the night before our wedding. I recalled my husband's feverish animation as we'd watched the magician and he'd spoken about trickery and cunning.

"We crave the deception. We want to see our world as a tiny bit more fantastical and awesome than it is. That's why we go to the theater, or movies, read books. The magician is much the same as a storyteller—a trickster who uses misdirection . . ."

"Vegas," I said quietly. "You named her after the club?"

"In memory of the night you proposed."

I glanced up at him. He grinned broadly, dimples showing. But through my groggy lens his face looked garish, like a clown's, his complexion shiny in the heat, hair too yellow-blond atop his bronzed face.

"Our respective second chances." His grin deepened. I hadn't noticed before how his eyeteeth were slightly longer than the rest. It gave him a malevolence in this shimmering haze. A bird of prey circled up high. It keened. A flock of lorikeets startled into the sky, colors harsh and bright. I swiped at the perspiration leaking down into my eyes.

"That's . . . sweet," I said. I felt totally drunk, to be honest. Worry slithered deeper. Was I getting ill?

He helped me into the boat, seemingly unfazed by my state. Maybe it wasn't noticeable to anyone but me? He fetched the cooler box and handed me a life jacket. I fumbled to do it up. He leaned over and buckled it for me. He untied the boat, pulled in the ropes, and started the engine chugging. He backed out of the mooring, and the motion forced me to sit down with a thump on the rear lounge seat. A pelican watched our progress.

We headed up the inlet, a dark wake swelling out behind us. Martin handed me a pale-blue ball cap to shield my face from the sun. I put it on and closed my eyes behind my shades, feeling the hum of the engine and the rock of the swell, drifting in and out of consciousness.

"There's cold water in that esky at your feet." His voice startled me awake. I opened the cooler, found a bottle of water among ice blocks, swallowed half the contents, and wiped my mouth. Martin was talking loudly over the noise of the engine, but his words droned on unintelligibly as the fogginess in my head suddenly worsened.

"Tidal," he said.

"What?"

"The inlet. It's tidal. The current flows up to the basin when the tide pushes in, then reverses and flows out to the sea when it pulls out."

"Oh." I felt even more dehydrated after the water. My tongue grew thicker, further slurring my attempts at speech, so I fell silent.

We entered a lake. It shimmered and danced with refracted sunlight. I shuddered at the sight of glassy bubbles of jellyfish everywhere just beneath the surface.

"Agnes Basin," he said. "From here smaller rivers lead off this basin in all directions . . ." Martin was pointing. Bronzed arms. Hair shining gold on his forearms. Handsome man I'd married, or was he ugly, too large . . . ? My thoughts were jumbling. I closed my eyes again.

"The estuary is like a maze. Can get really turned around and lost in these swamps if you don't know your way about." He steered the *Abracadabra* into a narrow channel. It was dark among trees that pressed close, the water an iron color. The boat slowed. Branches scratched at us. Water slapped against the hull. Thick reeds drifted with the tide. Martin angled up to a dock beneath a big gum. Behind the dock was a shallow bay. The bank of the bay was tangled with trees that sent gray, elephantine roots into the water. He dropped the anchor with a loud splash. Mosquitoes buzzed.

How long had it been since we'd left the jetty near the sales office? I'd lost all sense of time. It seemed to have gotten darker, or maybe it was just the somberness of the vegetation.

"Why are we stopping here?"

"Nice and private," he said. "And listen."

Strange noises came from the tangled mangroves—a scream of birds, fluttering sounds. A haunting call. Squabbles and cackles. A fish jumped next to the boat and slapped back into the water. I startled.

He laughed at me. "This is a dock we built. The abandoned farmhouse is along a trail from here. It's where we'll construct the eco-lodge.

A network of boardwalks—interpretive trails—will fan out from the lodge into the swampier portions of the land. I'll take you to the viewing platform near the old homestead after lunch."

He opened the cooler, took out containers of cold chicken and potato salad. He dished the food onto plates, poured chilled wine into real glasses, added ice. He handed me a plate and a glass.

I blinked at him. I couldn't quite believe I was actually here. I'd been plucked out of a wintry softness and dumped into this strange antipodean land that was hot and harsh and angular and filled with strange discordant sounds. Perhaps I'd wake up and still be on the plane . . .

"Cheers, El." He held up his goblet. Light danced off the liquid. Ice clinked against the glass. Thirst gripped me by the throat.

We sipped. I sipped again, this strange thirst making me desperate. I drank deeper. He watched me. I took yet another big swallow. Clouds thickened in the sky above us, blotting out the blinding haze. The iron-dark water turned black. A brooding menace pressed down over the mangroves.

Light flashed in the sky. I glanced up. Thunder rumbled and folded into the faraway boom of surf. Wind stirred. It brought a fetid smell out of the forest. I was not seeing what Martin saw in this place. I did not see beauty. I could not imagine here what the brochures showed. A terrible fear rose inside me. I'd done something awful—made a big mistake.

"No worries, been thundering most afternoons lately," Martin said. "Pressure systems building every day in this unseasonable hot spell. Should break and rain soon enough."

He topped up my glass. I sipped more of the cold drink and ate a bit. I felt a little better. He put down the back seat and gave me a blanket to lie on, which I did, staring up at eucalyptus leaves. My eyes began to close, and I finally felt free to allow the fatigue to wash over me. The world began to fade with the gentle rock of the boat upon the turning of the tide.

◆ ◆ ◆

I woke with a shock.

I was lying on the bottom of the boat. It was dusk. Massive bats swooped down on the boat and then back up into the tree above. More hung there, squabbling. Confusion flared through me. Then panic. I scrambled up onto my knees, pulled myself up onto my feet. Unsteady, I hung on to the boat's awning support.

"Martin?" I called into the darkening mangrove shadows.

A scream sliced through the air. My heart beat fast. Some kind of bird. Prehistoric-sounding. I looked up. Beyond the twisted silhouette of the forest canopy, the sky was slashed with vermilion streaks and angry blades of orange. I dropped back to my knees. Limbs wouldn't work. I retched over the side of boat, a dry heave. Bitter bile soured the back of my throat.

Martin! My voice was hoarse.

With a crashing sound, he appeared through the bushes at the end of the dock. He carried a flashlight and a stack of signboards. I read the words on the top placard as he clumped along the wooden dock toward the boat.

STOP AGNES MARINA! ACID WASH KILLS.

"Where have you been?" I demanded, trying to stand again. "Where did you go . . . where are those signs from?"

"Welcome back." His voice was cool. Displeasure contorted his face. He climbed into the boat and dumped the signs with a clatter on the bottom of the boat.

I looked at them next to my bare feet. When had I taken my shoes off? The tops of my feet were red and swollen from mosquito bites. Next to my toes was an empty bottle of rosé. Hadn't we been drinking white? A wine goblet lay on its side, rolling slightly back and forth with

Martin's movement on the boat. I touched my face. It was bitten and lumpy, too. Itchy. My lips were chapped.

"I wanted to show you the homestead," he said brusquely as he climbed out of the boat to untie the yellow-and-blue ropes. "I wanted you to see the view over our land." He angrily tossed in the ropes, climbed back into the boat, and positioned himself behind the wheel. The engine coughed to life. "You really shouldn't drink so much wine on top of jet lag and the cider, Ellie."

"What?" I pressed my hand to my damp brow. I couldn't process. I couldn't *remember*.

"Put your damn life jacket on." He reversed away from the dock, bubbles churning up from the propeller. "A bottle and a half? You're going to feel it in the morning. And look at you covered with bites. Not even sober enough to put on the repellent I gave you."

"But I . . . didn't drink—"

He reached down, snagged the rosé bottle up from the deck, held it up for me to see, wiggled it at my face. "Empty to the last drop."

My mouth indeed tasted sour with old wine. I felt drunk. He stuck the empty bottle and goblet into a compartment along the side of the boat, right next to an aggressive-looking fishing gaff that had the name *Abracadabra* down the side. He angled the bow back into the channel. Martin increased speed, the dark water swelling into a *V* behind us. Trees reached out to grab us. Bats swirled and filled the vermilion sky. Shrieks and screams tore through the air.

My gaze dropped to the signboards near my feet.

STOP MARINA DEVELOPER.
KILL MARTIN.

"Fucking protesters," he mumbled. "They've been inside that old homestead. That's private property—*my* property. If I get my hands on them, I . . . I'll cut those fuckers to shreds, cut 'em with a knife. Stick my gaff in them. Make them bleed and feed 'em to the muddies."

I cringed at the rawness of his anger, at his cursing. It was frightening because it seemed directed at me as much as the protesters.

"I didn't drink all of that wine, Martin," I said softly. I'd only had a few sips that I could recall. I had no memory of what had happened next. I'd just woken up at the bottom of the boat. He didn't reply.

I tried to reconstruct the events of the day. But I could barely even remember starting to eat the chicken and salad.

The boat entered the basin. Martin swung it around sharply. I lost balance and fell against the side. Pain sparked through my knee.

I pulled myself back up and sat gingerly on the rear seat. "I know I didn't drink all that wine, Martin."

He said nothing, didn't even look at me.

"I *know* I didn't," I said louder. But I wasn't sure. A soft panic swelled inside me. This had happened before. A couple of times. In that dark space between Chloe's drowning and my attacking Doug with a knife in the restaurant when I'd seen him through the window dining with his mistress, the woman with whom he'd been cheating on me. I'd tried to slice them both. It was the public breakdown that had precipitated my hospitalization. I suddenly lurched for the gunwale and threw up over the side.

"Fuck, Ellie!" He wiped something off his sleeve. "Downwind next time, please."

THE MURDER TRIAL

Now, February. Supreme Court, New South Wales.

Barrister Peter Lorrington rises for cross-examination. Lozza's stomach fists. She has described to the court how she and Gregg arrived to find Martin's body. And while the prosecution is not permitted to ask leading questions at this stage, a defense barrister can—and will—in the cross. Lorrington will need to seed his defense strategy early, either directly or indirectly, and Lozza knows she's vulnerable. She and Gregg are the weak links in the Crown's case. Lorrington will grill her mercilessly right out of the gate in an effort to undercut the integrity of the entire homicide investigation and seed reasonable doubt. She can feel the gazes of her fellow officers in the packed gallery.

Lorrington consults his notes, then glances up. Lozza faces him squarely and swallows.

Silence in the courtroom grows heavy.

Lorrington's words come suddenly, like machine-gun fire. "Senior Constable Bianchi, did you touch the body prior to the forensic unit and pathologist's arrival—did you move it in any way?"

Lozza hesitates. "The body had already been moved—cut free by a teen diver."

"But did *you* touch it?"

"Constable Abbott slipped into the water," she says carefully, unwilling to throw her partner under the bus. "He accidentally bumped the body, and the decedent rolled onto his back."

Lorrington rubs his chin pensively. "So *this* is how you determined it was a homicide?"

Irritation sparks through Lozza. She calms herself. The barrister is stirring, winding her up, trying to make law enforcement look guilty of something.

"This is how I came to see the gaff stuck into the chest, and the other puncture wounds, ligature marks, plus the rope tied around the decedent's ankles."

Konikova rises. "Your Honor, I fail to see the relevance—"

"I'll come straight to the point, Your Honor," Lorrington barks. "Detective Bianchi, you and Constable Abbott were the first officers on the scene, is that correct? The first officers to lay eyes on the body of Martin Cresswell-Smith?"

"Me, Constable Abbott, and Constable Mac McGonigle, who skippered the launch to the site, yes, sir," Lozza says.

"So just to be clear, the body was moved by an ordinary duty officer before a properly designated detective and a qualified forensics team from State Crime Command could arrive, is that correct?"

Lozza clears her throat. "As I stated, Constable Abbott slipped and bumped the body."

"So that's a yes?"

"Yes," she says slowly. "But I am a trained detective, sir. I served on the State Crime Command homicide squad for five years." As Lozza spoke, she saw the trap. She'd walked right into it. Lorrington would circle back to her legacy on the murder squad later in the trial. He was going to drag her personally through the muck to save his client from a guilty verdict. Her chest cramps. She forces herself to keep her gaze locked on Lorrington's.

"And how long was the wait before Detective Sergeant Corneil Tremayne and the rest of the forensic team from State Crime Command did arrive?"

"Two hours and twenty-three minutes," says Lozza. "They deployed from the Sydney area, flew into Agnes Basin via helicopter, and were brought into the channel by boat. There was a storm. It delayed them for a period."

"And what did you at the crime scene do during that period?"

"Constable Abbott cordoned off the area around the body. I left the jetty and went up the trail to where there is an old, abandoned farmhouse."

"Alone?"

"Yes," Lozza says quietly, her mind going back to that day, to the horrific scene she'd found. "I went alone."

THEN

ELLIE

Over one year ago, October 26. Jarrawarra Bay, New South Wales.

Light streamed in through open blinds, flat and searingly bright. The room was hot. My head pounded. My whole body hurt. Birds—awful birds in brilliant colors—flitted and screeched from branch to branch outside the window.

With a jolt I realized I was in my new house. My new bedroom. Naked beneath a tangle of damp sheets. I could taste the sourness of old alcohol and vomit in my mouth, and a metallic tinge . . . *blood?* I touched my tongue to my bottom lip. It was swollen, cut. My pulse quickened. Cautiously I turned my pounding head to the side. My clothes lay in a crumpled pile on the floor. A sense of horror dawned. I reached under the sheet and felt between my thighs. Sticky. Swollen. Sore.

I scrunched my eyes tightly shut as fear rose and circled like a tangible creature. Disjointed shards of memory sliced through my brain. Thunder. White lightning. Pummeling rain—the scent of it on dry soil. Martin pulling his truck into a driveway. Bats in the tree above the garage. Him half carrying me up some stairs. Then . . . nothing. A black hole. My fear tipped toward terror. Was it happening again? The blackouts?

I pushed myself up into a sitting position, caught sight of myself in the mirrored closet doors across the room. I was in a double bed and barely recognized the woman with the tangle of dark hair who stared back at me with puffy eyes, dark circles, a cut lip, red insect bites all over her face.

I put my hand to my brow.

Think, dammit! Remember.

But I couldn't.

I glanced at the pillow beside me—dented where a head had lain. A bottle of water had been placed beside a digital clock on the bedside table. Condensation formed on the outside. Still cold. It hadn't been there long. Had Martin put it there? The clock read 2:56 p.m.

The sound of a vehicle reached me through the open window, wheels crunching over gravel.

I stumbled out of bed and staggered to the window. I blinked out into the harsh light. I was on a second floor. Down below, the driveway was empty, a garage door open. Relief pinged through me. Martin was gone with the truck. I couldn't let him see me like this—I had time to pull myself together, figure things out.

In the adjacent bathroom I found that my cosmetic bag had been placed on a white marble counter. Everything was white, from the tiles to the fresh towels. My cosmetic pouch had been emptied, my tooth-brush and toothpaste placed neatly in a cup next to the basin. I avoided my reflection while I hurriedly brushed my teeth and cleaned the sour taste out of my mouth. I took a scalding shower. As soap made contact with my private parts, my skin burned. I tensed. Whatever had happened last night, sex had been aggressive. A memory surfaced—or was it a nightmare? Me trapped, restrained, fighting someone off. I shook off the image. I did not want to acknowledge to myself that it might not be from a dream. Edgy, I toweled off and combed the tangles from my wet hair.

The mirrored cabinet above the basin housed the rest of the contents from my cosmetic bag, including my bottle of painkillers and . . . *the container of Ativan tabs.*

I stared at it, my heart beating faster. Martin. He'd unpacked my cosmetic bag. He'd seen my pills. I opened the drawer beneath the counter and felt a wash of horror. He'd also found my backup stash of pills from my suitcase. He'd put them all into this drawer.

A mix of rage and anxiety crackled through my chest. How *dare* he go through my things? Surely he should respect my privacy? Surely there were boundaries even within a marriage? Doug had always given me space. I couldn't imagine Doug ever unpacking all my things, especially my cosmetics. Or was I wrong? Did people do this?

I exhaled forcefully.

Whatever my feelings, Martin had now seen all my drugs. I snatched the Ativan container from the cabinet, opened it, and hurriedly swallowed a pill, desperate now to take the edge off the full-blown panic attack threatening me. I replaced the container and saw he'd also put my bottle of multivitamin capsules in the cabinet, so I popped one of those, too, followed by a headache pill.

Wrapped in a towel, I went into the bedroom and slid open the mirrored closet door in search of clothes. The first side I opened was Martin's. I stared bemused at the impossibly neat stack of T-shirts. Color-coded. And his hangers holding button-down shirts had been placed at precisely even intervals. It was creepy. Cold. Too organized. How had I not noticed this streak in him before? Probably because we hadn't lived together yet. After we married he'd stayed at my place only on occasions. The rest of the time he was back and forth between winding up his business and his apartment in Toronto.

I opened the other half of the closet. He'd hung and folded my clothes, too, including my bras and panties in matching color groupings. A chill crawled down the back of my neck. Everything of mine had been touched and ordered by him.

I found a sundress, and as I pulled it over my head I felt the Ativan taking effect. It was a relief. Once dressed I did my makeup, trying to minimize the puffiness of my eyes and the redness of the mosquito bites. Then I wandered downstairs in bare feet.

Everything downstairs was white. The room was open plan, clean lines, minimalist. Huge pieces of abstract art provided the only slashes of color—streaks of bloodred, black upon yellow. Glass sliding doors opened onto a lawn that rolled down to trees along the river. The Bonny River, I presumed. I could see the mouth, where the brown bled into the aquamarine sea. Beyond the mouth was a rocky point where waves crashed and foamed, spray blowing white into the wind.

I padded into the living room, the white tiles smooth beneath my feet. "Martin?" I called.

Silence echoed through the hollowness of the stark house.

"Martin!" I called louder.

No answer.

I saw a closed door to my left. I tried the handle. Locked. Martin's office? Why would he lock it? My feeling of disquiet deepened.

The kitchen was huge. Again, all white, even the dishcloths. No dirty plates in the sink. No lingering coffee cups. The wine fridge was fully stocked with an array of whites and rosés plus two bottles of prosecco. A small craving pinged through me as I studied the chilled bottles, but I opened the main fridge, instead, in search of cold water. This fridge contained ciders, beer. I found bottled water. I opened the cap and swigged, but I was stopped by a sudden sense of being watched. I lowered the bottle, turned. The sensation of being observed intensified.

"Martin?" I said softly, but I could see no one there.

I went to the sliding door and stepped out onto the patio facing the river. The air was heavily scented with the sea. The sense of being watched lingered. I glanced up into the trees. As I did, two sulphur-crested cockatoos screamed and swooped down at me. I gasped and ducked. They fluttered, cackling into the sky. My heart hammered.

I turned in a slow circle, seeking the source of my unease. There was a vacant lot to my left—a tangle of drab vegetation. To my right was a neighboring property. I studied the second-story windows of the house that looked into our yard. A sheer curtain moved, possibly stirred by the hot breeze because I could see no one. The background noise of raucous birds was intense.

I walked over the coarse grass and down the slope toward the boathouse that Martin had said would be ideal as my studio.

Everywhere, droplets glimmered in the sun. It had clearly rained heavily last night. It was making the ground steam. Gum trees dripped. The blades of grass were sharp-edged under my feet, like everything else in this place was sharp.

Inside the studio the walls were also bright white—a kitchenette, a tiny bathroom, a daybed. A lone black-and-white clock hung above the bed. The clock was the exact same design as the one I'd seen on the wall of the living room in the main house. The boxes I'd shipped from Canada were stacked in front of the kitchenette counter. Glass sliding doors opened onto a small wooden deck that narrowed into a dock that led into the dark river.

I walked toward the daybed. It was covered in a white quilt. From the indentations it looked as though someone had lain on it recently. Sticking out from under a corner of a pillow was a piece of dark fabric. I lifted the pillow. It was a hair tie, a scrunchie. I picked it up.

The fabric of the scrunchie was deep green with skeins of gold thread braided through. A long strand of auburn hair had been trapped in a skein. Wavy hair. I frowned as a memory surfaced—Lennin watching us argue from the sales office window. It was followed by an earlier memory—the brunette with the Martin doppelgänger. I recalled the way the man I'd thought was Martin had looked right through me. A doubt began to whisper in my head.

No, Ellie, no, do not do this again.

I'd started going really crazy when I'd begun to suspect Doug was having an affair. I'd started seeing signs everywhere.

But you were right, Ellie. He was having an affair. You found out in the end.

Yes, but some of the things were imagined.

Right, like you imagined the man in the garage was Martin. But he was a doppelgänger, not Martin. So the brunette you saw with him means nothing to you.

But what about the brown hair trapped in this scrunchie on this bed?

I lifted the scrunchie to my nose and sniffed. As I did, I heard a noise. I froze. Listened. Heard it again—a thud.

Quickly pocketing the scrunchie, I exited the studio. No one on the lawn. I could see no movement through the big glass windows of our house. I made my way to the garage along the fence of the neighboring property. I entered the side door. It was dim inside. No truck. Martin had not yet returned. As my eyes adjusted I saw the garage interior was as neat as Martin's closet. A wet suit hung from a hanger. A stand-up paddleboard leaned against the wall. Tools hung in an orderly fashion on the wall above a worktable. A fishing knife lay on the table next to a gaff like the one I'd seen on the *Abracadabra*. Perhaps it was the same one.

I exited the garage, and immediately that sense of being watched grew powerful. I stood still, shaded my eyes, and carefully studied the windows of the house next door above the fence tangled with jasmine.

The curtains twitched again in the window on the second floor. I tensed as a woman appeared, then quickly retreated out of sight. I stared at the empty space, wondering why on earth she hadn't just waved hello.

"Hey!" I called as I went up to the fence, suddenly angry at being spied on and made to feel uncomfortable in my own yard. "Hey, hello!" I called up from the jasmine-tangled boundary.

Nothing moved.

I cursed and went back inside the house, intending to phone Martin and find out where in the hell he was and ask him what was up with the neighbor.

I located my purse upstairs, rummaged around inside it, found my wallet, my passport, boarding passes, plane tickets . . . no phone.

I emptied the contents of the purse onto the bed.

My phone was gone.

I spun around. It wasn't on the bedside table, not in any drawers, not in the bathroom. I hurried back downstairs and came to a halt in the middle of the living room, my head pounding. The white house felt clinical, like a cage. When had I last used my phone? Sydney Airport? Maybe I'd lost it there. I had no idea how to reach Martin. I couldn't see any landline phone in the house, either. I rattled the handle of the locked door to what I presumed was Martin's office. Definitely locked.

And even if there was a landline in there, I couldn't recall Martin's mobile number. I usually just hit his contact details in my cell. Did anyone remember phone numbers these days?

I found my sandals, went outside again, and made my way back to the garage. The thudding I'd heard earlier had sounded like it had come from behind the garage.

I reached the corner of the garage and heard a crack of twigs. I froze, listening, my heart beating irrationally fast. Why was I feeling scared? It was the constant screaming of birds that was grating on my nerves. I proceeded around the corner . . . and stopped dead.

Martin stood there covered in blood. A massive knife in his hand dripped with blood. Shock registered on his face. He took a quick step toward me.

I screamed, and stepped backward.

His face cracked into a grin. He laughed and waggled the knife at me. "You startled me, Mrs. Cresswell-Smith."

Another memory slammed through me—my hands trapped above my head, my thighs being forced open. My mouth turned dry. I took another step backward.

His features shifted again, darkening now. He took another step toward me.

"What are you so afraid of, Ellie?"

THEN

ELLIE

My brain cracked into primal mode. I spun to flee. But Martin lunged forward and clamped his bloody hand around my arm.

"Stop!"

I whimpered, shaking. Tears burned into my eyes. His fingers dug into my skin.

"Ellie," he said very quietly, darkly.

"Please . . . please let me go." My voice was hoarse.

"Step away from the wall, Ellie."

I didn't move. Couldn't.

"Ellie. Focus. Look at me."

Slowly I turned my head. He pointed the tip of his knife at the brick wall. "See that? You need to move away from that. Now."

I tried to focus. His blade tip pointed at a spider with a shiny carapace and hairy legs, which were raised at me, its fangs back—poised to attack.

"It's poisonous," he said quietly as I stared at the spider. "A funnel-web. One of the most venomous in the world. You need to step away—you were going to put your hand right on it."

My gaze went to his knife, the blood. There was more blood on his arms and on his shirt. He let me go and I hurriedly moved away from the wall. He set the knife on a wooden table. A fish-cleaning station. A big fish that had been sliced down the middle was splayed open on the table, moist flesh glistening in the sun. Entrails curled in a pink and bloody heap beside the fish. Shiny scales stuck everywhere. Fat flies buzzed over the kill. Next to the table was a stainless steel counter with a basin with a tap.

"Zog went fishing," he said. "He brought us a bonito. I was cleaning it. You spooked me—I had earbuds in. Was listening to music." He paused, and a frown furrowed deep into his brow. "Are you okay? You didn't think I—"

"I got a fright." I wiped my mouth with a shaky hand. "I . . . I was looking for you. I called you. I . . . heard a thump."

"Must have been me chopping that bonito's head off." I noticed his wireless headphones resting on a small wooden shelf that had been affixed to the garage wall above the fish-cleaning station. I couldn't seem to find words. I was still thinking about the rough sex, the sense I'd cried out for him to stop—yet I wasn't sure what had happened.

"Why don't you go inside, Ellie, and I'll take care of the spider and finish up with the fish here. Then we can maybe go for a walk? I can show you around?"

His voice was kind, his eyes gentle.

I tried to speak, but my mind had collapsed in on itself, and this fact alone scared the stuffing out of me. It was like I was still drugged.

"Ellie?"

"Your truck," I said abruptly. "Where is it?"

"The ute? I loaned it to Zog to haul his boat out of the launch. His is being repaired. It's why he gave us such a big guy." He nodded to the splayed fish.

"Who's Zog?"

"He owns the Single Fin. A surf shop on the beach road. I'll take you past there when we go for a walk." He paused. "Okay?"

"I couldn't find my phone."

"Oh—I'm sorry." He wiped his hands on a rag, then reached into the side pocket of his cargo shorts. "Here you go." He handed me my phone. "I thought I'd do you a favor while you were sleeping. I took it to get a new SIM card—had it all set up for Australia."

I took the phone and stared at it. Not only had he unpacked my clothes and cosmetics, he'd gone into my phone. "Thank you," I said quietly.

"You still feeling off?"

I thought about the raw skin of my private parts, the tenderness between my thighs, my blank memory. The stash of pills he'd seen. Cautiously I said, "I'm just really jet-lagged."

A smile returned to his face. "But last night was good."

I blinked.

"The sex," he said.

I swallowed. "I . . . I was really tired."

"You don't remember?" Worry darkened his eyes.

Heat seared into my cheeks.

"Hey, it's okay, El. I'm not surprised. You went out like a light. All that wine." He paused. "On top of those pills."

Heat deepened in my face. I didn't remember more wine—any wine. But I had tasted old alcohol in my mouth this morning. And I couldn't argue the pills. He angled his head, watching me intently. "Are you sure you're doing okay?"

No, I'm not sure of anything right now.

I nodded. "I . . . I think I'll start unpacking some of my boxes in the studio."

I needed to ground myself. Those boxes I'd shipped over the ocean contained my art supplies and paintings and sketches as well as framed photos of friends and family, plus other knickknacks that helped define who I was, what I did. I wanted to unpack everything, hang the pictures and photos up on those clinical white walls and stamp something of myself on this place—something that might help make me feel more real, because I couldn't shake the growing distance I felt between my normal self and reality. I couldn't quite absorb this new land yet, the scope of this adventure, and how I'd gotten to be here so fast. Neither could I shake the lingering fuzziness in my brain. Perhaps it really was just a serious wallop of jet lag, but I didn't like the cool fingers of paranoia starting to scratch at the edges of my consciousness again, trying to get in. I didn't like the disquiet I was feeling about my own husband.

"Great idea," he said, and turned back to the fish.

I cast another glance up at the neighbor's window. No one was there. I proceeded down to my studio on the water, trying to shake the sensation of being trapped and watched. Like prey.

THEN

ELLIE

Martin took me to the headlands first.

"It's a good place for surfers to come check the swell," he explained. "You also get an amazing view of the small boats trying to get in or out of the Bonny River when the bar is breaking. It becomes quite the spectator sport. See down there?" He pointed to where the mouth fanned brown into blue sea. "That's where the boat launch is. And over there—" He swung his arm northward. "Those sheer orange cliffs in the distance—that's the Point of No Return."

"And straight out ahead of us?" I asked.

He grinned. "The Tasman Sea pretty much all the way to New Zealand."

We left the lookout and wended along the cliff path that ran in front of high-end houses full of glass windows overlooking the sea. Exotic birds darted everywhere. I stopped to watch a "cocky" drink from a stone birdbath. It was bombed by a flock of lories. Everything seemed to be fighting here, and loud about it. Martin pointed out a kookaburra pecking in the grass among a flock of pink galah birds. He took me onto a little trail that led down to the beach, carving switchbacks through the cliff scrub. A rabbit darted across our path and Martin explained how domesticated rabbits had gone feral and become a problem.

"Shooters are occasionally hired to exterminate them—safer than poison."

"What did you do with the funnel-web?"

"Killed it. Before it kills us."

I shot him a glance.

He laughed. "The funnel-web might be responsible for all spider-bite deaths in this part of Aus, but no fatalities have actually been recorded since the introduction of an antivenin in the eighties." He took my hand and helped me down the last steep pitch to the beach. Small stones dislodged by our feet rolled down the incline to the water.

"You've just got to be cognizant of your surroundings, that's all. You can see its web easily if you know what to look for. It spins a series of fine trip lines that radiate out from a lair which is shaped like a funnel. The spider lives deep inside the funnel, and when an insect stumbles into one of the trip lines, the spider rushes out at extreme speed, grabs and bites the prey, then drags it down to the bottom of the funnel into its home, where it sucks the living juices out of its prey."

The idea of being murdered after innocently walking into a soft line of silk gave me a dark feeling. We reached the sand, took off our sandals, and strolled hand in hand along the shore, like in the movies. Afterward we sat in the dunes for a while, watching the waves and the sinking sun while I sipped hot coffee from a flask Martin had brought in a small backpack. He didn't want any.

"I had a mug before leaving home," he said.

The surfers off the point were having a rough time in the crashing waves, most of them heading back into shore as the sun lowered. I thought of Chloe drowning at a famous surfing beach. Memories of Doug resurfaced. Our old life, the old me, seemed so far away. What had happened to me? Who was I now?

What had I come to?

It's not forever, Ellie. You're here for an adventure. You came because you fell in love with this man and want to share his dream.

I glanced at him. His profile. His strength. His substance. He turned to me and smiled, and I glimpsed his dimples, the Martin I loved again. Yet the eerie sensation lingered that I'd made a mistake.

My mind turned to the brochure with my dad's name on it. The deception. I opened my mouth to mention it again, but bit back the words, preferring to avoid confrontation again, at least for now. I'd circle back later when I'd fully recovered from this weird jet lag and thickness in my head.

"What are you thinking?" he said.

"I . . . I was thinking about maybe trying to go back into the waves." I surprised myself—the words just tumbled out of my mouth, and the idea took hold. "Perhaps if I did—if I faced my fear of rough water, it would clear some of the mental blocks I've got around losing Chloe. That swim in the Cook Islands was like a first step. Maybe . . . maybe I am ready for the next."

He observed me intently. "Perhaps you're right, El. Maybe you *should* try."

I nodded. "Maybe. Eventually."

"You might stop blaming yourself for Chloe's death."

My gaze flared to his. Acid burned into my throat. It was fine for me to say, but out of his mouth it veered toward accusatory.

"It must have been so awful when they found her little body . . . The police questioning you on top of it all, as if they thought you could be guilty. As if you could have let her go on purpose."

Perhaps Martin *did* believe I was to blame.

"Yeah," I said quietly, darkly.

He fell silent, and I sensed tension continuing to build around him. After a few moments: "I saw all the pills, Ellie."

"You shouldn't have gone through my things," I said, facing the sea.

Waves crashed. The wind turned cool and blew harder.

"Is that why the wine went to your head so fast yesterday?" he asked. "Is that why you passed out—because you drank on top of more meds?"

I positioned my coffee cup in the sand. I *wanted* to come clean. I wanted nothing to hide between us. I glanced at him. His eyes were as blue as the sky behind him. It felt as though I were looking right through his head into the heavens. He looked worried, concerned.

"Look, maybe I shouldn't have unpacked your things. I'm sorry. But I was just trying to help, trying to make you feel welcome. I thought you'd be grateful. And once I saw the pills I couldn't unsee them."

I nodded.

"That Ativan—it's a benzodiazepine. Benzos are highly addictive. I mean, highly." He paused. "Ellie, I know you've had problems in the past, but I thought you were good now."

"I am. I stopped the pills. Honest. But my fear of flying remains a problem, and I need some meds to avoid a full-blown panic attack in the air." I hesitated. "The last time I had an anxiety attack the pilot had to make an emergency landing. The crew thought I was having a heart attack. I just couldn't have that happening again, especially while flying on my own."

He regarded me in silence for a while. "You took benzos on our Europe and Vegas trips?"

I nodded. "Small doses. And only for flying. But I was worried about coming here with a new medical system and . . . having to go through a new doctor and . . ." My words faded.

"You were afraid of a relapse? And you wanted to feel secure, with a big backup supply?"

"Maybe. I think so. And in case we have to fly somewhere again."

He pursed his lips and studied the sea for a long while. "What are the side effects?" he asked quietly.

"Nothing much if I take just small doses."

"And with a bigger dose?"

"When they wear off I can feel shaky . . . sort of panicky sometimes."

"See? This is why they're addictive, El, because then you'll want more in order to stop the withdrawal symptoms, and it becomes a vicious spiral."

He was right.

"I'm sorry," I said softly. "I'm not who you thought I was. I'm a bit of a mess still."

He took my hand in his, laced his fingers through mine. "We'll do this together, okay, El? We'll be open with each other. If you keep talking to me, I can keep helping you. A team, right? Our second chance—" Emotion caught his voice and shone in his eyes. "I don't want to blow this."

"Neither do I."

"I'm truly sorry I pushed you yesterday. I should have seen how badly you needed to sleep after you landed. I . . . This is why you *need* to talk to me. I hadn't realized." He squeezed my hand tightly.

Emotion surged into my throat. Martin leaned forward and kissed my cheek. So gently that I knew with sudden and firm conviction that my nightmare had been just that—a stupid, terrible, feverish dream that had probably grown out of jet lag, dehydration, the aftereffects of wine and the Ativan plus some rough and exuberant but good and healthy sex that my fogged-up brain just never encoded into memory.

"I'll stop the pills—I promise," I said. And I felt better for voicing it.

"I'm here for you, okay?"

I nodded, reached for my mug. I took another sip of coffee, and a feeling of benevolence and warmth bloomed through my chest. I actually felt happy having gotten that out of the way.

"It's getting late," he said as the sun slipped into the sea. "How about stopping for a bite at the Puggo on the way home? We can do Zog's fish on the barbie tomoz."

"Puggo?"

"The Pug and Whistler," he said with a grin. "Puggo for short."

I laughed, suddenly light inside again. "Of course it is. Is nothing in this country safe from hypocorism?"

"Hypo-what?"

"Turning words into diminutive or cutesy-folksy forms."

"That's your degree in literature talking." He chuckled, got to his feet, and held out his hand.

I allowed him to pull me to my feet, and I punched him playfully on the arm. "Tease."

But as we started up the dune path toward the road, I lost my balance and stumbled in the soft sand. He stopped and eyed me.

Sweat prickled my skin.

"Are you all right?"

"Yeah, just feel a bit . . . odd again."

Concern reentered his eyes. "We can go right home."

"No. No, it's fine."

"Are you sure?"

"Of course."

He placed his hand at the small of my spine and guided me up the dune path and onto the sidewalk. There was a public washroom off the sidewalk with a mosaic mural on the wall. Beside it was an outdoor shower where surfers rinsed off their wet suits and boards. I suddenly became conscious of a brown sedan parked across the road. I stilled.

A man in the driver's seat watched us. As I stared at him he powered up the window. I frowned. I wasn't sure why the car had caught my eye in the first place. Maybe it was just that eerie sense of being observed. I'd read somewhere long ago that our bodies can be aware of things when our brains aren't. Perhaps my unconscious had picked up something.

When we reached the end of the beach road, I glanced back. The dark sedan had pulled out of its parking spot. It was coming slowly up the road behind us.

THEN

ELLIE

I was so absorbed watching the car following us that I tripped on the uneven paving of the sidewalk.

"You okay?" Martin asked.

"I wish you'd stop saying that," I snapped. "You make it sound like there's something wrong with me."

"You're stumbling a lot, El."

"It's nothing. I wasn't paying attention."

"Did you take another one of those Ativan before leaving the house?"

My chest cramped.

"Ellie? We need to be open, remember?"

"I . . . needed something after—after that spider, seeing all the blood on you. It made me panicky. I needed to take the edge off."

"Do you have any pills on you now?"

Guilt washed hot up my throat. "No," I lied. "I'm going to be fine. I told you. It's just . . . I need to wean myself off them slowly." I'd been here before. Tapering was better than cold turkey. This was a medical fact. Going cold turkey could spark a resurgence of psychiatric symptoms that had lain dormant during the drug use. From experience I knew this could lead to severe anxiety, PTSD symptoms, OCD, depression. The last time I'd weaned myself off the meds I'd done it with the help of a psychiatrist because I'd been in the hospital after stabbing Doug—a court-mandated thing.

Martin nodded. We walked in silence, and I sensed the shift in his mood. He was worried. Perhaps he'd take all my meds and destroy them. Perhaps I should hide the pills before he could.

"You know, I think we should go fishing tomorrow," he said with a glance up at the sky, which was turning a soft indigo in the increasing twilight. "Weather should be good. It'll get your mind off the meds."

A statement. Not a question.

"I . . . was hoping to settle into my studio properly, get back to work. I have that deadline looming."

"You'll like it—you'll see. A mental break will be good. We'll go out to the FAD. It's not far off the continental shelf. Where the blue water is, where the giant pelagic swim. It'll be great."

"What's a FAD?"

"Fish aggregation device. A man-made object—usually some kind of buoy tethered to the deep ocean floor with concrete blocks. They're deployed by state fisheries up and down the coast and used to attract oceangoing fish like marlin, tuna, dolphin fish, sharks. The fish tend to congregate around the FADs, swimming in varying orbits and at varying depths around the device. They're funded by fishing license fees. Like a fish magnet."

The brown car passed us and crawled slowly up the street. It turned into the road where we were headed. I noticed the registration plate— QUEENSLAND. SUNSHINE STATE—maroon characters against a white background. The numbers were covered by dirt, but I could make out the last three letters: GIN.

We turned onto the street and I saw it again, parked ahead under a large gum with peeling bark. My pulse quickened. I stopped.

"Do you see that car?" I said to Martin.

"The brown Corolla? Yeah."

"It's following us."

He frowned. "What do you mean?"

"It was parked across from our house when we left. And then I saw it across the street from the surfers' shower when we came up from the beach. It followed us slowly, passed us, and now it's waiting ahead of us."

His frown deepened. "Why would someone follow us, Ellie?"

"I don't know—you tell me."

We resumed walking, but at a slower pace, and he studied the Corolla intently as we closed in on it. He seemed worried, but I wasn't sure whether it was about the car, or about me.

"It's a common model," he said as we neared. "Did you happen to see the plate of the one parked outside our house?"

"No."

The sedan suddenly pulled out from under the tree and drove quickly to the top of the road. Brake lights flared. It turned right and was gone. Wind gusted, flinging bits of bark at us. A flock of lories took flight with wild squawks.

"It was probably a different Corolla outside our house," he said. "The one up ahead was probably just some guy driving slowly to check the waves, and then he pulled over to answer his mobile—could be any number of explanations."

"I think someone was following us back home, too. In an orange Subaru."

He stopped dead. "What?"

"Yeah. It was a flat orange color."

"You mean—like one of those Crosstreks?"

"Yes."

Blood drained from his face. An unreadable look formed on his features. A vibrating energy, a palpable sense of purpose, coalesced around him. "Are you certain?"

"Yes."

"Did you see the driver of the orange Subaru? Or the plate?"

"No. But I think the plate was a BC one—blue and white."

"What about the driver of the brown Corolla—did you get a look?"

"Only a glimpse. He powered up the window as soon as I stared at him."

"He?"

"A guy, yes."

"Would you recognize him if you saw him again?"

I considered this. "I don't think so. His face was in shadow."

"Weird," Martin said.

We continued to the pub, but a cloud had descended over Martin. He walked faster, his shoulders forward like he was angry. I struggled to keep up. My breathing deepened. My anxiety grew sharper.

I lagged back.

While Martin was ahead I dug in my pocket and quickly popped a sublingual pill under my tongue.

He stopped, turned. "What's up?"

"Nothing. I had a stone in my shoe."

THEN

ELLIE

The wooden sign for the Pug and Whistler swung on metal chains in the slight breeze. The building had a historic facade and a fenced beer-and-wine garden out back. Fairy lights were strung from the gums, galahs fed on the verge, and flies buzzed over a scattering of patrons seated at tables along the front veranda.

I stopped beneath the sign. Carved into the wood was a figure of boy with a surfboard under his arm. The boy's face was turned to the sky, and he was whistling. Behind him followed a fat and merry-looking little pug. The Pug and Whistler.

"Rabz—the owner, Bodie Rabinovitch—had a pug," Martin said, following my gaze.

The sign—the place—looked friendly. My spirits calmed. Just a little. Or the Ativan was working. Nevertheless I shot a quick glance over my shoulder to ensure the Corolla was nowhere among the deepening twilight shadows.

Martin drew back a PVC strip curtain that hung across the door. We entered and the thick plastic strips clacked into place behind us. They reminded me of a butcher's shop. But the curtain seemed to keep the heat out because the interior was cool. Dimly lit. Busy. Lots of chatter. An old-fashioned jukebox in the corner played upbeat music. Surfboards and fishing memorabilia decorated the walls.

"Hey! Marty!" A woman came out from behind the bar, wiping her hands on a cloth. "How are ya?"

"Rabz." Martin gave her a hug. "This is my Ellie. El, this is Rabz. A local fixture. Ex–pro surfer." Martin grinned.

Rabz's gaze met mine. Her eyes were a rich brown. She'd attempted to restrain her mass of long brown hair in a loose braid that hung over her shoulder, but tendrils escaped and curled prettily around her face. Her deeply tanned olive skin was offset by an orange artisan-looking shift that hung loosely over her athletic body. Leather sandals. An armful of silver bangles and beads. A nose stud winked as she moved.

And what I felt was an odd stab of jealousy.

Rabz extended her hand. "Heya, El. Good to finally meet you."

Her grip was strong, like she was trying to make a point she didn't have to. She smelled like essential oils—patchouli with a hit of jasmine and lime. Something dark and uncomfortable began to unfurl along the edges of my mind.

"Cute place you have," I said. It came out patronizing. Perhaps I'd intended it to be.

She eyed me, then smiled, but it didn't quite reach her brown eyes. "Thanks. We just renovated, so I'm glad you like it."

We seated ourselves on barstools while Rabz began to pour beer from a tap, angling the glass carefully to get the head just so. She set the beer in front of Martin. "On the house—your usual." A smile at me. "What can I get for you, Ellie?"

I opened my mouth, but Martin said quickly, "Pinot gris."

The darkness at the edges of my consciousness snaked closer. I'd been about to ask for something nonalcoholic, but suddenly I felt I could use an alcoholic boost.

Rabz set a chilled glass of white wine in front of me. She leaned across the bar toward Martin. I could see her tanned cleavage. She lowered her voice and said to Martin, "Those are the greenies I was telling you about. In the back booth by the jukebox. They've been coming in almost every day for the past two weeks, drinking themselves into a froth over your Agnes project. I'd steer clear of them right now if I were you guys."

I turned to see four guys in the back booth. One of them—a wiry, dark-haired man with deep-set eyes, met my gaze. My pulse jolted with the intensity that radiated across the room. The slogan painted in bloodred on the side of the shed shimmered into my mind.

DEATH TO THE CRESSWELL-SMITHS!
KILL MARTIN.

Quickly I turned back to face the bar. I took a deep gulp of my wine as Martin's vitriol echoed in my brain.

"If I get my hands on them, I . . . I'll cut those fuckers to shreds, cut 'em with a knife. Stick my gaff in them. Make them bleed and feed 'em to the muddies."

I sipped again, relieved at how quickly the wine was softening my edges. My mind began to drift. I listened to the music, the voices growing louder in the pub.

I heard Martin order pies and chips with peas.

Time slowed, turned elastic. I took another deep swallow of my drink. A fly buzzed near my glass and I swatted it clumsily away. I felt Martin watching me. I felt the men in the booth watching me. I noticed Rabz glancing at me every now and then.

I finished my wine and motioned to a young server to bring me another. I started on my second glass as a tall and slender blonde approached the bar. She wore a camisole and denim shorts. Her white-blonde hair was cut in a short wind-ruffled style. Sexy hair, I thought, taking another sip. She had a lovely neckline. Lovely shoulders. Lovely big blue eyes. Elegance and athleticism.

"Hello, Marty," she said. "This must be Ellie?"

Marty.

He cleared his throat. "Willow, hi. Yeah, this is Ellie. Willow is a"—he turned to the woman—"what do you call it again?"

Willow laughed. "Wellness coach." She proffered her hand. "Willow Larsen." Her Australian accent was flat and thick, but not unattractive.

"And there I thought you were a fortune-teller," Rabz said as she set a glass of wine in front of Willow. "Or a diet coach. Or some kind of medium."

Willow laughed again and took the wine. She had a nice laugh. "A major building block of wellness is nutrition, so yeah, you could say I dabble in diet along with the occult." She glanced at me. "I read tarot cards. Tea leaves. Auras, too." She brought her glass to her mouth, sipped. "Coffee grinds at a push."

Dana's words crawled through my mind.

"Your aura is weird after you've been with him. Dark. Wrong. Something is badly off . . ."

I considered asking Willow what she felt about our auras right now, but I knew it was the wine tempting me. I refrained.

"I have an online business," Willow explained to me. "But I also offer consults at my home. My background is psychotherapy—I'm a trained therapist at the root of it all." She glanced at Rabz. "So yeah, Rabz, no worries. Most people have trouble describing what I do. I just refer to myself as a holistic healer." She took another sip of her wine while standing at the bar. "Nice to finally meet you, Ellie," she said. "We wondered if Martin had made you up." She threw him a grin but he didn't return a smile. She hesitated, holding his gaze. "Well . . . my friend Gregg is waiting." She gestured toward a booth where a good-looking man with sun-bleached brown hair sat. "Join us later if you like?"

"Thanks," I said. "We might take you up on that."

"And if you ever want a reading, El, I'm the second house up on the Jarra headlands. The one with all the glass. Stop by. Even if it's just for a cup of tea. Or glass of wine. Or if you just want the lowdown on this place, because believe me, there's plenty of it." Her gaze ticked to Martin.

"Thanks. I will." And I meant it.

"She seems nice," I said to Martin as she left us.

But Martin was focused on Rabz, who was setting two plates in front of us, each with a steaming meat pie, hot chips, and tiny peas. She poured Martin another beer and I realized I'd finished my wine. How many had I had? Two? Three? Rabz nodded to my glass and I said yes.

Martin tucked into his food, clearly ravenous. I picked at mine. He seemed to be avoiding eye contact with me.

"Martin?"

His gaze met mine. I felt undercurrents. Was he judging me for my drinking? Or was it the greenies upsetting him?

"You haven't said a word to me since she brought the food—" I reached for my fresh glass but my motor skills were off and I bumped it with the back of my hand. It toppled over. Shock crashed through me as wine splashed over the counter. I lurched up and lunged for the glass to stop it from rolling off and onto the floor, knocking over my barstool in the process. It toppled back onto the floor with a violent smash.

People stopped talking, turned.

"Jesus, Ellie!" Martin grabbed a napkin and tried to sop up the spill. Rabz hurried over with a dishcloth, calling for the young server to help.

"I . . . I'm so sorry, I—" I was shaken. Sounds around me turned into a droning noise. Everything seemed unsteady.

Martin's eyes turned thunderous. He righted the stool angrily while I braced against the bar for balance. The whole pub was swaying.

"Please don't worry," Rabz said quickly, lightly, trying to defuse things. "Happens all the time." She motioned to the server to bring me another drink.

"Yeah," snapped Martin. "I'm sure it happens all the time—people get drunk *all the time*. And she doesn't need another."

"I'd like another," I replied, determined to save face, to prove it was an accident. "I was just clumsy." But even I could hear the slurring in my words. I should go to the bathroom. I should splash water on my face. I let go of the bar, but my knees gave out under me. I grabbed for the counter again, knocking my plate off. It smashed onto the floor, breaking into shards and sending tiny green peas rolling everywhere.

Martin swore. I felt his hands on me, holding me up. His grip too tight. I heard noise, music, talking, laughing—all the sounds running into each other. I felt far away.

"Better take . . . home . . . ," Martin was saying something to someone. ". . . too much to drink again."

"I . . . only . . . had one hand half . . ." My words came out in a mumble.

Martin supported me with the help of Rabz. I heard Rabz say, "Have you got your ute here?"

Martin said, "We walked."

"Take my car. It's outside. You can bring it back later."

We stumbled outside. It was dark. Fairy lights swinging. Hot wind. Distant booming surf. I heard bats fighting in the tree overhead. A car lock beep. He helped me in.

"Were you drinking before we got here, Ellie? Or is it the pills?"

I shook my head. The world whirled. He buckled me in. The engine started. I rested my head back and closed my eyes. The whole world was tilting, spinning, round and round, faster, faster. I was going to throw up.

"I said, did you take more pills?"

"Wh . . . what?"

"Ativan—more benzos?"

But I couldn't make out words anymore. I felt the car turn. I was sinking into the dark . . . beautiful, dark, silky soft oblivion.

THE MURDER TRIAL

Pretrial forensic evaluation session.

We're back on the subject of my mother's death. It's my second appointment with the forensic psychologist in his Sydney office. I walked out on the last one when I felt he was trying to trick me. After sleeping on it I decided to return and follow through with the next appointment.

I need this trial to go the right way. My way. And after all, mental trickery goes both ways, right?

"You were nine, Ellie," he says. "You were in the house alone with your mother. At what point did you realize she was in trouble that day?"

"I'm not sure."

"Let's try and go back, shall we? What do you remember doing right before you realized your mom was in trouble?"

"I . . . I think I was drawing in my room."

"You've always liked drawing?"

I nodded.

"Do you recall what you were drawing?"

An image flares through my mind. Vines strangling a little girl who was walking through a forest searching for her dad, who was a big strong woodcutter with magical powers.

"No."

He studies me. I hold his gaze.

"Did you mother call out to you?"

"I . . . No. I just heard a thump and something break. I went to see what happened. I found her lying on the floor in her bedroom."

"Where exactly on the floor?"

"Between the bed and the wall. Near the nightstand."

"What did you do?"

"I tried to wake her. I shook her. There was foam coming out of her mouth. Nothing would wake her."

"Was it the first time you'd found her like this, Ellie?"

I feel heat in my head. "No. I'd found her like that twice before already."

"What did you do those times?"

"I phoned my dad."

"And this time—did you call him?"

"I . . . I can't remember. I just remember him arriving. Later. After the ambulances and a fire truck. Lots of people with big boots in the house and lots of equipment."

Slowly he says, "So did you call the emergency responders—dial triple zero?"

"It's 911 in Canada."

"Did you call 911, then?"

I swallow. My face goes hotter. I can't remember. I really can't. "I think so. Yes. How else would they have gotten there?"

He writes something in his notebook and nods. He opens a folder and reads some kind of report. I wonder if the lawyers somehow got hold of the old coroner's report. It would all be in there, what happened and when with my mother. The only reason he's asking me must be to see how I react.

He looks up. "How did your father treat you afterward—when you learned she'd died?"

I rub my knee. I feel nine again. I feel so small, and sad, and scared. I feel tears coalesce in my eyes. I feel all these things, but the memory of the events is not clear. Just the feelings.

"Did he make you feel safe, Ellie? Did he make you feel loved?"

"No," I say quietly, and I think of the little girl in my drawing, looking for her woodcutter father in the forest. Her father, who was big and strong, should have come with his ax to cut away the evil vines trying to strangle her and drag her down into the loamy earth where she would rot alone.

"He sent me away. To my mother's sister's house at first, because he was busy working and traveling a lot. And then I went to a boarding school."

"Did he love your mother?"

"He was always worried about her, fussing over her, taking her to doctors, or arguing with her about drinking or the pills."

"How did that make you feel?"

I hold his gaze. "How do you think?"

"Maybe you thought she stole all the light."

My stomach tightens. "Maybe," I say with a shrug.

"Did it change after she was gone?"

"No. Like I said, he basically dumped me—left me entirely. Just paid for my care and sort of forgot I was there."

"How did that make you feel?"

"Christ," I say as I get to my feet. I walk to the window. I look out. The playground is empty today. It's raining. Just a man walking a very tiny dog. "How do you think it made me feel? I hated him. I loved him."

"Do you still hate him?"

I waver. "Yes. And no. Conflicting feels."

"He's a domineering man, has a very commanding presence, no?"

I nod.

"Was your first husband like him at all?"

"Oh, I see where you're going, Doc." I turn to face him. "You think even though I hate my father I'm attracted to men like him? Out of some childhood need. Or genetic echo. Like my mother was attracted to my dad—you think this weakness runs through my DNA? That. And a susceptibility to addiction."

He says nothing.

"Maybe it does. I don't know."

"What about Martin?"

"What about him? He's dead now, isn't he? Doesn't matter what I feel about him now."

"Except it does. If they put you on that stand."

I smile slowly. "Well, there's your answer to the legal team right there, Doc. Yes. I wanted him dead."

THEN

ELLIE

Over one year ago, October 27. Jarrawarra Bay, New South Wales.

"Ellie! Hold the damn boat steady!" Martin yelled at me through the open window of his truck as he pulled the empty boat trailer up the concrete ramp. I stood barefoot in knee-deep water struggling to hold tightly on to the bowline of the *Abracadabra* so the boat wouldn't float away or come broadside onto the sand. He'd left me to hold the boat while he took the trailer to find a parking spot.

"She's drifting, Ellie! You're letting the current swing her around— she'll run aground, damn you!"

I winced at his words but was too afraid to respond. Already my muscles ached and the polypropylene rope burned my palms. The tide was pushing in hard and the currents swirled powerfully around my calves. I couldn't hold the *Abracadabra* at the correct angle for much longer. She was swinging sideways.

"I didn't listen to the 'captain.'... We were going out from the river mouth, and big waves started to break over the sandbar... My brother was hit, broke his back..."

Anxiety sank deeper talons into my heart. I shot a terrified look at the sandbar at the river mouth. Waves were breaking on the bar, getting bigger. Spectators were starting to line the tops of the cliffs to watch. My thoughts looped around to Chloe. My heart began to hammer.

I felt her slippery little hand in mine, water swirling around my legs. Suddenly I was back in the Waimea Bay being tumbled and churned in monstrous surf. I felt her slipping from my grasp. Tears burned into my eyes. This was a mistake. My head hurt. I could barely remember anything about our visit to the Puggo last night, apart from arriving at the pub and meeting Rabz and Willow. After that everything was a blank, and while Martin had been as sweet as sugar this morning, I felt something very wrong had happened.

I looked out to sea again. The waves were getting even bigger. Rolling in more consistently. Wind whipping now. A glop of foam slapped against my face. I blinked, but it stuck near my eye. I had no free hand to swipe it away or to wipe my nose, which was starting to run. The tide pushed harder. Panic started. Amping higher with each beat of my heart. Any minute I would tip into a full-throated attack. I thought of the pills in the pocket of the cargo pants Martin had loaned me for fishing. I couldn't reach them without letting go of the rope.

"Need help?"

I whipped my head around to see Rabz in her jogging gear. She had her hands on her hips, bright-yellow shorts, was breathing hard, cheeks pink, her hair gloriously wild in the wind as it fought to free itself of her hair tie.

I nodded, desperate, close to tears. Rabz took off her runners, tossed them up onto the bank, waded into the water, and expertly pushed against the side of the boat, bringing it round. Her muscles rolled smoothly under sunbrowned skin. Silver bracelets jingled. By repositioning the craft we were able to use the new angle against the current to hold the boat in position. It eased the strain on the painter line and thus on my arms.

"Thank you. More than I can express."

"Hey, no worries." A curious look entered her dark eyes. I noticed the tiny freckles spattered over her nose. Her long, thick lashes. We stood close, side by side, her tanned arm contrasted against my less toned and very pale one. I could smell her scent. That soft hit of patchouli and lime or bergamot.

"How are you feeling this morning?" she asked.

I gave her a blank look.

"You made quite the dramatic exit from the Puggo last night," she prompted. "Martin drove you home in my car. Don't you remember?"

Heat flared into my face. She regarded me steadily. Something darted through her eyes, and a slight smile curved her mouth as she took in my gear—my royal-blue windbreaker, Martin's oversize cargo pants, my pale-blue Nike ball cap. My ponytail blew over my shoulder, and strands of my hair had stuck to the lip balm on my lips. Rabz thought I was a loser—I could tell that was what she was thinking. Inside her head she was laughing, mocking me. In this environment she had the upper hand. She was in her element, and I was a fish out of water.

"So where are you guys headed, then?" she asked.

"Fish aggregating device."

"The FAD?" Her brows crooked up. "Zog said they were hauling heaps of tuna off the FAD early this morning, but it's getting a bit choppy now." She glanced up at the sky. "Weather is turning. The sea at the FAD can go from safe to suicidal in minutes. You guys should have gone out earlier."

Anxiety tightened in my chest. I glanced up at the people gathering atop the cliff, watching the bar. Kiteboarders whipped across Little Jarra Bay.

Finally I saw Martin coming toward us. Relief rushed through me, but flipped right back into tension as I noticed the angry roll of his shoulders as he strode toward our boat. A man called out to him. Martin stopped to address the man, who had a boy with him.

"Zog and his son," said Rabz, following my gaze. Zog's kid looked about twelve. Zog was wiry and nut brown with sun-streaked hair. We had yet to eat the fish he'd given us.

"Oh, look—" Rabz raised her hand and waved to someone up on the headlands. "There's Willow." She pointed. "See that big flat-roofed house with all the glass windows?"

I squinted. I could make out a woman standing in front of the big windows with a telescope. Blonde. Slender. She waved back. I wondered how long Willow had been watching us through her scope, whether she'd seen the distress on my face.

"She can see everything with that piece of equipment," Rabz said. "The telescope comes with the 'architecturally designed' house. What does that mean, anyway—'architecturally designed'?"

"She doesn't own it?"

"God, no." Rabz adjusted her position. "Here, let me hold that awhile." She reached for the painter line.

I let her take the yellow-and-blue rope and checked my palms. They looked raw and they hurt.

"She rents. Most of those houses up there are holiday homes. Owners live in Sydney, or in China, or some other country. Lease them out for a bomb. It's pricing us locals right out of the housing market. But Willow earns good money from her chicanery." Rabz chuckled. Her nose stud winked.

Was that a note of rivalry?

"Thank you, Rabz," Martin said in a great big bellow of a voice as he marched up to us. "Ellie was running us aground there." He laughed. It sounded harsh.

My mouth tightened. "If you'd at least shown me how to—"

"Get in, Ellie, while Rabz is holding her steady. Climb up over the side."

I hesitated, then moved into deeper water as Rabz turned her head. The wind caught her scent. And I froze. Slowly I looked around and stared at the back of her head. Suddenly I knew exactly what had been niggling at me before we'd arrived at the Puggo. And what had given me that sinister feeling upon meeting Rabz. Not a doubt in my mind.

My gaze shot to Martin.

They have a secret.

From me.

"What's the bloody holdup, El? Get in."

THEN

ELLIE

Every muscle in Martin's body was taut as he fought to hold the *Abracadabra* steady in the channel by powering the engine forward, then reversing, his gaze riveted on a distant set of swells rising like giant, swollen, silent ribs across the sea, gathering in size as they rolled toward us. I sat at the back of the boat and clutched the gunwale, unable to breathe. People lined the cliff. I saw the houses, including the glass one Willow had waved from. Could she see us? Could she read the desperation in my eyes? Would she send help? Martin's words from the night I'd met him, when he'd spoken about his brother, surged back into my mind.

"You need to time everything just right—it's when most boating accidents happen—going in or out when the bar is breaking. I didn't listen to an order . . . the boat hit a wave as it was breaking, and we went nose-up into the air and the boat flipped over backward. My brother was hit, broke his back."

Martin suddenly gunned the engine, and we surged forward, bow lifting, stern settling into the sea. The motor roared as we headed up the face of the first wave. It began to curl at the top. We smashed through the foam lip and smacked down onto the powerful shoulder as the wave crunched behind us in a foamy roar. Martin immediately gunned for the next one coming at us. The bow lifted again and we went up the face. The *Abracadabra*'s nose crashed through the curl. Water washed over the bow and down the sides, and I heard the engine cough, stutter. But suddenly we were through. The engine choked a few more times, then growled smoothly again. My heart drummed in my ears. The thundering of the waves was suddenly behind us. The rigidity of shock released me from its grip. I started to shake like a leaf.

I shot a glance back at the waves we'd come through. While we'd been powering through them, they'd appeared so monstrous. Deadly. Like Waimea. Like when they'd pummeled me down into the deep and snatched my baby right out of my hands.

Martin looked over his shoulder.

"El, you doing okay?"

"You did this to me on purpose, you idiot!" I screamed at him. "You *knew* this would happen."

"What?"

"Are you *trying* to terrify me?" I yelled over the engine. "You're mad, you know that! Totally mad. This is how your brother almost died!" Adrenaline fueled my anger, and it rode up into white-hot rage as I suddenly thought about Rabz, and what I'd realized back at the boat launch. "Do you have some fixation with your brother, with your father? Are you trying to repeat the accident? Just like you're trying to develop Agnes to prove something to them?" Fury burned tears into my eyes. My knuckles were white as I clutched the sides of the boat. "What in the hell are you trying to do to me, Martin? You *know* I am afraid of powerful water. Is *this* who I married? Are you trying to kill me?"

He blinked in shock. He freed one hand from the controls and reached for me. "Ellie—"

"*Don't!* Do not touch me." I cringed backward in the boat.

"Just—" The radio crackled and he swore. We were nearing the orange cliffs. He glanced up at the massive rocks. Waves smashed and surged at the foot of the sheer walls. "I need to log in with marine rescue before we go into the lee of the cliffs. They block radio signal to marine rescue."

He reached for the radio mouthpiece, keyed it.

"Calling Jarra Bay Marine Rescue, calling Jarra Bay Marine Rescue. Jarra Bay Marine Rescue. This is vessel AIS387 November, AIS387 November, this is AIS387 November. Do you copy?" He waited. Cliffs loomed closer. Waves heaved and sucked at the base. Skeins of foam ribbed the surface of the swells. We seemed to be getting pulled closer. He repeated his call, then said, "Come in, please, over."

The radio crackled to life as a distant voice arrived in our boat.

"This is Jarra Bay Marine Rescue. Copy, AIS387 November. Can you go to channel sixteen?"

Martin switched channels. I watched his movements like a hawk. If something happened to Martin out here, I wanted to know how to call for help.

He keyed the radio. "This is AIS387 November. We're heading out from Bonny Bay to fish the FAD. But if I hear that the fish are going off at the shelf, I'll call in again before we head over that way. Over."

I swallowed and looked out over the Tasman Sea. Clouds were gathering along the horizon to the east.

"Copy, AIS387 November. Estimated time of return?"

"About four p.m."

"Righteo, sixteen hundred. How many on board?"

"Two adults on board."

The boat lolled and was sucked on a massive backwash swell from the cliff. Water slapped at the hull. Martin steered our prow to face the direction of the swells so they wouldn't hit us broadside. We entered the shadow cast by the cliff. The voice on the radio started breaking up.

Martin signed off. He eyed me. My heart pounded. I waited for him to say he was not trying to kill me, or terrify me to death. He didn't. I didn't provoke him further, either, because it struck me how alone we were out here. Nothing but sea in all directions. I was at his mercy.

No one would know if I fell overboard or was pushed. I swallowed and looked away.

"Hold on," he said.

Before I could register, he suddenly increased engine power, angling our prow into the incessant swells. Wind increased as we continued to gather speed. I held my ball cap down on my head. He engaged full steam ahead, and the bow rose and bashed forward against the swells, again and again and again, like they were made of concrete. The regular beat of the impacts jolted through my bones, through my jaw. Through my brain. I clenched my teeth and tried to brace my body in ways that would lessen the force as we *thump, thump, thump, thump*ed for miles straight out into the ocean, each smack rattling my kidneys. Wind drew tears from my eyes.

I looked back. Jarrawarra Bay, the headlands, the orange cliffs, were all vanishing away into a pale blue haze over the landmass that was Australia. He saw me looking.

"See those hills north of Jarrawarra?" he yelled and pointed. "That's the mouth of the Agnes River up there. Boaters can go all the way up the inlet to the sales office from here."

Land vanished completely into the hazy mist. Then there was nothing but heaving swells ribbed with foam as the sea went from gray green to a deep cobalt.

A few terns wheeled up high, and an albatross began following our boat.

◆ ◆ ◆

The boat lurched. I opened my eyes a crack. My lids were swollen. My lips thick with salt. I was on the bottom, lying on my side. Bottles— wine cooler empties—rolled around me.

I heard a yell again.

"Ellie!"

I blinked and tried to get up. I fell as the boat rocked. I was drunk. I was going to throw up. The bow was rising and falling dramatically on the passing sea.

"Ellie! *Help* me, for God's sake!"

I turned my head, saw Martin. Shock slammed through me. He had his rod base rammed into the leather holder belted around his waist. The top of the rod was bent almost double as he fought a massive fish. The line screamed as the fish took line and dived in an effort to flee. I watched in a confused daze, trying to figure out what was going on. When the fish seemed to tire, Martin began to furiously wind it in again. His brow dripped with sweat. His face was red.

How long has he been at it? How long has he been yelling to wake me?

"It's foul-hooked. Grab the net, Ellie, for God's sake!"

I looked around the boat.

He swore viciously. "Bring me the fucking net! It's in the side compartment there, with the gaff. Bring the gaff, too."

I scrambled up onto my hands and knees and reached for the net. I gripped it with one hand, and with my other I pulled myself into a standing position. The boat pitched and lurched violently back and forth. Martin had let go of the controls. We were going in a circle, and the waves were beginning to hit us broadside. I clung to the targa bar for balance as I held the net out to him. But the boat tipped as a swell surged against the side. My support hand slipped. I dropped the net in order to grab for support with both hands. The net hit the top of the gunwale, then toppled overboard. It floated briefly on the heaving sea. Then sank.

The fish was now thrashing and fighting for its life at the side of the boat, bashing against the hull.

"Jesus. Gaff! Hurry, dammit!"

I got back down onto all fours and scrabbled to get the silver gaff. I handed it to him. He snatched the gaff from me and swung it down toward the fish. The boat tilted as another swell broadsided us and

Martin lost balance and missed solid aim. The hook of the gaff dragged a trough through the back of the fish. Blood poured red into the water, trailing pink in the skeins of foam. The fish wriggled to free itself of the treble hook, which I could now see was stuck into the outside of its gill. Another swell hit and the *Abracadabra* yawed and pitched me straight into Martin. He stumbled backward, jerking the rod up as he struggled to regain balance. The treble hook that had been foul-hooked into the side of the fish's gill ripped free. The fish dived. The hook jerked back into the air. And rebounded at Martin. He screamed as it came at his face.

Horror rose in my throat. I started to faint.

THEN

ELLIE

Two hooks from the treble hook lure had sunk into Martin's throat. The fake purple squid designed to hide the hooks and attract fish dangled below the hooks in his neck. The rod and reel had gone overboard. They were being sucked down into the ocean, and the force was pulling on the line and on the hooks in Martin's throat, tearing skin. He wrapped the fishing line around his hand in an effort to stop the line from ripping the hooks through his skin, but the rod was going deeper and the line was cutting into his hand.

"The knife," he whispered hoarsely, terror in his eyes. "The knife. It's on my hip—cut the line quick—quick."

I stared at the blood welling around the line cutting into his hand. And a strange, dark, and evil seed cracked open somewhere down deep inside my subconscious. It began to unfurl and ooze up into my conscious mind . . . *Martin is at my mercy.*

"Ellie," he pleaded. "Help me."

I shook myself and reached for the knife hilt at his hip. I drew the knife from the sheath. The boat lurched, and I tipped toward Martin, blade in hand. I couldn't stop myself or the knife. The sharp end of the blade sliced across his arm, slitting through his sleeve and cutting skin.

He yelled. The boat rocked back, and I stumbled backward and fell into the captain's seat, the fishing knife still in hand. I stared at him, trying to balance my brain, feeling very drunk. I grabbed the targa bar, pulled myself up. I planted my feet wide, keeping my knees bent and supple so I could move and sway with the boat. We were going around in another circle, and the swells were broadsiding us again. One big wave could send us both overboard. There would be no one to rescue us. I *needed* Martin back at the wheel. I *had* to free him if I wanted to get home safely. I had to be careful, though, be both slow and steady yet work fast because the line was slicing deeper into his hand, and his arm was now dripping blood where I'd cut him. His complexion was white, his eyes glassy with fear.

I fought to bring the focus back into my vision, and I brought the blade up to the taut line at his neck, worried I was going to pitch forward and sink it right into his throat, and that dark seed, that inky secret part of me, could almost visualize doing it, wanted to do it. To punish him for terrorizing me.

I sliced through the fishing line. The rod suddenly whipped free as it was snatched into the sea and sucked into the deep, swirling, foamy blue. A wave hit the hull and the knife was knocked out of my hands. As it flipped backward, the blade cut across the backs of my fingers. The knife hit the floor. My heart thudded as I saw my own blood welling. It wasn't bad. *Focus.*

Martin staggered to the controls and sank onto the chair, the lure dangling down from his neck. He reset the course of the *Abracadabra* so we now had the swell at our back.

"What . . . what does my throat look like?" he croaked. "Is . . . is it bad?"

I fought a wave of nausea and took a closer look at the damage. Bile surged into my throat. I couldn't see properly because his neck was bleeding now. "Wait." I wiped my bloody hand on my pants and reached for my backpack. I took out my sweatshirt and pressed it gently to Martin's throat, mopping up some of the blood so I could see better.

"Two of the three hooks have gone right in, barbs and all. And they've ripped some skin where they were pulled."

"My arm? What about my arm?"

I pushed up his sleeve. The cut was clean and it wasn't deep. I pressed on it and tightly wrapped a bandanna from my backpack around the wound.

"Reel in the lines," he ordered as he steered us back toward land.

With shaking limbs and blurring vision, I struggled to wind in all the lines. I hooked the lures safely into the rod eyes near the reels so they wouldn't swing around and snare anyone else. My hands were slippery with blood. It was my blood, his blood. It stained my jacket and pants. I adjusted my cap and got blood on that, too. I set all the rods back into the rod holders while Martin kept the *Abracadabra* on course. I collected the fishing knife and the gaff from the bottom of the boat and stashed them carefully in the compartment that ran along the side so we wouldn't stand on either the blade or the sharp gaff tip and incur more injuries.

Martin ordered me to sit down, and he increased speed. We began to bang and thump toward home. I saw him wince each time we hit a big swell.

"Aren't you going to radio in your injury?" I yelled over the engine and the wind.

"And have a whole bloody entourage of ambulances waiting? No fucking way." Vitriol laced his words. I hated the way he was cursing. I honestly had not heard him do this before—not in Canada. Not on our trips, either.

"But that would be good, right?"

"This shit with hooks happens all the time—just need someone to push the barbs through the flesh, cut off the barbs, and pull out the shanks. I can drive to the hospital. They can do it there."

"I can drive you."

"No, you bloody can't! You're fucking three sheets to the wind. Jesus, Ellie."

"Martin, please don't swear."

He mimicked me in a child's voice: "Martin, please don't swear." He shot me a chilling look. "How about you stop popping pills and getting completely blotto every time you face a tiny bloody challenge, huh, Ellie? How about that? This is your fault, you know that?"

"It's not my fault."

"If you'd been sober, if you hadn't been sneaking pills and downing wine coolers while I was fishing, you could have gotten that net under the fish instead of losing it overboard. We would have been going home with a fish instead of a fucking hook in my neck."

I fell silent, my heart thumping in my ears. Horrified by his language, his vitriol, by how ugly he looked with that rage twisting his face. My gaze fell to the wine cooler bottles that had rolled to the back of the boat. I shifted my gaze to the sky. A vague memory stirred. I'd asked him if he'd brought water. He'd told me to look in the cooler. All I'd found were the cold alcoholic drinks. I'd refrained from opening a bottle. But after more than three hours of trolling back and forth around the FAD buoy with no water, under the relentless sun, with salt drying my lips, I'd buckled and reached for an ice-cold cooler because it was part fruit juice and I was desperate. That was the last thing I recalled before waking up on the bottom of the boat. Humiliation and anger burned into my eyes as a vehemence rose inside me. *Hatred*—that's what I felt. It was pure white and black and dark and hot. Hatred for this man. My husband. I truly abhorred him right now. I felt I could kill him, wished I had.

When we neared the Point of No Return, I could see the surf had risen even higher. Throngs of spectators lined the headlands in the late-afternoon sun. I could hear the roar of the breaking waves. Getting into the river mouth was going to be worse than getting out.

THEN

ELLIE

People came running down to the boat launch as we limped in on the *Abracadabra*. Martin threw the bowline out to Zog as he waded into the water to meet us. Zog began to pull us into the shallows. His son grabbed the gunwale and helped guide us in until we bumped up onto the sand.

The young brunette from the standup paddleboard rental place came running over the lawn toward us, two men following behind her.

"Willow saw you in her scope," Zog said as he and his son held the *Abracadabra* steady while I tried to climb out. "She said you guys looked like you were in trouble—are you good, mate?"

Martin was holding my sweatshirt over his neck. Blood covered his arm.

"God, you're bleeding, Martin," Rabz said as she hurriedly waded into the water, worry tight in her face. "Ellie, you're all covered in blood. What in the hell happened out there?"

A woman covered her mouth as Martin removed the balled-up shirt from his throat and showed them all the monstrosity of a purple squid lure that dangled from the hooks in his neck. Someone swore.

"Do you need an ambulance?" yelled someone with a cell phone from the grassy bank.

"No ambulance. Please," Martin said as I clambered over the side of the boat and fell with a splash onto my butt in the water. I scrambled up onto my feet and waded to shore. I started up the road, wet shoes squelching.

"Ellie?" said Willow, coming up behind me. "Are you okay?"

"It's her bloody fault!" yelled Martin after me. "She did this! Bloody drunk!"

I began to run. Willow ran after me as I crossed the lawn in front of the SUP rental place, aiming for the shortcut river trail to our home. Blood boomed in my head. My whole body shook with a cocktail of rage and shame and horror. I stumbled, still feeling spacey, and I still couldn't figure out how or why or what exactly had transpired out at the FAD.

"What happened?" Willow asked as she caught up behind me.

I put my head down and walked faster, tripping every now and then on raised bits of grass.

"Ellie—" She reached for my arm and turned me to face her. "What happened out there?"

"We shouldn't have gone out. *He* did this. On purpose. He *wanted* to scare me. Damn him . . . he . . . he knows I'm afraid. Damn him!"

Willow's gaze lowered over my shaking, wet body. I was smeared with blood. I had to look as drunk as I felt. I probably appeared to her like a loose cannon, a wild madwoman dangerous to my own husband and to myself. Someone you shouldn't take out on a boat alone because she would cause trouble. They could all see it—that was the message they were getting. That was the message Martin was screaming about down at the launch—Ellie the lunatic. Ellie the psycho. Ellie with an addiction problem. They would all have seen the empty cooler bottles rolling around in the bottom of the boat. And one thing I was learning fast about Martin was that he had pride. Arrogant, alpha-male, chest-thumping pride. And God help anyone who undermined that and made him look foolish. He was the kind of man who blamed his tools or his employees—or his wife—when he got a hook in his neck because *he* had foul-hooked a fish and screwed up. As nice as he'd seemed back in the Cook Islands lagoon, he actually got off on making me scared.

I took in a deep and shuddering breath and said, "I . . . I'm sorry. I need to be alone right now."

She eyed me in silence for a moment. Then quietly she said, "Why don't you come and see me tomorrow, okay? Or whenever. Because you look like you could use someone to off-load on." She glanced over her shoulder at the small crowd gathering around the *Abracadabra* at the boat launch, and I sensed her assessing the situation, computing. She turned to face me. "I'm trained, Ellie. I can help." She paused. "At the least, I can help you get help."

I stared into her clear eyes and wanted to cry. I wanted to fold myself into her and let her hug me. And just hold me. Like I'd wanted someone to hold me when my mom had died. I missed Dana. I missed my old friends and my old life. I even missed my goddamn father, which was pathetic. Because he'd failed to hug me all those times I'd needed him most after my mom overdosed. I swiped moisture from my eyes with a trembling, bloodied hand and nodded, not trusting myself to speak.

"But you're okay right now?" Willow asked. "Physically—you're not injured anywhere?"

I shook my head. My hand wasn't badly cut. It wasn't even worth a mention.

She moistened her lips. "How about emotionally?"

Tears suddenly streamed down my face. I didn't trust myself to speak.

"Let me walk you home."

I took a step backward, shook my head, and held up both my hands, palms out, and I turned and staggered toward home.

She called out behind me, "Come and see me, Ellie! Or call. Anytime. I mean it—day or night, okay?"

I nodded and kept going.

When I blundered down our driveway, I saw the curtains in the window next door twitch. A shadow moved. That woman in the window again.

Watching.

THEN

ELLIE

I entered through the open garage door, palmed off my Nike ball cap, and threw it into the corner, onto the concrete floor. I kicked off my bloodied sneakers, shucked out of my bloodied and wet windbreaker, and tossed them into a crumpled heap on top of the cap. Breathing hard, I wriggled out of the bloodstained pants and threw the pants onto the pile. Heart thudding in my chest, I marched out of the garage's side door wearing just my panties and damp T-shirt. The woman watched from the window as I crossed the lawn. I flipped her a finger. She ducked back into the shadows.

Inside the house I marched straight for the wine fridge. I uncorked a top-of-the-line sauvignon blanc and filled a big glass. I gulped down half the contents of the glass, refilled it, then carried the glass and bottle into the living room. I plopped my butt down onto the sofa, drank deeply, topped up my glass again, and reached for the remote. I clicked on a mindless Netflix series and thought of Dana and began to cry. I finished my drink and poured yet another, desperate to get numb, to blunt the images of blood flashing through my brain, to quell the rage in my heart that was tipping me toward violent and heinous thoughts of stabbing Martin to death. I was frightened of myself, of my own mind.

My own thoughts. I wanted to hide from *me—this terrible me who was emerging like a demon inside my own body.*

I considered taking another pill, then recalled I'd left some pills in the pockets of the pants in the garage. I decided against going outside to retrieve them. I refused to allow that freak woman in the window to see me stumble drunkenly over the lawn. Instead, I fetched another Ativan from upstairs, came back down, finished the bottle of wine, opened another, and settled back into the sofa, still in my panties and damp T-shirt. Finally a calm descended on me, and I began to feel as though I could manage myself.

That's when Martin came in the front door. I didn't even tense. It was like he was in a time and place removed from my present.

He walked slowly into the kitchen, eyes fixed on me as he set his keys on the granite counter. He stared at the drink in my hand; then his gaze went to the empty bottle on the counter. His mouth tightened. He had a fresh bandage on his neck. I saw another bandage around his arm where the knife had cut him. He looked pale. Strange.

I waved my glass at him. "So they got the hooks out." My words came out slurred. My head was spinning, but in a nice, delightful way. "Here'sh to the good docs at the hoshpital." I raised my glass in cheers and took a swig. "How'd they do it?"

"They pushed the hooks, including the barbs, right through my flesh," he said coolly. "Following the natural curve of the hook until the point and the barb poked out the other side. Then they cut the points and barbs off with bolt cutters, then drew the shanks back out the way they went in. Luckily the hooks missed vital parts."

"Yeah. Lucky. And the arm? Stichesh?"

"Several." He came slowly toward me. As he neared, a shiver of warning prickled over my skin, but I held my ground. He seated himself on the ottoman close to me, within arm's reach of my wine bottle. The lights in the neighbor's house went on—I saw the flare of light through the narrow floor-to-ceiling window between the living room and the kitchen. It had gotten dark outside. I hadn't noticed the time passing. That woman could probably see right into our living room at night.

"We should get blinds. That woman ish always watching." Again my words ran into each other, but I didn't care. I took another sip.

"What woman?"

"That biddy next door. Watch, watch, watch, then she ducks behind lace curtains."

He frowned.

"You've seen her, right?"

"No."

This irritated me. "Of course you have to have seen the watcher next door."

"Ellie—"

"Wait—" I wobbled my finger at his face. "Just you wait before you go Ellie-ing me." I set my glass clumsily on the coffee table and leaned forward. "What in the hell were you trying to prove taking me out like that? In that bad weather—the swell so high, the wind so strong? Going so far out? For so long—with *no* water to drink? Were you trying to scare me? Or kill us both, or what? Even Rabz said we shoulda gone out earlier."

He regarded me in simmering silence.

Be careful, Ellie. He looks dangerous.

"Is it a power thing, Martin? Is that what this is? Ish this something I'm just learning about you? And you know what I think? I think you set me up to drink wine coolers by not bringing water. Did you set me up? Did you intend to return me to the boat ramp drunk so everyone could see—a whole cliff full of onlookers, a whole heap of witnesses at the boat launch? Did you tell all the doctors at the hospital your wife had done this to you because she was drunk?"

His face turned puce. His features looked weird. I didn't recognize him.

Stop, Ellie. Stop now.

"When we went for a walk yesterday, Martin, you told me that people would line the cliff when the waves on the bar started breaking. You knew there would be tons of witnesses there."

"No one forces you to get drunk, Ellie. No one is forcing you to take pills. You're an addict. You're ill. Do you understand this? You have a problem and you need help. You know what I did? I asked the doctor at the hospital for a referral for you, to a medical professional who handles addiction issues." He set a card onto the coffee table next to the wine bottle. Dr. Kenneth Marshall.

I felt a change happening in me—the Shame Monster rearing its head, unfurling its big dark body inside my chest, awakening through my haze. Everyone in town was learning fast that Martin Cresswell-Smith's wife was a drunk, an addict. First my apparent scene at the Puggo. Then at the boat launch. Now the doctors at the hospital. *Poor Martin.*

"So why did you take me out in that weather, then? Even Rabz said—"

"Because I wanted to distract you from the meds, for heaven's sakes. I wanted for us to do something together, to get you out of the house, away from the bloody pills."

"Liar."

He blinked. Shock showed on his face. It spurred me.

"You *wanted* to terrify me. And this morning when you brought me breakfast in bed, why did you not mention my behavior at the Puggo? You acted like nothing was wrong, like nothing bad had happened. You're messing with my head—you *want* me to think I'm mad." I reached for my glass, took another fortifying swig, and waved the glass at him. "You know what thish ish, Martin? It's called *gaslighting.*"

The word hung.

Air quivered, hot. The fan up high in the vaulted ceiling whopped slow paddles of air.

"Go to bed," he said softly, darkly. "You're out of it and you're being paranoid, psychotic. We'll deal with this in the morning—"

"No. No, we deal with this right now." I jabbed my fingers on the coffee table. "Why are you doing this to me? I wanted a fresh start here, a clean happy new life—"

"Except it's not clean, is it, Ellie? You arrived all drugged up right out of the airport gate, and now you want to blame *me*? No one is doing anything *to* you. You're doing this all by yourself."

"Is it because of Rabz?"

His face paled. He went very still.

"I want to know, Martin, right now—tell me now. How long have you been screwing Rabz?"

Silence.

The fan paddled. The air simmered.

It's the truth. I nailed it. Bull's-eye. I could see it in his eyes, in his face, in the reaction of his whole body. It was like I'd touched a live wire to his skin and electricity was crackling through him, invisible, but there, building.

A tiny thread of fear unfurled in my gut.

"You're drunk."

"Do you want to know *how* I know?" I asked, more quietly. My instincts told me I should back down, go upstairs, stop. But why should I stop? This was my marriage, my life. I'd come all the way over here to this strange land for this man, and I had a right, a duty, to see this through. I needed answers.

"There was a hair tie—a scrunchie—left on the daybed in *my* studio. It was the exact same scrunchie Bodie Rabinovitch was wearing today. Same skeins of gold through green fabric. You slept with her in the space that was to be my office? I could smell her in there, Martin. Her smell was on the scrunchie . . . that weird patchouli, herby, jasmine scent she wears. And one of her hairs was still stuck in it—a long, dark, wavy hair. That's her hair—I'd bet my life DNA would prove it was

Rabz's hair. And I could tell, I could *feel* something between the two of you in the Puggo. A woman knows these things, Martin—she knows."

"If there was a scrunchie left in your studio, if it belongs to Rabz, it would be because she and a group of friends from the Puggo came around to help me move your boxes in there when they arrived. And why would they do that? Because they are nice. They all are. The whole bunch. I was in the Puggo one night a couple of weeks after I arrived in town—I'd been eating there regularly—and I mentioned I'd bought a house and your boxes were arriving." He watched me closely as he spoke. His body was unnervingly still, his eyes pale, cold. "I was telling them about you, Ellie, my lovely wife from Canada. They were keen to hear about you, and they offered to come round and help when the truck arrived with *your* boxes." He paused.

I swallowed at something I could see in his eyes. Something I didn't like.

"And look at what they see now." He held his hand out to me. "See what my 'lovely' wife looks like, see who she *really* is—a neurotic addict. Can't you see? Abusing substances like this is making you suspicious of everything."

"Liar."

Everything in his face compressed. His eyes narrowed.

"Stop," he said. "Now."

I didn't recognize his voice.

"You brought her into my studio, Martin," I said very quietly. "Into *my* house—"

"Our house," he said.

"*I* bought this house. It was with my funds—"

He lurched to his feet and grabbed a handful of my hair at the top of my head and yanked up so fast I felt roots tear from my scalp. I screamed and surged to my feet to stop the resistance. He fisted my hair, tightening his grip. It felt as though my scalp was ripping right off. My eyes burned. Terror punched my heart. I didn't move, didn't dare make a sound. I was breathing hard.

He let go, and as I crumpled down toward the floor, he kicked me in the bum. The force of his foot lurched me forward in a drunken, ape-like flailing as I used my hands to try and stop my head from slamming straight into the kitchen counter. I hit the counter with my shoulder and fell onto my side on the floor. My temple smacked against the tiles. He took two fast strides toward me, and before I could catch my breath, before I could scrabble away along the bottom of the counter, he reached down and grabbed a fistful of my bangs and lifted me up again. I screamed in pain, in shock. He let go and raised a hand. As I went down, his backhand smashed across my mouth. My head spun. My body whirled. I slammed back down onto the floor on all fours, blood pouring from my lip. Snot ran out of my nose. I was shaking, terrified that if I made another sound he would kill me.

He clamped his big arm around my neck, holding me still on all fours, and he ripped off my panties. He got down behind me and I heard him undoing his pants. Tears ran down my face. I scrunched my eyes shut, every molecule in my body screaming to try and flee again, but I didn't dare make a noise or move.

Clutching my neck so I could barely breathe, he thrust into me from behind. Pain sliced through me as he rammed repeatedly into me with animal grunts.

He came inside me with a violent thrust, his balls pressing hard against my buttocks.

It seemed to release everything in him. He withdrew and dropped me to the floor. Wet between my legs, I curled into a fetal ball, shaking. And I knew now that my nightmare after the first night I'd spent in this house had not been a nightmare at all. It had been real. The sex had been aggressive and it had not been consensual and for whatever reason the memory of it had not encoded into my brain properly.

He pushed at me with the toe of his shoe.

"Get up," he said, stepping over me as he zipped up his pants. "You look disgusting. Clean up and go to bed. You're a drunken mess."

I couldn't move.

"Go!" He raised his foot to kick. I cringed more tightly into a ball, snot and blood dribbling over my chin as I mewled. He stopped.

I waited. Time stretched. I could hear wind in the gum trees outside. I wanted to go home.

He crouched down and gently moved damp, sticky hair away from my tear- and bloodstained face. He traced his finger softly over my cheek. I was too afraid even to flinch away.

"You should go upstairs, sweetheart."

I lay there stunned.

"Come on, I'll help you up." He put his hands under my arms and drew me to my feet. I could barely stand, my legs were shaking so hard. "Go upstairs."

I hesitated, then reached for my phone on the marble counter. But he placed his hand firmly over mine.

"No," he said quietly. "Leave it."

I didn't dare cross him. Not now.

I went upstairs without my phone. I entered the dark room and went across to the window. I looked out into the street. I could see that Corolla again. Parked in shadow across the street. Someone was inside. Watching.

I put my hand on the windowpane.

Help me.

The headlights came on. I heard the engine. The car pulled out of the parking space and drove down the street. Brake lights flared at the corner. It turned and was gone. Bats shrieked and fluttered in the dark.

THE MURDER TRIAL

Now, February. Supreme Court, New South Wales.

I watch from the dock as Lorrington winds up to cut Lozza down. I don't feel bad for her. It's them or me.

"So, Senior Constable Bianchi, to be clear," Lorrington says in his resonant baritone, "neither Constable Abbott nor Constable McGonigle accompanied you to the abandoned homestead—you went to the house alone?"

Lozza speaks clearly into the microphone. "That's correct, sir."

"Two hours and twenty-three minutes—that's how long you were all alone with the evidence before a trained team could get in."

"Objection!" Konikova says, lurching to her feet again. "This serves no purpose other than—"

"Withdrawn." Lorrington makes as though he's about to sit; then suddenly he rises again to his full height and clasps the sides of his lectern. "Did you touch anything inside the house?"

"Just one item. I used gloves. I replaced it as I'd found it."

"What item was that?"

"A baseball cap. A pale-blue Nike ball cap."

Lorrington straightens his spine, squares his shoulders, and tilts up his chin. "Why that one object and no other?"

Lozza wavers. *Mistake.* The jury notices her indecision. "I . . . At first I wasn't sure what the object was. I wanted to see—to be certain."

"To be certain that it was a baseball cap? Did you know anyone who owned a cap just like it?"

"Yes. Ellie Cresswell-Smith was seen by several witnesses wearing a blue cap and windbreaker when she and her husband left the Bonny River boat launch in the *Abracadabra.* It was the last time anyone saw him alive."

Lorrington nods slowly. He appears to be consulting his binder and puzzling over something. I like my lawyer more and more. A consummate thespian.

"Had you personally met Martin Cresswell-Smith prior to his disappearance?" he asks more quietly. The jurors almost lean forward.

"Ah, we met briefly. On the beach. It . . . it's a small town."

"Did you *like* Mr. Cresswell-Smith, Senior Constable Bianchi?"

Konikova surges to her feet. "Objection. Your Honor, I fail to see the relevance of this line of questioning."

"Your Honor." Lorrington swings to face the judge. "We plan to demonstrate the relevance."

"Then please don't delay in getting to the point, Mr. Lorrington. Some of us are thinking of lunch."

"Yes, Your Honor. I'll repeat the question. Senior Constable Bianchi, did you *like* Mr. Cresswell-Smith?"

"I'd barely met him."

He holds her gaze for several beats. "Did you, Senior Constable Bianchi, at any time, either on or off duty, stalk Martin Cresswell-Smith?"

"No."

"You didn't park outside and watch the Cresswell-Smith house?"

Lozza goes pale.

A rustle whispers through the gallery. The court artist's chalk flies over her paper. Reporters scribble furiously.

Quietly, she says, "I once watched the house for a few moments from a police vehicle."

"Why?"

My pulse quickens.

"I . . . had reason to fear for his wife's safety."

"You felt Mrs. Cresswell-Smith was in danger?"

"From her husband, yes."

"Why?"

"I'd seen bruises on Ellie."

"And you assumed they were from him? Did that make you angry?"

Lozza's mouth thins. Color creeps into her cheeks. "As I said, I feared for his wife's safety."

Lorrington moistens his lips and nods. "Violence against women or children—this makes you very angry, does it not, Senior Constable?"

"It should make anyone angry."

"How angry?"

"Objection!" says Konikova, coming to her feet. "Again, I fail to see the relevance to the case at hand."

"Mr. Lorrington, do we have a point?" The judge glances at her wristwatch.

"Your Honor, I put it to this court that Senior Constable Bianchi—a lead investigator on this case—was a biased investigator with a personal vendetta that blinded her to other avenues of inquiry from the moment she saw those bruises." He swings to face Lozza in the box.

"Senior Constable Bianchi, you have a scar on your forehead."

Movement rustles in the gallery. The sketch artist flips a page. Lozza's face goes deep red. Her eyes narrow.

"How did you get that scar?"

"Objection!" shouts Konikova, her eyes flashing with anger now.

"Your Honor," counters Lorrington, "that scar goes to this detective's history of aggression and tunnel vision on the job. It goes to the fact she once beat and kicked a suspect in her custody to the point she had to be hauled off by fellow officers—such was her rage. The man had to be admitted to hospital. He had to have surgery. And why?" Lorrington raises his finger high in the air. "Because the suspect in the senior constable's custody had a history of violence. And he'd just beaten to death his wife while their small child hid under the bed and saw the whole thing. And when Senior Constable Bianchi learned about the child, she just snapped." He clicks his fingers with a snapping sound. "Like that. Blinded with rage, she became violent herself. Is that not so, Senior Constable Bianchi?"

Lozza is sweating. She's vibrating. She looks like she's going to explode out of that box and hit him. What Lorrington has just wrought in front of our eyes is a beautiful thing because each and every juror can see right now that Lozza Bianchi is about to snap again. In front of them all. Just like that. And they're waiting for it—they *want* her to. This is surely not a woman they'd want investigating them. She would surely not give them a fair shake if she can so quickly be blinded like this.

"Constable Bianchi?" Lorrington says more quietly. "This incident is on record, is it not?"

"Yes, sir," she says through clenched teeth.

Murmurs rise in the gallery. I glance over. The officers look pumped, angry. Battle lines are forming. I can smell the tension—the adrenaline, testosterone. It's thick and hot in the room.

"Did you adopt that little girl from under the bed, Senior Constable Bianchi?"

Konikova explodes to her feet. But as she opens her mouth, Lozza says, "That is completely off base, sir. My daughter has no place in this trial. Shame on you."

A reporter hurries out the courtroom door.

Slowly, quietly, Lorrington says, "It has every place. You lost your job as a detective with Crime Command after that incident. It was swept under the rug because it was bad publicity for the New South Wales force. It's why you took a quiet job down the coast. But then you saw the bruises on Mr. Cresswell-Smith's wife. And you were quick to judge him. Perhaps too quick?" He faces the jury.

"I put it to this court that Senior Constable Lozza Bianchi in fact developed an instant and vehement *dislike* for Martin Cresswell-Smith. I propose she even had something of a vendetta against him right from day one. Because of her own history. Ms. Bianchi in her past capacity as a homicide detective has demonstrated a predilection to irrational anger and extreme violence, and I put it to this court that she had an agenda. A bias. And she should have been removed from the case. It was not a fair or clean investigation." His gaze swings back to Lozza.

"And it wasn't your only error on this case, was it, Senior Constable Bianchi? You also delivered a package of contraband drugs to the Cresswell-Smith home, did you not?"

Melody Watts, the reporter from the Sydney nightly news, now surges to her feet. She makes for the door, bows her head to the coat of arms behind the judge, and quickly exits the courtroom. I can picture her going out to talk into the camera on the stairs.

I imagine Lozza's little adopted daughter hearing the news about her angry-cop-mother at school.

THEN

ELLIE

Over one year ago, November 1. Jarrawarra Bay, New South Wales.

Willow sat opposite me in her living room with her endless view over the sea. Except the view was covered in clouds. Rivulets of rain squiggled down the windows, and I could hear the thud and boom of the waves on the rocks below. Occasionally a glob of foam would shoot up into the sky and waft down to settle like frothy snow on the spiky shrubs outside.

I'd come for two things. Martin had taken my cell phone, and I wanted to hire a PI to follow him, so I needed to use someone's phone or computer to find one. And I wanted off-the-books help quitting the drugs. Willow had said she was a trained therapist. I did not, however, want to tell her about the abuse. It was still too overwhelming. Private.

"What happened out on the boat, Ellie?" she asked.

"I . . . I'm not exactly sure."

"You don't remember?"

Shame was a vise around my throat. I wrung my hands. "I . . . I've got blank spaces in my memory."

She watched my hands as I spoke. I tried to hold them still.

It had been raining for two days, and I'd been holed up in my bed most of the time—my memory playing devious tricks with my recall of the events that had led to Martin striking me. He'd left for work early on both days and taken my phone so I couldn't call anyone. He said it was until I was in a better position not to embarrass myself. I had no vehicle, so I couldn't drive away. I felt humiliated. Demeaned. I kept replaying in a loop the horrified faces of all those onlookers at the boat launch. They'd all watched me clamber over the side of the boat and fall into the water, then stagger drunkenly off over the lawn while Martin yelled after me. Everyone had seen the blood, the empties in the boat—bottles I didn't remember putting there.

The first day after Martin assaulted me, I took painkillers and more meds. Lots more pills. Yesterday I'd flushed nearly all my pills down the toilet. The only way for me to figure my way out of this situation would be with a clear head. I also wanted proof Martin was having an affair with Rabz. Physical proof I could use. Photographs taken by a PI.

Her eyes, intense, bored into mine. The trained therapist in her was seeing through me to something deeper.

"Why?" she asked. "Why the blank spaces?"

"I need to figure that out," I said. "Yes, I take lorazepam. Yes, I like my wine. But this feels . . . like something more unusual, and the only way I can get to the bottom of it is to start with a drug-free, booze-free, clear head. Because then if I continue experiencing these spells, I'll know it's something else."

"Like what?"

I cleared my throat. I knew what she was doing—asking all the questions so I'd come out with it myself. I was a therapy veteran.

"Like . . . he, my husband, might be drugging me."

She blinked. "Are you *serious*?"

I cringed. I was fearful of articulating this because it seemed absurd. It underscored the fact that I could be clinically paranoid, that I really could be losing my mind. I rubbed the back of my hand. She continued to watch carefully my every little body movement. I stopped.

"El? Talk to me."

I glanced down at my hands and bit the bullet. "Maybe . . . The thing is, I . . . I'm beginning to think I've been duped. Conned. I'm beginning to think Martin married me for my money because I'm a Hartley." I looked up slowly. "I think he's gaslighting me. Maybe even drugging me."

"Do you really believe this?"

I inhaled deeply. "I've been lying in bed for two days going over it all. Rehashing the weird little things I might have overlooked during our intense courtship."

Like the doppelgänger incident.

Like how he wasn't registered at the Hartley Hotel when I went to return the cuff links.

Like the way he'd disappear until I grew desperate to see him, then suddenly reappear and say he needed me to make a decision at once and then he'd sweep me away on some trip.

Like the orange Subaru outside my apartment.

The way he isolated me, brought me here, far away from everything I knew . . . the way he terrorized me with the fishing trip even though he knew all about my past and my mental vulnerabilities.

"It's like he was one Martin before he got the funding for the Agnes Marina project, and a completely different Martin after. He no longer needs to be nice. I think he . . . tricked me into this, but the weird thing is *I* was the one who proposed to him. *I* was the one who suggested we go into a business partnership with my father's money. He even protested and argued against it, but I insisted. I *wanted* to help him finance everything. I wanted to move out here away from my family and friends. I wanted to help with the Agnes development. I *gave* him everything, Willow. Voluntarily. It was all my idea. I asked for it all. It's my fault."

She studied me in silence. Waves boomed. Rain ticked against the windows.

"You're really sure about this?"

I nodded. "I'm so . . . ashamed that I might have let this happen."

She edged forward on her seat and clasped her hands together. "Ellie, some people can be deviously clever that way. Con artistry says more about ourselves and how we see the world than it says about the con artist. The genius of a trickster lies in figuring out precisely what it is we want or need most to hear, and then that's how they present themselves to us—as a vehicle for delivering our deepest desire. They show up in the guise they're needed when they're most needed."

I considered how Martin had just shown up in my life on that chill January night. In my path on the way to the bathroom. How he seemed to say all the right things about life and children and art and parents that made me believe he was the answer to everything that I'd been looking for right at that moment. I'd lived in the public eye, thanks to my father. Stuff had been written about me, especially after Chloe drowned, especially after I went off the rails. It was all still probably accessible in online archives. I'd even been arguing loudly with my father in the Mallard Lounge that night, everyone listening. With a simple Google search anyone could have learned some very personal things about me. I felt sick.

"We *want* to believe what a con artist tells us, Ellie," she said softly. "They manipulate our reality. And if this is truly what you think it is, a long con, the kind that takes weeks, months, or even years to unfold, it requires manipulation of reality at a far higher level, and it plays with our most basic core beliefs about ourselves."

I fiddled with a thread on my capri pants. "You seem to know an awful lot about this."

"I had a patient once. A smart—very smart—woman, a widow who'd been sucked in by someone on an online dating site. It's sadly not uncommon. People use sites like that to troll for victims. They can learn a lot about them; then they use that information to lure their prey and suck them dry."

I glanced up. Her words made me think of that funnel-web spider with its trip lines and silk lair.

"I could be wrong, still."

"Yes. I hope you are, Ellie."

"My friend Dana warned me. My dad warned me. Yet I was convinced they were all just bitter because I'd finally found something good, something I believed I deserved. A decent man. A second chance."

"Is he physically abusive—is he a bully? Does he have a mean streak?"

I looked out the window. I couldn't voice it.

Quietly she rephrased her question: "*Did* he hurt you, Ellie?"

I touched the silk scarf around my neck that hid my terrible bruises, and I realized too late that my involuntary movement had given me away.

"Maybe I deserved it," I said very quietly. "I abused him verbally, too. I cut him with a knife. And . . . and I *wanted* to cut him, Willow. I wanted to hurt him, kill him, even."

She absorbed this for a moment. "Ellie," she said quietly, "no one *ever* deserves to be struck. Abuse is *not* your fault, no matter your internal thoughts. Violence is not acceptable."

I sat silent.

"How badly did he hurt you?"

"It won't happen again."

"Why?"

Because I won't fuck up again. I won't get drunk again. I won't take pills again. "I won't let it."

"You need to go to the police."

"I . . . I will. If he does it again, I will."

The intensity in her eyes turned hot, and I sensed the shift in her energy. She looked like a tightly coiled spring ready to explode. It made me uneasy. I hated confrontation. She was going to insist on bringing in the law, and I wanted to be careful and make sure I was ready and in a place where he couldn't get to me if and when I did.

"I will," I said again. "But not here, not now. I want to go to the police back home. I want to file for divorce from home. Where he can't hurt me. And I need to be off the meds. I need your help, Willow. Will you help me get off the lorazepam? I need to taper. I flushed most of the meds down the toilet, but I kept just enough for a week or two. I want you to keep the pills for me and give me only enough for each day, should I need them."

She stared at me. I could see her brain racing.

"And *this* is why you think he won't hurt you again—because you'll be clean?"

"He'll see that I'm trying. I'll tell him. I'll show him."

"Ellie, if you think he's drugging you—how's that going to help?"

I leaned forward. "Because if I'm not drinking, and not taking meds, and then if I do have another episode, I'll go straight to a doctor and have my blood tested." I paused. "I will have evidence of what is in my system. It could be the proof I need that Martin is drugging me."

"So you think your abuse of substances is making it easier for him to mess with you."

"He could be using it to veil whatever he's doing to me."

"Once a guy hits you, it's—"

"No." I raised my hand. "I need a clear head in order to properly assess my situation. I want to be one hundred percent certain I'm not imagining all this stuff out of some drug-induced paranoia. And if I go to the police here, Martin will use my public episodes to explain away my 'mad' accusations. I can see it—he'll say any bruises on me are because I fell when I was drunk. Everyone at the boat launch saw a drunk, Willow. They saw the blood. They saw the rage in my face. He told the doctors at the hospital his drugged wife cut him. People saw me at the Puggo—even you saw me there. The cops will believe his story over my story. They will side with him."

She eyed me, nodded slowly. "Do you want to tell me how the pills started?"

I told her. Everything. From how I'd lost Chloe to what grief had done to me and how I'd struggled to cope with that, right up to how I'd come to be institutionalized. She listened patiently while the rain fell.

"See?" I said. "I have a history—drug abuse, mental illness, violence, memory loss. He can use all that against me if I lodge a complaint or file a charge. Doug sure did when he filed for divorce. Martin could even have me locked up again, maybe even get power of attorney because we're in business together and he'd need my signature on things. He'd have full access to all my funds."

A look of doubt creased her brow. "You don't think that's a stretch?"

"Honestly, I don't know anything for certain right now."

She watched me, her face tightening into something that looked like anger. I felt it, too, coming off her in waves. I feared that now I'd armed Willow with information against a man who'd assaulted me, she'd take actions on her own initiative—actions I wouldn't be able to stop. Things would avalanche out of my control. She swore softly, got up abruptly, and put a kettle on. "Have you spoken to anyone, Ellie— called a friend? Family? Told anyone else?"

"This morning I called my friend Dana."

She glanced up. "In Canada?"

I nodded. "Right after I flushed the pills. My call went to voice mail. She won't return it."

"Why not?" She poured hot water over tea leaves in china cups. Her bracelets chinked. I envied her grace, her beauty.

"We fell out. It was over Martin."

"So Dana really didn't like him?" She carried the teacups over.

"Hadn't actually met him, but—" I glanced at the crystal ball on the buffet, the tarot cards on the coffee table, the Himalayan rock salt lamp on the bookshelf, the tiny wind chimes in the kitchen, and said, "Dana claimed Martin had a bad influence on my aura. She said it was dark after I'd been with him."

Her brow ticked up. She half smiled, raised her cup from the saucer, and sipped.

"Did you ever feel Martin had a bad aura?" I asked.

"I've never tried to read Martin. Don't really know him other than from the Puggo and from hearing the local enviro group go on about him and his project—your project." She paused. "You know, El, from what you've told me, I think that you were barely recovering from grief and PTSD when you met Martin—not that one ever fully 'recovers' from these things, but rather finds a new kind of normal. And now you've had a setback. You should talk to someone. A professional."

"I'm talking to you. You said you were a therapist."

"I'm not practicing. I don't have a current license. I stopped years ago in favor of life coaching and these so-called woo-woo pursuits." She tilted her chin toward the tarot cards.

"Why?"

"Why the tarot and tea leaves and coaching instead of therapy? It's more fun. As a coach I get to make healthy clients even better. I work with the conscious mind. I work with goals and specific timelines within which to achieve those goals. As a psychotherapist I worked with pathology, illness—I worked with the unconscious. I worked with open-ended outcomes, seeking to understand the why as a primary aim. The list goes on. For me coaching has also been more . . . lucrative." She smiled. "And a lot more flexible with my online business component. I can travel. Do it long distance from anywhere in the world." She tipped her cup toward me, and her smile deepened into a grin. "Some of my fiercest competition comes from Roma fortune-tellers in Bulgaria."

I laughed. We finished the tea, and as Willow cleared the cups, I said, "So will you help me?"

She hesitated. "What was the trigger, Ellie? What caused Martin to suddenly snap and hurt you—was it just the issue with the hooks on the boat, and getting drunk?"

I studied her for a moment, then said quietly, "That was the other thing I wanted to ask you about. I need a PI."

Surprise flickered across her face.

"I believe Martin is having an affair. I accused him, and that's when he struck me."

Her mouth opened. She blinked. "What?"

I cleared my throat. "He's sleeping with someone behind my back, in my own house. I need to look up a private investigator. I want someone to follow either him or his mistress. I need photographic evidence of them together. If he can arm himself with my mental history, I need to arm myself as well. With anything I can find."

She'd gone dead still.

"Willow?"

"With . . . Who do you suspect he's sleeping with?"

I hesitated. "You . . . promise you're not going to go and say anything to anyone? Not yet."

"I promise."

"Rabz. I think it's Rabz."

THEN

ELLIE

When I left Willow's house, it had stopped raining and I had a plan.

I'd given her the bulk of my drugs, and I'd committed to quitting drinking. Willow would be like my sponsor. She'd keep my secret. For now. Because I knew that if this went sideways, she was the kind of woman who'd go straight to the cops and demand action.

She'd also said she'd find me a PI and I could pay the investigator in cash via her. It would help keep it a secret from Martin.

Our conversation replayed in my mind as I walked down her driveway toward the gate.

"Are you sure you want to help me like this, Willow?"

She got up and went to stand in front of the big view windows. She stood there a long while, in silence, her arms folded tightly across her stomach, as if gathering herself. She finally turned to face me.

"I knew someone like Martin once," she said. "Some guy who was violent with my mum. He moved in after my dad went to prison and he beat her, sometimes senseless." She rubbed her mouth. *"He supplied her with drugs, too. Some bad stuff. I was seven when she died from an overdose—so I know what you're talking about, Ellie, when you say that was what happened to your mom."*

I tensed.

She inhaled deeply. "I was about to go into the system when my father got out and 'liberated' me. We lived on the streets, hustling. He taught me things. Other street people taught me, too. Mostly how to survive. Then he died homeless. I fought out of that bad childhood, El. I went into counseling, and I guess the crusader in me wanted to become a therapist myself, and to never let this happen to anyone else. Or to be there to help them if it did."

I suddenly felt my own problems pale in comparison. I felt foolish. I felt my privilege. I stared at her. We never really did know people, did we, when we saw them passing by on a street?

She gave a rueful smile. "I like to think I do it all for him, and for my mom. Mostly it's for me."

My eyes burned. "I am so sorry. I—"

She raised her hand, stopping me. And gave a smile. "Just let me help, okay? I need you to get away from Martin, so it's for me, too. You can pay me back one day by paying it forward."

I reached her garden gate beneath an arch overhung with jasmine. The smell of the flowers damp from the warm rain was fecund. Heady and full with promise. Suddenly I had hope. I had a friend.

I opened the gate. It creaked. I stopped and turned to look back at her house. Willow stood framed by an upstairs window. She had a phone to her ear. She smiled and waved.

I waved back.

Then I stepped onto the sidewalk and saw the brown car at the end of the road.

I paused and watched as the car pulled out and drove away. Yes, I thought. I wanted answers. I was going to get a PI and find out what was happening.

No more passive Ellie.

THEN

ELLIE

Over one year ago, November 14. Jarrawarra Bay, New South Wales.

It was midday. Two weeks since my visit with Willow. Unseasonably hot. From my bedroom window I could see heat shimmering off the road—even the birds seemed to have fallen silent. My T-shirt stuck to my back as I opened Martin's closet. I had the fan going in the bedroom, all the windows open wide. Tense, I moved carefully, quickly, trying to put everything back exactly as I'd found it. Otherwise he'd notice.

I was off the meds, off the drink. I was doing everything a "good wife" should do. Making dinners. Getting exercise, sleep. Looking my best.

I'd organized my studio, hung up my photographs and art, and was focusing on my work. When I'd struggled with withdrawal symptoms, I'd called Willow. We'd gone for long beach walks on those occasions. Or out for coffee at the Muffin Shop. Never the Puggo. Both Martin and I were avoiding the Puggo, even though Martin insisted there was nothing between him and Rabz. I'd told him I believed him, lulled him into a false sense of security. Meanwhile, Willow had found me a PI. I was having Martin followed.

For his part my husband had done a complete 180 and couldn't be nicer. It was as though all the bad things had never happened. Almost.

I pulled open his underwear drawer and felt around at the back.

Martin had unlocked his office and invited me to look at the company spreadsheets. He was right—the presales were going gangbusters. The environmental report was solidly in our favor. The shire council had given the first phase a third reading. The rest of the red tape was sorting itself out. Yet he'd relocked his office after showing me out.

And it remained locked while he went up to work at Agnes every day.

He still didn't trust me. Not fully.

Then five days ago he'd suddenly announced he had to go to Sydney for two weeks. Some emergency with the banks and meetings with an ad agency. He'd left two hours later, rushing to catch the small plane from Moruya. I'd spent the last two days searching for an office key without fear he might walk in.

There *had* to be a spare key somewhere. Or perhaps he'd taken the only one with him?

I opened another drawer and fingered around the back.

Yesterday I'd hunted everywhere downstairs. Today I'd continued the search upstairs. I opened his sock drawer next. One by one I checked inside his neat balls of socks. Then I felt around the back of the drawer. My fingers touched metal. My heart quickened. I stretched in deeper and closed my hand around something. I'd found it.

His keys.

I fished them out. Three keys on the ring. I stared at them, sweat prickling over my brow. It wasn't wrong for me to go into his office. It was wrong that he locked his space off from me—an equal shareholder in *our* company.

I hurried downstairs.

Outside the office door I stopped and calmed myself. No pills. Just deep breaths. He was not due back for another week. I had plenty of time to do this. Nevertheless I still glanced quickly around the room, a residual memory lingering—the echo of a sense of being watched. I could see nothing out of the ordinary.

I unlocked the door, pushed it open. Entered.

It was stifling inside. All the windows were closed. I clicked on the fan. It thrummed to noisy life. I put the setting on high. Wind ruffled edges of papers on his desk. His office was as neat as his closets. I fingered the keys in my hand, thinking.

When he'd shown me in here I'd noticed he kept keys for the filing cabinet in a locked drawer beneath the desk. I slotted the smallest key into the lock of the desk drawer. It clicked over smoothly. Guilt pinged through me, followed by a bite of determination. I opened the drawer.

THE WATCHER

The app for the CCTV cameras alerted the Watcher with a ping—the motion sensor had detected the subject had breached a critical area in the house.

The Watcher reached for the phone, clicked open the app, and watched the live footage being streamed from the Cresswell-Smith house.

Ellie Cresswell-Smith entering her husband's office.

She must have found a key.

The Watcher zoomed and watched closely as Ellie opened a drawer under the office desk. She was visible through the open office door. Wind from a fan blew her long dark hair. She glanced over her shoulder, looking back into the living room, her eyes large and dark. She was afraid she'd be discovered—she knew she shouldn't be in there. But she didn't know about the camera in the wall clock that could see her through the open office door. Nor did she know about the camera in the clock in her studio, or in the digital weather clock beside her bed.

Ellie returned her attention to the drawer and located a small box. She set the box atop the desk and opened it. From the box she removed some keys. She went over to the file cabinet and unlocked the drawers containing files. She riffled through one folder after another, then took a folder out.

The Watcher zoomed yet closer. The label on the file was just visible: AGNES HOLDINGS.

Ellie set the Agnes Holdings file on the desk and opened it. She tensed and quickly bent her head closer as she appeared to scan columns of figures with her finger. She looked up. Sweat gleamed on her face. She returned her attention to the spreadsheets, and stiffened. Her finger paused. Quickly she turned the page and scanned the next sheet. She moved faster and faster, flipping through the pages. She ran both her hands over her hair as if catching her breath, as if trying to comprehend what she'd just seen. She went back to the cabinet and removed another manila file folder. She opened it. A document fell to the floor. She picked it up.

Her whole body went still. Dead stone still. Blood drained from her face.

Hurriedly she began to scramble through the other files, being untidy now as she flipped through them. She found another document that halted her. Holding the document in her hand, she sank slowly onto a chair and covered her mouth with her hand.

THEN

ELLIE

I stared at the rental agreement I'd found for a luxury villa in the Cape Verde islands. In Martin's name. For two adults. The rental period for a year, with option for renewal. The date of occupation was next month. The wind from the fan chilled my sweat. Goose bumps pricked along my arms.

With the agreement was a folder from a travel agency in Sydney. According to an invoice, Martin had bought two one-way plane tickets to Cape Verde via Singapore, then Frankfurt. The flight from Sydney Airport departed in just over two weeks.

Two weeks?

I glanced at a calendar on the wall. Perhaps he was keeping it as a surprise for me—there was enough time to still tell me that the two of us were going somewhere. But even as my brain sought for an alternate answer, I knew there was only one. This ticket was not for me.

My breathing became shallow. I felt dizzy. Panic clutched my stomach. My mind spun toward thoughts of medication, but I'd given my pills to Willow. And on some deep-down survival level I knew I needed every ounce of clarity to deal with this. Understand it. Comprehend and process this.

Hurriedly I flipped through the other papers . . . I stalled.

He's mortgaged this house?

To the max. Blood drained from my head. I—*we*—had paid out-right for it. What had he done with the money he'd borrowed on it? We'd closed the sale at $4.56 million. I'd put the money up for it, but we'd purchased the property in our company name. Yet according to these papers, he'd taken out a mortgage on the house in his personal capacity? I read the document more closely—as closely as I could, given that my vision wasn't registering the details.

The new mortgage agreement included insurance. On *my* life.

A sick cold leaked into my gut. I glanced up and stared out the window. I didn't want to think what this could mean.

A crack sounded in the living room.

I froze. Listened.

But nothing more came.

It was probably another branch cracking off one of the gums out-side—I'd left the sliding glass door open due to the heat. When the weather got too dry, the gums shed branches as a means of survival. The trees were called widow-makers, I'd learned, because they so often killed people with the sudden dropping of massive limbs.

I glanced over my shoulder through the office door into the living room. I could see the clock. It was almost 3:00 p.m. I had no reason to fear Martin would suddenly walk in. He wasn't due back for at least another nine days.

Focus.

I returned my attention to the papers and opened a manila envelope with the word *CONFIDENTIAL* marked on it. Inside was a consultants' report. Commissioned by Agnes Holdings. It was not the report Martin had shown me. I scanned the summary, my heart beating faster and faster with each sentence. This report had determined that digging canals into the mangrove swamp would lead to acid sulphate in the soil, which would create acid problems in the groundwater, which in turn would mobilize arse-nic in the soil and result in massive habitat destruction. Fish—all sorts of marine life—would die on an epic scale. An example of similar destruction in another development was cited. Limestone walls in the channels would be required to neutralize the acid. The cost of the development would skyrocket. I flipped the pages. Words blurred. *Habitat destruction . . . population of fish eagles decimated . . . environmental impact . . . yellow-bellied gliders . . . frogs . . .*

I sat back, breathing hard. The development was dead if this report got out. But Martin had quashed it, hidden it. He'd commissioned a second, newer report—the one he'd shown me had downplayed any potential problems. If the shire council had seen this, or the prospective buyers had known, those presales would have dried up completely. We could be legally liable. This was fraud. I lurched to my feet, paced, then dragged my hands over my hair. What was Martin doing? Was he going to get on a plane and run? Leave me holding the bag? Had he ever intended actually going through with constructing this project? Or had it just been a way to fleece buyers out of deposits—the proverbial swampland-in-Florida scam?

No. That couldn't be.

I sat myself at his desk and powered up his desktop. His computer was password protected, but I'd watched carefully when he'd shown me what now appeared to be fake spreadsheets. The monitor flared to life and I typed in the password I remembered seeing him use. It failed. Because I was nervous. I'd missed uppercasing a letter. I tried again.

The system booted up.

My heart thudded as I accessed our online banking accounts—Martin had the sites bookmarked, and his computer remembered the access code. A security question came up.

"What town were you married in?"

I typed "Las Vegas."

It denied access.

I typed "Vegas."

It failed.

My hands hovered over the keyboard. I had one more attempt. If I failed again the site might lock me out. I frowned. Then opted to ask for another question instead.

"Where was your father born?"

I typed "Melbourne."

The banking accounts opened. Sweat pearled and dribbled down my stomach. The fan ruffled my hair. I could not believe what I was seeing. Our Agnes Holdings account contained a total balance of five thousand dollars and eighty-five cents. My temperature rose. I began to shake. The last time he'd shown me, it had registered over thirty million in short-term investments, and a good portion of that had come from presales deposits.

I clicked on Recent Transactions.

I stared, aghast. Since the day he'd shown me the bank balance, he'd been siphoning off funds in chunks at regular intervals. I clicked on the details of those transactions. The monies had been transferred to a numbered account offshore. I was unable to access that account.

I sat back. My head spun. I'd been lured into a web and sucked dry. More than thirty million gone. I'd been cleaned out. Willow's words flooded into my brain.

"We want to believe what a con artist tells us, Ellie. They manipulate our reality. And if this is truly what you think it is, a long con, the kind that takes weeks, months, or even years to unfold, it requires manipulation of reality at a far higher level, and it plays with our most basic core beliefs about ourselves."

The memory of Dana's warning sliced through me. I cast my mind back to the orange Subaru parked outside my apartment in Vancouver. The same model and color in the underground parking garage. The "doppelgänger." Who had kissed a woman with long, wavy auburn hair whose face I couldn't see.

I felt dizzy. I was going to throw up.

I cast my memory back further, to that winter's night ten months ago when I'd literally tripped into Martin's arms at my father's hotel. *Drunk. Vulnerable.*

I'd been so loud in arguing with my father. I'd felt people all around our table listening. Someone could easily—likely—have heard my father offering me capital for a project, any project I wanted. Could Martin himself have been seated behind us and overheard? Or had someone at the bar eavesdropped on me telling Dana how much money my father would give me? An image struck me—The Rock making a call on his phone, his dark eyes fixed on me. I felt sick. Someone in that bar could have arranged for me to fall into a trap later that evening. Could Martin have been waiting, like a spider, with a fine web of false narratives with which to trap my heart?

I swallowed as Martin's impassioned words crawled up from the depths of my soul.

"When we step into a magic show, we arrive actively wanting *to be fooled. Magic is . . . It's a kind of willing con. You're not being foolish to fall for it. If you* don't *fall for it, the magician is doing something wrong."*

He really had conned me. He'd baited, hooked, and played me over months—taking me to Europe on a wild whirlwind trip. Paying for everything. Then vanishing for weeks at a time and suddenly reappearing. He'd tricked me into giving him everything, including my hand in marriage.

And I'd been eager for it. I'd *wanted* what he'd offered. I felt sick. I glanced at the life insurance policy attached to the mortgage. And a darker thought struck like a hatchet. Could he kill me?

Something sounded in the living room.

I stilled. Listened. I heard it again—footfalls on tiles.

Martin.

I scrabbled to gather up the papers on the desk, cramming them back into folders and envelopes. Pieces wafted to the floor. I bundled the files into my arms and lunged for the filing cabinet. A shadow darkened the doorway.

I froze.

"Ellie?"

I spun around.

THEN

ELLIE

Willow.

She stood in the doorway, her gaze flicking over the mess, the papers and folders in my arms.

"What on earth are you doing?" she asked.

I couldn't speak for a moment. I'd thought she was Martin. I hurriedly finished replacing the papers and files and locked the cabinet. "You surprised me," I said. "I . . . I didn't hear you coming in."

"That fan is loud," she said. "The slider was open. I knocked first."

I held my arm out. "We can talk in the living room."

But she remained in the doorway to Martin's office, looking at me. My face felt beet hot. I was sweating, shaking.

"Is everything okay?"

No, it's not fucking okay. "Yeah. Fine. Please, I'd like to lock up here." I stepped closer to her, into her space, attempting to usher her out.

"I thought you told me he didn't allow you in here."

"He's been different since I've quit the medication. Our . . . our relationship has improved." My voice cracked.

"Ellie—"

"Look, I haven't forgotten that he struck me, okay? I . . . Can we please just talk outside of this office?"

I backed her into the living room and shut the door and locked it behind me. I slipped Martin's office keys into the pocket of my shorts. Her gaze followed my hand. I noticed only then that she carried a big bag and that a manila envelope stuck out of it.

"What are you doing here?" I asked. "You spooked me."

"I told you—I did knock. But no answer. The sliding door was open, so I figured you had to be in here somewhere."

"Yeah, well." I pushed my damp bangs off my brow. "I told you I wanted proof. I was looking for . . . stuff."

"What did you find?"

"It's nothing." My brain reeled. I was trying to process, trying to decide how much to tell her, how it might help or hinder me. "What have you got in there?" I nodded at the manila envelope sticking out of her bag.

Her mouth tightened. "It's from the private investigator. I thought you'd want to see it stat."

"What is it?"

Willow wavered. "Are you sure you're okay, Ellie—you want to see this now?"

"Yes," I snapped.

"Shall we sit down?"

I glanced around the white cage of this "architecturally designed" brand-new home on the banks of the Bonny River—the house that now belonged to the bank, unless I died; then it was all paid up and went to Martin. I pressed my hand against my stomach.

She touched my arm, eyes wide, gentle. "Ellie?"

"My studio," I said. "Let's . . . let's talk in my studio."

I still felt watched in here—I couldn't explain it. I'd read, however, that this sensation was real. And after I'd seen what was in Martin's files, my paranoia couldn't stretch far enough. I trusted nothing. And right now I felt like this room had eyes.

◆　◆　◆

"It's looking good in here, Ellie," Willow said as she entered my studio behind me. I slid open the glass door that led onto the little dock. I shuddered as I caught sight of the river mouth where it fanned into the sea—the channel where we'd navigated the waves breaking on the bar.

I was 100 percent certain now that Martin had been trying to terrify me. He was a sociopath. A glib liar. A trickster. A cruel and power-tripping sadist who got off on control. I was certain, too, that he'd raped me more than once while I'd been drugged. And yes, I was pretty certain now that he *had* been drugging me, and he'd stopped when I'd declared my abstinence and given all my pills away—I'd made it difficult for him to con me into thinking I was addling my own brain.

I motioned for Willow to sit on the daybed.

Before she sat she peered closely at some of the photos I'd framed and hung on the wall above the bed.

"Who's with you in this photo?" she asked.

"My friend Dana," I said flatly.

She glanced at me. "The one who doesn't like Martin?"

"Yeah, the friend I lost over him." Dana had been right about Martin. She'd sensed the changes he'd wrought in me right off the bat.

"Yet you still hang her photo here."

"She finally returned my calls," I said. "She accepted my apology. We're working on being friends again."

Dana and I had spoken for over an hour across the oceans while I'd stared wistfully at that photo of the two of us shot in the Mallard Lounge on the night I'd met Martin. While I had listened to her voice, a dissonance had started crackling along the edges of my subconscious again, something about that image of Dana and me at the bar that night—a just-hidden sense of something important, overlooked—but I couldn't place it.

"So what's in the envelope?"

Willow seated herself on the daybed. I sat across from her, a small coffee table between us. She opened the envelope and extracted several glossy photographs. She hesitated. "Are you sure, Ellie?"

"Just show me."

She placed the photos on the table and spread them out to face me. Glossy. Big. In my face. I couldn't seem to make my brain register what the photos depicted. Time stretched. Hung. A buzzing sounded in my ears. A spider ran along the edge of the table, and Willow smashed it.

I didn't flinch.

"Redback," she said. "I hate those things. The females kill their mates after mating."

Her words circled around and around my head as I stared with vile hatred at the images of Martin, my husband, my business partner. With Bodie "Rabz" Rabinovitch. There he was, getting out of a rental car in Sydney with Rabz. Martin's hand resting at the small of her back. A gesture I knew well. Rabz's face thrown up to the sky as she was laughing. Him grinning. Light dancing in his eyes. Sunlight gold on his hair. I drew one of the images closer. Martin and Rabz kissing. In what appeared to be an underground garage. Another photo captured them entering a hotel, his arm around her shoulders. Another had snared them eating ice-cream cones as they strolled near the Sydney Harbour Bridge, the iconic opera house in the background. I picked up a print that had been shot from outside a building, clearly with a massive telephoto lens. Through the hotel window Martin and Rabz could be seen in an intimate embrace. Rabz partially undressed.

I swallowed and set the photo down. "So . . . Rabz also went to Sydney."

"I'm sorry, Ellie."

I inhaled deeply.

"At least you know, El." Emotion glittered in Willow's pretty blue eyes. Her jaw was tight. "At least you have proof."

I moistened my lips, trying to realign everything in my head. The puzzle pieces, the odd little niggles—they were all slotting tightly into place, and the big picture emerging was terrifying. He'd been gaslighting me, no doubt. Was he trying to kill me—or trying to make me kill myself? Was that his endgame—some final plan before he left for the Cape Verde islands in two weeks?

"There's something else, Ellie."

"What?" My voice came out papery.

"The PI also learned that Rabz has sold the Puggo. The new owner is taking over next month."

I put my face into my hands and rubbed hard. "He used me, Willow. He's taken everything from our bank account. He's fleeing with the presales deposits. He's mortgaged our house. He's totally sucked me dry, and he's going to leave me holding the bag of this Agnes Holdings mess. I could go to prison. And she's going with him?" I surged to my feet, began to pace. "That's what the sale of the Puggo must mean. Rabz is going to the Cape Verde islands with my husband. There's no extradition treaty there, I bet. I—"

"*What* did you say?"

"I said there's no extradition—"

"You said Cape Verde islands?"

"I found two plane tickets in his office. Departure date is in just over two weeks. To the Cape Verde islands. I also found a rental agreement for a luxury villa."

"Are . . . are you sure?"

"Yes I'm fucking sure!" I paced faster, rage fueling me. Martin had beaten me down. He'd nearly stolen my identity—my very concept of self. But not quite. I was still here. I'd found this stuff in time. I now stood at a fork in my own road. Two choices faced me: Collapse and concede. Or get him. Get him back. Show him he should not have dared cross me.

I spun to face Willow. "I could kill him. I so badly want to kill him."

She sat there, deathly pale. "I cannot believe this," she said quietly. "Rabz? He's running off with *her*? She's like a fixture in Jarrawarra—I can't believe she'd do this."

"I should have taken that knife and plunged it in properly." I raised an imaginary knife into the air and brought it down repeatedly in a stabbing motion. *Stabbity, stabbity, stabbity.*

"Ellie—" She surged to her feet and took hold of my arm. "Stop it. Stop now."

"Fuck off, Willow. Don't touch me."

Shocked, she stepped back.

I came to my senses at the sight of her face. I was breathing hard. I unclenched my fist and pushed my hair off my face. "I mean it," I said more quietly. "I'm going to get him. I'm going to nail him so hard he'll be sorry I ever tripped into his arms."

"What are you going to do?"

"Fight back. And you know what else? If he did this to me . . . this level of a long con like this—my bet is he's done it before. He had to have built up to this kind of brazen act. There have *got* to be more victims out there. Victims in all sorts of ways. For starters, all those people who put down significant presale deposits for Agnes Marina land that's never going to be developed, for a project that is doomed by environmental standards. And now their money is gone? I'm going to war, Willow. I'm going to rally a goddamn army and bury that bastard." I pointed to the photos on the table. "And those—those are going into my portfolio of evidence."

"Are you going to the police?"

"First I'm going to pack my bags and clear out of this house before Martin returns from Sydney. He's dangerous. There is so much at stake here—he's taken more than thirty million from me—I fear he'll try to stop me, or worse. I need to be gone before he gets home. And I've got nine days. I'm going to search the rest of the house, and I'm going to copy the computer evidence and scan all the files and save it all to a flash drive. Then I'm flying back to Canada and going straight to my father's lawyers. I'm going to get the best damn legal advice from a safe place, and go from there. Because my bet is Martin's victims are scattered all over the world, and Canadian law enforcement can work globally with Australia and other jurisdictions."

"I don't know, Ellie. If he's run off with presales, that's a crime *here*, in New South Wales." She looked visibly shaken. "You should go to the local cops. And if he's dangerous—"

"What are they going to do? Honestly? Whisk me into some kind of witness protection before they've taken the time to investigate whether 'mad drunk Ellie's' accusations even have substance? No, this is bigger than the Jarrawarra community police. I need to get out of here, and I have a week within which to do it."

"What can I do?"

"I need you to leave, Willow. I need to be alone. I need to think."

"Ellie—"

"No, please. Go." I looked at the PI's photos on the table and my throat constricted. "I need to process this."

She glanced around the room, worry darkening her blue eyes, hesitation in her movements. Her gaze settled back on mine. "I can't quite absorb all this. Why don't we get out of here, go for a walk?"

"I need to be alone."

She angled her head.

"I'm not going to take pills, Willow. I promise. I'm going to gather the files, pack my suitcases, and buy an air ticket home, and then maybe I'll go for a long walk on my own. I'm thankful for the photos." I pointed at the glossy evidence. "I owe you. And the PI. But I need to process."

She left, and I glanced at the photo of me and Dana above where Willow had been sitting. And that sinister feeling wormed deeper and deeper into me.

THE MURDER TRIAL

The shrink asked me if Martin was like my father. I hate that he's right about this—I *am* attracted to men like my dad. Big and powerful and commanding, and I want them to love and treasure me and make me feel safe and special. Like a princess. Like some vestigial childhood fairy-tale thing I can't shake, someplace in my kid psyche where I got stuck. The place that wants storybook happy endings.

"So if you wished ill on Martin, do you also wish ill upon your father?"

A discordant jangle begins in my head—two parts of me being forced together in the mirror.

"My father is not violent toward me."

He assesses me. I haven't answered his question. I'm getting panicky again. He's closing in on the hidden and secret places in the basement of my soul again. I feel the rustling of discontent, the discordant alarm bells going off in my body. Agitation.

"I can see this question makes you uncomfortable, Ellie. We can move on if you like. You called your mother weak."

"She was. I despised her for that. For leaving me."

He watches me for a few moments. "If you despise those parts of your mother, and you believe on some level you are like your mother, does this mean you despise those traits in yourself?"

"So is this where I'm supposed to say yeah, but by taking drugs, self-medicating, I numb myself to this truth?"

"What about Doug? Did he give you the attention you needed?"

"What are you saying?"

Silence.

Panic flicks longer tongues through my belly. "Doug and I loved each other. But it fell apart after we lost Chloe. The grief was too big. Everything we had was built around being Chloe's parents."

"So he wasn't there for you when you needed him most?"

Anger surges—basal, rudimentary anger. Incompletely articulated. Dark. "He's a jerk, okay. He started having affairs."

He glances up sharply from his notes. "More than one?"

"I . . . Right after Chloe was born—he lost . . . interest in me."

"Sexually?"

I fiddled with my hands. My face started going hot. "I was carrying a lot of baby fat. I wasn't sleeping, not looking good. Breastfeeding was rough. Stressful. I was worried I wasn't doing it all right." Emotion coalesces in my eyes. "I wished my mother had been there to guide me. I had all the money in the world, but it couldn't buy the things I needed. I . . . I was lost. Scared."

He consults his notes again. "I see you were diagnosed with postpartum depression. You were clinically depressed well before Chloe drowned."

"Where did you get that from?"

"Transcript of the police interview in Hawaii," he says.

"You have no right."

"The opposing legal team will have the same access to these transcripts, Ellie."

THEN

LOZZA

Over one year ago, November 16. Jarrawarra Bay, New South Wales.

Lozza caught a last wave and rode it all the way into the shallows, where Maya, her eight-year-old daughter, was already waiting with her board. The sun was sinking toward the horizon, and the low-angled rays cast a beaten-copper glow over the sea. The early-summer breeze, warm and rounded against her skin, sent a fine spindrift off the backs of the waves. It was her first surf of the season without a wet suit, and it felt like heaven.

She slid off her board and allowed it to float for a moment, catching her breath as Maya came paddling over. Lozza's muscles ached, and her eyes burned from salt and wind and sun. But this was exactly the kind of mental scrub she'd needed after a long week working on a strike force that had resulted in a biker gang drug bust up the coast. Since moving to Jarrawarra, Lozza had discovered that surfing with her girl was a far better tonic than the booze she'd once habitually sunk into after a tough shift on the homicide squad back in Sydney. Her life there had spiraled into a self-destructive cycle after she'd lost her husband. It had ultimately cost Lozza her coveted position as a detective on an elite investigative squad with State Crime Command. But her boss, her team of brothers in blue, had protected her from losing her badge entirely. They'd kept "the incident" out of the press. And the quiet demotion to the policing backwaters of the South Coast had pretty much saved Lozza. It had allowed her to clean up and adopt Maya. It had brought Lozza closer to her own mother, who'd moved into the beach house Lozza rented to help out with Maya when Lozza worked long hours or was called out at weird times.

Jarrawarra had been the best decision in the entire world. She was finding her essence in this place with its wild ocean and empty beaches in the off-season, and the great fishing. She was sending down firm roots and discovering a way of life she hadn't even known she'd been looking for.

"Did you see my last ride, Mom? Did you see I got barreled?" Maya beamed. Her eyes glittered with fierce excitement.

"I sure did, kiddo." Lozza grinned at her daughter as she reached into the water to undo the Velcro strap that secured her board leash to her ankle. Looping the leash over her thruster, she tucked it under her arm, and she and Maya waded through the shallows and onto the hard-packed sand. Small birds scattered as they made their way up the beach toward the dunes where they'd left their gear.

"Are we gonna have that leftover pizza?" Maya asked, breathing hard at her side as she scrambled to keep up on her skinny brown legs.

Lozza smiled. Her kid's thoughts were never far from food. Something they had in common.

"Yep. But I get the anchovies."

"Blech!"

Lozza laughed. That was the moment she saw the woman sitting up in the dunes. Her waist-length hair—ebony brown—fluttered like a pennant in the wind. She hugged her arms tightly around her knees. Pale skin. A beach towel draped around her shoulders.

She was watching Lozza and her daughter. Or more likely the sunset behind them. Yet Lozza felt that acute sense of being very keenly observed. It made her hesitate slightly.

Her inclination was to give the woman space. But her and Maya's gear was next to the path through the dune grasses, right where the woman sat. So Lozza continued up the beach with Maya in tow. As they neared, Lozza noted the woman had no board with her. Not a surfer, then. She was also beautiful. The kind of beautiful Lozza could never even dream to be.

"How are ya?" Lozza said as she set her thruster on a patch of dune foliage, fins up. It was casual—what any local would say. She grabbed Maya's towel, tossed it to her kid, and picked up her own. She began rubbing her tangle of hair.

The woman glanced up and something inside Lozza stilled. The woman's eyes were big, and an improbable cobalt color. Like the deep-blue pelagic waters fifteen klicks into the Tasman Sea where the big migratory and predatory fish—marlin, tuna, bonito, great whites—moved deep in the clear, sediment-free currents. But it wasn't the color. It was something else—a look of raw desperation. Need.

Lozza had spent enough years as an interrogator to have become adept at reading tells, both overt and at the micro level. It was now second nature to her. And something about this woman screamed *fear*.

The rescuer in Lozza, the goddamn gladiator in her DNA that had pushed her to become a cop in the first place—the same impulses that had also gotten her into serious trouble—made her say, "Nice evening, huh?" Because now she was curious, and fishing.

"Uh . . . yeah, it is," the woman said, her gaze latching on to Maya. "It's gorgeous."

American. Maybe. But there was also something about the way the woman was staring at Maya that made Lozza feel uncomfortable for reasons she couldn't articulate.

"Going in for a quick splash, then?" Lozza asked, noting the woman's bikini straps beneath her tank top. "Water's pretty warm—it's our first session this year without a wettie." She smiled.

The woman hugged her knees more tightly against her body as her gaze flashed toward the ocean. That's when Lozza noticed the aging bruises around the side of her neck. And along her collarbone. And on her arm. Wind gusted and ruffled the woman's fringe. Lozza saw a cut on her temple and another yellow-green bruise around it. Lozza's breathing slowed. She'd seen bruises like that before.

A soft inner war rose inside her—a battle between giving this woman privacy to deal with whatever it was that seemed to be conflicting her right now and satisfying her own curiosity, which was sliding into concern territory. She hooked her towel around her neck, the wind now chasing tiny goose bumps over her skin.

"So, you in Jarrawarra on holiday, then?"

"No. I . . . I'm new in town. Arrived last month." She gave a nervous laugh. "Seems like an eternity ago already, though."

"Are you from America?" Maya asked as she draped her towel around her skinny shoulders like a Batman cape.

"Canada. West Coast."

"I've never been to Canada," Maya said, giving a gap-toothed grin that made the woman fixate on her in that odd way again.

"I didn't know we'd had any Canadians move into town," Lozza said, delving deeper.

"Should you—I mean, have known?"

She gave a shrug. "I'm a cop. One might expect a local copper to know what's what in a small rural town like this."

The woman recoiled. Her neck tightened. "A *cop?*"

Lozza's interest was 100 percent now. Something was going on here—a darker undertow.

This was the moment Lozza should have perhaps walked. It was also the instant she could not, because she'd already crossed some invisible and indefinable line. So she proffered her hand. "Laurel Bianchi," she said. "But everyone calls me Lozza."

"Or Lozz," Maya offered.

"And this is my daughter, Maya."

The woman hesitated, then accepted Lozza's hand. "Ellie."

Her hand was cold and fine boned. Smooth skin. No rings. "Well, then, Ellie, welcome to Jarrawarra Bay, New South Wales."

Lozza waited for a last name. Ellie said nothing.

Lozza picked up her thruster, hooked it under her arm, wavered, then said, "Does Ellie have a surname?"

She paled, looking as though she'd rather bolt.

"Hey, no worries. See you next time—enjoy your swim. Come on, Maya-Poo. Pizza's waiting."

Maya gathered up her board and sandals and began to scamper up the dune path ahead of Lozza.

"Is . . . is it safe? I mean, right now?" Ellie called out behind them.

Lozza stopped, turned. "What?"

"Is it safe to swim in this part of the bay right now, at this time of evening with maybe sharks coming out and all? I heard they feed at dusk, and that there are rips here sometimes. And . . . I . . . I guess I expected other swimmers to be out. But the beach is deserted."

Lozza frowned, momentarily puzzled.

"I *can* swim," Ellie said forcefully. It sounded off-key. "I just haven't swum in, you know, big waves for . . . for a while."

Lozza looked at the ocean. Surf crunched and boomed off the reef, spumes of spray catching gold rays. The tide was pushing into the mouth of the little creek and churning sand into the water, turning it cloudy and brown.

"Never mind," Ellie said. "I feel stupid for asking."

"Hell no. It's smart. To learn how to read the sea, to learn where the rips tend to form and what to look for." She hesitated. "Hey, Maya! Hold up. Come back here a minute."

Maya came running back down the path.

Lozza set her board back down. "Come on." She tilted her head toward the sea. "We'll go in with you. Just a quick one before the sun sets. You obviously came down to the beach in that getup because you wanted to go in."

"Mom! What about the pizza?" Maya held her hand out, palm up.

"Pizza can wait twenty minutes. A quick swim with Ellie, then you can have extra ice cream for dessert—deal?"

Maya beamed and put her board down. Going back into the water was no real hardship for Maya Bianchi. The ocean, surfing, swimming, ranked right up there behind food and spiders—Maya's priorities in life.

Ellie opened her mouth in a perfect *O* of surprise, then glanced over her shoulder as if expecting something to come barreling over the dunes. She bit her lip, turned back to face Lozza and Maya.

"Are you guys sure?"

"Course we're sure."

THEN

LOZZA

Lozza and Maya stayed where Ellie could stand waist-deep as they duck-dived into breaking swells, popping up on the other side. Lozz was puzzled by Ellie. She seemed strangely fearful of the sea yet fiercely determined, yanking the triangles of her bikini back into place each time she came up out of a dive. Her bruises looked like she'd been through hell not that long ago. And the way she kept fixating on Maya in the waves was . . . odd.

After a few dives, a veil seemed to clear from Ellie's face. Her movements changed, became looser. She smiled at them, and a light began to shine in her eyes—a spark of mad exhilaration almost.

"It's so amazing to be with the two of you in the sea like this," Ellie said. "Mother and daughter. In the waves."

Lozza frowned, her curiosity deepening.

"Look!" Maya suddenly pointed at a freakishly large set of swells soldiering steadily in from the distance, growing in size across the bay as they neared. "Big set coming in."

Ellie went rigid.

"It'll be fine," Maya said to her.

"It will," added Lozza. "Just follow our lead, okay? As soon as a wave is almost upon us and starts to curl at the lip, that's when you dive in, and at the bottom of the wave, right down, deep, and we'll pop up the other side . . . The first one's coming. Are you ready?"

But she'd frozen, her face bloodless, features stricken.

Lozza realized Ellie was not ready for this. But she *had* to be, because now there was no way out other than facing the wave and going straight through it. If she tried to wade back to shore and the wave broke on her back, or if she allowed the wave to suck her up to the lip and dump her over the falls, it would be worse.

Maya, who was closer, saw, too. She grabbed Ellie's wrist and yanked her close. "Hold your breath, Ellie! I got you!"

They gasped, and they all dived headfirst into the powerful, rising surge of water. The force tore at Lozza's hair, peeling back her eyelids as water pummeled over her skin. Pressure that made her ears want to pop pushed down as she swam forward under the crushing washing-machine churn of green water filled with sand. They all popped up like corks on the other side into a skein of foam while the breaker crunched behind them and rolled toward the beach. Maya still held on fast to Ellie's hand. Lozza gave her kid a thumbs-up and glanced out to sea to gauge how far away the next big wave was.

"Another big one coming," she called out to Ellie. "We can start wading toward shore now, but as soon as that wave nears, we turn around and face it again. We do the same thing, dive under and back out toward sea. Then we wade closer in to the beach again, and repeat for the next one—ready?"

Ellie nodded.

The wave neared, and under they went again.

When they popped out the other side, it was sheer exhilaration Lozza saw in Ellie's face. Ellie looked at Maya's hand on her wrist and laughed out loud, her eyes wild. It made Maya laugh, too, but Lozza remained unsure about what she was witnessing. Something was weird about this woman.

They repeated the process—wading back toward shore, facing the next wave, diving under it, turning around, and wading in some more—and soon they were in the ankle-deep shallows and the big set had passed.

"Thank you," Ellie said breathlessly as she tugged her bathing suit back into place. "I . . . I've been unable to do that for such a long, long time. Thank you both so much."

"You mean . . . play in the waves?" asked Maya.

Ellie nodded, grinning. Droplets glinted on her dark lashes. "Sort of like . . . getting back on a horse after a terrible riding accident. I've wanted to try again for so long, and—" She froze as a movement up on the beach caught her eye. Her face went ghost white. Her features turned rigid. She hurriedly waded out of the sea toward the beach.

"Ellie?" Maya called after her.

But when Ellie reached the hard sand, she started to run up the beach, her buttocks wobbling beneath her scrap of bikini.

Lozza shaded her eyes and peered up into the dunes to see what in the hell had spooked her.

A man.

He sat where Ellie had been seated earlier. Next to Lozza and Maya's gear. Big man with blond hair that gleamed gold in the setting rays of the sun.

"Come," she said quietly to Maya.

They caught up to Ellie. It was instinct driving Lozza now. Her cop impulses had linked Ellie's bruises with Scary Man before her brain had even begun to articulate the thought.

"Martin," Ellie said breathlessly as she reached the man. "I . . . I didn't expect you back. What . . . what's going on? Why're you back so soon?"

"Cover yourself, Ellie," Martin said quietly, holding out Ellie's towel to her. Australian accent, but with a hint of Canadian.

A chill trickled down Lozza's spine. Every molecule in her body snapped alert. She picked up her own towel and exchanged a look with Maya. Her daughter sensed it, too. She'd gone quiet as she gathered her towel and draped it around her skinny body.

Lozza cataloged the male quickly. A slight wave in his dense blond hair. Pale-blue eyes offset by tanned skin that was evenly toned and unlined. Strong face. Wide jaw. Built like a rugby player—bit on the thick side. Handsome bugger if one was into that look. He didn't even look at Lozza. His gaze remained locked on Ellie. Wedged into the soft sand at his side were two stainless steel wine goblets and a small esky.

Shivering, Ellie took the towel from him and wrapped it around her shoulders. While the wind had picked up and the air had cooled—as it so often did just before sun slipped into the Tasman Sea—Ellie was not cold. She was shaking for some other reason. A hot and dangerous energy began to cook in Lozza's chest. She felt her jaw tighten.

"G'day, mate," Lozza said as she hooked her towel around her neck.

"Who's your friend, Ellie?" Martin said without acknowledging Lozza.

Angry. Dangerous.

"This is Lozza," she said very quietly. "She's a cop."

Martin's gaze snapped to Lozza. He regarded her for a moment, his features inscrutable.

"Lozza, this is Martin," Ellie said.

Martin smiled. His canines were pointed. It was the coldest smile Lozza had ever seen.

"Lozza Bianchi." She held out her hand. Martin glanced at Lozza's hand but did not take it.

"Martin Cresswell-Smith," he said. "I'm Ellie's husband."

And there it was, some sort of battle line drawn in the soft Jarrawarra dune sand between Lozza the cop and this dangerous-looking man who Lozza realized must be the developer of the Agnes Basin project. She'd seen that name on the signs.

She noticed his ring. While Ellie was not wearing a wedding band, Martin sported what looked like a platinum ring inset with a bloodred stone. A ruby, if the fancy bronze Rolex on the man's wrist was anything to go by.

Lozza lowered her rejected hand, and a sinister taste crawled up her throat. She glanced at Ellie. But Ellie turned away, no longer willing to meet Lozza's eyes.

Terrified. Doesn't want to displease her husband.

A soft, steady drum began in Lozza's heart. This woman was not in a safe place. Wind shifted and gusted hard. Lozza could smell smoke from a distant wildfire.

"You okay, Ellie?" she asked.

"Yeah, yeah, fine."

She still wouldn't meet Lozza's eyes.

Lozza lingered. The man watched her.

"Come, Maya," she said quietly.

Martin and Ellie remained silent as they took their leave.

As Lozza and Maya made their way up through the dunes, Maya said, "He's scary. He's a bad man."

"Yeah. He is."

THEN

LOZZA

As Lozza drove home with Maya, their boards strapped onto the roof, she chewed on her lip and turned over in her mind the enigma that was Ellie and Martin Cresswell-Smith. The woman's bruises. How terrified she'd acted when she'd spotted her husband in the dunes. How he'd controlled her. The look in his eyes.

The woman was in trouble.

But where did Lozza's cop boundaries lie between interfering without official reason and her own deep-down personal drivers around domestic abuse? Of all people, Lozza needed to walk the line carefully. The reason she'd been demoted was because she'd acted badly in response to violence. She'd used violence herself.

The reason the social workers had finally allowed her to adopt Maya was because Lozza had gone to great effort to demonstrate that her slate was clean and to show she could be a responsible and nurturing single mother to a child who herself had been orphaned by domestic violence.

Lozza had only to slip slightly and there were people who'd see to it she was stripped of her badge after what had happened on the murder squad.

She shot a glance at Maya, who was fiddling with the radio in search of a new tune. She owed it to her kid to keep her job, to keep her reputation sterling. She owed it to Maya to be a good example as a human being. And the one thing Lozza was realizing was that more than anything in this world, she wanted a happy home, a warm home for her daughter. She wanted Maya to live in a world where there was no violence. Where she didn't have to hide under a bed and be scared.

Lozza turned her car onto the road that took them past the Puggo. The place was hopping, and through the open car windows came the mouthwatering scent of burgers cooking on the barbie. Her stomach grumbled—surfing always built up her appetite.

Lozz slowed, checking the cars parked outside to see who was there. She half expected to find her partner's truck outside. The Puggo was Gregg's second home. It was also ground zero for gossip. A thought struck Lozza.

If anyone would know anything about the Cresswell-Smiths, it would be Rabz.

"Hey, Maya, how about takeout burgers off the barbie and chips instead of warmed-up pizza?"

"Are you *serious*?"

"Yes."

"Can we get extra chips?"

Lozza grinned. "You betcha." She found a parking space along the curb farther down the road beneath a giant lilly pilly tree. The Puggo was a licensed establishment, not a place for minors, but while she waited at the bar for the takeaways, she could quiz Rabz, or whoever else was in there. "You okay to wait here?" she asked Maya.

"Are you kidding? For burgers and chips?"

Lozza left Maya in the car listening to an audiobook and hurried up the street. She passed a beat-up dirt bike parked a few vehicles behind hers. It didn't look roadworthy, and she took note of the Queensland registration. Cop habits died hard. Her stomach grumbled audibly as she climbed the stairs to the Puggo veranda, and she reckoned she'd order extra chips for herself as well.

Lozza pushed through the PVC strip curtain and entered the pub. Her eyes adjusted and her spirits lifted with the boisterous atmosphere.

No sign of Rabz.

Instead, there was a new guy working the bar—young and tanned, with long dreads and a happy face. He was chatting and laughing with two women bellied up to the counter. Sue and Mitzi. Old-timers from the local board riders club. She went up to the bar, said hello to the women, and placed her order with the young barkeep. He called it into the kitchen.

"Rabz not working tonight?" she asked him.

"She's away in Sydney," said the bartender. "Won't be back for another week or so."

Mitzi and Sue were yabbering about the greenies in a booth in the back corner of the pub.

Lozza followed their gaze. Mitzi turned to her. "Every evening it's the same thing. They come in to plot ways to stop the Agnes Basin project, then get shit-faced and lose the plot." She chuckled. "This evening they're all afire over some enviro report which apparently clears the way toward shire approval."

"Who did the enviro consult?" Lozza asked. She was personally against the development of that area herself.

"The dodge brothers," said Sue.

"Yeah. Word is you can slip those dodgy brothers a bribe and they'll write anything you damn want in a report," added Mitzi. She reached for her beer, swallowed heartily, and wiped her mouth with her hand. Inside, Lozza smiled. Mitzi was salt of the earth. A longtime local who took no crap and never minced her words. "Stinks if you ask me. I reckon those Cresswell-Smiths are crooks, and so is half the council plus the mayor if they're buying into a dodge brothers report."

"Do you know the couple at all?"

"I know they're intent on destroying Agnes Basin." She finished her beer, plonked her empty glass on the counter, and pointed for a refill. "Word is it's Ellie's daddy's money that's being used to fund the project, and she basically doesn't know what in the hell her husband is doing with it."

"I reckon the missus is not altogether there," said Sue, making a drinking motion with her hand. "Boozer and drug addict is the word around town."

Lozza frowned, and her curiosity was piqued.

The barkeep set two containers of hot food to go on the counter in front of Lozza. "Did you say Ellie Cresswell-Smith?" he asked.

"Yep," said Mitzi.

"I was wondering who she was. Someone left a package here for her yesterday," said the barkeep. "Some bikie with a bald head and ink down the side of his neck."

"A package? Here?" said Lozza. She was solidly hooked now because she and Gregg had spent the past few weeks helping out on Strike Force Tinto, a law enforcement operation that had zeroed in on an arm of an outlaw motorcycle gang that had run a drug operation out of a town to the north.

"Yeah. This dude came in asking for 'Ellie'—said he had a delivery for her. But Rabz hadn't left any instructions about a delivery, so the guy asked if he could just leave it here with me for Ellie to pick up."

"And did she pick it up?" asked Lozza.

"Nah, it's in the office," said the barman. "Package has her name on it. Figured I'd leave it for Rabz to deal with when she got back."

Lozza paid for her order and took her leave.

Outside, the bats had started bickering like old witches in the tree—it was getting dark. Orange poop collecting on the sidewalk stuck under her flip-flops. As she neared her RAV4, she heard voices. A male and a female. Arguing. Their tone was low but angry, the kind of sound that invites one to listen closer. Lozza stilled. Listened. The woman raised her voice. "No," she commanded. "Get out of here! Stop. Leave me alone!"

Lozza moved forward fast. Beneath a tree along a fence, she saw a man grab a woman's arm. The woman jerked herself free. With shock Lozza recognized her.

"Willow?" she called out. "Everything okay?"

The man stepped back hurriedly into the deeper shadows. He was bald, his pate shiny. Black T-shirt, black jeans. Biker boots. In his left hand he held some kind of carry bag.

Lozza strode up to them carrying her takeout boxes. "Hoi! Mate! Step away from her. Now."

"She . . . she's police," Willow said loudly. "You better listen to her, mate."

The man shot a glance at Lozza wearing her sarong and flip-flops, her takeout boxes in hand. His features were obscured by the gloomy light. A bat flitted through the air. The man spun around, slung the bag across his body, and stalked toward the beat-up dirt bike parked near Lozza's RAV4. He straddled the bike in one smooth motion and kicked it to life. The streetlight caught a tattoo down the side of his neck. The man gave full throttle and roared down the street, popping a wheelie before disappearing around the corner. A kangaroo bounded in his wake and went crashing into bushes.

Lozza went up to Willow. "Are you okay?"

She was shaking. "What an asshole." Her voice came out quavery. "Thank you," she said.

"Who is he? What did he want?"

"I have no bloody idea who he is. He came out of nowhere, accosted me as I walked past. Said he wanted to buy me a drink and wouldn't take no for an answer. He tried to grab me, and that's when you arrived." She rubbed her upper arm where the man had touched her. "Good timing—thanks, Lozz."

Lozza hesitated. "You headed to the Puggo? You going to be okay?" As she spoke, Gregg appeared from the shadows and came down the street. "What's going on?" he said.

"Some arsehat accosted Willow," said Lozza.

"Are you okay?" Gregg touched Willow's arm. An intimate gesture. Lozza felt her jaw tighten. Of course Gregg was interested in Willow. She was single. Sexy as all hell. As much as Lozza hated to admit it to even herself, she was more than slightly attracted to her buff partner. Gregg might be a rookie cop and not a very good one yet, but he had life experience. He'd worked in the construction industry before signing on with the NSW police force. He was good with his hands, at fixing things. At problem-solving. He was also good with kids. That ranked pretty high in Lozza's books. In his spare time he ran a surf school and helped coach nippers at the lifesaving club. And yeah, Lozza was jealous right now. She'd never have the looks of a Willow or an Ellie or a Rabz. Maybe that was part of why she liked being a cop and carrying a gun. It gave her purpose. A power that those other women didn't have.

"I . . . Well, I'll see you guys. Have fun."

"Yeah," said Gregg.

"Thanks, Lozz," said Willow.

"Hey, no worries." She headed to her car while Gregg and Willow walked toward the Puggo.

"Way to go, Mom!" Maya said as Lozza handed her the takeout boxes. Maya sneaked a handful of fries from the bag, and Lozza allowed her kid to stuff a few into her mouth as she reached down to start the ignition. The bartender's words resurfaced in her mind.

"Some bikie with a bald head and ink down the side of his neck . . . This dude came in asking for 'Ellie.'"

She stopped short of starting the car, swallowed her mouthful, and said, "Can you wait here a sec, Maya? I forgot something at the Puggo. I'll be right back—you can start eating if you want."

Before Maya could reply, Lozza was jogging back down the sidewalk toward the Puggo. She dusted french fry crumbs and salt off her chin and entered the pub. She noticed Gregg and Willow in a booth, talking with heads bent close. She went straight to the bartender.

"That package for Ellie Cresswell-Smith, I'll take it—I'll deliver it to her house."

The barkeep looked uncertain.

"Hey, I'm a cop. How wrong can it go?"

The barkeep laughed. "You'd be surprised." He took Lozza into the back office and handed her a small package. It was wrapped in brown paper. Across the top was scrawled, ELLIE CRESSWELL-SMITH. Lozza shook it. It rattled. Like pills in containers.

"You got CCTV in here?" she asked.

"You mean inside this office?"

"No. Out front."

"Yeah. CCTV of the exterior of the premises and doorways."

"Do you still have the footage from the day this package was brought in?"

"You think it's drugs or something?"

"What makes you say that?"

A shrug. "I dunno. Like I said, the guy looked like a bikie. Plus, there was that news of that bikie drug bust the other day. But yeah, the footage wouldn't have been overwritten yet. I could pull it for you, but maybe later?" He jerked his head toward the door. "I got a heap of customers waiting. And, I dunno . . . maybe I should check with Rabz that it's okay?"

Lozza studied the package. Ellie's name. "Yeah, you do that. I can return in uniform and make it official."

The barkeep wavered. "I'm sure Rabz will be fine—I'm sure it'll be okay."

"Okay, locate the footage later, save it for me. I'll come by and pick it up tomorrow."

Lozza jogged back to her car. It would be easy enough to find the address for the Cresswell-Smith developer couple. She tucked the package behind her seat on the floor. Maya watched her.

"What's that?" she asked.

"Just something I forgot."

THEN

LOZZA

Over one year ago, November 17. Jarrawarra Bay, New South Wales.

Lozza's entire day had been swallowed by an ex-con who'd attempted to blow up his wife's lover's car with a homemade pipe bomb. It was now dark, and she was still in uniform and exhausted by the time she parked her marked Holden Commodore in a space outside the Puggo.

Lozza went inside to collect the CCTV footage. Rabz was apparently still in Sydney, so the bartender handed over a drive containing the clip captured by the CCTV camera outside the Puggo.

"The bikie is on there," the bartender said. "You can see his tat pretty clearly when he turns his head. It's a hummingbird on the side of his neck."

She thanked the barman, got back into her police vehicle, and drove to the Cresswell-Smith house on the Bonny River. The house was in darkness save for a lone light in a window upstairs. No boat or trailer in the driveway. The big garage door was open. No vehicle inside, either.

She switched off the ignition and watched the house for a while. The wind blew even harder than it had this morning. She reached for the package she'd picked up from the Puggo last night. As she got out of her vehicle, she saw a shadow move across a lighted window next door. A curtain twitched. Someone was watching.

In her uniform she walked up to the front door of the Cresswell-Smith home. The door was made of thick wood and carved with an aboriginal-looking design. A thick pane of glass ran down the side. A motion-sensor light flared on as Lozza reached for the doorbell.

The bell echoed inside. No one came. The place felt empty. She rang the bell again. It ding-donged inside. No answer. She tried once more. Nothing. The upstairs light must have been left on accidentally when the couple went out.

But as Lozza turned to leave, in her peripheral vision, she caught a fast movement inside the house. Her pulse quickened. She cupped her hand against the glass pane and peered in. Dark. She couldn't see. She considered using the flashlight on her duty belt but refrained. This wasn't a crime scene. Apart from her gut instincts, she'd been given no reason to intrude. Yet she felt a whispering sense of unease as she peered into the shadows inside. She was certain she'd seen something move.

She waited a few moments, rang the bell again. No answer.

There was nothing more she could do here. She'd return with the package tomorrow because she really wanted to see what was inside now. She planned on hanging around and watching while Ellie opened it.

Lozza had started back up the driveway when the silhouette of a woman appeared in the lighted window next door again. Lozza stopped and looked up. Wind gusted and dry gum leaves crackled over the paving. An owl hooted softly. The curtain was pulled back and the window opened. A woman leaned out.

"You looking for the Cresswell-Smiths?" she called out to Lozza. She sounded old, but Lozza couldn't make out her features. *Must be a new tenant in that house,* she thought. As far as she knew, the property was used by the owners only during the height of the summer holidays.

"Do you know where they are?" she called up to the woman.

"They went fishing with the boat early this morning. The wife came back on her own. Came up the shortcut path from the river. She's in there—inside the house. The wife."

Lozza glanced back at the house and frowned. She studied the lone lighted window upstairs in the Cresswell-Smith home.

"Are you sure?"

"Saw her arriving home just after it got dark—about half an hour ago. She looked strange."

"What do you mean?"

"She was stumbling about near her studio and knocked over the rubbish bin. The metal lid clattered, which is what made me look out the window—thought it might be that possum back. I saw her. In her ball cap and jacket. She startled when I put the lights on and ducked around the side of the studio. I switched off my light to watch from the darkness because I thought it was odd. She went up the garden and into the house via the sliding glass door. It's still open. You can see from my other window."

Nosy woman.

"So she's alone in there?"

"Far as I know. Never saw the husband come back. The truck and boat, neither."

Lozza stood there, her gut firing signals to her brain. She'd need to cover her ass if she went onto their property uninvited.

"Are you worried she might actually be in some kind of trouble?" she called up to the neighbor. If the woman claimed fear for Ellie's well-being, it would give Lozza more reason to enter the property through that open garage door and go around the back.

"Her husband hits her."

Lozza's pulse spiked. "What?"

"I've seen it. Through the bottom window between their kitchen and living room. I saw him strike her and try to strangle her once. And last night I heard screaming."

"Last night? What time?"

"About seven, I think."

After they'd returned from the beach. I should have done something—but what?

"You didn't call triple zero—report it?"

"Not my business. Each to his own, I say."

Lozza swore to herself. "So you think she's in there and in danger right now?"

"Maybe. Something is definitely weird."

"Thank you." Lozza entered the garage and came out the side door onto a lawn in darkness. The glass sliding door of the house was indeed open. A sound reached her—a crackle of leaves, then a snap of a twig. Followed by a sudden crashing through the bushes on the vacant lot on the other side of the lawn. Her heart raced.

Carefully she crouched down and set the package at her feet. Peering intently into the shadows of the vacant lot across the lawn, she unclipped the strap on her holster, freeing up access to the Glock 22 .40-caliber semiautomatic pistol at her hip. She slid her flashlight out of her duty belt, clicked it on, and panned the bushes. She jerked with adrenaline as her beam hit two glowing eyes.

Bloody possum.

Lozza drew in a calming breath and scanned the rest of the property. At the bottom of the lawn, behind trees and beyond a small boathouse, the river moved dark and shiny, reflecting a sliver of moon. Hairs prickled up the back of her neck. This place felt wrong. Ominous. She left the package near the garage door and crossed the lawn.

She stepped onto the patio and called in through the open door, her hand near her sidearm.

"Hello? Anyone home?"

Silence oozed out of the house. Her skin crawled with a sense of something evil.

"Hello!" she yelled louder.

Silence.

Lozza entered the house, every molecule in her body primed. She panned her torch beam across the living room interior. "Anyone home? Ellie Cresswell-Smith, are you here? This is Senior Constable Laurel Bianchi of the Jarrawarra police. I've got a package for you."

From outside came a sudden loud crashing in the dry bushes. Too big for a possum. She hurried out and scanned the bushes with her flashlight. A car door slammed on the other side of the vacant lot— Lozza couldn't see it through the vegetation. An engine started. Tires spun in gravel. The car sped into the night. Her heart hammered.

Hastily she reentered the house, this time with sharpened purpose.

Using her flashlight, she found a light switch, clicked it on. Bright light flooded the interior. It was stark inside, all white and oddly sterile. Two empty wine bottles stood on the kitchen counter. One empty wineglass. Lozza crossed the living room into the kitchen area. She saw broken glass on the floor. Red streaks down the side of a cabinet.

Ellie?

She moved toward the staircase. There was a small puddle of blood on the bottom stair. Lozza shone her light up the stairwell. Streaks of what looked like blood smeared the stairwell wall.

She moved fast up the stairs, made straight toward the door where the lone light glowed.

"Ellie!" she called out as she entered the room.

Lozza stalled.

The bed was a tangle of white sheets—blood on them. An empty wine bottle lay sideways on the nightstand. A female's clothes littered the floor near two suitcases that looked like they had exploded their contents. A trail of blood led to the bathroom. She saw a bare foot sticking out of the bathroom door. Lozza rushed forward.

Ellie lay naked on the tiles, eyes closed, unmoving, her skin a deathly blue-white color. A pool of blood congealed under her head. Her forehead was gashed open. A pill container lay on its side near her outstretched hand. Pills had scattered across the floor. A mobile phone with a cracked screen lay wedged behind the toilet base. Lozza moved fast toward Ellie. As she crouched down, she registered the words on the pill container in bold black print: **CONTROLLED DRUG. HYPNODORM.**

She felt for a pulse as she keyed the radio at her shoulder.

THEN

LOZZA

Lozza panned her flashlight carefully over the dry sand of the unpaved road behind the vacant lot next to the Cresswell-Smith home.

The paramedics had responded quickly. Ellie was now in the hospital and apparently still in a coma while doctors worked on her. Lozza had bagged the contraband drugs and called in the incident to her station. And while she'd had access to the premises, she'd walked slowly around the Cresswell-Smith home, taking photos of the blood, wine bottles, broken glass. Upon calling it all in to her own station, Lozza had learned that marine rescue had activated a search for the Cresswell-Smiths' boat.

Apparently the *Abracadabra* had logged on with Jarrawarra Bay Marine Rescue at 5:49 that morning. Marine logs indicated that the boat was headed out to the FAD. But the *Abracadabra* had failed to log off, which had triggered a response.

There was no sign of the boat. Martin Cresswell-Smith was not responding to radio calls or calls to his mobile.

He appeared to be missing.

Lozza stilled as the beam of her flashlight caught something.

Fresh tire tracks.

She crouched down and took photos with her phone, the flash bright in the darkness. She looked up and scanned the row of houses opposite the vacant lot as she replayed in her mind the sound of someone crashing through these bushes. The sound of a car door slamming. An engine starting. Tires spinning as a vehicle sped away. She thought of the shadow she'd seen through the glass next to the Cresswell-Smiths' front door. Her mind went to the blood. Ellie on the bathroom floor. The pills.

A man exited the front door of a house across from the lot. He wheeled his recycling bin down his driveway. Lozza pushed to her feet and went across the road to talk to him.

"Evening, sir, I'm Lozza Bianchi with the Jarrawarra police."

"Officer," he said, parking his recycling bin outside his gate. "What's up?"

"Your house looks right at that vacant lot—did you happen to see a vehicle parked there earlier?"

"You mean a brown car?"

"So you did see a vehicle?"

"Well, yeah." Wind gusted and dry gum leaves crackled across his driveway. A bat flitted under the boughs. "It was a Corolla. I saw it because it near killed my cat as it sped out of there. Bloody idiot."

Lozza's pulse quickened. "You sure it was a Corolla?"

"Yeah. I've seen it before. Parked down that street a couple of times with a guy just sitting inside like he was watching that developer's house. Creeped my wife out. She said if we saw it again she was going to call you coppers."

"Any chance you saw the rego?"

"Part of it was covered in dirt. But I did see the letters *G-I-N*. I think."

"Yellow plate?"

The glow from the streetlight caught his frown as he seemed to cast his mind back. "Nah. Maroon on white, I think."

"Queensland?"

"Could be, but definitely not the black on yellow of a New South Wales rego."

Lozza thanked the man. She retrieved the package marked for Ellie, which she'd left on the lawn near the side door of the Cresswell-Smiths' garage, and got into her Commodore. Lozza checked her watch, then called her mother.

"Hey, Mom," she said, "I'm probably going to be home a bit late tonight."

"Everything okay, love?" her mother said.

"Yeah. Something's come up at work. New case. Missing person. Can I speak to Maya?"

"She's in the bath."

Lozza smiled and felt a warmth in her heart. "Tell her I'll tuck her in when I get home, and remind her that her project is due at school tomorrow."

Lozza killed the call and drove down to the dark and deserted Bonny River boat ramp. A lone white Toyota Hilux was parked in the lot beside an empty boat trailer.

She exited her marked vehicle and walked slowly around the ute and trailer. A slice of moon provided a silvery light, and an owl hooted softly.

If, as the woman next door had said, Ellie and Martin Cresswell-Smith had both gone out to sea in the *Abracadabra* early this morning, and if the boat had never returned, how had Ellie gotten back home?

What had happened between 5:49 a.m., when they'd logged on with marine rescue, and 7:40 p.m., when the neighbor had seen Ellie coming up from her studio boathouse?

THEN

LOZZA

Over one year ago, November 18. Jarrawarra Bay, New South Wales.

"Take a seat, Lozz."

Sergeant Jon Ratcliffe—the Jarrawarra station boss—motioned to a vacant chair in front of his desk. He'd called Lozza into his office first thing this morning.

She hesitated, then took a seat. She had with her the package she'd taken to the Bonny River home yesterday evening. She positioned it on her lap, along with the photograph of the "bikie" taken from the CCTV camera outside the Puggo entrance.

"Catch me up," Jon said, leaning forward. His eyes were a dark beetle brown, intense. He was a big and imposing man. He ran a tight ship and held fierce command of his officers, but Lozza knew him to be fair. This was a small town, so she'd associated with him outside of work, too. He had a big family—five kids—and a heart of gold underneath that uniform and gruffness. "Run me through what happened at the Cresswell-Smith home yesterday—why were you there?"

Lozza moistened her lips and explained it all as best she could. And she was honest. She showed her superior the photo of the bikie.

"This is the guy who delivered the package. I saw him ride off on a dirt bike. I recalled the Queensland rego because it didn't look road-worthy. I ran the registration earlier this morning, given what happened yesterday. It came up stolen." She paused. "And a neighbor said the vehicle I heard fleeing the Cresswell-Smith home also had a Queensland plate. I don't know if that's relevant."

He regarded the image of the man, then leaned back and clasped his hands behind his head. He eyed her for a moment. "What's inside the package?"

"I don't know, sir."

"Given the circumstances—missing husband, his wife with a history of drug abuse and now in a coma—open it."

Her pulse quickened. She set the box on his desk, and Jon handed her a pair of scissors.

She'd already photographed the package.

She put on some gloves and carefully cut the tape. She opened the top. Inside were five containers, all with the same label as the one she'd found with Ellie Cresswell-Smith on the bathroom floor. Jon got to his feet and came around the desk.

"Hypnodorm," he said. "Controlled meds."

"Looks like the same stuff she overdosed on."

He glanced down at her. The potential implications hung heavy in the room. She, a cop, had apparently delivered black-market pills to the house of a woman who might yet die of an overdose from the same meds.

Jon rubbed his chin. "Log those into evidence. Have them tested. Let's hope this doesn't become an issue, Lozz," he said quietly. "At least this isn't a murder case, which could go high profile. So far it's just a person missing at sea—a man who could still turn up. Coupled with spousal abuse and a drug-addiction problem."

He reseated himself behind his desk. "Canvass the place. And find that bikie."

"Yes, sir."

Lozza got up, exited the room, and shut Jon's office door quietly behind her. She felt sick. Her gut told her there was nothing simple about this case.

THEN

LOZZA

Gregg was waiting for her outside in the car park.

"You drive." She tossed him the keys. She wasn't in the mood.

He caught the keys. "What did the boss man say?"

"He said to get our arses out there and canvass residents." She wasn't inclined to discuss her meeting with her superior with rookie Gregg right now.

She slid into the passenger seat and reached for her seat belt. Gregg started the vehicle and pulled out of the lot. The day was bright. Hot already. But clouds were building over the northern horizon. He drove toward the headlands. There were several residents who lived there who had telescopes and routinely watched the ocean in the morning. One of them was Willow Larsen. They aimed for her house.

Gregg fell oddly silent as they neared. She glanced at him. He cleared his throat.

"I was with Willow," he said.

"What?"

"I was with her. In the morning. Before six a.m. yesterday. I saw them—the Cresswell-Smiths—going out in their Quinnie."

"And when were you going to tell me this?"

"I just did."

Lozza's blood pressure went up. She looked out the window and tried to breathe deep.

They drew up outside a gate under a jasmine arch. Willow's lime-green VW Bug was parked on the street outside. Lozza hesitated. "So you're sleeping with her?"

"What difference does it make?"

"I didn't say it made a difference. I'm just asking."

"It's not really your business, Lozz."

"Just want to know what I'm dealing with before we go in there."

"And if I was—how's that going to change our interview?"

"It means I'm doing the talking." She got out of the car and banged on the door.

Gregg followed suit and said, "Chill, Lozz. It's not like I'm delivering drugs or anything."

She cursed under her breath and opened the garden gate.

THEN

LOZZA

Willow opened the door wrapped in a turquoise kimono with a dragon embroidered on the back. Her feet were bare and her hair was tousled—clearly they'd woken her.

"Hey." She looked at Gregg, then Lozza. "What's going on?"

"Martin Cresswell-Smith is missing," Lozza said. "Gregg says you witnessed his boat going out to sea."

She frowned, looked confused. "Yeah, we both saw the *Abracadabra* going out. Martin and Ellie were on board. What do you mean he's missing—where's Ellie?"

"She's in the hospital. Drug overdose."

"*What?*"

"Can we come in, Willow?"

But she seemed frozen for a moment. "Is . . . is she okay?"

"She's in a coma right now."

Willow's hand went to her mouth. Her eyes watered. "Oh my gosh," she whispered. "How . . . how did this happen . . . if they both went out on the boat?"

"This is what we're trying to figure out," Gregg said quietly. "Can we come in for a moment, Willow? We need to interview anyone who saw them going out."

"Sure, sure." She stepped back, allowing them to enter.

"Sorry if we woke you," Lozza said as they followed her into a stunning living room overlooking the sea.

"No worries. I worked late last night. I do readings online in time zones across the world. Sometimes that means crazy hours. Take a seat. Can I get you guys coffee, tea?"

"No. Thanks," said Lozza. "We shouldn't be long."

They sat and Lozza got out her notebook. "Describe what you saw, please," she said.

"I saw them quite clearly through the scope." Willow nodded to the telescope on a tripod in front of the huge picture windows. "Gregg was with me. He saw them, too."

Gregg grunted.

"What time was that?" asked Lozza.

"It was . . . just before six, I think. I was making coffee when I saw a boat heading out into the bay. I went to the scope to get a better look. I saw it was the *Abracadabra*. Saw the name clearly. And I saw Martin and Ellie on board."

Lozza scribbled in her notebook, feeling hot and clumpy in her big boots with her stupidly frizzy ginger hair and peeling sunburned nose while Willow sat across from her in her pretty kimono and elegant home. Despite her late night and the shadows under Willow's eyes, she still managed to look sexy.

"What were they wearing?" asked Lozza. "How did you know it was them?"

"I could see. Martin had . . . I think a tan shirt. Cargo pants. The same as he wore fishing the other day when they got into trouble on the bar. Bare head. Ellie had a pale-blue cap on. A royal-blue jacket. Her hair was tied in a ponytail. I noticed because it's so long and was blowing in the wind. They were headed toward the Point of No Return. I was surprised to see them because Martin was supposed to be away on a business trip. And there were whitecaps on the sea. It was windy. Not ideal fishing weather . . ." Her voice faded.

Lozza glanced up. "Anything else?"

"No. I don't think so."

"Thanks," Lozza said, closing her notebook and coming to her feet.

"Is Ellie going to be okay—can she have visitors yet?" Willow asked.

"She's unconscious. Don't know yet."

Worry creased Willow's brow. "I . . . I don't understand. What . . . what does it mean that Martin is missing?"

"The boat is gone," said Gregg as he stood up. "Martin and the boat."

"So how did Ellie get back?" asked Willow.

"We're trying to figure that out," Gregg said.

Willow frowned at him. "I'm going to call the hospital. I need to see her."

"Did you know Ellie well, Willow?" Lozza asked.

"We're friends." She sniffed her emotion back. "Ellie has confided in me, as a friend." She hesitated. "I . . . Look, it's not my place to say anything because . . . it's personal. But . . ." Willow's frown deepened. "Given the circumstances, it might be relevant. Ellie . . . she'd just gotten proof that her husband was having an affair."

"What do you mean?" Lozza's interest was suddenly piqued.

"She'd hired a PI to follow Martin and his mistress, and Ellie had recently received photographic evidence. She told me she was planning to leave him—return to Canada—before he got back from his business trip. But he must have come back early. Which makes it really strange that they'd even go out in the boat together. Especially since Ellie had such an awful experience the first time they went fishing. It doesn't make sense. None of it."

"Did you see the photos?" Lozza asked, her brain racing now.

Willow nodded, hesitated, then said, "Ellie had also apparently found proof her husband was moving money out of their joint account.

She feared he'd married her in a rush to get access to her money. She even thought he might be drugging her." Willow swore softly, rubbed her face, then said, "Ellie found a receipt for two plane tickets to the Cape Verde islands. The departure date was in two weeks, and they were not for her." She paused. "I . . . I can't believe this. They only got married in May. In Las Vegas. It was a whirlwind thing, Ellie said."

Lozza stared at Willow. "You mean Martin was getting ready to bolt?"

"I'm not sure. It seems that way."

"With his mistress?" asked Gregg.

"That's what Ellie feared."

"Who's the mistress, Willow?" asked Lozza.

Willow looked out of the window, clearly conflicted.

"Willow—" Gregg pressed. "This puts *everything* in a different light. If Martin is lost out there"—he flung his arm toward the picture windows overlooking the sea—"it could be a life-or-death situation. The clock is ticking. But if he's not—if he's bolted—there are search-and-rescue volunteers out there right now, good people risking their lives and losing employment hours searching for him. We need to know if there's a chance he's fled the country with some woman or something."

"Rabz," she said quietly. "It's Bodie Rabinovitch."

As Lozza and Gregg walked back to the Commodore parked on the street, she said, "Let's go find Rabz at the Puggo."

"My thoughts exactly," said Gregg, pushing open the gate. "Who'da thunk—Rabz?"

"So is Willow's witness statement consistent with what you saw of the *Abracadabra* going out?" Lozza asked.

"Yeah. Two people. One Quinnie. Ellie in a blue jacket and pale-blue cap, hair in a ponytail. Martin with no hat. Around six a.m. I was going to have a coffee, then leave, go home, get ready to go to work."

They got into the car, and Lozza said, "There were those two suitcases in the Cresswell-Smith house when I found Ellie unconscious in the bathroom. Women's stuff. All over the floor."

"Like she'd packed?" He leaned forward and started the engine.

"Yeah. Maybe she was about to leave for Canada, like she'd told Willow, went for a last swim on November sixteen, which is when I saw her on the beach, and suddenly Martin was back. There in the dunes. Ellie looked shit-scared when she saw him. And he looked like bottled pressure ready to blow. Something evil about him. Even Maya said so."

Gregg pulled into the street. "Maya was with you?"

"Maya and I swam with Ellie."

He shot her a glance. "Why?"

"That's the weird thing. She was sitting next to our gear when we came out of the surf. She seemed both terrified of the water—the waves—yet determined to go in. And because she was clearly scared . . . I don't know, I offered to go in with her."

"Lozza the savior."

She gave a shrug. "I felt sorry for her. And then I saw her bruises. It's consistent with her neighbor saying Martin hit her. This is starting to look really weird."

Gregg swore. "Yeah, it's sus all right."

"So maybe Martin comes back early. He sees her suitcases packed. They have a fight that night, the suitcases get trashed . . . but then why go out in the boat together early the following morning?" Lozza said. "And now she's in a coma. And he's vanished." She paused, thinking. "We need to confirm whether Ellie did in fact purchase an air ticket for Canada. And for what date. We need to know a lot more about those two."

As they turned into the road that led to the Pug and Whistler, Lozza's mobile rang. She glanced at the caller ID. Jon Ratcliffe. She connected the call.

"Bianchi."

"Lozz, Ellie Cresswell-Smith has regained consciousness. I need you guys there."

Excitement crackled through Lozza. She hung up.

"Detour," she said. "Hospital."

THEN

LOZZA

"What happened, Ellie, after you and Martin went out in the boat?" Lozza asked. She sat in a hospital chair beside Ellie's bed. Gregg propped his butt against the windowsill, his arms folded over his chest, a notebook in one hand, watching. Late-morning sun streamed in behind Gregg, tiny dust motes dancing in the hazy rays.

Ellie appeared confused. Her gaze flickered around the hospital room, and she touched her hand to the bandage on her head. "I . . . I don't recall going out in a boat."

On their way to the hospital, Lozza had checked in with marine rescue. Still no sign of the *Abracadabra* or Martin. And the other Jarrawarra Bay police officers who'd been canvassing residents around the boat launch and along the ridge had confirmed what Gregg and Willow had reported seeing—all had witnessed Martin and Ellie Cresswell-Smith heading out to sea in their Quinnie shortly before 6:00 a.m. No one had seen the boat return.

"Ellie, your husband is missing. He's been gone since early morning yesterday. Helicopters, fixed-wing aircraft, marine rescue boats, volunteers, police, have all been combing up and down the coast in search of Martin and signs of the *Abracadabra*. Anything you could say might help—time is critical."

Ellie blinked, frowned, then winced as the movement appeared to hurt her. Her eyes were red-rimmed and watery. Hollows had sunk below her cheekbones, and her complexion was so pale her skin looked almost translucent. Lozza had thought she was dead. She still couldn't quite believe she'd arrived just in time to save the woman's life. If it hadn't been for the drug package . . .

"Ellie, do you know where Martin might be?" she asked again.

"I . . . I don't know what you're talking about."

"Do you know why you're here, Ellie?" Gregg asked from his window perch. Lozza heard his duty belt squeak as he repositioned himself against the windowsill.

Ellie's gaze shifted to Gregg. She flinched against the sunlight and turned away again. She closed her eyes for a moment and tried to moisten her lips. Lozza offered her water with a straw. Ellie sipped slowly. It clearly hurt to swallow.

Lozza tamped down her frustration and put Gregg's question to her again. "Did the doctors tell you why you are here, Ellie?"

"They told me I'd overdosed." She touched her bandage again. "The doctors . . . said I had a cocktail of drugs in my system. Alcohol, GHB, and something else—I don't remember taking them."

"What else did the doctors tell you?"

"They said I probably fell under the influence and hit my head in the bathroom. Or in the kitchen before I went up to the bathroom. They gave me stitches. They said I had vaginal bleeding and tearing . . . I have no recollection of anything. They also say I have some retrograde amnesia and that memories prior to my . . . accident might or might not return."

Lozza swore to herself and glanced at Gregg. He shrugged a shoulder. This was the first time Lozza had heard of vaginal trauma. Her mind went back to what the neighbor had said about witnessing Martin hitting his wife and hearing screams. She thought about the bruises, the allegations of a mistress, and the other things Willow had said.

"Okay, here's what we do know, Ellie," Lozza said quietly, leaning forward. "And maybe going through it all will jog some memory. Several witnesses, including Constable Abbott here, saw the *Abracadabra* leaving Bonny Bay early yesterday morning. According to Jarrawarra Bay Marine Rescue records, the *Abracadabra* radioed to log in at 5:49 a.m. At that time the *Abracadabra* informed the volunteer radio operator that there were two adults on board and they were heading out to the FAD. Their estimated time of return was six p.m. That was the last anyone heard from the boat. Do you recall any of this, Ellie?"

Ellie stared blankly at her. "I'm sorry, I don't remember any of it."

Frustration bit through Lozza. "Okay, here's what else we know. Your neighbor saw you come home in the dark, around seven forty p.m."

"That woman next door who watches everything from her window?"

"She saw you from an upstairs window," Lozza said. "She reported you stumbling and bumping over a rubbish bin near the boathouse studio, then she saw you going over the lawn and entering your house from the rear sliding doors. How did you get back to shore if the boat is gone?"

Ellie frowned and touched her bandage again, as if confirming it was still there.

Lozza pressed. "Your neighbor said you looked wet and that you were wearing a baseball cap and a windbreaker—the same items of clothing you were seen wearing that morning while heading out in the boat."

Ellie began to look frightened. She glanced at Gregg.

"I arrived at your house at 8:02 p.m., Ellie," Lozza said. "The rear sliding door was open. I found you unconscious in the bathroom. There was broken glass downstairs, blood smears in the kitchen, blood at the base of the stairs, clothes all over the bedroom floor, open suitcases, some blood on the bedsheets." She paused, thinking again of the noise in the vacant lot and the Corolla that had sped off in the dark. "Can you remember what happened at your house?"

Ellie was quiet for several moments. Her eyes flickered and Lozza tensed in anticipation, but Ellie shook her head. "I'm sorry. I have . . . it's all just a black hole."

"Was anyone else with you inside your home?" Gregg asked.

"I'm sorry. I don't remember."

Lozza moistened her lips and nodded. "Okay. Now, I do have to bring this up—it could be relevant. Do you recall having a fight with your husband the night prior to going out in the boat?"

Ellie hesitated. "No."

Lozza watched her eyes. The woman was lying. She remembered something. Even a hint. Or perhaps Ellie just expected from habit that this was something that had occurred.

"Ellie, you've just mentioned vaginal tearing. Do you recall having aggressive intercourse that might have caused the vaginal trauma?"

Tears coalesced in her eyes. "No," she whispered. "I only know what the doctors have told me."

Gregg inhaled deeply behind Lozza. Uncomfortable.

Lozza said quietly, "Ellie, I came to your house with a package that had been left for you at the Pug and Whistler. It contained the same black-market prescription medication that you overdosed on. The package had your name on it. What can you tell me about that package?"

She gave Lozza a blank look. But the pulse at her neck increased in tempo. Her breathing became more shallow. "I . . . I don't know anything about a package, or those drugs that the doctors said were in my system—I don't take them. I used to take Ativan, but I'd stopped."

Lozza showed her the photo of the bald man in a leather jacket with the tattoo on the side of his neck. "Do you know this man?"

Ellie peered closely at the photo. Sweat broke out on her brow. She swallowed. "I . . . I've never seen him. Who is he?"

Again, Lozza felt she might be lying.

"This man left the drug package for you at the Puggo. He has a hummingbird tattoo on the side of his neck, and he rides a dirt bike with Queensland plates."

Ellie looked frightened. She said nothing.

"Had you ever received packages from this man before?"

"I told you, I don't know who he is! Maybe Martin does."

"Martin is missing, Ellie," Lozza said.

Ellie raised a hand to wipe her mouth. She was shaking. She looked even more pale. Lozza felt the clock ticking. Any minute a doc or nurse was going to barge in and shut this questioning down.

"How do you think you got back from the boat, Ellie?" Gregg pressed again.

"I don't know!" She glowered at Gregg. "I *told* you. Do you have any idea how this feels—to have you guys telling me all this, to think I might have been raped or something, and have absolutely no recall? Do you know how *vulnerable* this makes me feel?"

"I'm sorry, Mrs. Cresswell-Smith," Lozza said firmly. "But your husband is missing and you've been in a coma. We need to ask you these things now. If Martin is still alive somewhere, his life could be in grave danger. Time is critical."

Ellie's gaze locked on Lozza's. Her jaw tightened and her eyes turned feverish beneath the bandage on her brow. "I hope you *don't* find him. And if you do, I hope he's dead and that he suffered."

Silence slammed into the room.

Lozza took in a deep, slow breath. She heard Gregg making notes in his notepad.

"Why do you say this, Ellie?"

"Because . . . I hate him."

She waited. Ellie offered nothing more.

"Do you hate him because you found out that he was having an affair? Or because you felt he married you for your money?"

Something in Ellie's eyes shuttered. Her hands fisted the sheets. "I need you to leave. Now," she said through clenched teeth. "I . . . I'm tired. I'm going to be sick. I—"

Quickly, before Ellie could reach for her buzzer and summon medical personnel, Lozza said, "Can we at least try and go back to the last point you *do* remember, Ellie? Do you recall meeting me on the beach? We swam together with my daughter."

"Yes," Ellie whispered. "I remember."

Lozza cleared her throat. "And then while we were in the water, you saw Martin up on the beach."

She nodded.

"You looked terrified."

"I . . . He wasn't supposed to be home. He'd been on a business trip to Sydney. I wasn't expecting him home for several days."

"And this frightened you?"

She looked puzzled, as if she really was trying to remember something.

"What happened after Maya and I left you and Martin in the dunes?"

"I . . . We . . ." She appeared confused again and trailed off.

"Take your time," Lozza said softly.

"I was afraid, but I don't remember why."

"Martin had brought an esky and wineglasses to the beach. You had a sundowner after I left, maybe?" Lozza said.

"Maybe."

"What did Martin bring to drink for this sundowner?" Gregg asked.

"White wine, I think."

Gregg made more notes. "How did you feel after the wine?" he asked.

"Um . . . buzzy, I suppose. I . . . I was very stressed. Perhaps . . . I had a bit more than I should have. To . . . to take the edge off."

"Why did you need to take the edge off?" Lozza asked. "Why did you feel so stressed that day?"

Ellie moistened her lips again and closed her eyes. Tears leaked out from under her lashes. Very quietly, her jaw tight, she said, "I. Can't. Recall. Things."

"Can you recall packing your suitcases?"

"Nothing. I can't remember . . . what happened before." Ellie suddenly lunged for the call button and pressed it to summon a nurse.

"Ellie, please, quickly, think, just one more time—do you have *any* idea where Martin might have gone?"

"No," she said, eyes still closed.

A nurse entered the room. She took one look at Ellie and said, "Okay, you guys need to leave. Now."

THEN

LOZZA

"She's lying," Gregg said to Lozza as she drove them to the Puggo to interview Rabz. "That retrograde-amnesia thing is suspiciously convenient."

"I agree—she's holding something back," Lozza said, turning into the street that led to the pub. She pulled into a parking space right outside the Puggo and switched off the engine. Gregg unbuckled his seat belt.

"Even if some of her memory does return," he said, "how do we know if she's going to share anything she's recalled? And we have no way of knowing for certain just how far back—or how selective—this 'retrograde' thing is, either." He got out of the vehicle. Lozza followed suit and slammed her door shut.

"Plus, there's the weird shit with the Corolla you said you heard bolting from their house."

"Yeah." Lozza glanced up at the CCTV camera as they passed under it.

And the bikie with the drug package, and the Queensland plates.

Rabz sat behind her desk in her office and twisted the strings of her apron. Her complexion was bloodless, her eyes puffy. Lozza and Gregg sat facing her on the other side of her desk.

"Yes," she said, "I've been seeing Martin."

"How long?" Lozza asked.

"Is this relevant? I understand you need whatever help you can get to find him, but—"

Lozz leaned forward. "The more comprehensive a profile of a missing person is, the more we can know about his or her state of mind, motivation, recent movements—it gives us more tools with which to find the person."

"Lozz is right," Gregg said. "If Martin has had an accident out at sea, or if he washed up somewhere, a good profile—knowing his state of mind—will give us ideas of how he might react, where he might go, what he might do."

Rabz looked down at her hands. "We've been seeing each other for a while."

"How long is 'a while'?" asked Lozza, watching Rabz's eyes carefully.

The woman's face reddened. "Before his wife arrived here."

Lozza said, "His wife's name is Ellie."

Rabz swallowed, nodded. "Before Ellie arrived in Jarrawarra."

"How long before Ellie moved to Jarra?" Gregg asked.

Silence.

"Rabz?"

A tear slid down the side of her face. She quickly swiped it away. "Since October last year. We met when Martin first came to look for land up at Agnes."

Lozza frowned, recalling Willow's words about the Vegas wedding. "I thought the Cresswell-Smiths were more recently married? Like in May this year."

Rabz hesitated, shot a nervous glance at the door as if desperate to escape, then said, "Martin and I started seeing each other before he even met Ellie. He met her in early January this year. In Vancouver."

Lozza exchanged a quick glance with Gregg. Her pulse quickened.

"Just to get this clear," she said, "you and Martin were dating *before* Martin met Ellie? And then you and Martin continued seeing each other long distance throughout their courtship and marriage? Then after they moved here, you and Martin continued the affair?"

She nodded.

A dark, inky thought that dovetailed with Willow's comments bled into Lozza's brain. "Did Martin marry Ellie for her money, Rabz? Is that what this is about? He loves you, but she's bankrolling your lives?"

"It's not like that."

"What's it like, then?" asked Gregg.

"Why don't you guys bloody well find him and then you can ask him yourself!"

Lozza and Gregg said nothing. They waited.

Rabz pushed a tangle of hair back from her face and said, "I'm sorry. I'm just wired—I'm so scared he's dead or something and I . . . I've had no one I could talk to, or share my worry with. We were in Sydney together and then he got a sudden call from her. She informed him that it was urgent that he come home right away. He flew back early."

"By 'her' you mean Ellie, his wife?" Lozza asked.

"Yes," Rabz snapped. "Ellie. He said he was going to leave her. We'd bought tickets to . . . we were going to go away together. Live abroad, travel the world. I don't know what was so important that he had to rush back for."

Quietly, Lozza said, "Here's the thing I'm not understanding. You and Martin start an affair around the time he develops an interest in a big expensive development in New South Wales. You're single, he's single—why not just make it official?"

She looked down, said nothing.

"And then he meets Ellie, who we've learned is some Canadian heiress—her father is one of the wealthiest men in the country. And Martin marries her very quickly, supposedly on a trip to Las Vegas, while you two carry on your secret affair. He and his rich wife form a partnership with funds from her daddy, and Martin Cresswell-Smith is suddenly flush with funds to proceed with the development. Yet he's planning to leave her and run away with you?" Lozza paused.

Gregg watched Rabz closely. "Looks to me like he's a gold digger, Rabz, and you knew it."

"He's wealthy in his own right," Rabz countered. "He'd made a mistake with Ellie, that's all. A terrible mistake. He'd realized it after she'd moved here. She was not what he thought she was. He was winding things up and selling his half of Agnes Holdings, and he was going to leave her before she freaked out and tried to harm him or something. She'd get high on drugs and hurl things at him. She stabbed him on the boat—a whole lot of people witnessed what she was like that day. Martin said he saw something truly frightening in Ellie that day. She tried to strike him with a cast-iron frying pan later. I . . . And now, with you guys here, with no sight of him, yet she returned from the fishing outing? I'm worried *she* might have done something to him. He'd never have taken her out fishing again. I know he wouldn't have. It made no sense that they went out in the boat again. Just after she called him home urgently. She must have lured or coerced him to do it or something."

Lozza thought of what Willow had said—that she too felt it unlikely her friend Ellie would go out in the boat with Martin again. Things were not adding up here.

"You mentioned you and Martin had bought plane tickets?"

"We were going to fly to the Cape Verde islands in just over two weeks. Martin had rented us a house there for a year."

"And you believe he was winding up his company—this big development project?" Gregg said.

"Well, he said he was off-loading his share of it, and leaving Ellie to handle the rest or sell or whatever."

"Did Ellie know that her husband was getting on a plane and vanishing in two weeks?" Lozza asked, testing Rabz.

Rabz looked embarrassed. "No . . . I . . . I don't think so. Why would she?"

"Are you aware that Ellie had hired a PI to follow you and her husband, and that she apparently has compromising photographs of you and Martin?"

Sweat beaded across Rabz's lip. She wiped it away with a trembling hand. "No," she whispered.

Lozza placed the CCTV photo of the bald man on Rabz's desk and pushed it toward her.

"Do you recognize this man, Rabz?"

She studied the photo. "No. Why?"

"This man came into the Puggo with a parcel for Ellie while you were away. He left the parcel here for her to pick up. Had he come in before?"

"I . . . I've never seen him. I'd recognize someone like that." She glanced up. "What's he got to do with this?"

"Maybe nothing," Lozza said. Her mobile buzzed. She ignored it and watched Rabz's face closely as she studied the photo again. Gregg's phone then buzzed. Gregg checked the caller ID and motioned to Lozza he was stepping out to take the call. She nodded.

"There is something else," Rabz said quietly as Gregg departed. "It might be important . . . given everything that has happened." She wavered, wiped her mouth again, then said, "The night before they were seen going out in the Quinnie, Martin called me from his house. He said there'd been a sudden change of plans. He could no longer meet me in Sydney to fly to the Cape Verde islands. He asked if I could join him at a hotel in Kuala Lumpur instead. He said he'd be leaving for KL

287

early and he'd wait for me there—send details. And we'd head to Cape Verde from KL."

Lozza frowned. "You think he might have bolted to KL?"

"He hasn't answered his cell. He said he'd text me the hotel details and he never did."

"Did he say why he was changing plans suddenly?"

"No. All he said was something had come up and he needed to take care of it. Then he hung up. Next morning he goes out in a boat with Ellie and never comes back."

Lozza considered Rabz in silence.

"Ellie is not what meets the eye, Lozz," Rabz said. "She might come across all demure and gentle and introverted, but that kind of woman can be the most dangerous when betrayed or wronged, because you least expect it. They can be deadly. Did you know that she stabbed her ex-husband when she caught him having dinner at a restaurant with his mistress? Do you know the police in Hawaii thought she'd drowned her three-year-old daughter in the sea at Waimea Bay?"

Surprise quickened through Lozza. "Her daughter drowned?"

"Ellie took her out into waves that were too big."

Suddenly Ellie's odd behavior in the sea took on new meaning. She held Rabz's gaze, saying nothing, waiting for Rabz to fill the silence again.

"If Ellie knew about our affair . . . I think she could have done something terrible to him."

"Lozza?" Gregg reappeared in the doorway, an intense look on his face. "I need to speak to you. Now."

Lozza stepped outside the office.

Gregg kept his voice low. "They found a body. Up at Agnes. Could be him."

THEN

LOZZA

Thunder clapped above them and Lozza winced. The sound grumbled over the mangrove swamp and rolled toward the sea. The storm had muscled in while she and Gregg had gone up the Agnes River with skipper Mac McGonigle and Barney guiding them to the gruesome find tangled into the lines of Barney's illegal crab pots.

It was dark now and pouring. And she was pretty sure it was Martin Cresswell-Smith they'd found floating in the little cove without his pants on. The body type and hair were a match. She'd recognized his ring from when she'd swum with Ellie.

Lozza had taken photographs. Gregg had cordoned off the immediate area around the floater in the small cove. They were now waiting for a forensic team, a coroner, and a detective from the murder squad, but the storm was holding them up.

Thunder cracked again and rain redoubled in force and volume. The drops struck the black water in the channel with such force they sent up a stream of backsplashes that looked like a shimmering waterfall under the glare of the boat spotlights and intermittent flashes of lightning. There was only room for two under the boat's targa cover, so she and Gregg sat out in the rain. Water dripped steadily off the bill of her cap. It ran down the back of her neck. Her hair was sodden. She wiped her face and checked her watch. Just over two since she'd called in the floater.

Gregg's gaze followed her movement. "That gaff in his chest—that's like a statement."

She nodded, thinking of Maya. Hoping she was finishing her homework. "Yeah. Personal. Overkill in those puncture wounds."

"And the missing fingers? Nothing makes sense," Gregg said. He sat silent for another fifteen minutes, and Lozza said a personal thanks for that. He'd been jabbering nervously since she'd returned to the boat from the abandoned house where she'd seen the pieces of severed finger, ropes, feces, windbreaker from Canada, and pale-blue Nike ball cap.

Lightning flared. Everything turned white silver. The image of the floater shot vividly back into her mind.

White skin against black water, the empty eye sockets, the nose-less face, the open, lipless mouth. Her brain circled back to the words they'd heard from Rabz shortly before they got this call.

"Ellie is not what meets the eye . . . That kind of woman can be the most dangerous when betrayed or wronged, because you least expect it. They can be deadly. Did you know that she stabbed her ex-husband when she caught him having dinner at a restaurant with his mistress?"

Lozza wasn't sure Ellie Cresswell-Smith could be capable of this. Did she have an accomplice? Had Ellie had a window of opportunity between when witnesses had last seen her and her husband—the victim—heading out in their Quinnie, and when Lozza had found her on the bathroom floor?

As the questions circled around and around in Lozza's brain, another half hour ticked down. The rain stopped. They heard the sound of a helicopter behind the clouds.

"It's them," said Mac.

She checked her watch again. A total of two hours and twenty-three minutes. She got up. The boat rocked. Soon they heard the sound of an engine coming up the channel. Bright spotlights winked in and out of view behind the tangle of mangrove trees. The radio crackled. Mac responded, guiding the arriving launch into their mooring along the jetty.

Lozza shielded her eyes against the blinding glare of the spotlights as the boat approached in the darkness. She could make out several silhouettes, glimpses of white—crime scene techs had already suited up and were ready to go. The boat moored on the opposite side of the jetty. Lozza climbed out and stood on the dock. Waves slapped and splashed against the pilings.

A man, a black silhouette against the row of spotlights atop the bar of the newly arrived police boat, climbed out. He approached her.

Something in the vestigial caves of Lozza's subconscious began to stir as the man neared. Something about his movements. Before her brain could interpret the recognition in her body, light fell on his face.

Lozza's heart stalled. She swallowed. Then swore viciously to herself.

"Lozz," he said.

"Corneil." Of all the murder cops from HQ, they had to send this one. Her nemesis. The one detective who'd lobbied hard to have her stripped of her badge after the "incident." A man who'd been married when she'd had an affair with him. A man she now hated with hot passion.

"Didn't expect to see you," he said quietly.

His voice was the same. Flat. Toneless. Like his face. Like his eyes. Unreadable. Expressionless. The homicide detective rarely showed emotion—just those watchful eyes. God knew what she'd ever seen in him. She'd thought she'd needed sex. But mostly Lozza had just needed to be held. It had started in the bathroom stall of a pub on a very drunken night exactly one year to the day after Lozza's husband's death. Her husband had been a firefighter, and she'd loved him more than the entire world. They'd been talking of kids. They'd had plans for the future. Then in the blink of an eye he was gone. Killed by a drunk driver.

Then came Corneil.

After Corneil came many rough cases, too many drunken nights, then ultimately a call where Lozza had snapped. A call where a brute had beaten his wife to death in spite of a restraining order she'd had on him. And it had happened while their little girl, just a toddler, had been hiding terrified under their bed.

A little girl who'd seen it all.

A little girl named Maya who'd been effectively orphaned by the incident.

A child who had forced Lozza to look hard into the mirror, to clean up. To question everything about life. And once she'd cleaned up, once she'd requested a transfer, once she'd been offered a position in Jarrawarra with the help of some compassionate superiors—*in spite* of Corneil's campaign against her—she'd applied to adopt Maya.

Corneil's battle against Lozza had been pure personal vendetta. Ugliness. He'd needed to kick back at her—at anyone—because his wife, on learning about their affair, had walked out on him. Corneil's wife had gotten custody of their three kids. He'd gotten nothing. He'd coped by blaming Lozza, and it had become like a sickness in him. And then he'd used the "incident" of her violence like a weapon with which to beat her down.

He hadn't succeeded.

She was here.

She had Maya.

She had her new normal.

Now he was fucking standing in it, in her face.

She lifted her chin and squared her shoulders.

"Are we going to be good?" he said quietly.

"Water under the bridge. Sir." She emphasized the last word.

"Since you're being seconded to this case, and since you'll be resuming criminal investigative duties, your detective designation will be reinstated. Temporarily," Corneil said.

It wasn't a rank. Lozza had never lost her detective designation while performing general duties. She just wasn't referred to as *Detective*.

"Right," she said. Corneil clearly hadn't let all the water flow under the bridge. He'd dammed up a little toxic reservoir of it.

Gregg approached.

"Gregg," she said, "this is Detective Senior Constable Corneil Tremayne from homicide."

"Detective *Sergeant* Tremayne," he corrected, proffering his hand to Gregg.

Resentment bit into Lozza. While she'd been pushed down the cop ladder into general duties and a remote backwater, Corneil had climbed up on the coveted city-based squad and become a sergeant. And now he was Lozza's boss on this case. On her turf.

I took this demotion for Maya. This is about me and Maya now, our new normals. Do not get sucked back into his aura and head games. I do not want what he has . . . or do I?

Gregg glanced at Lozza—he could clearly sense the tension. "Constable Abbott," he said, shaking Corneil's hand.

"Where's the body?" Corneil asked.

"This way, sir," said Gregg, leading the way, whereas last time it was Lozza who'd had to bushwhack in for Gregg before he'd gone and fallen in, then puked all over the place.

She held back a moment and watched the two men ahead of her. Already Gregg was sucking up to the new man on scene.

THEN

LOZZA

Over one year ago, November 19. Jarrawarra Bay police station, New South Wales.

Lozza entered the briefing room clutching an armful of files and a triple-shot mug of coffee. It was midmorning and she'd gotten maybe an hour's sleep, if that. She and Gregg and Corneil had stayed at the Agnes crime scene until almost dawn.

The mood in the room was somber yet crackling with electric anticipation.

Corneil had taken up position in front of a board on the wall. A monitor had been wheeled in. On a table in front of him was a laptop. Gregg had gone and seated himself right in front of Corneil—like an eager teacher's pet. Jon Ratcliffe sat at a desk in the corner. He was here mostly to observe. This was happening on his watch, his turf, with the assistance of his officers, but the investigation itself was being run out of State Crime Command.

"Thank you for joining us, Senior Constable," Corneil said as Lozza entered.

She nodded and kept her mouth shut. She found a seat at a desk beneath the window, set down her files, and took a giant swig of caffeine.

Also present in the room was a female officer in plain clothes whom Lozza did not recognize, plus Constable "Henge" Markham, who was tall and skinny and a whip-fit hydrofoil surfer and Constable "Jimmo" Duff, who had a Kevin Costner face and a way with the ladies that made up for his squat stature. The Jarrawarra-based team was small, but it was supported by the full resources of State Crime Command, including the state forensics services unit, additional murder squad detectives out of HQ, and technical support from the fraud and cybercrime units. Corneil could ramp up or down at any given point plus call on additional specialized units for assistance.

Corneil scrawled along the top of the crime scene board: **STRIKE FORCE ABRA**, the name he was giving to this homicide investigation.

He tapped his black marker pen against the palm of his hand and faced the group.

"Okay, good morning. I'd like you all to welcome Detective Constable Sybil Grant from Crime Command."

Sybil—the cop in plain clothes—nodded unsmilingly. She had a tan face. Clean look. Dark-blonde hair pulled back into a tight ponytail. She carried an aura of experience.

"This will be brief. Things are still evolving, and right now, time is of the essence. Ellie Cresswell-Smith has identified the ring we found on the deceased as being her husband's. Mrs. Cresswell-Smith has also positively identified the body from one of the kinder photographs that DC Grant showed her this morning, just before she was discharged from the hospital. The autopsy is in progress. It will likely provide positive DNA identification, but we are presently working on the assumption that the body found floating in the Agnes Bay channel belongs to Martin Cresswell-Smith."

"Where's Ellie now?" asked Lozza. "You mentioned she's been discharged."

"DC Grant brought her back here, to the station. She's being held and is awaiting questioning. We also have officers at her home executing a search warrant. While the house is not the murder scene, we have a warrant to seize Martin Cresswell-Smith's computers and any other communication devices we might find in order to further our investigation."

Corneil quickly ran through the facts to date, including how the Cresswell-Smiths were seen going out in the boat, but only Ellie seemed to have returned.

"Latent and patent prints from the abandoned farmhouse are being processed," said Corneil. "Same with the biological and other evidence. The boat is still missing. There's no sign of the Rolex Daytona that Mrs. Cresswell-Smith said her husband always wore. We're also looking for the male with the tattoo that left a package of contraband at the Pug and Whistler addressed to Mrs. Cresswell-Smith. At this point she is our key person of interest, but we're working from the possibility she has an accomplice."

Gregg said, "That was not a calm, organized killing. There's overkill in all that stabbing. And the gaff left in the chest? Like some kind of statement."

Lozza rolled her eyes internally. The rookie was posturing in front of the big shot from HQ. It kind of made her sick, but she had to confess she'd been there. They'd all been probies once. They'd all sought to jockey and impress.

"It's possible it started out controlled," Sybil—DC Grant—said. "But then it could have devolved into uncontrolled passion." She pointed to an image of the pruning shears up on the screen. "Cutting off fingers—that smacks of torture. Of someone seeking information. As do the ropes and the chair found in the abandoned homestead."

"The guy was scared," added Jimmo. "He shat and peed his pants."

"Maybe he didn't give up what his assailant wanted," said Lozza. "Maybe Martin Cresswell-Smith refused, his captor was enraged, and snapped."

Corneil held her gaze. She cursed to herself. She could *feel* in his gaze that he was reminding her that she, too, could have—had—snapped. Become enraged, violent.

"So my question," Gregg said, "is why try to dispose of him underwater like that? If someone was trying to hide the body, why did they leave the ropes and pruning shears, and all the other evidence, in plain sight inside the house?"

"Because maybe something went wrong?" offered Henge. "Like, there was a plan, and it changed on the fly. In a rush. Maybe the suspect or suspects were disturbed and fled in a hurry."

"Any idea of time of death, or how long the body was in water, yet?" Sybil asked.

Corneil said, "Preliminary estimate from the pathologist is that he was killed sometime late on November seventeen. He was in water maybe twenty-four hours. Those muddies work fast."

Lozza knew this to be true. You could leave massive fish heads in a crab pot late at night, and come early morning the bait would be all but gone.

Corneil continued. "So between five forty a.m. November seventeen—the time the Cresswell-Smiths were seen going out in the *Abracadabra*—and seven forty p.m., when the neighbor saw Mrs. Creswell-Smith stumbling home, she conceivably had a window of opportunity, if the pathologist's preliminary estimate holds up."

"She could also have taken the drugs and purposefully passed out, sort of as an alibi," suggested Gregg. "The alleged memory loss could be a convenient tool. Except things went wrong and she fell and hit her head."

"Or," said Henge, "she could have used the overdose simply to misdirect suspicion from herself while also working with a coconspirator. Because a woman like that—heiress with tons of money all her life—people like her hire others to do dirty work."

"Maybe the bikie," suggested Gregg.

Lozza juggled the various puzzle pieces in her head but did not offer too much input. She preferred at this point to stay out of Corneil's crosshairs. Jon had obviously already told Corneil about Lozza delivering the drugs. If he had a chance, he'd use that against her.

"Okay," said Corneil. "Assignments. DC Grant, you're on victimology. We need everything we can find on Martin Cresswell-Smith—who he was, what he did, where he comes from, who his friends and family are, what his beliefs are, who his enemies are, what he was doing before he came to Australia, any criminal record anywhere."

"On it, sir," said Sybil.

"Constables Markham, Duff, the greenies are yours. Bring the ringleaders in. Constables Bianchi, Abbott, since you both already have history with the wife, I want you two to handle the initial interview with Ellie Cresswell-Smith."

It did not escape Lozza's attention that Corneil had not referred to her as a senior constable. The guy was a jerk.

"When DC Grant brought Mrs. Cresswell-Smith into the station from the hospital this morning," Corneil continued, "she learned that Mrs. Cresswell-Smith had booked a flight out of Moruya Airport that left yesterday. She missed it because she was in hospital. Mrs. Cresswell-Smith made clear to DC Grant that she intends to purchase another plane ticket and return to Canada as soon as she can. So find something we can use to keep her in the country. She's our number one. I don't want to lose access to her." He paused. "Any questions?"

No one responded.

"Right, let's get to it," Corneil said. "We've got photos of Martin Cresswell-Smith's missing bronze Rolex Daytona out with Crime Stoppers and the media. It's worth seventy thousand dollars, give or take. If anyone tries to hawk it, I want to know. We've also got the rego and hull identification number of the *Abracadabra* out there, plus photos of a similar Quinnie model. If anyone tries to sell a boat with that HIN number, I want to know about it. Plus, we've got a BOLO on this man—" He tapped his Sharpie on an image on the board of the bald bikie with ink on his neck. "Who is he? How is he connected to Ellie Cresswell-Smith? How are they both connected to the black-market prescription drugs? Why was that package left so openly at the Puggo with Ellie's name on it?" He met the eyes of each officer in the room. "We meet back here at the end of the day to debrief. The clock is ticking. Get me something."

THEN

LOZZA

"Thank you for coming in," Lozza said as she seated herself at the table opposite Ellie. Gregg took the chair to Lozza's left. "How are you feeling?"

The woman looked weak. Thinner. Very pale. Dark circles under her eyes. She still had a bandage on her brow. Lozza wondered if they were doing the right thing, bringing her in like this right out of the hospital.

Ellie's gaze met Lozza's for a brief moment, then twitched up to the camera near the ceiling. Clearly she was aware they were being observed. So was Lozza. She could feel Corneil's eyes on them.

"I don't remember anything more, if that's what you mean," Ellie said. "And I didn't come in. I was brought in."

Defensive.

Lozza nodded to Gregg. He pressed the "Record" button.

"Interview with Ellie Cresswell-Smith, November nineteen, 11:02 a.m., conducted at Jarrawarra Bay by Senior Constable Laurel Bianchi with Constable Gregg Abbott present." She gave their ID numbers.

"I'm very sorry about your husband, Ellie," Lozza said quietly. "I understand you've made a positive ID based on photographs."

She nodded.

"Could you speak out your answers for the recording, please," she said.

"Yes," said Ellie with a flash of her eyes to the camera again.

"We're still awaiting a positive DNA—"

"It's him. I know it's him."

Lozza held her gaze. "You're very certain."

Ellie swallowed. Her nose pinked. "I could tell from those photos. I don't have any doubt."

Lozza nodded. "Okay, and you do understand that we need to ask you some questions as we conduct our investigation into what happened to your husband?"

"Yes."

"Do you have any idea what might have occurred?" she asked.

"I already told you everything I know at the hospital. I didn't go out in the boat with him."

"But we have multiple witnesses who saw you going out, Ellie. Including Constable Abbott here. He saw you through a telescope."

Her eyes ticked to Gregg.

A muscle on Gregg's jaw pulsed.

"Let's start with your memory of your husband's premature return from Sydney, shall we? What brought him home early?"

"I don't know. I don't recall if he told me."

"Did you perhaps phone him, tell him to come home?"

"Why would I? I was packed and ready to leave. I had a plane ticket. I wanted to be gone before he returned."

"So you remember that now?"

She looked nervous for a moment. "I . . . guess I do. Bits must be coming back."

"Why did you want to be gone?"

"He was having an affair. I'd gotten proof. I didn't want to confront him because he could be violent. I'd also come to realize he was a con artist. He'd stolen everything I'd brought to the marriage. I . . ." Her voice faded and she stopped speaking. Two hot spots had formed high on her cheekbones.

"What was he doing in Sydney?" Lozza asked.

"Screwing his mistress and getting ready to flee the country with my money—hell knows. I plan to deal with the legal ramifications from home."

Lozza's gaze held hers. "His mistress being—"

"Oh, please, don't patronize me. You people are searching my home as we speak. You probably already found the photos of my husband and Rabz that were in my studio. I'm sure you've already questioned her and everyone else who knows me and Martin, plus everyone who saw the boat going out, plus my neighbor. What else do you want from me? Am . . . I'm not a *suspect* here, am I?"

"We need to cover some bases, Ellie." Lozza opened her file folder and extracted a few photos taken at the murder scene. "Do you recognize these?" She pushed toward Ellie the images of the blue windbreaker and the ball cap stained with blood.

"Yes. They're mine. That's blood on them."

"Blood?"

"Martin's, mostly. And probably some of mine. From when I stabbed him."

Lozza blinked. "You're admitting you stabbed your husband?"

"When we went out on the *Abracadabra*, right after I landed in Jarrawarra, I had an accident with the knife and cut Martin. I was wearing that jacket and cap. I left them in the garage. Ask anyone who was at the boat launch that day. Martin had gotten a foul hook in his neck, and . . . we both had blood on us. Witnesses on the cliff saw us coming in. Martin went to the hospital, so the doctors know about it, too. You'll probably find my fingerprints on the fishing knife and gaff, too, because I picked them up with my bloodied hands that day."

"How do you know about the gaff?"

"It was in one of the photos Detective Constable Sybil Grant showed me in order to identify the body."

Lozza leaned forward. "Ellie, how did your jacket and cap end up in the derelict farmhouse at Agnes?"

"I don't know."

"You were wearing these items when you were seen going out with Martin on the *Abracadabra* on November seventeen."

"I . . . I didn't go out with him again. I wouldn't have."

"I told you—you were seen by several witnesses, including Constable Abbott."

"Well, then, I can't remember it. And I really can't understand why I would have gone out with him again. I hated the boat. The first incident terrified me. Martin *wanted* it to terrify me. He won."

Lozza said slowly, "So how do you *think* your jacket and cap with Martin's and your blood got to the abandoned house in the mangroves at Agnes Basin where Martin was killed?"

"I have no idea."

Gregg said, "Had you ever been to that abandoned farmhouse, Ellie?"

Her gaze ticked nervously to Gregg. "I don't know. Maybe."

"Maybe?" asked Lozza.

She inhaled deeply. "The day I arrived in Jarrawarra, Martin drove me up to Agnes and took me into Agnes Basin and into that channel on the *Abracadabra*. We had lunch and I . . . I passed out in the boat. In retrospect I think he might have spiked my wine or my water, and maybe even the cider he gave me right after I landed, because I kept on having these episodes. I think he was gaslighting me—trying to make me go mad, or feel like I was going mad, so it would look normal if I overdosed on drugs or something. Then he'd cash in on the insurance he took out on me, plus he'd own everything I'd invested in Agnes Holdings."

Lozza clicked the back of her pen in and out. "Okay, let's go back to that day Martin took you down the channel. Did you moor the boat somewhere?"

"Next to a dock. There was a path from the dock to an abandoned house. He told me that. We had lunch in the boat, and I passed out, then woke up in the bottom of the boat when it was getting dark. He was furious and he had protest banners which he said he'd found in the old house. He said the 'greenies' had been on our private property." She glanced at the camera again. Lozza had a sense Ellie was playing to it. Perhaps she was playing all of them. Rabz's words sifted into her mind.

"That kind of woman can be the most dangerous when betrayed or wronged, because you least expect it. They can be deadly."

"Up until that point I'd never seen Martin so furious. He said if he got his hands on those greenies, he'd . . ." Ellie paled as she appeared to recall something. She cleared her throat. "He said he'd cut 'those fuckers' with a knife, stick his gaff in them, and feed them to the muddies."

Gregg and Lozza stared at her. The air in the room grew thick. An invisible energy crackled around them. Very quietly, Lozza said, "You remember this, yet you can't recall if you might have gone along that trail and into the old farmhouse with Martin?"

Ellie swallowed. "I not only passed out, I blacked out, Detective. With my blackouts I can be doing things, but I don't know what I did. I have no recall because the events that occurred during a blackout-drunk period are not encoded into memories in my brain. My doctor told me this once. I blacked out on the boat, then I woke up on the bottom. That's all I know. And that's when Martin said those things. It shocked me . . . to think that the man I'd married had turned so mean. I'd not until that point in our relationship witnessed this very, very ugly side to Martin. He was one man back home in Canada, and another man entirely in Australia. It was like he'd hooked me, and he no longer had to pretend."

"Your doctor told you this about the blackouts?" Gregg asked.

"My therapist."

"Why were you seeing a therapist?" Lozza asked.

"I could tell you that's personal, and privileged. I could also tell you it was because my daughter drowned when she was three years old, and I couldn't bear the grief. It was killing me, and I was coping in all the wrong ways." Her mouth tightened and her eyes turned shiny. "Look, I know you're going to go digging up my entire life and you're going to find out all the horrible things about me that are going to continue dogging me for the rest of my life, like how I was institutionalized for a while. So there you have it. Grief, loss, can all but kill you. It can drive you mad. But I did not kill my husband, Detectives, and I'd like to leave now."

Lozza regarded Ellie for a moment, thinking of something else Rabz had said.

"Do you know the police in Hawaii thought she'd drowned her three-year-old daughter in the sea at Waimea Bay? Ellie took her out into waves that were too big."

"Ellie." Lozza leaned forward. "Can we go back to the clothes you said you were wearing when you first went out on the *Abracadabra*—the clothes that had your blood and Martin's blood on them. You said you left them in your garage?"

She shifted in her chair and wiped her nose. "Yes."

"And you don't know how that jacket and cap ended up at Agnes Basin?"

"No. I left them in the garage with the cargo pants and shoes."

Lozza made a mental note to check for the shoes and pants.

"And I don't know what happened to them or how they got to Agnes."

Lozza rubbed her chin. "So the blood on the—"

"It's mine. And Martin's. I *told* you." The hot spots on her cheeks deepened. The atmosphere in the room was getting closer, warmer. Edgier.

Lozza said, "So there is a chance that you visited the abandoned house shortly after your arrival in Jarrawarra—you just don't remember it?"

"Yes, that's right. I might have. I don't know. I can't recall either way, but it's possible."

Lozza cursed to herself. Ellie had just driven a bus through any potential case to be made against her so far. If she'd been at the murder scene—inside that old house—she could claim that any DNA or fingerprints or hair or fiber evidence found at the scene might have come from an earlier time. Or from the earlier boating incident with the knife. She had a defense.

Lozza pushed two more photos toward her—the fishing knife and gaff marked with the boat's name.

"Do you recognize these?"

Ellie drew them closer. "Yes, that's the knife I used to cut Martin free of the fishing line when he got foul-hooked. And that's the gaff I handed to him."

"So you definitely touched this knife and gaff."

"Yes, I told you. While I was cutting the line from Martin's rod, the boat tilted and I slipped and cut his arm, plus the back of my hand."

"How about this—do you recognize this?" Lozza showed Ellie another crime scene photo.

"That looks like the rope from the *Abracadabra*. It's the same colors as the bowline Martin made me hold on the day we went out. It burned my hands."

Lozza inhaled deeply. This meant any DNA that showed up on the ropes from the crime scene that was a match to Ellie could also be argued to have come from earlier incidents. Crown prosecutors would not be happy. Lozza eyed her, and the sinister sensation of being played intensified. Was this woman a deception artist herself? Like she claimed her husband was? Could it be wildly possible she'd used that first day out on the boat to set up a scenario that would later undermine any police evidence found in a crime? Lozza was getting a feeling that maybe this was less an interview with Ellie Cresswell-Smith than it was Ellie laying out a future defense on the record. An inkier thought struck Lozza—could Ellie have set out to swim with her and Maya in the sea that day? Could she have wanted for some reason for Lozza to see her bruises and meet her husband and sympathize? Could that have been part of some ploy, too?

Lozza showed Ellie the photo of the bald man with the neck tat again. Once more Ellie denied knowing anything about him or any package with drugs.

"I'd like to leave now," she said.

"Just a few more questions," Lozza said. "Who was the PI you hired to take photos of your husband and Bodie Rabinovitch?"

"Look, I'm really tired. I'm not feeling well. I'd like to go and buy a plane ticket and go home." She started to push her chair back.

"Please stay seated, Ellie."

"You can't force me, Lozza. I know my rights. If you want to hold me, if you want to ask any more questions, you're going to have to arrest me and go through my lawyers. I've been as cooperative as I can, and I'm in a very bad place with the mess Martin has left me. I need to go home to Canada and to meet with my legal team there."

Lozza sucked in a deep, long breath of air, assessing her. "Fine."

"Fine what?"

"Fine. Go."

Ellie hesitated, then got up and went to the door. She reached for the handle, paused, turned back to face Lozza and Gregg. She wavered, then said, "There was a car following us. I noticed it soon after I arrived in Jarrawarra."

Lozza and Gregg exchanged a glance. "What kind of car?" Lozza asked.

"A brown Toyota Corolla," Ellie said. "It has a dent in the back and a Queensland plate. I remember the last three letters of the plate because they spell GIN, like the drink."

Lozza's heart sped up. "You certain it was a Queensland rego?"

"Yes. I even pointed the car out to Martin. He looked really worried when he saw it."

"Did he know who was in the car?"

"No. He suggested it was a common model and color, and said it was probably different cars I was seeing. But I could tell he was worried about it." She then stepped out the door and left.

On impulse Lozza followed her out into the street.

"Ellie?" she called out.

The woman turned. Sunlight caught the shine in her dark waist-length hair.

Lozza went up to her and handed Ellie her card. Quietly she said, "If any more memory returns, please call me. Nothing is too small or too insignificant."

Ellie eyed her. The memory of their time in the waves shimmered between them. Seemingly unsure, Ellie glanced again at the card.

"I can see you're scared, Ellie. I know Martin hurt you. I understand the confusion and shame around substance abuse."

Ellie's big blue eyes watered, and Lozza felt she was going to say something. But she stopped. This woman was either very, very alone or very smart and dangerous. Lozza wanted to give her an opening to reach out. In whatever way. Good-cop/bad-cop–style—and right now she was playing good cop.

"If you do see that Corolla again, let me know. Okay?"

Ellie nodded, turned, and walked down the road.

Lozza watched until Ellie disappeared around the corner at the end of the street.

She turned to go back into the station but stalled. She looked up. Corneil stood in the window. Watching.

THEN

ELLIE

I entered our house followed by Willow, who'd brought me home from the travel agency where I'd purchased another ticket home. I'd called Willow from there. After being grilled by the police and still feeling so weak, I'd suddenly felt so alone, scared. I needed her company. My flight left in two days. I had to cope until then. The cops had told me I could return to my house—it was not a crime scene. They'd photographed everything, and they'd taken Martin's computers and the files and papers from his cabinet. His office was a mess, drawers still open, things scattered all over the floor.

I stopped and stared, my heart beating fast.

The lock on his office door had been broken. I felt bile rise up the back of my throat. At least I'd made copies of everything. I walked slowly, dazedly, into the living room and sat down.

"Can I get you something to drink, eat?" asked Willow as she set her purse on the kitchen counter near where Martin had raped me. Concern creased her brow.

"Water, thanks."

She brought me a glass. I sipped with a shaky hand, odd and indistinct, disjointed memories slicing through my brain.

"I can stay awhile," Willow said. "I can stay overnight—stay until you leave, if you like?"

I stilled as I saw the blank space on the wall.

"The clock."

"What?"

"They took the clock." I set my glass down and came to my feet, my heart racing. I made for the sliding glass door.

"Ellie? Where are you going?"

I yanked open the door and marched over the lawn toward my studio. Willow hurried after me.

I entered the studio and stilled.

The clock was gone from here, too. I spun to face her.

"Why would the police take the wall clocks?"

"I . . . I have no idea."

"There was a clock there." I pointed. "It was exactly the same design as the clock in the living room. Both gone."

Willow stared at me like I was going mad.

My mouth turned dry. I scanned the rest of the room, and froze. They'd also taken the framed photo of me and Dana. The one that was shot the night I met Martin.

I exited the studio and strode back up the lawn, sweat breaking out on my skin.

Willow hurried after me. "Ellie! Just calm down. And then when—"

I whirled to face her. "*Calm down?* My husband has been brutally murdered and I seem to be a suspect. And I can't recall anything. Why should I calm down, Willow, why?"

"I'm just saying—"

"I need you to leave. Please. Thank you for fetching me, for all your help. I truly appreciate it. But I need to be alone now."

She wavered, unsure. "Okay . . . okay." She went to retrieve her purse, hesitated. "If you need me, I'm just a call away, all right?"

I nodded, shaking inside, feeling suddenly overwhelmed.

Willow went to the door. I waited until she was gone, then retrieved Lozza's card. It displayed her work phone number and a mobile number. I dialed her mobile.

It rang once.

"Bianchi."

"It's Ellie. Why did you guys take my clocks and that framed photograph from my studio?"

Lozza told me to hold while she checked. I paced up and down, up and down, horrible shards of memories slicing into me. Martin grabbing my hair. Kicking me. Striking me . . .

"Ellie?"

I tensed. "I'm here."

"Our logs indicate no clocks or framed photos were taken from your house. The warrant covered only computer equipment, files, communications devices."

I hung up and stared at the wall where the clock had been, blood thudding in my ears.

THEN

LOZZA

Over one year ago, November 20. Jarrawarra Bay, New South Wales.

Lozza tossed and turned in her bed. She'd thrown her windows open wide, and outside, the sea heaved and sighed under the moon. She rented a house on the beach on the less tony side of the Bonny River. It was run-down, made of weatherboard, had peeling paint, and was freezing in the winter. But it had a suite for her mother, and having her mom come live with her in Jarrawarra had been a big part of the reason Lozza had been cleared to adopt Maya. The arrangement worked for Lozza's mom, too. She'd been widowed, and helping with Maya had given her a new lease on life.

Lozza punched a pillow and lay back. The heat was humid, thick. She'd come home late and had an early start tomorrow, but her brain wouldn't stop churning the details of the case. Her thoughts turned to Ellie and what it must've been like to lose her daughter. She thought of Maya's mother, killed by Maya's abusive father. And how Lozza herself had lost it when she'd tried to take him into custody while Maya—who'd been three years old, like Ellie's daughter—had cowered under the bed.

Lozza's violent reaction that day had almost cost her everything.

But she'd fought for Maya when no one else had wanted the kid. And when Maya's father had died in prison, Lozza had gained everything.

She tossed onto her side. The red glow of the numbers on her alarm clock read 3:25 a.m. She bashed her pillow into shape again. Nothing about the case was making sense.

Her mobile rang. Lozza glanced at the clock again. It was 3:50 a.m. She reached for her phone and connected the call.

"Lozza? It's Ellie."

She sat up abruptly in the dark. "Ellie?"

"I . . . I need help—I need to talk to you."

"*Now?* Do you know what time it is?"

"It's urgent. It's about that framed photo that went missing."

Lozza frowned and glanced at the clock again. "Are you on medication, Ellie? Have you been consuming alcohol?"

"Damnit, Lozza, listen to me. I phoned Dana, my friend in Vancouver. She was in that photo with me. Something about it had been bugging me before it vanished. And when it disappeared, it really started to eat at me. So I phoned Dana—it's almost eleven a.m. in Vancouver now, but still yesterday—" Lozza could hear movement as Ellie spoke, a noise like a printer in action. A rustling of paper. "I asked Dana if she still had digital copies on her phone." More noise. Printing again? "She did. More than one. She just sent them to me, and—"

Silence.

"Ellie?"

"Shit," Ellie whispered. "Oh shit!" Lozza heard movement. "I . . . there's a car outside. I . . ."

Lozza heard noises. Ellie moving around her house?

She swung her feet over the side of the bed and reached for her pants.

"Oh God . . . Help, I need help! I need to get out of—" Lozza heard the phone drop with a clatter, then a scream followed by a crash and a horribly gut-sickening thump—like the sound of a body slamming into a wall. Adrenaline speared through her blood. Lozza tugged up her pants. She was already wearing a T-shirt. She hurried to the door with the phone pressed to her ear. "Where are you, Ellie? What's going on?"

More thumping. Glass shattering. Muffled sounds.

Lozza found shoes, took her weapon from the safe, checked and loaded it, stuffed it into a holster, and hurried out to her vehicle with the phone still to her ear. She heard nothing more.

Sliding into the driver's seat, she fired up her engine, put the phone on speaker, and set it in the cup holder. She drove fast for the bridge that would take her over the river. From there she'd cut down to Bonny River Drive. A kangaroo, eyes bright, stopped dead in the middle of the road. She swerved, heart hammering. She had no idea if Ellie had called from her home, but guessed she had because of the printer noises. Perhaps she was back on meds and had passed out. But it had sounded a lot worse.

THE MURDER TRIAL

Now, February. Supreme Court, New South Wales.

A woman with thick auburn hair tumbling to her shoulders takes the stand.

I know very well who she is.

Her testimony will turn jurors against me. My heart beats fast. Lorrington's team looks tense. This woman is the reason the police came to my door in riot gear. Lorrington is going to have to work hard to swing this back around.

"Can you state your full name and place of residence for the court?" asks Ms. Konikova, the birdlike Crown prosecutor.

"Dana Bainbridge. I live in Vancouver, BC, in Canada."

The jurors shift in their seats. Some sit up straighter. In my peripheral vision I see the same happen in the court gallery. Everyone is prepped for a climax. All are fully vested in the battle of these narratives. They're ready for an end.

"Ms. Bainbridge," says Konikova, "Do you recall receiving a phone call around eleven a.m. Vancouver time on November nineteen just over a year ago?"

Dana leaned toward the mike. "I do."

"That's a long time ago—why do you remember that phone call specifically?"

I feel Dana's attention being pulled to me in the dock. Like the others, she's probably been advised not to look. And she doesn't. She keeps her eyes firmly on the prosecutor, clears her throat, and says, "Because it was from her—from Ellie. And it stuck in my mind because it would have been close to four a.m. her time the next day. I thought she might be in trouble, and it jolted me."

"What did she want?"

"She asked if I remembered a photograph of us that the barman at the Mallard Lounge had taken on her father's birthday."

"The Mallard Lounge is where?"

"In the Hartley Plaza Hotel on the Vancouver waterfront. The hotel is named for her father—it was one of his development projects."

"And what was happening at the Hartley Plaza when you were there?"

"The AGORA convention. It's an event hosted annually by the Hartley Group, which is Ellie's father's company."

I'm going to throw up. I watch Lorrington's profile intently. His jaw is tight. He knows what's coming now.

"What is the AGORA convention?"

Dana is nervous. She reaches for her glass of water with a trembling hand, sips, and says, "Ellie referred to it as a sort of 'pitch-fest' or speed-dating event designed to introduce investors to people who need equity financing for various projects, mostly development projects, real estate, that kind of thing."

The prosecutor consults her notes. "And the patrons in the Mallard Lounge that night, were they part of the AGORA convention, too?"

"A lot of them looked like they were. Business attire, conference name tags, that sort of thing."

"So all people hungry for money?"

"Objection." Lorrington rises. "Leading the witness."

"I'll rephrase," says Konikova. "What was the primary goal of most of the hotel occupants that night?"

"Well, people seeking money. Or to loan or invest it and make a profit from it."

"And why were you and Ellie there?"

She clears her throat. "Ellie had come off a bad dinner with her father when I happened to call her. She suggested I come over, and I was keen to join her for a night on the town. I met her in the Mallard, where she'd had dinner, and we drank a lot more. Then we asked the barman to take some photos of the two of us together."

"Is this one of the photos, Ms. Bainbridge?"

A photograph comes up on a screen for everyone to see. It's been enlarged tenfold and sharpened. My breathing begins to deepen. I feel my chest rise and fall, but I'm not getting air.

"Yes," says Dana.

I feel the moment build. It swells. I glance around the court. I need to get out.

"Can you please tell Your Honor who is in that photo, Ms. Bainbridge?"

"That's me. And that's Ellie."

"And in the background, among the other patrons of the Mallard Lounge, do you see anyone else you recognize?"

"Yes. I recognize the person seated directly behind Ellie at the bar."

My scalp is shrinking. The more I try to control my breathing, the faster my chest rises and falls. I'm going to hyperventilate.

"Is this person in the courtroom now?"

"Yes, ma'am."

"Ms. Bainbridge, can you point to this person?"

Dana points.

THEN

LOZZA

Lozza roared down Bonny River Road and screeched to a halt outside the Cresswell-Smith home. Lights blazed inside. The front door was wide open.

The woman from next door came running into the road in her nightgown, a mobile clutched in her hand. "Thank God you're here—I called triple zero. He took her! I saw it happen! He took her in his car."

"*Who* took her? What happened?" Lozza heard the wail of sirens in the distance. Emergency response was on its way. More sirens sounded from an opposite direction, growing louder.

"I . . . I . . . didn't know what to do," the woman sobbed.

Lozza steadied the old woman by the shoulders. She looked her dead in the eyes, spoke calmly, clearly. "Tell me what happened. Everything."

"There . . . was a scream. A terrible scream. It woke me—I was sleeping with the windows open because of the heat. The most awful sound I've ever heard. I . . . I looked out the window. There . . . there was a car in their driveway, over there." She pointed to the driveway. "Both the driver's door and the passenger doors were open, engine running. Headlights on. Then I heard crashing and banging, and he came out struggling to drag something very heavy. He came out the front door and tugged it across the lawn to the car and—" She shuddered and wrapped her arms tightly around herself, her cell phone still gripped tightly in her hand. "It looked like a body. I think it could have been a body wrapped up in a blanket or sheets or something and tied up with rope. I think it was her—the wife—inside. He really struggled to get his load into the back seat of the car. When I realized what might be happening, I hurried downstairs to find my phone. I couldn't find—" She swiped away tears. "Oh, God, I couldn't find it at first. Then I did. It had gone down between the cushions on the couch. I called triple zero. But when I went to the window again, the car was already backing out of the driveway."

"Did you get a look at the assailant?"

"Dressed all in black. He had a balaclava over his head."

"What kind of car?"

"Brown. I think it was brown."

"A sedan, hatchback, ute, what?"

"Sedan. One of those . . . those . . ."

"Corolla? Was it a Toyota Corolla?"

"Yes, yes, I think it could have been."

"Did you see the rego?"

She shook her head.

"Which way did it go?"

"To the right." She pointed. "It sped off that way. I heard tires screech at the end of the road."

The sirens grew louder. Lozza's mind raced. Bonny River Road was shaped like a crescent. Going either north or south would lead a driver to the Princes Highway, which was the only road that ran up and down this section of coast. If the assailant had turned north here on Bonny River Road, it was likely he intended to head north when he hit the A1.

She ran to her vehicle and climbed in. She needed a full highway patrol response. Breathing hard, blood racing, Lozza dialed for backup from a neighboring jurisdiction that had a bigger force and staff on night duty. As the phone rang on speaker, she spun a U-turn across Bonny River Road and hit the gas.

As Lozz sped toward the highway, she explained the nature of the emergency to dispatch and gave her name and rank. "I'm in pursuit, heading north onto the A1. If I lay eyes on the vehicle, I'll call it in."

It was a gamble. The Corolla could conceivably turn south. Or it could duck into a side road before it reached the A1 and lie low in a quiet neighborhood. But her instincts told her a kidnapper would want to get away and fast. It was the assailant's bad luck that the Cresswell-Smiths had a nosy neighbor, or the kidnapper could have been long gone.

Lozza hit the highway. She put her foot down on the gas, then swerved violently for three kangaroos that bounded across the road and vanished into the gum forest. Close call. Sweat dampened her brow, and she thought of Maya and all the reasons she'd left the murder squad in the big city. A semi came barreling toward her from the opposite direction, headlights and running lights bright as the rig punched a tunnel through dark forest. It roared past and shuddered her little car. Lozza gripped the wheel tighter, driving as fast as she dared. She had every intention of going home to her daughter. Alive.

Another truck roared past, headlights blazing. A memory flashed like lightning—the sight of Martin Cresswell-Smith's pale body floating in the swamp—his buttocks barely breaking the inky surface. Martin lolling onto his back when Gregg bumped him. The sightless sockets, the shredded lips, the nightmarish work of the muddies, his groin seething with sea lice. The knife with blood. The ropes. The chair. The feces. The severed digits. The smell. She focused as she rounded a bend. If the person who had killed Martin Cresswell-Smith now had Ellie, she feared the worst for her.

Another, deeper part of Lozza's brain still couldn't see the pieces adding up—she still felt Ellie was playing them.

What was she missing?

Who was the man from the Puggo—the bikie—who'd delivered the drugs Ellie had overdosed on?

Lozza saw it suddenly as she rounded a curve. Red taillights. The Corolla. She increased speed.

THEN

LOZZA

Lozza gained on the red lights up ahead. As the vehicle came into better view, she saw it was definitely a Corolla. With a dent in the rear and the registration **QUEENSLAND 549-GIN**. Her heart sped up.

She leaned harder on the accelerator, which increased the risk of hitting an animal and obliterating both the creature and herself. Every molecule in her body was focused and ready to slam on the brakes.

Trees whipped past as she went faster through the tunnel of gums. Without taking her eyes off the road, she used her voice-activated system to call dispatch again.

"This is Senior Constable Lozza Bianchi. I have eyes on suspect vehicle. Repeat, eyes on suspect. Brown Toyota Corolla. Queensland 549-GIN. Headed northbound on A1 between Jarrawarra and Keelongong. We're about two klicks south of Keelongong intersection."

She swerved around a sharp bend, tires screeching. Lozza's heart shot into her throat as she felt her wheels skidding on fine sea sand. She pulled back into control. The Corolla driver ahead seemed to realize he was being chased and picked up speed, skidding and swerving around another curve in the narrow road.

Lozza eased back slightly. There was nowhere to go until the intersection, which was now about one klick ahead. Highway patrol would hopefully have had time to deploy road spikes.

The red taillights disappeared from view behind trees as the Corolla rounded another curve.

As Lozza followed, she caught sight of the Corolla again. It suddenly hit the brakes, swerved violently, then fishtailed. The car had collided with something. Brake lights stuttered as the Corolla slid sideways again and veered onto the dirt verge. It bounded over the sandy verge, then spun as it pulled back onto the road. Whatever it had hit went hurtling down a bank. Lozza clenched her teeth as a sick feeling filled her.

Her phone rang.

She slowed a little more and connected the call.

"Roadblock in place. Spikes deployed. Stand down, Officer, repeat, stand down. Under control . . ."

She killed the call and eased off the gas, her heart thudding against her ribs. Her T-shirt was wet from perspiration. She rounded another bend and saw the pulsating red and blue lights of law enforcement vehicles at the intersection ahead, the colors bouncing off the silvery trunks of gum trees. But her adrenaline kicked up again—*the Corolla was not slowing down*! It continued to barrel at high speed straight toward the strobing lights.

Horror rose into her throat.

She slowed and backed off even more, a feeling of dread leaching through her veins as the inevitable played out in slow motion in front of her eyes.

Suddenly the Toyota swerved, almost flipped, corrected, and veered off the highway to the right. It bounded down a sand track and disappeared into the black forest. All Lozza could see through the trunks were intermittent flashes of light from the fleeing vehicle's headlights. Lozza called it in.

"Suspect heading east down a dirt road through the forest—" She saw a sign for the Keelongong campsite. "Track could lead to the campsite near the beach." She turned down onto the sandy track and followed after the Toyota.

The road was rough, the sand soft in places, bogging down her tires, causing them to spin. She heard sirens wailing behind her and also coming from somewhere up ahead. She guessed responders were approaching from the beach direction to head the Toyota off from the east.

Her headlights darted off ghostlike gums. Glowing eyes watched her from the woods. She spotted the taillights of the car ahead.

The fleeing driver hit the gas and punched and bounced faster along the sandy road at reckless speed. The vehicle disappeared from view again as it went behind trees, then as Lozza came around a stand of dense ferns and trees, she heard a loud explosion. Her heart sank to her stomach. The sound was followed almost instantly by another explosion ripping through the forest. Bats burst from the trees. They swooped and fluttered in front of her headlights. As she neared, she saw the orange flickering glow of a blaze through the trunks of the trees. Behind the fire the bar lights of a police vehicle strobed, and Lozza realized with horror what had occurred. The getaway car had crashed head-on into a highway patrol cruiser.

She took her vehicle closer, stopped, flung open the door, and ran stumbling over roots and ruts toward the fully engaged vehicle fire. Smoke roiled black and acrid through the trees. Heat radiated at her. She heard the fierce crackling of flames. As she neared, another explosion sent a whoosh of white fire and sound into the air. Heat blasted at her. Her heart stalled. She stopped, stared, and she put her hands on top of her head as if to press the horror back in.

Ellie.

She was still in there.

Lozza heard more sirens coming from the other side of the blaze. A fire truck also approached from behind her. A firefighter ran up and took her arm.

"Ma'am, please, you need to back away, ma'am."

"The victim is—she's still in there."

"Ma'am. Back away. Now."

THEN

LOZZA

She was dead.

Ellie Cresswell-Smith had perished in the fire along with her abductor.

Lozza had failed. This thought, the weight of it all, circled and pressed down on her along with all sorts of questions as she sat shivering on the back bumper of an ambulance with a blanket around her shoulders. Despite the heat, shock and her own perspiration had made her cold.

Pale dawn seeped through the smoky forest. The vehicle fire had spread rapidly through the surrounding drought-dry brush and highly combustible eucalypts. It was only being brought under control now. Smoke burned her nostrils and the back of her throat.

A spark from the crash had likely ignited spilled fuel. The highway patrol officer had been pulled free of his vehicle before it became engaged, but officers from the vehicle traveling behind him were unable to approach the fully engulfed Toyota Corolla. The highway patrol officer had been taken to the nearby hospital with non-life-threatening injuries.

Firefighters were now attempting to control the ensuing wildfire before investigators could even begin to go in. Gregg handed Lozza a coffee. She looked up. His eyes were kind. His rugged face and smiling eyes had never been such a welcome sight.

"Thanks," she said, taking the cup from him.

"Did you call Maya—let her know you're okay?"

She nodded, sipped.

Corneil approached. The sergeant's features were as flat and inscrutable as always. A helicopter thudded up ahead.

Lozza had already explained to Corneil the events in detail—how she'd received Ellie's call at 3:50 a.m., heard screaming. How she'd gone to the Cresswell-Smith house, then given chase. Corneil had taken notes. Lozza felt this wasn't going to end well.

"Why did she have your personal number?" he asked now.

"I gave it to her. After we interviewed her. You saw me giving her my card. You were watching from the window."

"Why did you give it to her?"

"In case she decided to talk or remembered something."

Corneil's brow crooked up. "Exactly what did she say on the phone?"

Lozza repeated her recollection of the call, again.

"Are you certain Ellie Cresswell-Smith was not in the home when you got there?"

Lozza's pulse stuttered. "I . . . The neighbor witnessed what looked like a body tied in blankets being dragged out of the house."

"Are you certain it was a body?"

Lozza cleared her throat. "I made the assumption."

"Assumption," Corneil said quietly as he reached for his phone. But as Corneil was about to place a call, one of the officers shouted.

"There's no one in here!"

Everyone looked. Lozza got to her feet.

"There's no one inside the vehicle!" The charred driver's door was open. A suited-up forensics officer had peered in. "Looks like the driver fled," he called out.

Corneil strode closer, calling out in return. "What about on the back seat? Where is the victim? Have you checked the boot?"

"Nothing in the boot. No human remains in the vehicle immediately apparent. Looks like there was no victim in here."

Gregg touched Lozza's arm. She felt like she was going to be sick.

"I was acting on the statement of the neighbor," she said quietly.

"You made an executive decision, Lozz," Gregg said. "There was no time to gamble with. We all would have done the same thing."

Except Lozza wasn't certain about that. Not at all.

Corneil strode back toward Lozza as he placed his call.

"Sybil," he said into his mobile, "are you at the Cresswell-Smith home now?" He listened, eyeing Lozza, his brows going lower. "And you're sure she's not still inside her home?"

He nodded and killed the call.

"House is empty," he said. "Evidence of an assault. Blood. Mrs. Cresswell-Smith's phone was found in the house. Neighbor's account remains consistent. But she's gone. Ellie Cresswell-Smith is gone."

THEN

LOZZA

Lozza drove slowly back along the Princes Highway. The sun was higher, and the road shimmered in the heat. Traffic was getting busier. She replayed the events in her mind, trying to see where she might have done things differently. A sick part of herself wondered again if Ellie Cresswell-Smith was really just a brilliant con who had set this up. But why?

What purpose would it serve?

Possibly to veil the fact that she had killed her husband—stage an abduction with an accomplice to pretend she was really a victim? But her scam had been exposed because Lozza had shown up in hot pursuit, and they'd crashed?

K9 tracking teams had been brought in. Another chopper deployed. Ground search and rescue assistance. The area was being scoured for the driver, who'd fled on foot, but the suspect had gotten a head start because everyone had been distracted by the fire, which had spread rapidly through the eucalypt forest in the wake of the explosion. Plus, the ensuing wildfire had obscured trace.

Lozza slowed as she neared the bend where the Corolla had hit an animal and almost lost control.

The memory flashed through her mind again as she passed the spot where she'd seen the injured animal rolling down the bank and into the woods.

Lozza's heart kicked as something struck her. She'd seen what she'd expected to see—an injured kangaroo being flung down the bank. But in her memory, the way it had gone down, the way the car had fishtailed—had she seen the rear door swing open for a moment before the Toyota Corolla had righted and gone around the bend? Lozza frowned and glanced up into her rearview mirror. The road was clear. She spun a U-turn across the highway and headed back.

When she saw where the Corolla tires had punched into the soft sand on the side of the road, she pulled off and parked on the verge. She opened the door and got out. The scent of eucalypts was strong, the sound of beetles buzzing loud. A truck rumbled by. Lozza approached the bank, a sensation building inside her.

She saw it, down at the base of some trees. The tawny brown . . . *not a kangaroo.*

A blanket tied with ropes. She saw a bloodied human hand sticking out from the folds. The top of a head with dark hair. It moved.

She was flung from the car. She wasn't inside when it crashed and burned.

"Ellie!" she screamed as she bounded and jumped sideways down the steep bank. The bundle moved again. The fingers twitched. Ellie was alive. Emotion seared into Lozza's eyes.

She dropped to her haunches. "Ellie, it's okay, I'm here. Help's on its way." Lozza reached for her phone and called it in. She then fumbled to untie the ropes, and she drew back the blanket around Ellie's face. Ellie stared up at her.

"Don't move," Lozza whispered. "I've got you. Help's coming."

She untied more ropes and carefully peeled back the rest of the blanket. Ellie moaned.

"Where do you hurt?"

329

Ellie moved her mouth. Her lips were dry. "All . . . all . . . over," she whispered. "I . . . my leg . . . broken . . . hip . . . hurts . . . was hit . . . back of head."

Lozza heard sirens wailing, louder, louder. Closer.

Ellie tried to talk again.

"Shh, don't say anything." She took off her T-shirt, and wearing only her bra, she pressed the shirt against the bleeding wound on the side of Ellie's head.

"I . . . I freed my hand," Ellie whispered. "Managed . . . to open the door . . . When . . . car swerved I spilled out."

Lozza nodded. "Yes, yes you did. Good job, Ellie. You're going to be good. Hang on."

Ellie tried to moisten her lips, moaned. Her eyelids fluttered. "The photo—"

"Shh, don't talk. Save your energy. The ambulance is almost here." They'd see Lozza's car parked up on the road. She smoothed hair back from the victim's eyes.

"I know who . . . person . . . in the photo . . . with me and Dana . . . All this time . . . she . . . targeted . . ." Her voice faded. Lozza's pulse quickened. The sirens grew deafening—they were almost here. Ellie's lids fluttered. She moistened her lips, trying to speak again. Lozza leaned close.

"Willow," Ellie whispered. "She . . . she was . . . in the bar that night. Listening . . . her and . . . they . . . they did it together."

THE MURDER TRIAL

Now, February. Supreme Court, New South Wales.

Dana Bainbridge is pointing at me in the dock. Everyone in the room is looking at me. Tension presses down. My throat closes.

Focus. Stay calm. Lorrington has got this.

I'm a victim.

Do not react.

Breathe.

"For the record," says the Crown prosecutor loudly into the mike, which makes her voice echo and bounce around the heavy silence in the courtroom, "Ms. Bainbridge is identifying the defendant, Mrs. Sabrina Cresswell-Smith. The *real* Mrs. Cresswell-Smith. Married to Martin Cresswell-Smith for the past fifteen years." She pauses. The court artist's chalk scratches furiously on paper. "Also known as Willow Larsen, among the many fraudulent aliases she has used with her husband in their cons around the globe." The prosecutor returns her attention to Dana.

"Ms. Bainbridge, are you certain that the accused is the same woman in the photograph?"

Dana leans close to the mike. "Yes. She was sitting right next to us at the bar counter—unnecessarily close because there was a vacant stool on her other side."

"What was she doing at the counter?"

"Eavesdropping while busy texting with someone on her phone. She was a brunette then."

"Did Ellie mention the woman to you at the time?"

Dana reaches for her water. She sips and carefully sets her glass down, using the moment to regather her composure.

"Not at the time. But when Ellie phoned and asked if I still had digital copies, she mentioned that she thought the woman at the bar had earlier been seated next to their dinner party. Ellie, by her own admission, was arguing very loudly with her father that night. Mrs. Cresswell-Smith would have heard Sterling Hartley making Ellie an offer of money for any project Ellie chose. Ellie said she'd hung a framed print of the photo on her studio wall, and something about it had begun to bother her. You couldn't see Willow—Mrs. Cresswell-Smith—very clearly in that framed photo. But she was much more visible in the copies shot with my phone." She sips more water. Her hands are still shaky. "Ellie said someone had taken the frame off the wall while she was in a coma."

"Did she say why she thought the framed photo was taken?"

I turn my head slowly and look at Ellie seated in the gallery next to Gregg. She's staring at me. Gregg, too. The Crown team has chosen to not put her on the stand. I'm betting it's because the Crown is worried she'll sink the case—it'll open her up to admitting she hated Martin and that she wanted to stab and kill him herself. Ellie on the stand would have given Lorrington the reasonable doubt we need.

My memory swings back to that fateful wintry night in Vancouver over two years ago. Martin and I were in trouble. Because we were under investigation in Europe for several scams, we'd moved to the States, where I began parting rich women from their money by giving spiritual readings. I soon learned faith healing was more lucrative—people will try anything and give everything to get well again when faced with death. But then I came under legal scrutiny in the US for selling my Magic Drops—a purported "cancer cure" made of water and some herbs and a few drops of peroxide, which I flogged at nearly $1,000 per tiny vial. Which is why we'd then relocated to Canada and shifted the Magic Drops sales online with various distribution centers we could keep moving around. But complaints had been filed in Canada, and an investigation opened there, too. We needed a new plan—one last big con that would enable us to retire to some island without an extradition treaty.

It was Martin's idea for us to scope out the AGORA convention for potential marks we could lure into another one of his real estate scams. When Ellie and her father sat down next to me, it was a gift. Manna from heaven. I texted Martin, who was working another part of the hotel, and told him to start googling everything he could find on Ellie and her father. I stuck beside Ellie when she and her friend Dana moved to the bar counter. The more I heard, the more I realized she was the perfect mark. I knew it would require commitment on both our parts. A long con. Many months. But if it paid, it would pay big. Our last job. One final score, then we could lay low.

So after Dana left the bar, Martin headed Ellie off near the washroom. We were in play.

I confess I was nervous from the outset. The role for my husband required seducing and sleeping and living with the vulnerable heiress, who was also beautiful. Gentle. Artistic. Rich. Loving. I feared—more than a little—Martin could fall for her. I stalked them so that I'd know if something started to go sideways. I followed them in my Subaru. I tracked Martin's movements. I had Martin install spyware on her phone so I would know their location whenever they went away together. I had cams installed in the Bonny River house, hidden in the clocks. Martin didn't know I could watch him and Ellie via an app. I was right. I *was* losing Martin. But it wasn't to Ellie.

It was to Rabz.

Little did I know that it would be our mark, Ellie, who would show me that my husband had been planning another final scam—a bigger one. Double-crossing *me*.

Little did *he* know that Ellie had outed his secret to me.

THE MURDER TRIAL

Detective Corneil Tremayne is in the witness box. I don't like him. I can't read him. I think he has a mean streak. In earlier testimony he already outlined for the court the forensic details of the investigation, but Lorrington has called him back.

"Sergeant Corneil," says Lorrington, "can you recap a few facts for Your Honor? The hairs found in the Velcro of the Nike ball cap—who did they belong to?"

The sergeant barely moves as he speaks. "As I mentioned earlier, they were synthetic hairs. From a wig."

"So they did not belong to the defendant."

"No, sir."

"The blood on the cap?"

"It's a DNA match to Ellie Hartley. The cap was bloodied in a prior incident and left in her garage."

"So not my client's blood."

"No, sir."

"The blood on the knife?"

"It was found to have been contributed by the deceased, Martin Cresswell-Smith. Plus, there were very small trace amounts that belonged to Ellie Hartley, also from the prior incident on their boat."

"Were any fingerprints at the old farmhouse found to be a match to the defendant, Mrs. Sabrina Cresswell-Smith?"

"Negative."

Lorrington nods slowly. "Was there any evidence at all that the defendant was at any time inside that house?"

"No, there is not, but she was working with a coconspirator who was inside the house."

"You're referring to this mystery 'bikie' who was seen accosting my client?"

"We believe he was working with Mrs. Cresswell-Smith. She used him to deliver contraband marked for Ellie Hartley as a way to make public her drug addiction and to pave the way to her possible death."

Murmurs come from the gallery.

"Detective," Lorrington booms suddenly, "you have not presented any physical evidence, any witness testimony, anything at all that actually links my client to this mystery biker. You have not presented any proof that she was instructing him. You have not even located this mystery man. Not only that, one of your key investigating officers, Constable Gregg Abbott, was sleeping with the defendant. Your other key investigator, Senior Constable Laurel Bianchi, has a history of violence, which she has confessed to in this very courtroom. She was forced out of Crime Command for physically assaulting and injuring a suspect in her custody. And she has the scar on her head to prove it. She also adopted the child who hid under the bed and witnessed the whole thing. Constable Bianchi is vehement—almost radicalized, one might say—in her personal crusade against male violence. Yes, she tried to leave her crusade and her tattered career behind in Sydney. Yes, she tried to lay low and rebuild in Jarrawarra. But then she met Ellie Hartley and saw bruises. By her own admission to the court, Constable Bianchi feared for the woman's safety. I put it to this court Constable Bianchi had a hate-on for Martin Cresswell-Smith right out of the gate, and was not an unbiased investigator. Constable Bianchi also personally delivered the contraband drugs to the home on Bonny River. This was not an objective investigation, Your Honor, nor was it a clean or fair one."

He turns to the jury. "Murder consists of two elements. As I stated at the outset to this trial, there must be a proven intention to kill. And it must be proven that the defendant did in fact kill." He pauses and meets the eyes of each jury member in turn. "I put it to this court that the prosecution has failed to provide evidence of *the* vital half of that equation. Yes, maybe it could be argued that the defendant—Mrs. Cresswell-Smith—wanted to kill the man she once loved, the man she'd lived with since she was around nineteen years old, the man who then cheated on her, who was embezzling funds she believed were hers, who was going to bolt with his lover to live in a country where there was no extradition treaty. Yes, it could be argued that Sabrina Cresswell-Smith was a con artist, that she defrauded and cheated people out of their money. It could even be argued that she'd come to despise her husband so deeply when she learned of his duality, his deception, his double cross, that maybe she did want to kill him. Perhaps she even intended to kill him. But"—he raises a finger into the air—"she didn't."

Lorrington pauses and lets that hang. "Detective Corneil," he says, turning back to the homicide cop, "is it at all possible that someone else could have hired the mystery biker or some other person entirely to kill Martin Cresswell-Smith—perhaps someone from his past who he'd double-crossed, or someone who was furious at being defrauded, or someone who'd posted signs all over Agnes Basin calling for his murder?"

Silence.

"Sergeant Corneil?" says Judge Parr.

The detective clears his throat. "It's possible, sir, but evidence of torture suggests—"

"'Suggests'!" Lorrington swings to the jury, his finger back in the air. "Did you hear that—'suggests'? This is all they have? A *suggestion*?"

As he turns to face Corneil, the court door is flung open. The barrister stalls. A legal aide comes rushing down the aisle and goes straight to the prosecuting side of the table. She leans down and whispers into the solicitor's ear. The solicitor whispers into Konikova's ear. At the very same time the journalist, Melody Watts, gets up and rushes out the door. So do two cops. Something is happening. What is happening?

Before Lorrington can speak, Konikova is up on her feet. "Your Honor, may we approach the bench?"

"What is this about, Madame Crown?" asks the judge.

"We . . . we have a late-breaking . . . development. We have new evidence, a possible new witness."

"Objection," barks Lorrington. He looks worried. I am suddenly afraid. "We were not informed of this."

"This is highly irregular, Madame Crown," says the judge.

"It's only just come to our attention."

The judge irritably wags her hand at them. "Approach."

THE MURDER TRIAL

Berle Geller watches television in her squat house with its corrugated tin roof that bakes under the Australian sun. The house is on the knoll of a derelict spread several kilometers outside the small rural town of Toomba in Queensland, close to the border with New South Wales. Flies buzz inside and a lazy fan paddles the air. A dog scratches itself at the foot of her recliner. Berle holds a tin of beer on her belly. Her husband is in the next room doing whatever it is that Herb Geller does, but Berle is glued to the reality show that is the Martin Cresswell-Smith murder trial. She's convinced Sabrina Cresswell-Smith is guilty, but she agrees with the TV pundits that all the evidence against her is circumstantial at best. Besides, Berle has sympathy for the woman. That husband of hers sounds like a right asshole. Bastard. She'd have stuck him with a knife, too. Lord help her, but sometimes she feels like sticking a knife in Herb. Berle knows what rage feels like. She knows the taste of betrayal and failure. She glances at the old wedding portrait of herself and Herb on the buffet. They had such dreams back then. Look at her life now. If she had a heap of money and her husband ran off with it, and with his mistress—

Melody Watts appears on the screen.

"Melody is back on, Herb!"

Herb grunts from the other room.

"You're gonna miss it!"

"I'm sure you'll tell me all about it," Herb calls from the other room.

The camera zooms in on Melody Watts. She stands in front of the courthouse doors. She's impeccably made up and sporting a fuchsia jacket that contrasts with her blonde TV hair. She's so pretty.

Berle kicks her dog with her swollen foot to stop it from scratching. She takes a sip of beer from her tin, riveted.

"When the Martin Cresswell-Smith murder trial resumes this morning, Justice Geraldine Parr is expected to summarize the central arguments. We anticipate that Justice Parr will outline the key points of evidence given by each significant witness, and she will explain to the jury the relevant laws and how they relate to the case at hand. The next step will be the jury deliberations."

The screen splits and shows the male anchor behind a desk in the newsroom. "Thank you, Melody," he says. "And NSW police have still not found an alleged accomplice or the missing *Abracadabra*?"

"That's right, Harlan. The mysterious 'bikie' with a neck tattoo continues to remain a key person of interest, and he continues to remain at large more than one year after the murder at Agnes Basin."

"Is there a chance Mrs. Cresswell-Smith will walk?"

"As I've told viewers, Mr. Lorrington has been underscoring the weaknesses in the Crown's case and presenting to the jury feasible alternate narratives. And as Lorrington told the court early in his opening statements, anything can happen in a jury trial. If jurors feel sympathy or identify with Mrs. Cresswell-Smith, or see her as a victim of her husband's, they are more likely to find reasonable doubt and render a verdict of not guilty. The defense legal strategy has been to acknowledge that while Mrs. Cresswell-Smith is a clever and accomplished con artist, she is not a murderer."

"Thank you, Melody," the anchor says. Melody signs off and disappears, and the screen fills with an image of a Quintrex cuddy cabin boat. The anchor says, "New South Wales police are still asking members of the public who might have seen a boat like this under suspicious circumstances to please come forward. The number for the anonymous tip line is at the bottom of the screen. Police are also still looking for this man—"

A photo taken from CCTV footage of a bald man appears. Berle lurches forward in interest. While she's watched most of the reporting on the trial, she hasn't seen this photo. The screen splits and shows a better rendering of the tattoo on the man's neck. Something begins to stir in Berle's mind. Her heart begins to beat faster. She takes another swig of her beer, fixated by the close-up of the tattoo. It's a rendering of a hummingbird. The screen flashes to a photograph of a fancy bronze watch.

"Police are also looking for a Rolex Daytona like this one." Berle coughs as she swallows her mouthful of beer.

"Hey, Herb!"

"What?"

"Get in here, quick." She's on the edge of her chair.

He comes around the corner in a sleeveless undershirt that was once white. Berle points her tin at the screen. "That! That watch. I've seen it."

"What are you talking about?"

"Our tenant, you idiot. That guy who rents the shack at the bottom of the farm."

"I don't deal with him, Berle. You're the one who wanted to lease that dive. I've barely seen his face. He doesn't come out when I'm around."

She pushes clumsily to her feet and waddles hurriedly toward the landline phone that squats next to their framed wedding photo.

"What are you doing?"

She guzzles back the rest of her beer, plunks down the empty tin, and picks up the receiver. She feels feverish, excited. "We're gonna be on TV, Herb. We're going to be *paid* to be on television. We're going to meet Melody Watts. In the flesh. Right here. She's going to come here."

"Are you nuts—who are you calling?"

"I'm calling the TV station. I'm calling Melody Watts. I've seen that watch on our tenant. He has that tattoo. He arrived over a year ago, and he parks that boat in the shed and just leaves it there with that old dirt bike of his. It's him. I swear it's him! He's been laying low on our farm the whole time!"

Herb stares at his wife. The flies buzz about his head.

"Berle," he says quietly, "if it's him, you should call that Crime Stoppers number, you should call the cops, not Melody Watts."

She puts the receiver to her ear. "We gonna be on TV, Herb."

THE MURDER TRIAL

Now, February. Supreme Court. New South Wales.

It's been five days since Justice Parr stood down the court after a highly unusual request from the Crown to bring forward late-breaking evidence and a potential new witness. Lorrington looks gray as court reconvenes this morning. He's not a man who likes to lose, or to be seen to be losing.

The court officer opens the door. Everyone goes dead still.

He walks in.

For a moment I fear I'm going to faint. He's come. I was hoping he wouldn't. It means one thing. He's turned state's evidence. Worry tightens. I shoot a glance at Lorrington. He *thinks* he still has a plan. But he doesn't, not now. He has yet to learn the depths of my deceit.

I have just become a barrister's worst nightmare—the client who has lied to him.

The new witness swears on the Bible and takes a seat in the witness box. Dark hollows underscore his eyes. He's tired. I bet the cops have been hammering him round the clock.

"Can you please state your name for the court?" says Konikova.

"Jack Barker."

There is a stirring in the gallery. The place is packed with officers. Ellie sits close to Gregg. I wonder if they could be holding hands. A lot could have happened in the year that my case has taken to come to trial.

Konikova says, "Mr. Barker, can you describe to Your Honor how you know the defendant?"

"We met after her father died on the streets in Sydney. She was homeless. We became friends, hustled together on the streets—classic three-card monte, shell games. Slept in parks. Doorways." He pauses and looks at me. "We were friends."

I see Ellie whisper something in Gregg's ear. She's realizing I'd actually told her the truth about my mother and father, my history, that day she came to see me. It wasn't just a con used to bond her to me. I learned to hustle on the streets. I learned from Jack. From my dad . . . *"Watch the shells closely, kiddo . . ."* *You should have watched my game more closely, Ellie . . .*

"So the two of you go way back?"

"Yes."

"Did you stay in touch all this time?"

"On and off after she left Australia—she called me occasionally over the years, and made contact again when she returned to Australia to live in Jarrawarra. She arrived several months before her husband and the mark came."

"The mark?"

"Ellie Hartley. She was the new mark. The new 'Mrs. Cresswell-Smith.'" He makes air quotes. "As Sabrina explained it to me, Ellie technically wasn't married to Martin because he and Sabrina already were—Martin had entered false information on the Nevada marriage forms."

There is a murmur in the gallery.

"Order, please, silence," calls the court officer. My gaze is riveted on Jack. I'm willing him not to go there—but he has to. Or why else would he be here right now?

"Can you explain to Your Honor why you went to Jarrawarra Bay?"

"Sabrina hired me."

"Can you describe to Your Honor what Sabrina Cresswell-Smith hired you to do for her?"

"She wanted surveillance on her husband and the mark. She paid well for it. I'd left the navy with a dishonorable discharge and needed cash badly. She—Sabrina—felt her husband was up to something, and she said she was worried. So I followed them and reported on their movements when they were outside of the house."

"What vehicle did you use to follow them?"

"A brown Toyota Corolla."

More murmurs in the gallery.

"Order! Quiet in the court, please!"

The sketch artist turns a fresh page, her gaze flicking back and forth between Jack and me and her sketch. Reporters scribble furiously. I can almost feel the news vans hovering outside waiting with their big satellite dishes on top. Heat presses into the room.

"Did Mrs. Cresswell-Smith ever ask you to do anything other than surveillance?"

"She asked me to deliver a package to the Pug and Whistler marked for 'Ellie Cresswell-Smith.'"

"Why?"

"She didn't tell me."

"Did you also follow a woman named Bodie Rabinovitch?"

He clears his throat. "Yes."

"Why?"

"Sabrina had been told that Martin was having an affair, but he seemed to be hiding it well. I'd previously only followed Martin when he was with Ellie. Or I'd follow Ellie when she was alone. When I followed Bodie Rabinovitch to Sydney, I captured both of them on camera."

"How did Mrs. Cresswell-Smith react when you gave her these photos?"

He looks down for a moment. I see the tension in his neck. "Angry," he says quietly.

"How angry?"

"Objection," calls Lorrington as he surges to his feet. "Calls for speculation."

"I'll rephrase. What did Mrs. Cresswell-Smith ask you to do next?"

Silence.

"Mr. Barker," says Judge Parr, "you must answer the question."

He inhales. "She . . . she asked me to drown Martin."

A reporter hurries out the door. The mouth of one of the jurors drops open.

I feel my body, my face, going hot.

"How?" asks Konikova.

"She came up with a plan. She recalled Martin from Sydney urgently—he told his mistress it was his wife calling. Sabrina informed him that Ellie was onto him and they had to take care of Ellie in a hurry and pull the plug on the scam and clear the hell out of Australia."

"What did she mean by 'take care of Ellie'?"

"Kill her."

"How?"

"Sabrina told Martin the best way would be to make it look as though Martin and Ellie had gone out on the *Abracadabra* and had an accident at sea. That way, when the boat didn't return, a marine search and rescue effort would be launched, but no suspicions of murder would be raised. The 'Cresswell-Smiths' would simply be a couple who'd vanished at sea. Martin was to acquire a truck and trailer in a hurry and drive the rig from Sydney to Agnes Basin. Sabrina would pick him up from Agnes Basin, then drop him at Moruya Airport, where he'd collect his ute and drive home to the Bonny River house as though he'd flown home early. She said there would be no way to coerce Ellie onto that boat, so Martin was to drug Ellie—give her enough Hypnodorm and GHB to potentially kill her. I was to then meet him in the dark morning in his garage, which he'd leave open—she told Martin I was an old friend who'd do anything on the quiet for the right price. She'd already given me the ball cap and jacket and wig outside the Puggo. She'd taken them from the garage. The plan was to leave the house very early and people would see what they thought they were seeing. Ellie and Martin Cresswell-Smith heading out to sea. As you can see, I am of slight stature. With the wig I could pass as Ellie from a distance."

"Where did the wig come from?"

"Sabrina bought it in Moruya. When we went out on the boat, Martin was to log on with marine rescue. Sabrina told Martin the plan was then for me to cover the boat name and registration markings with false ones, throw Ellie's jacket and cap into the water near the FAD, and then we'd head up to the Agnes inlet mouth. Once in the inlet, we'd dock and load the Quinnie onto a trailer. Sabrina told Martin she would bring Ellie up to Agnes in the Corolla. She'd either be dead or comatose. We'd sink her body into a channel, where the muddies would finish her off. Then Martin and I would drive the boat and trailer back up to Sydney, where he'd get on a plane and leave the country ahead of Sabrina. I'd carry on north and hide the boat and trailer. Everyone would be searching for the lost couple at sea while Sabrina drove to Melbourne and boarded her flight to join Martin."

"But that didn't happen, did it?"

He sips water. "No. That was the story for Martin. Her plan was to double-cross him. I was to drug Martin out at sea and dispose of him overboard, far offshore. Along with Ellie's jacket and cap. I was then to slap on the false rego, then go up Agnes inlet and continue with the plan to drive north and dispose of the boat and trailer. And while we went out to sea, Sabrina would transfer all the funds from their joint offshore account—Martin had already moved it all in there. That's what Ellie had seen when she got into his office. And then Sabrina was going to drive to Melbourne and leave the country before it was even known that the *Abracadabra* was missing."

"But that didn't work, either, did it?"

"No."

"What went wrong, Mr. Barker?"

Silence.

"Mr. Barker?" says Judge Parr.

He rubs his brow. "As soon as Martin and I were seen going out—me dressed as Ellie—she accessed the online account and found that Martin had already taken all the money out of their joint offshore account. He'd robbed her blind. She panicked. Was furious. She called me on my mobile and told me to change the plan at once. She needed the account details from Martin. He'd been drugged already. So she told me to take him up to the abandoned farmhouse at Agnes and hold him there so she could drive up and get the information out of him herself when he came round."

"What about Ellie Hartley?"

"Her intent was still to dispose of Ellie in the channel—both bodies in the channel at that point, once she'd gotten the account information out of Martin."

"Was it Mrs. Cresswell-Smith who tortured Martin?"

He swallows. I feel sick. I know this is the end. Lorrington looks at me. I can see it dawning on him. I feel Ellie in the gallery looking at me. I feel all the cops staring at me. And the reporters and jurors. I sense the cameras outside, hovering.

"Mr. Barker," says the judge again.

"Yes. She cut off his fingers while I went to get Ellie."

"And did you 'get Ellie'—Mr. Barker?"

"The cop—Constable Bianchi—arrived and surprised me. I was inside the house. I managed to flee out the glass sliding door with the clock cameras and the framed photo from the studio that Sabrina ordered me to get as well, but I didn't have time to get Ellie."

"What did you find when you arrived back at the abandoned house empty-handed?"

"She'd killed him."

Gasps come from the gallery. Lorrington fires a look at me. I meet his gaze and do not blink. He's vibrating.

"And did Mrs. Cresswell-Smith get the account information out of her husband?"

"He told her Ellie had taken the money."

"Had she?"

"I don't know. Sabrina killed him in a blind rage."

"Is that why Sabrina went back to abduct Ellie?"

"Yes, and also because Ellie had phoned her friend and was acquiring a copy of the photograph. That photo was proof Sabrina had been in on the con from the day Ellie met Martin at the Hartley Plaza Hotel. She still had the mirroring app on Ellie's phone. She could see and hear everything Ellie did with that phone. She'd heard Ellie tell Dana she was going to tell the cops right away. She was afraid she'd be exposed, and now for murder."

"What happened after you saw that Mrs. Cresswell-Smith—Sabrina—had killed her husband, Mr. Barker?"

"I helped her put his body in the channel. She went back to Jarrawarra. I took the boat on the trailer north to Queensland and laid low."

"One more question, Mr. Barker—you seem to be familiar with boats, in that you were able to take the helm of the *Abracadabra* and navigate her up the coast and into the inlet?"

He leans toward the mike. "I mentioned already that I was in the navy. I know boats. And the sea."

Silence swells loud into the room. It shimmers and crackles at the edges like a dry forest waiting for a spark.

"Mr. Barker," says Konikova slowly, quietly, "why are you telling all this to the court?"

"Because I didn't kill Martin Cresswell-Smith. Sabrina Cresswell-Smith claimed to her lawyer that I had. And now I've been caught, I don't want to take her rap." He flicks a glance at me. "A friend doesn't ask another to serve life for something he didn't do."

Lorrington glowers at me. His face is bloodless. His eyes are hot. He knows me for what I am now. A liar. A con.

You, too, should have watched those shells more closely, Mr. Lorrington, I say in my head, channeling my father's voice. *Life is a shell game, and in a shell game only the tosser wins. You're either the tosser or the loser.*

NOW

ELLIE

February. The Bigwig Pub, New South Wales.

Dana and Gregg are with me. We're gathered in the dark, cool, intimate pub across from the courthouse with some of Gregg's fellow police officers, some reporters, friends.

Jugs of beer and sparkling water and bottles of wine are brought to the table along with plates of food. The big television screen behind the bar has the volume turned up so we can all hear. On the screen we can see Melody Watts in the newsroom at a table with one of the SBC-9 News anchors, and he's quizzing her on the "stunning" turnabout in the Martin Cresswell-Smith murder trial and the record-quick and unanimous verdict from the jury that found Mrs. Sabrina Cresswell-Smith, a.k.a. Willow Larsen, guilty on all counts.

"The matter has now been stood over for sentencing at a date to be fixed," Melody Watts tells the anchor. "Negotiations around extradition proceedings will also likely begin because Mrs. Cresswell-Smith faces additional fraud charges in the EU, the UK, the States, and in Canada."

The anchor turns to the camera. "And this brings to a close our coverage of a murder trial that has mesmerized television audiences not only here in Australia, but also in Canada and the US, where the

Cresswell-Smiths had strong ties and left a legacy of victims in their wakes. The battle between Mr. and Mrs. Cresswell-Smith ended ignominiously in a house of horrors in the dark mangrove swamps of the Agnes Basin estuary. The proposed marina development is now dead, and the land has been ceded to the state for a nature reserve on behalf of the Chloe Foundation created by Ellie Hartley in honor of her daughter, who drowned in an accident at age three in Hawaii."

Everyone looks at me suddenly. I feel my cheeks heat. Gregg's eyes are alive with emotion, hot with it. I give an embarrassed shrug. "Something good has to come of it all."

Gregg kisses me fiercely on the cheek. He whispers in my ear, "You rock, you know that, Ellie Hartley?"

"This is Melody Watts signing off for SBC-9 News. Thank you for listening."

And with that, it's over. A whole violent and terrifying chapter of my life as a victim. But I fought back. I dug deeper than I could possibly have imagined, and here I am. My injuries from the car accident during my abduction over a year ago have healed. My lawyers in Canada managed to put a freeze on the monies Martin and Sabrina stole. Bit by bit the funds are being retrieved. Legal maneuverings around the fraudulent presales are ongoing. I have new friends. I have reclaimed my Hartley name. I am now Doug-free and drug-free and clearheaded. I am finally well.

"Ellie Hartley?" calls the server over the noise of the group. "There's someone outside who wants a word."

"Who is it?"

"A woman. She didn't give her name."

I push my chair back and stand up.

"Want me to come?" Gregg asks.

I shake my head and make my way through the packed pub. I step out into the balmy night. A woman comes forward. With surprise I see it's Lozza.

"Hey," I say, nervous suddenly.

"Congratulations," she says, her hands in her pants pockets. It's not a congratulatory tone she's using, though.

I hesitate. "Why . . . why didn't you join us?" But I think I know why she's not inside with the rest of us. Lozz has the hots for Gregg, and she doesn't feel like watching the two of us get tipsy and close tonight. She's also smarting, I bet, from all the news coverage about her incident on the murder squad. She tried to protect her kid from that, and failed. Lorrington rubbed her name in the mud. I think of how I swam with her and her daughter in the waves, how I knew she wanted to help me. How convenient it was that she saw my bruises and met Martin. And brought me that package. And in so doing, Lozza probably saved my life. I owe her. But I just want her to go away right now. Because she sees me. In a way that others don't.

"I need to get home to Maya," she says.

"Okay, good. I . . . I should go." I point my thumb over my shoulder at the pub entrance. "People waiting for me."

"Your daughter never did stand a chance, did she, Ellie?"

My heart skips a beat.

"I . . . I don't know what you mean."

A car goes by. A drunken, happy group of revelers sways down the opposite sidewalk.

"It's why they didn't put you on the stand, isn't it?" she says. "You. A key witness. *The* key witness. Because you wouldn't have stood a chance with Lorrington. You'd have given him all the reasonable doubt in the world, not so, Ellie?"

"I don't know what you want, Lozza. But I don't like your insinuation." I turn to go back inside.

"I spoke to the investigating officer in Hawaii. He sent me transcripts."

I freeze, unable to move.

"Your in-laws, Doug Tyler—your ex-husband—they're the ones who asked the cops to look into the possibility you drowned her. They told the cops you'd been diagnosed with serious postpartum depression after Chloe was born. It's right there in the transcripts. Your in-laws said they'd been worried you might actually hurt their grandchild in order to get more of Doug's attention."

"He didn't give me any attention. My marriage broke up," I snapped. I was sweating. I could feel panic rising. I needed an Ativan. I needed to walk away from Lozza but couldn't.

She takes a step closer. The light from the pub sign falls on her hair, making her look orange. "You know what I think, Ellie? I don't believe you have it in you to kill someone. Your aggression is secret. It's passive. You don't pull triggers." She pauses, her eyes holding mine. "But you are an enabler, I think. Maybe the sea did grab your daughter, but when she reached for your help underwater, maybe, just maybe for a second, you couldn't reach back. Or you stopped yourself. And then she was gone. Maybe, just maybe, you didn't call 911 when your mother overdosed. Maybe you just sat there with her until you were certain she was dead. Because you wanted all Daddy's attention for yourself."

I try to swallow. "You . . . you're mad."

"I spoke to your ex-husband and his new wife. Doug Tyler told me he'd come to suspect you enabled your mother's death."

"You can't ever prove that. I don't even remember what happened that day. I was only nine years old."

She steps even closer. I can't breathe. "When did you really find out that the woman in that photo of you and Dana was Willow?"

A buzzing starts in my brain.

"Was it before you went to visit Willow to ask for her help in hiring a PI? Did you already suspect then that she was working with Martin? Did you *want* her to find out about Rabz? Because you knew it would make her angry, maybe even dangerous to Martin? Is that why you also told her about the plane tickets to the Cape Verde islands—because the dark enabler inside you, Ellie, wanted to see what she'd do? Did you think she might kill Martin?"

"You need to leave. How *dare* you? I did nothing. You're totally mad."

Gregg appears from the pub. "Everything okay?" He frowns, looking from Lozza to me.

"That's right, Ellie. You did nothing." Lozza nods to Gregg. "Everything's fine. I was just telling Ellie goodbye."

Lozza turns and walks slowly down the street. I'm shaking. I watch her go. I watch the way the streetlights turn her hair to fire. My last session with the forensic psychologist oozes to life in my mind.

"Do you know about the Karpman drama triangle, Ellie? It's a way of mapping the destructive interaction that can occur between two people locked in conflict." He draws an inverted triangle on a piece of paper, and he writes a role at each point on the triangle.

Persecutor.

Rescuer.

Victim.

He looks at me. "The person who adopts the role of the Victim in a dysfunctional relationship is all 'Poor me, woe is me.' She or he feels hopeless, powerless, ashamed, unable to make decisions. Unable to find joy in life. And if she's not being persecuted, the Victim might actively seek out a Persecutor. But she will also try to find a Rescuer to save her, but in so doing the Rescuer will perpetuate the Victim's negative feelings about herself. Sometimes in a relationship a couple will actually shift between these roles—the Victim for a time might become the Persecutor. And then the Rescuer." He pauses.

"Which one are you, Ellie?"

And it strikes me. The three of us—Willow, Lozza, me—we're like those three points. The Persecutor, the Rescuer, the Victim.

Lozza stops, turns around, and calls out to me. "If you ever think of coming back to Jarrawarra, Ellie, I'll be there. I'll be watching you."

"What was that all about?" says Gregg softly.

"Nothing. Nothing at all. Let's go back inside."

He places his hand at the base of my spine and escorts me back toward the pub. The pressure of his palm is both gentle and firm. Both sexual and benign. Both controlling and charmingly chivalrous.

But at the door I cast a final glance over my shoulder.

She's there. At the corner. Standing under a streetlight in an orange halo.

Watching.

ACKNOWLEDGMENTS

Once more I have been blessed to work with editors Alison Dasho and Charlotte Herscher, who always bring to the table brilliant ideas and a deft touch. Thank you both, deeply. Also a big thanks to my Montlake team for giving me some wiggle room and understanding with deadlines while our family struggled through a challenging year. I love you all, and am honored to be a part of this team. Jessica Errera and Amy Tannenbaum, thank you both for shepherding me through the process of bringing another book into the world—I hope there shall be many more! And a big heart full of gratitude to Melanie and Jay White for sharing a slice of their Australian life with us. Our adventures on the South Coast of your sunburned land seeded the germ of this story, and later, while I was polishing it, my soul cried while watching it all catch flame from afar. I am glad you are safe. And thank you, Melanie, for your careful Australian contextual read. A big thanks, also, to the rest of my dear family. I will not be able to think of this story without also thinking of my mother, who passed during the writing of it. We miss you, Mom.

ABOUT THE AUTHOR

Loreth Anne White is a *Washington Post* and Amazon Charts bestselling author of thrillers, mysteries, and romantic suspense, including *In the Dark*, *The Dark Bones*, *A Dark Lure*, and the Angie Pallorino series. A three-time RITA finalist, she is also the Overall 2017 Daphne du Maurier Award winner, and she has won the Romantic Times Reviewers' Choice Award, the National Readers' Choice Award, and the Romantic Crown for Best Romantic Suspense and Best Book Overall. In addition, she's an Arthur Ellis finalist and a Booksellers' Best finalist. A recovering journalist who has worked in both South Africa and Canada, she now resides in the mountains of the Pacific Northwest. When she isn't writing, you'll find her cross-country skiing, open-water swimming, or hiking the trails with her dog (a.k.a. the Black Beast) while trying to avoid the bears. She calls this work because that's when the best ideas come. Visit her at www.lorethannewhite.com.